ALSO AVAILABLE FROM
CATHERINE COWLES

For a full list of up-to-date Catherine Cowles titles,
please visit catherinecowles.com.

Chasing SHELTER

CATHERINE COWLES

Chasing
SHELTER

CATHERINE
COWLES

sourcebooks
casablanca

Published by Sourcebooks Casablanca, an imprint of Sourcebooks
P.O. Box 4410, Naperville, Illinois 60567-4410
(630) 961-3900
sourcebooks.com

Cataloging-in-Publication data is on file with the Library of Congress.

Printed and bound in the United States of America.
LSC 10 9 8 7 6 5 4 3 2 1

FOR EVERYONE STRUGGLING TO BE PERFECT.
ALL YOU NEED TO BE IS YOU.
THAT'S WHERE THE MAGIC IS.

PROLOGUE

Ellie

EVERYTHING WAS *VERY* PINK. NO, THAT WASN'T RIGHT. I MIGHT'VE liked it then. It would feel like strawberry starbursts or those bright flowers I saw everywhere when Dad took us to the Mediterranean. But this was one step above nothing at all.

"Do you like it?" my mom asked, wringing her hands like she was squeezing water from a dishrag. Not that she did that often—or ever.

I looked around the room, taking in every detail: the thick curtains with swoopy edges the designer said were *scalloped*, which just made me think of potatoes, and the plush duvet with its delicate, pale pink flowers. That pink was everywhere. But it was the only color I got. One step above nothing.

"It's pretty," I said softly. It just wasn't...me.

Mom's shoulders slumped, and I felt like the world's biggest jerk. She moved into my space and wrapped an arm around me. "I tried," she whispered.

My lips pressed together in a hard line. I was getting good at it.

Tightening my mouth so all the truths I held inside didn't break free. Wouldn't spill out like oil polluting the sea. "It's okay."

When the designer asked what I wanted for my new room, I'd said rainbows. Dad had squashed that faster than I could blink.

"I'm not having that sort of ridiculousness in our home. That isn't the kind of thing someone of station uses in décor."

Home. That was the only ridiculousness. Nothing about this penthouse apartment with its views of Central Park was homey. I knew that much.

I'd been in places that felt like a home. My friend Kate's apartment in Brooklyn was full of chaos and light. Her artist mom let her *draw* on her bedroom walls. I wasn't even allowed to have a poster.

"I really like the window seat." That much was true. I broke out of her grasp, unable to hold my disappointment and her hurt at the same time. I crossed to the cushioned bench upholstered in the same pale pink flowers as my bed.

I'd wanted huge splashes of color in my room. The brighter, the better. But at least I still had my window.

When I leaned against the pillows and rested my head against the glass, I could see into the park—Linc's and my escape. Not that he needed it much anymore. He was a senior now, ready to escape and find his freedom. And I'd be here. Alone.

Mom followed me over to the window, staring out into the park as if she could find her freedom there, too. But she didn't venture out much anymore. As if it hurt too much to go.

Sometimes, it felt like she was fading in front of my eyes, turning into a ghost I could only see at certain moments.

Her hand sifted through my hair, strands that seemed to change color depending on the light. It was mostly light brown with hints of blond, but the light hit strands of red every so often. Mom called it *magic hair.*

"It's boring, huh?" she asked.

My brows rose in surprise as I looked up at her.

Mom's lips twitched the barest amount. "You can be honest. There isn't a speck of real color anywhere. And my girl is rainbows."

Pressure built in my chest, and the sudden urge to cry hit me. Not because I was sad but because I remembered what it was like to feel like my mom *saw* me. Know she was on my side.

"I'm gonna spill something, and Dad's gonna get mad," I mumbled.

Mom's mouth pursed. "You know what? I think we need to mix it up a bit. I saw a rainbow comforter at a store a few blocks over. We'll get that and some rainbow pillows. I think it'll look great with the flower curtains and window seat."

"Really?" I asked, hope bleeding into the word. Mom *never* went against Dad's wishes.

Her pale green eyes, so similar to mine, sparked with a little more life, a hint of fight. "I think we should paint a mural on the wall. A rainbow over your bed."

My jaw went slack. "Paint a rainbow on the *wall*?"

A laugh bubbled out of her. "What? Afraid to get your hands dirty?"

I thrust my chin up. "Never." I wasn't like Dad, afraid to do things myself.

Mom's hands snaked out, and she tickled my sides. "Are you sure? You might get covered in rainbow splatters."

I shrieked, flopping back onto my bed as she tickled me in earnest. I rolled and writhed, trying to escape the attack. "I'm gonna splatter you with rainbows."

A chuckle sounded from the doorway, deeper than it had been even a year ago. When I caught sight of my older brother, he looked more like a grownup than a teenager. He'd bulked up from playing hockey in a local league—much to our father's chagrin—and had just a hint of dark stubble on his face. Kate's older sister, Angeline, told me his hazel eyes were *dreamy*. Gross.

"Threats in the form of rainbows. Watch out, Mom," Linc said, eyes gleaming.

Mom grinned at him. I hadn't seen that kind of smile in months. "I can take it." She straightened and pulled me to sitting. "We're going to paint a rainbow over Ellie's bed. Want to help?"

Linc's dark brows almost hit his hairline before a look of unease flickered across his face. He covered it quickly, and an answering grin spread. "I'm in."

"The hell you are," a new voice boomed from the hallway.

It wasn't a yell, exactly. It never was. But the tone made my stomach churn because Dad's punishments were crueler and more clever than the typical stuff. He didn't spank or ground. He took the things you cared about most.

A class or club you loved. Access to your favorite friend or the library. Only for him to replace them with things he thought you needed to be an *appropriate* young lady. Stuff I hated. My life got a little smaller every time.

Dad's dark eyes flashed, and Linc moved instantly, stepping between us and him. That telltale muscle in Dad's cheek pulsed in a staccato beat, his dark gaze moving to Mom. "We discussed this, Gwyn."

Mom wrung her hands again, that nervousness bleeding back into her. But she didn't back down. "I know. But this room isn't really Ellie. She's six. She needs color, life."

The continued pulse in Dad's cheek was the only thing that gave away his anger. I'd gotten good at looking for it. It was my sign to run for one of my hiding spots.

As if Linc had read my mind, he held me tighter and moved closer to Mom...preparing.

One corner of Dad's mouth lifted in something that looked a lot like a lip curl a Disney villain would make. "So noble."

Linc's eyes flashed. "You don't need to be a dick just because your six-year-old has the audacity to be a kid."

Dad only took one step, but the power behind it had me sucking in a sharp breath. He glared at Linc. "I'm the one who's keeping you. Those clothes, your tuition, this *house*...it can all go away in a single second if I want it to."

Linc's jaw clenched, making sharp angles appear where more rounded curves had been.

"And you," Dad spat, turning to me. "I spend thousands of dollars redecorating your room and you want to ruin it with sloppy finger painting?"

My legs started to tremble. There were so many things I wanted to say. I hadn't wanted thousands of dollars spent on designers and fancy, stuffy decorations. I just wanted my room to feel like *me*.

"You're an ungrateful brat," he snarled.

"Philip," my mom said on a gasp as I started to cry.

"A *sniveling* brat, apparently," Dad muttered.

"Enough," Linc barked, lifting me into his arms.

I pressed my face into his neck, trying to hide the tears.

My father let out a sound of disgust. "She's weak. Just like her mother."

"Philip," Mom whispered. "Let's discuss this privately."

"Mom, don't," Linc said, his voice tight.

"It's okay," she assured him. But I heard the lie in her voice. I'd gotten good at that, too, hearing the way untruths turned voices just a little higher, tighter.

"It's not," Linc gritted out.

At least he was honest. Linc never hid what he was feeling. He let it play out on his face and in his voice and words.

"Take care of Ellie," she whispered, heading for the door, knowing Dad would follow.

As they stepped into the hallway, I heard his angry words. Mean ones that cut her down like vicious blows. Threats that made her bow to his every wish. Sometimes, he seemed worse than any villain in my storybooks. Because he was smarter, too. And the good guys never won.

The cruelty in Dad's voice only made me cry harder. Linc's hand moved over my back as he sat us on the edge of my bed. "It's okay, El Bell. Everything's going to be okay."

"It's not," I hiccupped, the words breaking through my sobs. "I shouldn't have said anything. It's my fault, ConCon. I should've lied better."

Linc muttered a curse. "No, you shouldn't have. You should say exactly what you think. What you feel. Fuck 'em if they don't like it."

My eyes went wide as I pulled back from my brother, settling next to him on the edge of the bed. "That was a bad one."

He grinned at me, but it was sad around the edges. "It was honest, though."

I rocked my feet against the floor, back and forth, again and again as I mulled over his words. "I hate them sometimes."

It was the worst kind of wrong: hate. Even hating my father, who could be so mean. But it was worse to feel that way about Mom. I wanted so badly for her to make it all stop, to take us away from the cold cruelty of this house and bring us somewhere with warmth, lightness, and air. A place I could breathe.

"I know," Linc said quietly. He curved his hand around mine and squeezed gently. "How about we make a promise?"

I looked up at him. "What?"

"That we'll never be like them."

I pulled in air as if I were drawing that vow into my very being. "We'll never be like them. Mean, or..."

"Not fighting for ourselves, for what's right," Linc said, his hazel eyes flashing a little more gold in the fading afternoon light.

"I wanna be strong. Like you, ConCon," I whispered.

Linc's expression softened. "You already are."

A ringing clawed at my ears, making me blink against the darkness in the bedroom. By the time my eyes were fully open, I wondered if I'd imagined it. But then the knocking began, followed by muffled voices.

I pushed up in bed, throwing off the stupid, pale pink comforter and sliding my feet into my slippers. I crept toward my door as if some invisible ghost might spot me out of bed and tattle to Dad. The voices got louder as I approached the door, and a shiver worked its way down my spine as my fingers closed around the glass doorknob.

I waited, listening, trying to make out the words. But everything was too muffled. I stayed there for a moment, my heart hammering against my ribs at just the *thought* of what I wanted to do. I closed my eyes and summoned my strength as I replayed the promise I'd made with Linc earlier today in my mind. Ever so slowly, I twisted the knob and slid into the hall just as Linc's door opened.

His gaze cut instantly to me. *"Go back to bed,"* he mouthed.

I shook my head and jutted out my chin. I was finding a little of the strength he had.

He let out a frustrated breath and then reached for my hand. We carefully moved down the hall, both aware that the wood planks might give us away if we stepped wrong. We tried to stay on the antique rugs that dotted the path.

I caught a few words as we approached the entryway. *Upstate New York. Bridge. Crime scene.*

A sick feeling slid through me, making me feel queasy and heavy all at once. I tried to fight off the nausea, but it distracted me enough that I stepped in the wrong spot. The floor creaked, and the voices went silent.

Dad stalked around the corner. "What are you doing out of bed?"

"I-I heard voices," I stammered.

"You guys weren't exactly quiet," Linc defended.

Dad ran a hand through his hair, giving it an unkempt look that was very unlike him. His jaw tightened, and that telltale muscle pulsed again. "Doesn't matter." His gaze moved from my brother to me and back again, a coldness creeping into every part of him. "There was an accident. Your mother's dead."

SEVERAL MONTHS LATER

I chewed the bite of pork tenderloin our chef had probably spent hours on and tried not to think about the little creature it had once been. The one time I'd told Dad I wanted to stop eating meat, he hadn't been thrilled. *"You don't want to eat like a normal person, then you'll get bread and water in this house and nothing else."*

I'd lasted three days. When I asked to eat with him again, he'd served the rarest cuts of meat for a week straight and sat there until I ate every last bite.

But nights like tonight were easier. He was focused on files as he ate while I stared out at the glittering lights of the city and the park's lit pathways. I told myself stories about a little girl who discovered she was really a fairy princess and the royal court that came to rescue her from the evil human who'd kidnapped her.

I was getting pretty good at the stories. They were all I really had now. Dad had stopped letting me have playdates with Kate, Linc had told Dad to jump in the Atlantic and went off to Stanford instead of Harvard like Dad wanted. And Mom...she was gone.

A burn lit at the backs of my eyes. I missed her. I missed the little glimmer of hope that she'd take Linc and me out of here. Somewhere we could be free. Even if it never happened, at least I'd had the hope. Now, I had nothing at all.

"Eleanor." Dad's voice snapped out like a whip.

My spine jerked straight as I took a mental inventory of what I might've done wrong.

"What is the meaning of this?" he demanded. He held up a piece of paper, but the sheet trembled, so I couldn't make out the words.

"W-what do you mean?"

"This." He slammed the paper down on the table, making the plates rattle.

Dad rarely let his temper show, so I knew I'd stepped in it. Whatever I'd done.

"I told you that you had two choices. The flute or the violin. A young lady does not play the saxophone."

I felt the blood draining from my head. The all-girls school I attended on the Upper West Side had a music program that started in second grade. We all got to pick an instrument. Everyone except me, apparently. But at the last possible second, I'd been a rebel. I'd been strong like Linc and picked the sax because it sounded cool.

I hadn't thought Dad would find out. It wasn't like he ever came to anything but the meetings with my teacher. He always played the working-single-dad card. I'd heard him too many times to count.

But I should've known. He had eyes everywhere. He probably got weekly reports on my behavior from people at the school.

"Eleanor."

That tone. It instantly had sweat rolling down my back and my hands fisting in my lap.

"I'm disappointed in you."

My mouth went dry, and my legs began to shake.

"Clearly, you aren't ready for the responsibilities I've bestowed on you. The privileges."

A sick feeling took root in my belly. *What else is left? What else can he take away?*

And then he said it.

"Until you can prove that you are worthy of the privileges I bestow on you, there will be no more weekly chats with Lincoln—"

"Dad, no! Please!" The tears were instant, streaming down my face in angry torrents. It didn't matter that Linc was working two jobs to cover his tiny apartment or taking extra classes to try to finish early. He always made our calls.

My father's cold look had me snapping my mouth closed. "He's already a bad influence on you. Overly emotional. Rebellious. I won't stand for it."

All the best parts of me were things Linc had instilled in me. Things he'd fostered. Because he was often more father than brother.

I'd have to pack those things. Hide them from the world until it was safe to take them out again.

"I'm sorry," I whispered. "I'll do better. I just…please don't take him away, too."

My father smiled then. Like when he won an especially brutal round of racquetball or closed a business deal. Because he knew he'd won. "I'm glad to hear that, Eleanor. Now, tell me. What will it be, flute or violin?"

I stared at the plate of half-eaten food, knowing I'd have to finish or risk hellfire for that, too. "Whatever you think is best."

Dad's grin only widened. "I've always been partial to the flute. Violin can be a little shrill, don't you think?"

Some part of me knew I answered. That I'd played the part he wanted me to play. But the rest of me? I buried it deep so no one could ever steal it from me again. The only problem was that *I* didn't have it either.

CHAPTER ONE

Trace

DAAAAAADDY." Keely's voice cut through our house like a heat-seeking missile. "My toothpaste exploded."

I didn't move for a second, just stared at the wall before I pinched the bridge of my nose in that spot just below my brow bone where headaches loved to form. Everything hurt. Whether from sparring with my foster brother, Kyler, or tackling a perp behind The Soda Pop after he tried to snatch cash out of an open register, I wasn't sure. Both options made me feel old.

"It's really everywhere."

The amused wonder in Keely's voice had me pushing to my feet. As cute as my kid was, she could leave destruction in her wake. I strode down the hallway, adjusting my empty gun belt as I moved. But I froze as I stepped into the doorway.

It looked like a murder scene, not a kid's bathroom. Red goo was *everywhere*. The sink, the mirror, and all over said kid's face.

I stared at her for a long moment. Her long, brown locks were in haphazard pigtails she'd attempted to tackle herself. Her green eyes, a couple of shades lighter than my own, looked up at me with a hint of wariness.

That flicker of uncertainty spurred me into action. "You just had to have the strawberry flavor, didn't you."

Keely broke into a fit of giggles, just as I'd hoped. "I dunno what happened. I just squeezed, and *BOOM*!" She threw her hands wide, making more red goo hit the walls.

I tried not to wince at the mess. "Gentle squeezes, remember?"

She sent me a sheepish grin. "I forgot."

I chuckled, grabbing her pink washcloth dotted with strawberries. "Bet you won't next time."

"Prolly not," she mumbled as I ran the cloth under the water.

I dabbed at my daughter's face, trying to get her clean while glancing at my watch. Five past eight. *Damn.* I scrubbed faster.

The thought of being late ground at me. Logically, I knew it wasn't the end of the world, but it reminded me too much of growing up. Of the time before I went to live with the Colsons. When I'd gotten to school hours past starting time, hungry and in stained clothes a size too small.

That would never be the case for my kid.

"Daaaad, too scratchy," she complained.

"Sorry, Keels." I instantly softened my movements, trying to get every sticky ounce of red gel off her. Laying the washcloth on the sink, I lifted and deposited her in the hall so she wouldn't step in the mess. "Arms up."

Keely instantly shot her hands in the air. I fought a laugh as I pulled her T-shirt covered in tiny rainbows over her head and handed her the toothbrush from the counter. "Go brush your teeth in my bathroom, then pick out a new shirt."

"Aw, man. That one's my favorite," she complained.

My lips twitched. "You want your friends to think you miss your mouth when you're eating jelly and toast?"

Her little nose wrinkled adorably. "Noooo. Do I have to use your gross mint toothpaste?"

"Mint isn't gross."

"It burns, and it tastes like a plant from Grams's garden."

I shook my head. "Lucky for you, I stocked extra strawberry in the hall closet. Just be careful."

"Yes!" She shot both hands in the air again and did a little dance down the hallway.

I laughed, but as I turned back to the bathroom, a groan replaced the sound. I glanced at my watch again. Five minutes. I could handle that. I'd become an expert in mess cleanup at record-breaking speed.

Pulling open the cabinet, I grabbed some paper towels and cleaning spray and got to work. As I cleaned, I realized the red toothpaste was leaving pink stains behind everywhere. It really did look like a crime scene.

My back teeth ground together as I scrubbed harder. My kid wouldn't have a bathroom with stained tile. I'd have to tackle it with bleach tonight.

I did the best I could with the time I had, wiping up the worst of the mess. I straightened as that heat-seeking missile cut through the air again.

"Daaaaaddy! It exploded again."

I dropped my head, pinching the bridge of my nose and rubbing the spots where pressure was building. I didn't make a habit of cursing, not in front of others, and especially not in my daughter's presence, but there was only one word that would do right now.

"Fuck."

Downtown Sparrow Falls still bustled with foot traffic as I turned toward the sheriff's station, but it wasn't quite as busy now that we'd hit early October, and tourist traffic was waning. The rock climbers, mountain bikers, and whitewater rafters seeking out Central Oregon's beauty would be replaced by skiers and snowboarders once the snow hit. But there was usually a lull in the fall that let all of us locals enjoy the peace of our town.

Turning into an open parking spot, I turned off the engine just as my phone dinged. I grabbed the device from my cupholder and took in the alert on the screen.

Kye has changed the name of the group to Trace's Bloodbath.

I scowled at the screen, and my fingers typed out a message.

> **Me:** *I was just asking if anyone knew how to get stains out of tile, that's all.*

I should've known better than to ask my siblings for help. They loved to roast me on a good day. Most of us might not be related by blood, but that didn't mean the seven of us weren't like any other siblings. Kye was the ultimate shit-stirrer, though.

> **Kye:** *I always knew you had murdery tendencies under that rule-following facade.*

> **Rhodes:** *I'm framing this photo. Or seeing if Lolli can make it into diamond art.*

My scowl deepened at my sister's text. She'd come to live with the Colsons at age thirteen after losing her family in a fire and was particularly fond of our grandmother—a woman infamous for creating inappropriate gemstone paintings. This one wasn't nearly dirty enough for her.

> **Me:** *That picture of my bathroom was shared in confidence.*

> **Fallon:** *I'm pretty sure Keels got toothpaste on the ceiling.*

If I'd thought Keely's bathroom was bad, it had nothing on mine. And I'd had no chance to clean it before I left to drop her at school. Just the thought of going home to that had me twitchy.

> **Me:** *Pretty sure it's worse than your glitter bombs.*

> **Fallon:** *Nothing is worse than my glitter bombs. That's why I hold all the power.*

My sister was the kindest, gentlest human being and had the most empathetic heart. But she had a creative vengeful streak. Once you crossed her, there was no going back. The combination made her perfect for her role as a social worker with Child Protective Services. But the fact that she went into volatile situations wasn't easy for any of us.

Kye: *Stay far away from me with that devil's breath.*

Fallon: *Depends, are you going to follow me on my home visits AGAIN?*

Kye: *If you go after dark to bad neighborhoods, I sure as shit am.*

My back teeth ground together. Fallon was determined to stand on her own, sometimes to her detriment. It drove Kye and me crazy, but him especially. The two shared a bond that went beyond words. When Kye came to live with us at sixteen, raging at the world and the horrific situation he'd come from, she'd been the only one who could reach him.

Fallon: *Then prepare for my can of whoop-ass.*

She dropped a glitter explosion emoji in the chat, and I knew Kye would be paying for his latest protective stunt.

Me: *If you jerks aren't going to help me, I'm going to work.*

Shep: *Watch out, he said the J-word. Might as well be an F-bomb. We're all in for it.*

Me: *I hate you all.*

I switched the chat to silent, noting that I hadn't heard from our siblings Arden and Cope this morning. Cope was up in Seattle, back to hockey training, his fiancée, Sutton, and her son, Luca, making the trip with him. And Arden was likely holed up with her fiancé, Linc, or lost in a painting or sculpture. But I still typed out quick texts to make sure all was good.

Making sure all was good with my siblings on a daily basis was a compulsion, and I knew it. But most of us had come from rough circumstances, making our way into the system through loss, neglect, or abuse. Even Nora Colson's two birth children, Cope and Fallon, had been through their share of heartache, losing their father and brother in a car accident at a young age.

It was a reminder that none of us made it out of this life unscathed. And recent events only made that more evident. The thought had twitchiness surging back to life. The urge to call the school just to check on Keely was strong, but I fought it back and climbed out of my SUV.

Striding toward the station's front door, I appreciated the slight chill in the air. After a summer of record temps, everyone was ready for fall. As I stepped inside, a man in his mid-twenties looked up from behind the desk with a grin. "Morning, Sheriff."

"Morning, Fletcher," I greeted. "Anything on fire today?"

"Just the mountain of paperwork from your arrest last night. Nice tackle, by the way."

I cracked my neck, trying to relieve some of the leftover pain from the move. "I'm getting too old for this stuff."

Fletcher shook his head, making his light brown hair flop over his eyes. He looked like a quintessential college quarterback without a care in the world. "Never."

I scoffed. "I'm thirty-six, not twenty-six. Practically geriatric for law enforcement."

"Whatever you say, Sheriff."

I waved him off. "I'm gonna go fill out that paperwork and probably ice my back."

I headed through the bullpen, the familiar din of various voices filling my ears. Some stopped conversing to say hello, others just gave me a chin lift. Will Wright pretended he didn't see me at all, as if that were some sort of power play. The deputy was power-hungry, and that sort of thing made an officer dangerous. But so far, he hadn't done anything I could fire him for.

"Hey, Sheriff," Beth Hansen greeted as she balanced an egg sandwich in one hand and a phone in the other.

"Morning, Beth."

"Left a sandwich on your desk."

"Thanks," I muttered. I'd managed Keely's breakfast this morning but not my own.

"Kiss ass," Will muttered.

Beth's eyes cut to him. "If you weren't such an ass, I'd get one for you, too. But it's hard for a zebra to change its stripes."

Frank Smith let out a guffaw at his desk as he patted his stomach. "Mine tastes mighty fine, Wright."

I shook my head and moved toward my office. I didn't have the energy to referee their antics. Besides, if I knew one thing for sure, it was that Beth could hold her own. And she wouldn't take kindly to me stepping in on her behalf.

Entering my office, I came up short when I saw my friend and second-in-command, Gabriel Rivera, sitting in a chair opposite my desk. "If you stole my breakfast sandwich, we're gonna have words."

Gabriel looked up, but there was no amusement on his face like I expected.

The grin slid from my face as I shut the door. "What happened?"

He stared back at me, giving it to me straight, like always. "It's your dad. He's out."

Blood roared in my ears, and my jaw clamped shut so hard it would be a miracle if I hadn't cracked a tooth. *Out.* Not out of the hospital or a day spa. Out of prison.

Where I'd sent him at the age of twelve.

A sentence he'd vowed to make me pay for.

Now, he would get his chance.

CHAPTER TWO

Ellie

I STEPPED ON THE BRAKE, MAKING MY NEW LITTLE SUV JERK slightly as I stopped at one of the three traffic lights in Sparrow Falls. That was three *total*. In the entire town. Just a little different than the hardscape of Manhattan.

But as I took in the main street through town, I saw why my brother had fallen in love with the place. Mountains and forests encircled it like a ring of protection, the air had a crisp clarity to it that made you feel like it was clearing away your troubles with each breath you took, and the shops and restaurants lining Cascade Avenue were absolutely adorable and unique.

A soft honk sounded behind me, and I realized the light had turned from red to green. Even the honking here was gentler. I switched my foot from the brake to the gas, and my car lurched forward.

I winced. I'd gotten my license at eighteen but hadn't needed to drive much in New York. I didn't even own a car until two weeks ago when I purchased the RAV4.

Bradley would've hated it. He would've insisted on something understated but astronomically expensive. A top-of-the-line Mercedes or Maserati. Something in black or metallic gray.

At the dealership, I'd swapped white for Ruby Flare Pearl at the last moment. My hands had started sweating just saying the name. It felt like my first true rebellion in years. And it felt good.

My fingers wiggled on the wheel. I was still relishing the lightness of my left ring finger, where the diamond solitaire used to sit. The one that felt more like a chain than a promise of forever. The only remnant of it now was a faint tan line I was determined to erase, along with all memories of the man my father had all but picked for me to marry.

Heading down Cascade Avenue, I passed The Mix Up, my one-stop shop to feed my cupcake addiction; The Soda Pop, a diner with the best burgers around; and the sheriff's station. I forced my gaze away from that building, images of dark green eyes that saw too much filling my mind.

Not today.

Today was for new beginnings and the first place that would be mine alone. I'd gone from my father's penthouse to an apartment with Bradley, never getting to make a place *mine*. But that all changed today.

I flipped on my blinker and made a slightly too-wide turn onto a side street. I'd need some driving practice before the snow came. Thankfully, my new rental was close enough to town that I could walk if needed—or wanted. As I moved away from downtown, the streets turned residential with enchanting Craftsman houses on lots with yards that said the people who lived there took pride in their homes.

Making another turn onto Lavender Lane, I grinned. The houses were a bit more spread out on this street, the yards bigger. I'd looked at countless rentals. Apartments over shops, guesthouses on properties outside of town, and, finally, this one. It was perfect.

The house had been painted lavender, matching the street name. Nothing about it was cookie cutter, from the garden gnomes decorating the front yard to the stained glass hanging in each window. The outside was a riot of color that called to a part of me I'd shoved down for far too long.

Turning into the driveway, I pulled to a jerky stop and hopped out, breathing in the Central Oregon air. I'd been to places with mountains before: Aspen, Vail, Tahoe, and even the Swiss Alps. But the air was different here, as if it had a scent all its own.

A horn sounded, and a familiar Range Rover pulled in behind my SUV. The passenger door was open before the engine was off, and a woman with dark hair and hypnotic eyes jumped out, her massive dog behind her.

Arden's eyes twinkled as she crossed to me. "Move-in day. How do you feel?"

I grinned at my brother's fiancée. "I'm excited. Ready to make this place my own."

"You shouldn't be jumping out of cars," Linc called, slamming the door to punctuate his point as he glared at Arden.

She just rolled her eyes. "Cowboy, the doctor gave me a clean bill of health a week ago. I can spar with Kye if I want to."

That was the wrong thing to say. Linc's scowl deepened, and his hazel eyes went stormy. "You still need to be careful."

"Do I?" she challenged.

"Vicious," he growled. "Don't make me tie you up."

Arden's lips twitched. "Promises, promises."

Linc's expression softened as he gently pulled her into his arms, grazing her temple with his lips. "Just want you to be careful."

A pang flared along my sternum as I crouched to give Brutus some scratches, anything to distract me from the longing taking root somewhere deep. My brother had found himself the best possible family. The Colsons were warm and accepting, the kind of people who always had each other's backs. And Arden and Linc needed that. Especially when my father had tried to tear them apart and ruin their happiness.

Brutus laid his big cane corso head on my shoulder, and I wrapped my arms around his gray body. He always seemed to know when I needed a little extra comfort and was the best at giving it.

"You need a dog," Arden said, cutting into my thoughts.

I looked up at her and grinned. "I do."

"Will Mrs. Henderson let you have pets?" she asked hopefully. "She had a couple of cats."

The woman who used to live here had moved into assisted living after she fell and broke her hip. But she wasn't ready to sell the place quite yet, allowing me to luck into this rental.

"She said I was welcome to as long as I pay the pet deposit."

Linc studied me carefully. As Arden fully recovered from her injuries at the hands of my father and his minion, Linc's focus had turned to me more often than I liked. He was too astute for his own good, and I was a horrible liar. Another reason I needed some space from him and Arden.

"Maybe you should wait a little bit. You've had a lot of change lately," Linc said gently.

Break up with my fiancé? Check. Leave my well-paying interior design job? Check. Move across the country? Check. Watch my dad go to prison? Check.

"Sometimes, it's better to just rip off the Band-Aid." At least, I hoped it was. I wasn't rocking in a corner. Yet.

Linc frowned. "Maybe you should stay with us for a little longer. And I'm putting a guesthouse in at the new build. You can have that all to yourself."

"Cowboy." Arden laid a hand on his chest. "Ellie's an adult. She wants her own space. This is good for her."

My brother's frown deepened. "I just—"

"Love her. So, it's natural for you to worry about her. But no one will mess with her in this house."

My brows pulled together. "Why?"

"She just means Trace has you on his patrol officers' drive-by list," Linc said quickly.

Trace.

Arden's brother and the most stunning man to ever see me at my worst. Those dark green eyes flashed in my mind again. So full of concern, with a healthy dose of pissed off.

"He doesn't need to do that," I gritted out as I pushed to my feet.

Arden looked from me to Linc and back again, then shook her

head. "I'm not getting between you two. El, we got groceries to stock your kitchen."

I grimaced. Just another new thing I'd be tackling in this era. Cooking. Living in New York meant restaurants on every corner and some of the best cuisine the world had to offer. Sparrow Falls had some delicious spots, but certainly not enough to sustain me seven days a week.

"She's going to burn the house down," Linc muttered as he pulled me into his side.

"I am not," I huffed.

Amusement danced in his eyes. "At least I learned how to boil water for ramen in college."

Because that was all he could afford. My brother had stood strong when our father cut him off. He'd gotten a scholarship and loans so he could go to the college of *his* choice. Not me. I'd toed the line, attending Columbia and living at home just like *Dad* wanted.

Anger surged. But not at my father, at *me* for going along with it. I'd wanted to study painting at Savannah College of Art and Design, but it was far too *hippie* for Philip Pierce's tastes. And I'd caved, not wanting to rock the boat. But I hadn't known I was kowtowing to a killer.

"Hey." Linc gave my shoulder a soft squeeze. "You okay?"

I lifted my gaze and forced a smile. "Peachy. Just thinking about what culinary masterpiece I'm going to serve you to make you eat your words."

Linc chuckled. "I'll believe it when I see it."

I set the final box in the living room and surveyed the space. As vibrant and quirky as the outside of the bungalow was, the interior was fairly...bland. Furniture in neutral tones with the occasional hint of color in the form of a throw pillow. It reminded me too much of my bedroom growing up, as well as the apartment I'd shared with Bradley and the aesthetic my design firm favored.

Rocking from my toes to my heels, I started envisioning what the space *could* be. The colors and textures I could use to bring it to life. The only problem? I wasn't sure what I wanted my life to be. And I'd gone so long without color that I wasn't sure what my favorites were anymore.

Color wasn't the only thing I'd gone without. I'd missed out on so many things. But I could only change one thing at a time.

I slid my phone out of my jeans pocket and moved to one of the bags from the massive haul I'd gotten at a catchall store. Grabbing a portable speaker from the bag, I hooked up my cell and opened my music app. It only took a couple of minutes of scrolling before my lips tugged up.

Boy Band Bangers.

I hit play, and *NSYNC's *Tearin' Up My Heart* filled the room. My preteen heart soared.

Sayonara, silence.

I lost myself in unpacking everything I'd purchased for my rental over the past few days and the suitcases of personal items I'd brought from New York. I'd left behind a closetful of clothes Bradley was likely shredding out of spite.

It didn't matter. That wardrobe was just as bland as the walls of my apartment. I'd get new clothes that fit the me I didn't quite know yet.

By the time I finished getting the bulk of my new belongings settled, I was a starving, sweaty mess. But Backstreet Boys were keeping me going with *Everybody*. I swung my hips to the beat as I made my way to the kitchen.

Looking around the room, I tried to decide what the easiest thing to make would be. Definitely nothing that required steps and assembly. Maybe I could take a cooking class for that.

I crossed to the fridge, opened the freezer, and grinned. Arden knew me well. The compartment was filled to the brim with frozen lasagna, bags of veggie stir-fry, and an array of other meals. But moving required one thing and one thing only.

Pizza.

Grabbing a veggie lover's from the top of the stack, I read the instructions. Seemed simple enough. I crossed to the oven that looked older than the Backstreet Boys bop currently playing from the speakers. I turned the knob to bake and set it to four hundred and twenty-five degrees. I quickly cut the pie out of the plastic wrapping and set it on the rack, which had certainly seen some use over the years.

After making sure the preheat light flashed on, I headed for the stairs. While the lot for my rental was large, the house was fairly small. It had two bedrooms and one and a half baths, with a tiny living room and office downstairs. But it was all I needed and more—because it was mine.

I snagged a fresh change of clothes from my room and headed for the shower. Turning on the water, I peeled off what I'd been wearing and left it in a pile on the floor. A smile that probably looked more than a little unhinged spread across my face.

I could leave my clothes in that pile all week if I wanted to. There'd be no arched eyebrows or wrinkled forehead and look of disgust from Bradley. No sharply barked command from my father that no daughter of his would be a slob. I could pick them up whenever I damn well pleased.

And as if *NSYNC could read my mind, *Bye Bye Bye* came on the second I stepped into the shower, seeping up through the floorboards. I belted out the lyrics as I shampooed my hair and washed my face. By the time I was ready to turn off the water, I felt better than I had in years, maybe ever.

Quickly toweling off and getting the excess water out of my hair, I reached for my underwear and grinned. They were totally ridiculous. An impulse purchase at one of the big-box stores I'd hit up in preparation for my move. I was pretty sure they were a kids' design, but I didn't give a damn.

The rainbows decorating them reminded me of what I'd wanted

to be back when I wasn't afraid to reach for it. I pulled them on and then reached for my bralette. The lace was a creamy white, but I'd find some brighter ones. There was a small boutique in town that might carry some things. If not, I'd order online.

Before I could dream up what colors to buy, an angry beeping blared so loud it resembled a tornado warning.

Do they get tornados in Oregon?

I didn't have the first clue, but I was already racing out of the bathroom. And that's when I smelled it.

Smoke.

"Shit, shit, shit!" I raced down the stairs toward the kitchen. Smoke billowed out of the oven in angry waves, and I tried to remember if this was the sort of fire I could put out with water. I spun around, trying to see if there was a fire extinguisher or a pitcher of some kind, as the blaring warred with the nineties pop.

I swore I heard something else, too. A banging. But I was too worried about potentially blowing myself up to seek out the source.

I should have.

Because I was frantically opening cabinets one second, and the next, a dark god of fury was striding into my kitchen. I gaped as the man hauled open the oven and sprayed something inside to douse the flames.

As he straightened, I took in the details I couldn't grasp before. Dark hair still damp from a shower. Green eyes like the hues found deep in the forest. Scruff dotting a jaw so sharp it could cut glass. And a worn Mercer County Sheriff T-shirt, the kind that was perfect for sleeping in.

"Trace?"

CHAPTER THREE

Trace

I DIDN'T KNOW WHERE THE HELL TO LOOK. EVERYWHERE MY EYES darted was skin. Too much damn beauty.

And she had ridiculous, sparkly rainbows on her panties.

Cute on top of gorgeous was not a good combination. Especially when it came to Ellie Pierce. She was all sunshine and goofiness. But the woman had secrets. And secrets weren't something I handled well.

"What the hell are you doing?" I growled.

Her mouth dropped open. "Trying to make a pizza?"

"You could've burned this house down. What are you doing in Mrs. Henderson's house anyway?" I wanted to ask what she was doing here half-naked, but my dick didn't need to be thinking about that any more than it already was.

"I, uh, live here."

Oh, hell no.

I paced to the window, opening it so the smoke could escape. The last thing I needed was Ellie living next door. She was walking temptation, and a mess all rolled into one. And that was something I needed to stay far away from when I had a daughter to think about. I needed safe, stable, and predictable. And Ellie was rainbow fireworks.

Fireworks and secrets.

Turning back around, I wanted to jab an ice pick into my eyes. Tan skin, pale green eyes, hair that couldn't quite decide what color it wanted to be, and curves for days. My dick twitched.

That was it. I was going to hell.

"For the love of God, put this on." I tugged off my tee and handed it to her.

Ellie flushed, the color deepening the apples of her cheeks and only making her look *more* beautiful. "Sorry, I, uh, just got out of the shower."

"You're making it worse," I groaned, pinching the bridge of my nose.

She tugged the shirt over her head. "Better?" Her gaze dipped to my chest, tracing lines I couldn't see. Information I didn't need.

"Not really," I grumbled.

Annoyance took over some of the embarrassment. "Has anyone ever told you that you're a grouch?"

"You're the one who almost set the neighborhood on fire."

"*You're* the one who broke into my house."

Heat flared because she had a point. "I have a key."

Ellie's eyes narrowed, a hint of fire slipping into her pale green irises. "Why do you have a key to *my* house?"

"Because I live next door."

Ellie's jaw went slack, and her eyes widened. "No, you don't."

Amusement replaced a little of my frustration. "Want me to show you the title?"

She let out a huff of air. "My damn interfering brother," she grumbled, moving around the kitchen in search of something.

I frowned. "What do you mean?"

"Linc insisted on touring every rental with me. He found something that wouldn't do for his little sister everywhere we went. Then he *happened* to hear about this one. But he just wanted me living next door to the sheriff." She snatched a set of oven mitts and a garbage bag, moving toward the fire zone. "So-called drive-by route. You drive by it all right. On your way home."

My eyes narrowed on her. "Why would he want you living next door to me?"

Ellie slid out the burned-to-a-crisp pizza and tossed it into the trash bag. "That's a damn good question. You'll have to ask him."

Linc and Ellie's father had recently proven he was the worst of the worst, but he was in prison now, and they were out of his reach. Unless there was something else. I knew it wasn't the first secret Ellie was keeping. Just like I knew she'd lied when she arrived in town a few weeks ago with a black eye, saying she'd hit herself with a suitcase by accident.

My hands fisted on instinct, anger surging in hot waves. Everything about the faint purple beneath expertly applied makeup had reminded me of another time. One I'd do anything to forget.

"There something you're not telling me?"

Her mask fell into place so fast it nearly gave me whiplash. Gone were the frustration and hints of humor, and in their place was a nothingness I hated with every fiber of my being.

"Linc is overprotective. You should know that by now since your sister can't sneeze without him calling three doctors to give her a checkup."

That much was true. I'd had my concerns when Linc and Arden got together, unsure if she'd ever be ready for a relationship like that. But he'd turned out to be everything she needed.

"You in trouble?" I asked, watching for any flickers of a lie on that beautiful face. I might've been blind to that sort of thing in my past, but I wasn't now.

Ellie lifted her chin, the movement slight but telling. "What I am is exhausted."

A non-answer. Not a lie, but not the truth either. And that ground at me—the idea that someone might be messing with her. It wasn't any of my business, but I couldn't stop the urge to step in, help, and shield her from whatever was headed her way.

I opened my mouth to speak, but the smoke detector cut out,

finally signaling that the smoke had abated somewhat. But it didn't leave us in silence. Instead, it left us with some god-awful pop ballad about promises and lifetimes. "What in the actual—?" I stopped myself from cursing. "What *is* that?"

A little of the fatigue left Ellie's expression, and her lips trembled as if fighting a smile. "What do you have against the classic vocal stylings of *NSYNC?"

My face screwed up. "I think I'd take Arden's ear-bleeding metal over this."

"You can't tell me you've never jammed out to *It's Gonna Be Me*."

One corner of my mouth kicked up as I winced at an especially high note. "I'm more of a *Bye Bye Bye* man."

"You missed that one earlier. I did some epic shower singing to that bop."

Ellie. Singing. In the shower.

I'd be needing one of those soon. A very cold one.

Ellie turned, surveying the room and sighing. "I just wanted a veggie lover's pizza on my first night in a house that's all mine."

The sorrow in her voice hit me square in the solar plexus, and I wanted to fix that, too. "It's the oven. Mrs. Henderson hasn't used it in years. The local church brought most of her meals. Otherwise, she ate with Keely and me. The oven needs to be cleaned out before it's used."

Ellie stared at the appliance like it was her archnemesis. "I should've thought of that. It looked…well-loved."

I barked out a laugh. "That's the kind way of saying it."

"I'll get some oven cleaner tomorrow. And a whole bunch of rubber gloves."

"You should have someone come out and look at it. Make sure it's safe to use." I stared at her. Noticing how her hair soaked through the cotton of my tee, making the fabric cling to her. How the strands appeared so much darker than before. The urge to touch them, to know if they were as soft as they looked nearly took me out at the knees.

"I will." Ellie turned then, the sorrow from her earlier words now in her eyes. "Thanks for riding to the rescue."

"Just glad I was home." I wasn't always. The nights Keely was with her mom, Leah, I usually stayed late at the station to catch up on paperwork. The thought of Ellie getting caught in a blaze while alone had a sick feeling taking root in my gut.

She started for the door. "Tell Keely hi for me."

That was my cue. It shouldn't have been hard to leave. The kitchen reeked of smoke, and I was freezing without a shirt and the window open. But my feet felt like lead as I headed for the door.

"I will. She'll be excited you're her new neighbor."

Ellie winced, and I knew she wasn't sure about having me next door. My kid, on the other hand? Ellie and Keely got on like two peas in a pod and had since Ellie braided Keely's hair at a Colson family dinner. That would only make things harder.

"Goodnight, Trace," Ellie said, hovering in the entryway as she waited for me to leave.

Hearing her say my name was beauty and pain all at once. "'Night, Blaze. Try not to start any more fires."

I stepped out onto the front porch but waited until Ellie shut the door, and then I waited a little longer until I heard her turn the deadbolt. When I forced myself to start walking, I pulled my phone out of my pocket. Tapping the contact I needed, I listened as the line rang.

"Hello, you've reached Firehouse Pizza. How can I help ya?"

I recognized the teenager's voice instantly. "Hey, Steve."

"Sheriff Colson, how's it hangin'? Looking for another meat lover's or a cheesy delight?"

I kept walking, even though a twitchy feeling had taken root in my limbs. "I'm actually calling in an order for my neighbor. You can put it on my tab, along with a twenty-percent tip. Veggie lover's to 365 Lavender."

"Someone finally rent Mrs. Henderson's house?" he asked over the din in the restaurant.

"They did." I knew he wanted more information, but I wasn't about to give it to him. The last thing I needed getting around town was that I'd ordered pizza for the new woman in the house next door.

"Well, I'll get that right in for you. Probably about thirty minutes or so."

"Thanks, Steve."

"No probs, boss man. I got your back."

I chuckled as I hung up but couldn't help glancing back at the purple house. I was an idiot for looking for flickers of movement in the windows. There weren't any.

As I walked up my front walkway, the door flew open, and Keely stood there in pajamas with brightly colored hearts. I fought back my scowl. "Keels, what's the rule about opening the door if you don't know who it is?"

"I knew it was you, *Daaaaaad*. I looked out the window." She giggled. "But you're nakey. What happened to your shirt?"

Wasn't that the million-dollar question?

CHAPTER FOUR

Ellie

I HID BEHIND THE CURTAIN LIKE SOME CREEPY STALKER, WATCHING as Trace made his way down my walk. His steps slowed as he put his phone to his ear. I didn't miss the way the motion made his biceps flex. My eyes traced the curve of the muscle, and I couldn't help but imagine how easily he could lift me. How he could—*nope, nope, nope.*

I was not going there. This was a man-free zone. One that needed to stay that way for quite a while. And I knew all the reasons why. They were infinite at this point. So, why wasn't I moving?

But I couldn't help mapping Trace's broad chest with my gaze as he turned toward his house, taking in the dusting of dark hair and broad shoulders.

I ripped myself away from the window. "No more being a dumb girl, Ellie."

Talking to myself probably wasn't a great sign, but it was better than drooling over a man who always seemed to look at me with a hint of wariness in his eyes. As if I were a wild animal that could turn on a dime. Maybe I was.

As I strode toward the kitchen, a new scent cut through the smoke. I sniffed, trying to catch it. Sandalwood and…black pepper?

I pulled the neck of the tee I had on to my nose and inhaled deeply. The aroma nearly made me stumble. Earthy and real. Unexpected. So very *Trace*.

I instantly released my grip on the cotton. "Now, you're sniffing him?"

I was an idiot. I forced my feet to move deeper into the scent of smoke. That would burn out the witchcraft of Trace's cologne.

Donning the one pair of dish gloves I had, I got to work cleaning up what I could. The oven's interior would have to wait until tomorrow when I could get the proper supplies and call a repair person out to make sure the fire hadn't damaged anything important. I'd replace the range if I had to. The last thing I wanted was poor Mrs. Henderson knowing I'd almost set her house on fire the first night. Not a good look.

As I finished mopping the floor where the extinguisher goo had landed, my phone dinged, cutting into the pop tunes no longer feeding my happy buzz. I leaned the mop against the counter and headed for the living room. If Trace had tattled on me to my brother, I was going to egg his house.

Disconnecting my phone from the speaker, I stopped the music and opened my messaging app. The moment I saw the name at the top, my stomach sank. I tapped on the text, seeing the string of messages I'd left unanswered. They started with apologies, promises that it would never happen again, moving to petulant guilt trips, and finally anger.

> **Bradley:** *You break off our engagement so you can move into a trashy house in the middle of nowhere?*

A chill skated down my spine, and my palms began to sweat. I suddenly felt far more exposed than I had standing in my kitchen with Trace in just a bra and underwear. I knew it was bait. Something to startle a response out of me when nothing else had worked.

I hadn't told Bradley where I'd moved, but it wouldn't be a

stretch for him to assume I'd gone to Linc. It also wouldn't have been the first time Bradley had put eyes on me. The driver he'd *gifted* me with in New York had reported my every move to my future husband. But when I caught sight of the email dossier, I hadn't said a word. Just played the good little girl and kept my mouth shut. No longer.

I wasn't about to let Bradley win. He'd already stolen too much from me. No, not stolen. I'd given it away. I'd become exactly what my father demanded of me and what Bradley expected of his future wife. I'd given up the pieces of me that made me who I was. Now, I couldn't even remember where I'd hidden them away.

My doorbell rang, making me jump and fumble my phone. I cursed as it hit the floor, part of me hoping it was smashed to bits so I could become one of those people who lived without one.

When I snatched it up, I saw that I wasn't so lucky. But as the bell rang again, I realized I might need to call 9-1-1. I unlocked the device and crept toward the door, hitting those three numbers on the screen, just in case.

"Who is it?" I called through the door.

"Firehouse Pizza," a youngish male voice called. "Got a delivery."

"I didn't order anything."

"It's a gift. From your next-door neighbor. Veggie lover's pie."

I stilled, a stinging sensation taking root in my nose. I carefully unlocked the door and opened it. The guy standing on my front porch looked no older than seventeen. As his gaze swept over me, stilling on my bare legs, I remembered what I was wearing.

I winced, heat hitting my cheeks. "Sorry, I, uh, wasn't exactly expecting anyone."

The teenager grinned. "Don't gotta apologize to me. Never gonna mind a beautiful woman answering the door in just a tee." One corner of his mouth kicked up further. "A tee that looks a hell of a lot like one of Sheriff Colson's."

Oh, crap. That was just what I needed. Some rumor that I was banging the sheriff getting back to Linc or the Colsons.

"It's not like that."

"Never is," the kid said, amusement lacing his words.

"My oven caught on fire and…never mind. It's a long story."

He chuckled. "Well, hopefully, the pizza helps. I'm Steve. Welcome to Sparrow Falls."

"Thanks," I mumbled.

"We deliver for free within town limits, and we've got more than just pizza. We've got pasta and salads and all sorts of stuff. I threw in a brownie for free because I knew you just moved in."

That shiver down my spine was back as I scanned the street. There was no sign of anyone watching.

"Sorry," Steve said, wincing. "That probably sounds creepy if you're not from a small town. Are you?"

I shook my head. "New York."

"City?" he squeaked.

"Manhattan. All my life." One that carried more scars than I wanted to admit.

"Whoa. Wait, you Linc's sister?"

Of course, my brother had already made friends within the teen gossip mill. "I am."

"He's the coolest. Paid me a hundred bucks to bring pizza out to Arden's place when she was recovering. That's baller."

It was my turn to laugh, and the release of tension was more than welcome. "He's not opposed to a bribe now and then."

"I am very bribable."

"I'll be sure to let him know."

"Thanks." Steve shot me a charming smile. "You need a tour around town, just stop by the shop and let me know."

"I'll keep that in mind." I took the pizza from his hands. "Thanks for this."

"Anytime. Just call."

"Will do."

I shut the door and locked the deadbolt, the scent of cheese and veggies filling the air. My stomach rumbled, and that stinging sensation in my nose was back. Trace must've been on the phone with the pizza shop as he walked away from my house. Trying to remedy the one thing he could.

It was such a simple gesture. Nothing over-the-top like Bradley's apologies or my father's bribes. This was simple kindness. An effort to ease the sting of a rough day in a new place. But it meant more to me than anything else I'd ever been given.

I suddenly didn't want to eat the pizza. I wanted to find a way to preserve it for eternity so I could remember how this felt. My stomach growled as if to argue with me.

"Okay, okay." I carried the pie into the kitchen and set it on the table. The room still smelled like smoke, but I had nowhere else to eat, so it would have to do. Flipping open the box lid, I snapped a picture of the pizza, marking the memory. Not for social media or to send to anyone. Just so I would remember.

Before I could sit, my phone dinged again.

Bradley: *Pizza? Really? Not sure you can afford those calories.*

My blood ran cold, and I suddenly didn't have any appetite at all.

CHAPTER FIVE

Trace

REACHED FOR MY COFFEE AND DOWNED A HEALTHY SLUG. THERE wasn't enough caffeine in the world for how I felt today. I'd tossed and turned until well after two in the morning, thinking about my new neighbor. And when I finally fell asleep, my dreams were full of her, too—dreams I didn't want to look at too closely.

My phone dinged, and I swiped it off the table.

Cope has renamed this group to Anyone Got Any Singles?

I frowned at the screen. What the hell did that mean?

Cope: *I heard from a little birdie that Trace did a striptease last night.*

My frown morphed into a scowl. Small towns.

Kye: *By little birdie, you mean one of Sutton's mom-friends, don't you?*

I knew he was right because a boy Luca's age lived down the street. The next time I saw his mom doing thirty in a twenty-five, I was giving her a speeding ticket.

Rhodes: *I'm sorry, I'm still stuck on the striptease part of this.*

Fallon: *No, it's the striptease AND Trace part of that sentence.*

Jesus. Did my siblings seriously think I was that much of a stick-in-the-mud?

Me: *There was a fire situation.*

Kye: *And you put it out with your shirt?*

Me: *It's a long story.*

Cope: *It always is. *wink wink**

Me: *You're the worst. I need to go check on Keely.*

Arden: *Lolli would be so proud of your striptease, T-money!*

Fallon: *Remember, make good choices. And if someone tries to pull down your G-string, just say no.*

Shep: *That was a mental image I did not need.*

"Daaaaaaddy!" Keely's heat-seeking-missile voice was back. But this time, it was followed by thundering footsteps that were far louder than a six-year-old's should be. The drumroll of feet hitting the stairs was followed by a stampede toward the kitchen.

"Keels, what is the rule about running on the stairs?" I called before she appeared.

"Don't do it 'cause I could get hurt," she yelled back.

"That's right. So, let's put that into practice, okay?" I always tried to be gentle with my girl, but I needed her safe above all else. Setting my phone down, I pinched the bridge of my nose. It was going to be a long day, and it wasn't even eight a.m. yet.

"But it was an emergency." Keely skidded to a stop in the kitchen's new threshold. Shep and his construction company had taken it down to the studs and rebuilt it, blending modern elements with the history of the Craftsman. But I wasn't thinking about what an incredible job my brother did with the remodel. I was too busy gaping at my kid's hair.

She sent me a wavering smile. "I think I made an oopsie."

It took everything in me to keep the panic I felt from my

expression. Keely had attempted something a little more ambitious with her hair this morning. Her pigtail braids were off-center, and one looked like it was sticking straight out thanks to some hair gel she'd clearly gotten into.

Keely's lower lip started to tremble. "Can you fix it?"

Hell.

That killed me every time. It didn't matter if it was a skinned knee or a lost stuffed animal. I couldn't handle Keely being upset. I glanced at my watch, nearly letting an audible curse slip free. We had eight minutes before we needed to leave.

"I got you," I assured her. But I wasn't so sure. Both Fallon and Rhodes had tried to teach me braiding, but my fingers didn't seem to have the dexterity. The best I could do were simple braids, and even those didn't look especially awesome.

"Thank you, thank you, thank you!" Keely smacked a kiss on my cheek as she dropped her brush onto the kitchen table.

I turned in my chair and assessed the damage. This wouldn't be easy. My hands worked at getting one of the rubber bands loose, almost losing a finger in the process. I grunted as it snapped against my skin.

"Hurry, Daddy. We're gonna be late."

I was well aware of that fact. Sweat broke out on my brow like I was trying to defuse a bomb. When I finally got the rubber band out, the braid didn't fall. "How much gel did you use, Keels?"

"Only half the bottle," she said, snatching a piece of my bacon.

Jesus.

I grabbed the brush and tried to gently work it through her hair.

"Ow, ow, ow!"

"Sorry." I winced. "It's just a little tangly."

I wondered if I should dunk her head in the kitchen sink, but we didn't have time. I worked as fast as I could, detangling as the clock counted down. By the time we hit three minutes, I'd managed to get her hair into loosely braided pigtails that hung on either side of her head.

"Done. Let's hit it," I said, pushing to my feet.

Keely felt her head. "They aren't spunky."

I grabbed her backpack and lunch box. "Spunky?"

"They're supposed to be spunky. Like they're happy."

"Happy hair?"

Keely bobbed her head in a nod.

"Maybe we can try for that tomorrow. But we gotta jet."

Keely's mouth thinned, a mixture of frustration and sadness swirling in her light green eyes. And hell, if that didn't make me feel like a failure. It seemed I was always letting her down about something. Hair wasn't a big one, but it only drove home the others. Like the fact that I hadn't been able to make it work with her mom.

We headed toward the door, Keely going straight through it as I paused to set the alarm. "Keels, wait," I called. Knowing that my birth father had gotten out of prison had my head on a swivel every time we stepped outside the house. But the only thing I saw when I moved onto the front steps was Keely's tiny shoulders shaking as she tried to hold in her tears.

Fuck.

"Hey, Colson fam," a musical voice sounded from next door as I locked the deadbolt.

Great. Now, Ellie would bear witness to my failings as a parent.

As I glanced over, I saw Ellie's gaze zero in on my daughter's face and instantly register her distress. Most people avoided a potential kid tantrum like the plague, but not Ellie. A second later, she was crossing the yard, headed straight for Keely.

"What's going on, bestie? Rough morning?"

Keely nodded, tears tracking down her cheeks. "My hair's sad."

The sentence didn't even make sense, but that didn't stop Ellie. "We can't have sad hair now, can we?"

Keely shook her head, and one of the rubber bands at the end of a braid slipped free, falling to the stone pathway.

"How can we make it happy?" Ellie asked, eyes only on my daughter.

"I-it needs to be spunky."

"I got this," Ellie said, pulling two rubber bands from around her wrist.

"We're gonna be late—"

"Daddy, pleeeease. I don't want sad hair."

Ellie's gaze flicked to me, her fingers already running through Keely's hair. "How much time we got, Chief?"

My mouth thinned. "I'm a sheriff, but—" I mentally calculated. If I drove five miles over the speed limit... "Five and a half minutes."

"No problem. I'll have you out of here in four." Ellie's fingers flew through Keely's hair, first creating two pigtails and then beginning to braid them in a style I'd never seen before. "These are called fishtail braids. They were my favorite when I was about your age."

"Who did them for you?" Keely asked.

The innocent question was like a knife to the chest. I was no good at this sort of thing, and her mom thought it was a frivolous waste of time. Leah's idea of loving Keely was trying to get her into a French fluency program at the age of six.

Shadows swept through Ellie's eyes. "My mom when she was up to it. Sometimes, my nanny."

"My mom says braids are silly."

Ellie's gaze cut to mine, searching. But I blanked my expression, not giving anything away.

"I guess they are silly, but they're also super fun. And I love braiding my hair. See?" Ellie ducked so Keely could see the thin braid serving as sort of a headband in her hair.

Everything about the woman was a work of art. From the braid in her hair to the outfit that looked perfectly put-together but uniquely her. She wore wide-leg pants in an olive green that hit mid-calf, showing off tan, toned flesh. Her sleeveless white top hit just above the band of those pants, revealing a sliver of skin I wanted to trace with the pad of my thumb. And countless necklaces ringed her neck, bringing in colors that felt more *her* than the rest of what she was wearing. Reds, pinks, blues, and turquoise in delicate beads I wanted to grab hold of to pull her close.

Hell.

"I love your braid, bestie," Keely said with a grin.

Ellie's fingers deftly wove a design I couldn't have mastered, even with hours to spend on it. "Thank you. It makes me feel like a princess in hiding."

"Can I be a secret princess, too?" Keely asked, wonder replacing the earlier sadness in her voice.

"I'm pretty sure you already are."

Keely giggled at that. "What were you doing at Mrs. Henderson's? Hiding from an evil queen?"

Ellie's lips twitched. "I actually live there now."

"For reals?" Keely squealed.

"For reals." Ellie fastened the second braid with a rubber band and straightened. "There we go. Two minutes to spare, Chief."

"Sheriff," I bit out.

Ellie beamed at me, and damn if that didn't hit somewhere in the vicinity of my chest.

"Daddy, look how spunky I am!" Keely twirled in a circle, sending her braids flying around her.

My kid was happy. That was what mattered. And Ellie had made her that way.

"Thank you," I gritted out.

"Why does it sound like you just had a wisdom tooth pulled?" Ellie asked, amusement wrapping around her words.

"Supergran says he's cranky because he doesn't go out dancing," Keely added helpfully.

A laugh bubbled out of Ellie, wrapping around me like husky silk. "Is that so?" she asked, eyes twinkling. "You know, I had a pretty good dance party to *NSYNC before you barged in last night."

"What's *NSYNC?" Keely asked, confusion in her voice.

Ellie made an exaggerated motion of stabbing herself. "You're tearin' up my heart. We're gonna have to work on your musical education, bestie."

"Dear God, please don't," I muttered.

Ellie just laughed again, and I wanted to drown in the sound. She offered a hand to Keely for a high five. "Just for that, we start today. I'll work on a mix of their greatest hits."

Keely jumped in the air, fists skyward. "Dance party."

"First, let's get you to class. First grade waits for no one," I said, a hint of gruffness taking root in my voice.

"Bye, Ellie!" Keely cried, running for my SUV as I beeped the locks.

"Have a spunktacular day!" Ellie called after her. "And thanks for the pizza, Chief."

"You're welcome," I gritted out as if a boa constrictor were strangling my words.

But I didn't let myself turn around. Didn't allow myself to take in the magic that swirled around her—the kind that could be volatile. I'd seen it firsthand with my mother. How they were reading you a bedtime story with all the voices one minute, and the next, on the roof of your cabin saying they could fly just like the dragon in the book, track marks running down their arm.

My childhood had taught me one thing. Magic wasn't worth the risk.

CHAPTER SIX

Ellie

BECAUSE I WAS APPARENTLY STILL IN MY DUMB-GIRL ERA, I tracked Trace's every move as he walked toward his SUV. Everything about him had sadness and anger written all over it. From the set of his shoulders to the tension radiating through his jaw. I just couldn't figure out why.

It was like I'd kicked his puppy, not put cute braids in his daughter's hair. Maybe he thought I was infringing on their time together. I could understand that. From what I'd gathered during my couple of Colson family dinners, Trace and his ex shared custody. Only getting your daughter for half the time had to be hard. But something niggled.

A little piece of doubt that told me there was more to the story.

Trace's engine starting had me jolting out of my musings. Keely waved from the back seat, beaming brightly. Trace might be cranky, sad, pissed-off hotness, but I wouldn't trade Keely's smile for anything, even if it came at the price of Trace's stern looks or clipped words.

I waved back and headed for the sidewalk. As Trace's SUV disappeared around the corner, I scanned the street, looking for anything out of place. I wasn't sure what I expected. A pissed-off Bradley jumping from behind a neighbor's bushes? He'd never deign to get his khakis dirty.

But I still looked. All I saw were normal morning happenings. A couple heading off to work. A mom loading three kids of various ages into a minivan. A sedan driving past with a man I'd seen come out of a house down the street yesterday. No Bradley. No private investigator with a long-lens camera.

I let out a long breath and headed toward town. Sleep hadn't come easily last night. I'd finally grabbed about three hours after finding a bat in the garage. I'd fallen asleep clutching it.

So, there was only one thing I needed this morning. Caffeine. And lots of it.

As I started walking, a breeze picked up. In just a matter of weeks, the temperature had dropped drastically, and I was thankful Arden had told me about the need for layers around here. I pulled a sweater out of my bag and slid it on as I headed toward downtown.

The streets were fairly empty since the tourist season was fading. Now, it was the sort of casual foot traffic that meant a predominance of locals going about their normal business. A bookstore called Sage Pages was opening as I passed, the older gentleman giving me a smile and a dip of his head.

"Morning," I greeted.

"Back at ya. Gonna be a beaut," he called.

It had taken me a little while to get used to the innate friendliness of Sparrow Falls' citizens. In New York, no one stopped to say hello on the street unless you knew the person—and maybe not even then.

But I found I liked the warmth of it. Nothing about it read false like you might think. Instead, it left you with the feeling that you were never completely alone as you moved through the streets.

I passed a few tourist shops, boutiques, and galleries before hitting my destination. The Mix Up. The bell jingled and the bustling noise hit me as I opened the door. The place was packed. While the citizens of Sparrow Falls were nice, they also weren't fools. They knew good coffee and treats when they tasted them.

"Hey, Ellie," a flustered but familiar voice greeted me.

Thea's brown hair had a little more blond now, and it flew around her in a wild tangle as she balanced a tray and unloaded plates.

"Morning. You guys are busy," I said, watching in awe as she spun to another table and deposited three plates while hardly looking.

"Try slammed. The college kid we hired was a no-show for the third time in two weeks, and someone special ordered three dozen scones at the last minute."

Thea managed the Mix Up for her soon-to-be sister-in-law, Sutton, while she and Cope were up in Seattle for his hockey season with the Seattle Sparks. But between this gig and her job at the local nursery, Bloom & Berry, I knew she had to be feeling the pressure.

"Can I help?" I asked.

Thea stilled, her green gaze cutting to me. "Seriously?"

I shrugged. "I don't have any plans until three. Put me to work."

"You want the register or dropping off orders?" Thea asked, not delaying.

I glanced at the long line of patrons waiting to place orders. "Why don't I deliver food? As long as I can take two plates at a time instead of your dozen."

Thea laughed. "Shep's always wondering how I don't end up covered in bakery goods every day. But the only time I spilled anything was when he snuck up on me." She sent a look toward a table housing her boyfriend to punctuate the point.

I grinned. "Such a troublemaker."

"I keep trying to tell people, but no one believes me," Thea muttered.

I'd been here for less than a month and already knew that Shepard Colson was the town's golden boy. The kind of guy who would help anyone who crossed his path, and just the sort of man Thea deserved after everything she'd been through.

"Tell me what to do," I said, stepping behind the counter.

"Wash your hands over there and grab an apron. Numbers on the tables will match the order tickets."

"Seems simple enough. Let's see if *I* can do this without spilling on myself or one of the customers."

"May the force be with you," Thea called as she turned to the waiting patrons.

I quickly stored my bag and sweater, then washed up and donned my apron. Crossing to the kitchen, I poked my head in to find an older man at the griddle. "Got any orders for me?"

Walter turned, grinning at me in his white chef's apron. "How'd you get roped into this circus?"

"I heard you pay in coffee."

He chuckled and gestured toward a station with two plates and a ticket. "I'll get you a cup while you deliver these."

"You're an angel."

"Tell Lolli that, would you? Never hurts to hear another woman has me in her sights."

A laugh bubbled out of me as I crossed to the waiting food. "It's hard to pin that one down, huh?"

Lolli Colson, or Supergran as Keely liked to call her, was the best grandmother and great-grandmother a kid could luck into having. She was brash, hilarious, and not afraid of the good kind of trouble. And just a month after meeting her, I was a little in love, too.

Walter let out a dreamy sigh. "She's a wild woman, but that's why I love her."

Something shifted in my chest, and the feeling wasn't entirely pleasant. It was like some sort of foreign entity invading. The sweetness of Walter's words wasn't something I'd ever experienced before. Even the longing in his tone was beautiful. But something about it made me uncomfortable, and I didn't want to look too closely at it.

I shoved the stew of feelings down and forced a smile. "Never seen a man more determined. You'll win her over."

Walter shot me a grin. "Danged straight."

I moved to grab the first duo of plates. They smelled delicious, and I suddenly regretted my breakfast of cold cereal. This would've been way better.

I carefully balanced the egg sandwich and cereal-crusted French toast and headed into the din. Conversations bled together as I wove through the tables, looking for number thirteen. I finally spotted it and made a cautious beeline.

I grinned as I approached the two familiar faces. "Playing hooky from the jobsite?" I asked as Shep looked up.

He chuckled. "We have a meeting with a prospective client in an hour. Thought we'd eat while we go over the pitch. Who roped you into this circus?"

"Your girlfriend," I said with a grin. My gaze moved to Shep's tablemate and second-in-command at his construction company. Anson wasn't exactly the warm, fuzzy type. He was a man of few words, but they were always important ones when he spoke. I'd learned that the ex-FBI profiler had been through his share of trials, but everything changed when he was around his girlfriend, Rhodes. His entire demeanor softened.

"French toast?" I asked him, knowing Shep wasn't a huge fan of sweets.

"Thanks," Anson said, the one-word answer fairly typical for the man.

I slid the egg sandwich in front of Shep. "Can I ask what he does in these meetings when he's so opposed to talking?"

Shep barked out a laugh. "You've got a point there."

Anson just scowled at us. I only grinned wider. "You look like Trace with that grumpy face."

Shep shook his head. "Speaking of Trace. You know it's making the rounds that he came out of your rental house shirtless last night."

Heat hit my cheeks, surely blazing bright.

"You know, if I was still in my past job, I'd analyze that blush," Anson muttered.

It was my turn to scowl at him. "I never should've poked the profiler bear."

Anson's lips twitched. "Now you know."

"I had a little, um, incident. My frozen pizza caught fire," I explained.

Shep's brows drew together. "And Trace's shirt went up in flames?"

I rocked back and forth from my heels to my toes. "I, uh, had kinda just gotten out of the shower when it happened and wasn't fully dressed, so…"

Anson burst out laughing, which surprised me so much that I gaped at the typically stoic man. Turning to Shep, I dropped my voice to a stage whisper. "Is he having a stroke?"

"There's a good chance," Shep agreed.

Anson wiped beneath his eyes. "Sorry, just picturing Trace coming face-to-face with a safety violation and you in all your post-shower glory. If anyone had a stroke, it's him."

That got Shep laughing. "Now that I know what really happened, I'm going to give him so much shit."

"Good. He needs to lighten up a little." And if that happened at my expense, I was good with it.

Shep shook his head. His mouth still formed a smile, but I didn't miss the hint of sadness in his amber eyes. "I'm not sure lightening up is in Trace's wheelhouse."

"And why is that?" I found myself asking. It was none of my business and a question I shouldn't be asking. And not just because I had no right to the answer. My no-man zone meant that the last thing I needed was to discover the root of Trace's demons.

Shep shifted in his chair. "When you come from the kind of background Trace does, control becomes important. Safety, too."

My stomach hollowed out. I didn't know Trace's history. Just that he'd come to live with the Colsons when he was twelve. But you weren't placed in foster care for happy, fun reasons. It was because of loss or something worse.

God, life could be a real dick. And not the good kind. But it was also a great equalizer. It didn't matter if you came from a background that meant you were struggling to get by or if you were part of the one percent of the one percent, life could still suck in the worst ways. And the people who were supposed to care for you could do anything but.

The image of a tiny Trace swirled in my mind, alone and defenseless. I suddenly understood him a little more. But that didn't mean I would stop trying to force him into a little fun and recklessness. All it told me was that he needed it more than ever.

"Good to know," I said softly.

I felt Anson's gaze probing the side of my face but didn't look in his direction. I knew my expression could give away too many clues for a man who was a master at discerning them all.

"You guys need any refills?" I asked.

"We're good," Shep assured me.

Anson just grunted his agreement.

I turned in his direction. "Next time I see you, the goal is twenty whole words. I believe in you."

Shep choked on a laugh as I raised my fist in the air. But I didn't miss the twitch of Anson's lips. "Victory!" I called as I backed away.

I got caught up in delivering food to a crowd made up of mostly locals. I'd met a few, but the majority were new acquaintances. I wasn't surprised when all but two already knew who I was. That was small-town life.

I slid a plate in front of a woman I didn't recognize, her eyes locked on me. "Here's that breakfast platter for you. Do you need any refills?"

"You're that Pierce girl, aren't you?" she asked, not much warmth in her voice.

Tension wound through my muscles. I'd never wanted to change my name more than I had this past month. "Ellie."

The woman's lips thinned. "You and your brother have a lot of nerve sticking around here after what your father put poor Arden through. The stress he put on the whole Colson family."

My hands fisted at my sides, my fingernails digging into my palms. "Well, seeing as Arden and Linc are engaged, I don't know how she'd feel about Linc taking off, but I'll be sure to pass along your concerns."

I turned on my heel and stalked off before I said something I really regretted. The problem was, I didn't disagree with her on the father front. Philip Pierce was a monster, capable of things I couldn't have imagined just a couple of months ago. And the thing that scared me the most was that his DNA wove through mine.

I startled as I nearly knocked into someone. Strong hands reached out to steady me. "Whoa, careful there, woman on a mission."

I looked up into kind, brown eyes I recognized from the aftermath of Arden and Linc's attack. "Deputy Fletcher," I greeted, doing my best not to look like a deer caught in headlights.

"I told you, call me Harrison." Those brown eyes narrowed. "Hey, you okay?"

"Just a hectic morning," I said, forcing a smile.

He didn't look especially convinced, but he didn't press. "I didn't know you worked here."

My smile became a little more genuine. "I don't. I just offered to pitch in because Thea's new hire was a no-show."

"Joey," Harrison groaned. "That kid dances to the beat of his own drum."

"I'm starting to think his drum never beats on time."

Harrison chuckled. "It does not. Thea'll have to hire someone else. I have no doubt."

As I glanced around the still-crowded bakery, I winced. "I hope she finds someone quick."

"I think I'll keep my orders to go until she does," Harrison said, nodding to the bakery bag and coffee on the counter.

"Smart man."

He smiled wider and shifted slightly. "I heard you're sticking around Sparrow Falls."

Goose bumps rose on the backs of my arms, but I did my best to shove down the sensation. Harrison wasn't a private investigator breaking my privacy. This was just the small-town grapevine, and I needed to get used to it. "I am. It'll be nice to be close to my brother, and I think a change of pace will be good."

Harrison nodded, shoving his hands into his pockets. "I'd love to take you out. Dinner? Maybe a little town tour?"

I braced as if we were about to get into a car accident. In a way, maybe we were. "Thank you. That's really kind, but I'm not dating right now."

Harrison arched a brow at that. Nothing about the gesture was rude or unkind, but he was clearly surprised.

"I just got out of something pretty serious. I need a little time to get my sea legs back," I explained.

Sympathy washed over Harrison's expression, softening the lines of his face. "I get it. Tell you what, the offer stands. You feel like you've gotten those sea legs back? Give me a call." He pulled out his wallet and handed me a business card. "My cell's on the back."

I took the piece of cardstock and shoved it into my pocket. "Thank you."

Harrison grabbed his food and coffee. "Good luck filling in for Joey."

"I'll take all the luck I can get."

He chuckled and saluted me with his coffee before heading for the door.

I rounded the counter and turned toward the kitchen, but someone blocked my path. Thea's green eyes twinkled as she grinned at me. "That looked like an offer of a date."

"Small towns," I grumbled.

"Hey, I just have eyes. Small towns have nothing to do with it."

"Do you know that half the people I served today knew who I was, where I was from, what I did for work, and probably had my social security number?"

Thea laughed. "I feel your pain. It tweaked me when I first moved here, but I'm used to everyone being in my business now." She studied my face, trying to read beneath whatever expression I wore. "So... did you say yes?"

I shook my head, fighting the urge to rock back and forth on my feet. "I'm not ready. I need a little time."

Thea's expression fell, but she instantly moved closer, squeezing my shoulders. "Take all the time you need. It's gotta be hard moving on from what you thought your life would be."

What I thought my life would be. I wanted to laugh at that. Not once in twenty-six years did I have control of my life. Not in any meaningful way, at least. It felt like every molecule of it had been decided for me, from what I ate to who I was set to marry. Telling Bradley we were over was the first time I'd stated what *I* wanted since the day I wished for a rainbow on my bedroom wall.

Sometimes, it felt like I'd died right alongside my mom. That my will to fight slipped away with her. Instead, I walked a tightrope, trying to keep everyone happy but me.

"I think I just need to stand on my own for a little while," I said, not agreeing or disagreeing with Thea's statement. Either path would give her information I didn't want her to have.

She squeezed my shoulders before releasing them. "I get it. And I'm always here if you need to talk."

"Thanks," I said, side-stepping her. "Better get the next order."

I dipped into the kitchen before she could respond. Walter had moved on to dishes now that we were through the worst of the breakfast rush. "One last order for ya," he called over the spray.

"You got it, boss."

"Now that's the kind of respect I love."

I chuckled as I grabbed a veggie scramble and headed for table five. I was already learning the map of the bakery and found weaving through the tables to drop off food or pick up empties was sort of a meditative practice.

As I approached table five, I took in the man sitting at it, poring over a newspaper. He wore a familiar Bloom & Berry T-shirt. A handful of years older than me, his tan skin had smile lines around his eyes, only accentuating the amber color.

"Veggie scramble?" I asked, holding out the plate.

The man looked up, his gaze sweeping over my face as if trying to place it. "That's me."

"Here you go," I said, sliding the meal in front of him.

"New to The Mix Up?" he asked.

I shook my head. "Not really, just helping Thea in a pinch."

"That's a good friend," he said. "I'm Duncan. I work with Thea at the nursery."

It was nice that he didn't share that he *owned* the nursery—a fact I knew thanks to Thea. Bradley never missed an opportunity to let people know his family owned the hedge fund he worked for.

"Hi, I'm Ellie. I've been meaning to come by Bloom. I just moved into a new rental property and really want to make a butterfly garden. Mind you, I don't know what goes into a butterfly garden, but it's the goal that counts, right?"

Duncan laughed, making the dark, almost-black beard around his lips twitch. "Good thing about coming into Bloom is that we can help you with that. I'm pretty partial to butterfly gardens myself."

He must've recognized the skepticism on my face because he let out another laugh. "Hey, a man can't like butterflies?"

Heat hit my cheeks. "Of course, they can. I just…it's a case of opposites. Burly mountain man and delicate butterflies."

"I'm gonna take that as a compliment."

"You should."

"Well, come by anytime. I'll be happy to show you around and tell you what those butterflies love."

"Thanks," I said, warmth lighting within me. "I really appreciate it."

"No problem."

I gave Duncan a nod and started clearing the rest of the empty tables, wiping them down. By the time I finished, it was after noon, and I was beat. When I reached the counter, Thea held out a to-go bag for me. "Lunch for my savior. I had Walter make your favorite."

"Tomato mozzarella panini?" I asked hopefully.

"You know it."

"Thank you. This is going to be perfect."

"I'm the one who should be thanking you," Thea said. "You saved my ass today."

I waved her off. "I was happy to help. Honestly, it was nice having a little purpose. Since leaving my job, I've felt a little all over the place."

"Well," Thea began, "what would you think about working here? Just until you figure out what you want to do permanently. I could use the part-time help, and you're great with the customers. The pay isn't bad—twenty-three dollars an hour."

She obviously hadn't seen me smack down the rude lady, but I also didn't think Thea would begrudge me for that. "Are you sure you want someone with no experience?"

"Pretty sure I can teach you what you need to know in an hour or two. Plus, I like you, which is a hell of a lot more than I can say for Joey."

I chuckled at that. "I'm learning he's a little flaky."

"Understatement of the century. So, what do you say?"

I mulled over the pros and cons for a moment and then grinned at her. "I'm in."

Thea let out a hoot and did a little dance. "You are saving me, Ellie Pierce. Thank you so much. I'll email you a preliminary schedule tonight, and you can let me know if it works. We've got two other fill-in folks, so it won't be full-time or anything."

"Part-time is perfect." It meant some structure, but not so much that I wouldn't have time to find my way, and I needed that.

"Okay, get gone before I find something else for you to do."

I laughed again. "I need to work on my leg strength. Being on your feet all day is hard."

"You'll get used to it. Don't worry."

I hoped she was right because, right now, a hot bath in the middle of the day sounded like heaven. I gave Thea a wave, ditched my apron, grabbed my bag, and headed for the door. The bell jingled as I stepped into the sunshine. Even though fall had hit, it felt a little closer to summer with the sun out full blast.

I was making my way down the street past the adorable shops when a shout caught my attention. I looked, trying to find the source, and saw a car speeding past. One second, I was trying to make out the words, and the next, I was stumbling back as something crashed into my chest.

I only had a moment to register the stinging pain before I was falling.

CHAPTER SEVEN

Trace

THE SHOUT CAUGHT MY ATTENTION AS I STEPPED OUTSIDE THE station. It didn't have a panicked edge, so most people would likely assume it was kids goofing off or some other shenanigans. But not me. It was as if every part of me was attuned to trouble, permanently braced for attack. Maybe because those instincts had kept me alive for so long.

The beat-up sedan that sped past was a cross between mustard yellow and a shade of brown that wasn't appealing in any way. The angle meant I didn't have a clear view of the license plate, but that didn't stop me from instantly memorizing every detail I could.

Color: yellowish-brown. Make: Nissan. Model: indiscernible. Identifying marks: rust spot over a rear wheel well and a broken taillight.

But then everything in me stilled. The front passenger window rolled down, and something flew out the window. I didn't hear the pop or crack that typically accompanied gunfire, but that didn't mean it wasn't.

I tracked the line of the projectile, and my blood went cold. I recognized the olive green pants. The sleeveless white top that revealed a sliver of tanned torso. The hair in every color that hung in waves around Ellie's face. But those pale green eyes had gone wide with shock.

Something hit her, and she stumbled back, falling to the pavement. I took off before I consciously gave my body the command, flying down the sidewalk faster than I had run since high school football.

The second I reached Ellie, I dropped to my knees, some part of me registering the lack of blood on her chest. Instead, a sticky yellow substance spread over her top.

"Ow," she groaned.

"Careful," I barked.

"Don't yell at me," Ellie shot back. "I didn't egg myself."

Egg. Not a bullet. Nothing that put her in danger of dying. A stupid prank.

Ellie struggled to sit up.

"Easy." I battled to gentle my voice. "Did you hit your head?"

My hands reached out on instinct, feeling her scalp for bumps or cuts.

She batted me away, her gaze jerking around, complexion paling as she saw the people looking at us. "No. I'm just going to have a nice bruise on my ass."

I sent Mr. Grigg a pointed glare that had him turning around and heading back into the tourist shop he owned. Ellie didn't need people staring right now. "Can I help you up? I can get you a T-shirt at the station—"

"That's okay," Ellie said, her cheeks flushing. "I just need to get home."

Fucking hell. I wanted to shank whoever had thrown that egg. "Please," I gritted out. "Let me help. You don't want to walk home like this."

Yolk bloomed across Ellie's chest, and she winced as she looked down. "Okay."

My hands wrapped around her slender, delicate wrists, the skin there just as smooth as I'd feared. "On the count of three, okay?"

She nodded.

"One, two, three." I lifted Ellie to her feet, not letting go until I was sure she was steady. "Come on." I placed my hand on her upper back, guiding her toward the station.

Ellie quickly scanned the street before dipping her head. "Everyone's staring."

"People around here have a hard time minding their own business. But they're not judging you, just the pricks who threw the egg."

Ellie's gaze flicked up to me for a brief second. "Careful. In some circles, prick could be considered a swear."

My jaw clamped shut, and a mixture of annoyance and relief washed through me. If Ellie was giving me shit, then her fire was returning.

"Don't worry, Chief, I won't tell."

"It's Sheriff," I ground out.

Ellie's berry-pink lips twitched. "Whatever you say."

I didn't move my hand from her back until I opened the door to the station and held it for her. As we stepped inside, Deputy Fletcher's eyes went wide. "Jesus, Ellie. What the hell happened?"

She forced a smile. "Omelet making gone awry?"

"Do I need to have a word with Walter?" Fletcher asked.

"I'm fine, Harrison," Ellie assured. "Just a stupid prank."

The back-and-forth ate at me, something about the familiarity of it. I'd had no idea my deputy knew Ellie beyond her name and relation to Linc.

"Put out an APB," I clipped, a bite to my words. Fletcher stiffened as I rattled off everything I remembered about the vehicle. "I want every free officer looking for that vehicle."

"You got it, Sheriff." Fletcher picked up his radio and began calling in the all-points bulletin.

"Come on," I said, guiding Ellie toward my office.

"Why are you so grouchy? I'm the one who got egged."

"Stop reminding me," I growled.

Ellie huffed out a breath as we made our way through the bullpen. Beth stood at the sight of us. "Shit, Ellie. Are you okay?"

Ellie forced another smile. "You know, they say egg makes a good face mask."

"Hit the streets and see if you can find anything that matches the description, eh?" I asked.

"On it, boss."

"You too, Wright," I called over to Will, who was pounding a breakfast burrito at his desk.

"Why? 'Cause your girlfriend got pelted with an egg? Isn't that a little below the department's pay grade?"

Fury built fast and fierce, nearly stealing my breath. I didn't deal with anger well. It reminded me too much that I was my father's son. Ellie must've read something in my demeanor because she leaned into me, her shoulder pressing against my arm as she dropped her voice. "Easy, Chief. I got this."

She leveled a glare on Will. "You obviously have no concern for the egg injustices of the world. Just look at half that breakfast burrito on your shirt. But what should we expect from someone who can't even swallow before he speaks?"

Frank laughed and then let out a hoot. "Burn, Wright. She got you good."

"And if you have a problem with the chain of command, you're welcome to walk right out that door," I growled. "As it is, I'll be putting you on traffic duty for the rest of the week."

Wright's face turned a shade of red that was almost purple, but he kept his trap shut.

"Come on," I gritted out.

Ellie followed me toward my office, and I ushered her inside. "I've got a bathroom through there." I pulled out my bottom filing cabinet drawer and handed her a tee. This one read *Sparrow Falls LEO Baseball.*

Ellie took the faded shirt, her fingers rubbing the fabric. "Careful, Chief, you're not going to have any shirts left before long. Not that the women of Sparrow Falls would mind."

Fuck.

The last thing I needed in my head was the knowledge that

Ellie was thinking about me shirtless. "I think I'm safe. Go ahead and change. And it's *Sheriff*."

Ellie rolled her lips over her teeth, fighting a grin. "Whatever you say."

I waited as she slipped into the bathroom. I tried not to think about her and what she was doing at that very moment, but my ears were too attuned to every sound: the water turning on and off, the paper towel dispenser. Rustling.

The rustling was the worst because I knew it meant Ellie was changing. I was going to hell for thinking about my neighbor changing when she'd just been through something that likely scared the hell out of her.

The door swung open, and Ellie reappeared. I didn't want to think about how good she looked in my shirt, but it was impossible to deny. Ellie had tied the oversized cotton in a knot at her waist. If you didn't know, you would've thought this was her plan all along.

"Thanks," she said. "Feels a lot better than my sticky shirt."

Hell. I was jealous of my own damn shirt in that moment. "No problem." My voice sounded deeper, a touch raspier. "How do you feel?"

Ellie arched her back, forming the perfect curve as her hand dropped to her ass, rubbing.

Jesus.

"Pretty sure my ass is going to be black and blue for a while, but nothing's broken."

My back molars ground together. "Did you get a look at the person who threw the egg?"

Ellie shook her head, the blond and red strands amid the brown catching the light. "No. They were all kind of a blur."

"Has anyone been giving you trouble since you got to town?" My question was typical, something I'd ask anyone who'd been a victim of this sort of attack. But I knew there was more to it. I wanted to know all Ellie's secrets, even if I didn't have the right.

She stared at me, unblinking. "Come on, Trace. My dad didn't exactly get me on the most popular list."

It wasn't the first time I'd heard her say my name, but something about how she said it now made it feel intimate, like a little secret that only the two of us shared. But I stalled on the second part of the sentence. "Have people been hassling you?"

Ellie rocked slightly from the heels of her feet to her tiptoes. "You know what he did. Helped the wealthy get wealthier by the shadiest of means. Helped the powerful escape punishment for the crimes they committed. *Killed* people who got in his way."

"Yeah, *he* did that. You had nothing to do with it."

She looked at me like I was a moron. "I'm guilty by association. Fruit of the poisonous tree. I don't blame them. I was raised in his home and benefitted from his misdeeds."

"You were a *child*."

Ellie shrugged, her gaze dropping to the floor. "People think I lived a charmed existence. They don't know that I was basically in prison for twenty-six years."

Everything in me stilled as my temper flared. Not at Ellie but at the possibilities of what she'd lived through. I struggled to get the words out without yelling. "What the fuck does that mean, Ellie?"

CHAPTER EIGHT

Ellie

THE WORDS SLIPPED OUT WITHOUT MY PERMISSION. A BRUTAL truth I didn't want anyone to know, especially Trace.

"You cursed, Chief. And it was the big one. Do you need to go to the bathroom and clean your mouth out with soap?" I was hoping for a laugh. Would've settled for a lip twitch. I got neither.

"Ellie…" His voice held the barest hint of a growl.

A shiver tracked through me, but it wasn't one of dread. If I were smart, maybe it would've been. Instead, my stupid nipples pebbled against the thin lace of my bra. "Nothing. It means nothing."

Those dark green eyes pinned me to the spot. "Saying you lived in prison isn't nothing."

I rocked forward on my toes. "Everyone has their stuff."

Trace didn't move his gaze from me. "They do. But I'm not talking to everyone. I'm talking to you."

I had no doubt that every suspect who went up against this man crumbled in seconds. It was like he saw just a fraction more than the rest of the world and could put together pieces the rest of us missed.

"People have made their displeasure with me known, that's all.

And some around here think Linc and I have done enough to your family and should leave. They don't tell Linc that because he can be scary, but they don't mind telling me. I guess I need to work on that mad-dog look."

"Who?" Trace demanded. There was so much authority in his voice.

My mind flashed back to the woman at The Mix Up earlier. "It doesn't matter."

"It matters to me."

My nose stung, and pressure built behind my eyes. Why was that simple statement almost more than I could take? "It's not your battle, Chief. Let it be, and it'll pass with time." I just hoped like hell I wasn't lying.

A muscle fluttered in Trace's jaw. "Sheriff. And I'm pretty sure that title *makes* it my battle."

I sent him a droll look. "Are you going to follow me around and make sure no one tugs my pigtails?"

"If I have to."

"You don't. Just let it go." I needed to leave before I spilled all my secrets to dark green eyes that promised respite. Safety. I'd gotten myself into the various messes I was currently in, and I needed to be the one to get myself out. "I need to get home to meet an appliance repair person. Thanks for the T-shirt."

"Ellie—"

"I'll wash it and drop it off later."

"Ellie—"

"Thanks again." I was out the door before Trace could say another word.

I barreled through the bullpen and nearly knocked into a man almost as tall as Trace and a little bit broader. His tan skin and dark features spoke of Hispanic origins, and his wide, amused smile relayed nothing but kindness. "Careful there, you could take someone out."

"Sorry," I mumbled.

The man glanced behind me, following the path I'd taken, and grinned wider. "Coming from Trace's office. In his tee, if I'm not mistaken."

I grimaced. *More* fodder for the rumor mill. "I was the victim of a drive-by egging."

The man's brows rose. "And it's not even Halloween."

"Guess it's just my lucky day."

He chuckled and shook his head. "Well, I'm glad Trace could help you out." He extended a hand. "I'm Gabriel Rivera, that cantankerous fool's best friend."

My brows lifted, and I couldn't help but study Gabriel more thoroughly. He looked a few years older than Trace, and the fine lines around his mouth told me he smiled more often than his bestie.

"It's nice to meet you. I'm Ellie." I left off my last name. Pierce was the last thing I wanted to be known by. I needed to look up how to change it legally.

Gabriel smiled wider. "Linc's sister?"

"One and the same."

"Pleased to meet you. I'm sorry your welcome to Sparrow Falls was less than warm, but I hope you'll stick around."

"No eggs will keep me away from The Mix Up's cupcakes or The Pop's double veggie burger with extra cheese."

Gabriel laughed. "A gal after my own heart. Well, minus the veggies. I'm a carnivore. Let us know if you need anything."

God, that was nice. Sparrow Falls was going to kill me with its kindness. "I will. Thanks. And nice to meet you."

"You, too." I headed out before someone else in the station could almost make me cry. I needed to pull myself together. Maybe I was PMSing. I wasn't usually such a weepy mess.

Stepping out into the sunshine, I adjusted my bag on my shoulder and decided to take a different route home. They weren't that different in terms of distance, and this way, I wouldn't have to pass the spot of the egging or risk running into anyone who'd witnessed it.

I tried to focus on the good things. Listing them off in whispers to the breeze.

"The air here smells like heaven." I inhaled deeply to punctuate the point.

"I got a job." One that would give me purpose while I figured out my greater one.

"I get a chance to start over." And that was the greatest gift of all. It wasn't too late for me. I'd almost gone down the road of living my life for people who hadn't even come close to earning that gift. But I'd pulled the emergency brake. I'd ended things with Bradley and stood up to my father. And now, I was making a life of my own.

I took in the bed of flowers still blooming on the corner as I turned away from downtown. They wouldn't last much longer with how cold it was getting at night, but I'd soak in their beauty until it faded, knowing it would return next year. And wasn't that what I was hoping to do? Become something that could bloom again after what felt like an endless winter?

My phone rang, cutting into my thoughts. I fished in my bag and pulled out the device, frowning as a familiar name flashed across the screen. "Hey, Sarah."

"Hi, El. How's the Wild West treating you?"

My assistant from the design firm I'd worked at was the one unapproved friend I'd managed to hold on to. Mostly because Bradley and my father had no say over who I worked with—much to their chagrin. Sarah was hilarious and adorable and marched to the beat of her own drum, no matter how hard our beige office tried to stomp it out of her. And I admired the hell out of her for it.

"It's good." Despite the egging, that wasn't a lie. "It's peaceful and easy, and they have amazing cupcakes."

"Better than Magnolia?" Sarah gasped.

I laughed at her shock at my disparaging our favorite bakery. "They are. But nothing compares to Magnolia's banana pudding. Never fear."

"Thank God. At least some things are sacred."

I grinned as I turned onto Lavender Lane. "You gonna tell me why you're calling in the middle of a workday?"

Sarah was quiet for a moment.

"Are you okay? Did something hap—?"

"I'm fine," she said quickly. "I wasn't sure if I should tell you or not, but Bradley's mom stopped by."

My steps stilled. I'd always liked Helen Newbury. While there was a formality to Bradley's family, just like there was in mine, Helen had a warmth to her. "What did she want?"

My tongue suddenly felt heavy in my mouth. I hadn't had contact with any of the Newburys since we'd broken up. That wasn't how it was played in my old circles, especially with the older generation. Emotions and messiness were things they swept under the rug. Even with people you'd known all your life.

"She was here to see Madison about a project at their beach house, but she chatted with me for a little bit. I got the sense she was hoping that what she said would get back to you."

My hand tightened around the phone as I picked up my pace again. "And that was?"

"That Bradley's having a hard time."

A million incredibly inventive curses flew through my head. Ones that would've made Trace's head explode. My face started to throb, and I swore I could still feel the spot where Bradley's hand had connected with my cheek.

It had only been a slap, open-palmed like something you'd see on a soap opera, but there'd been enough force behind it to leave me nursing a black eye. But the shock and confusion were worse. The fact that someone I'd promised to spend forever with was capable of laying hands on me in anger.

It just went to show how lacking I was in the judgment department. Bradley. My father. Who knew what else?

"You know my opinion on the matter," Sarah went on when I didn't say anything. "That tool can weep in his Wheaties for all I care. But I wasn't sure if she would call you and wanted you to have a heads-up."

Sarah didn't know what had happened. No one did. She only knew that I'd ended things with Bradley and was over the moon about that choice.

"You're a good friend."

"Sometimes," she said with a laugh. "I gotta get back to work before Madison sends me another death glare, but let's catch up this weekend."

"Sounds good," I said, catching sight of the lavender house on Lavender Lane. "Don't let the bitches get you down."

Sarah giggled. "It was easier when we stood against them together."

"I believe in you. Battle evil for us both."

This time, she let out a soft snort. "I'm getting the death glare because of you."

I could picture Madison's pinched face as she stared at Sarah in derision. "Later, sweets."

"Later."

I shoved my phone into my pocket and scanned the street as I approached the house. No one sat in a vehicle watching my place. No one even walked the sidewalk. I wasn't under surveillance. And in a month or two, Bradley would move on—hopefully, to someone who had the same boring life plan he did. Someone who wouldn't trigger the sort of violence in him that I had.

My stomach twisted. Why did that feel like a lie?

"I'm sorry, Ms. Pierce," the woman in her mid-forties said as she straightened from where she was crouched in front of my oven. "This baby is toast."

I groaned. "I worried you might say that."

"We offer a discount on new appliance purchases when we can't fix something. Ten percent off."

"That's nice of you," I mumbled. "Could you point me in the direction of an oven that's not going to break the bank but is also a similar value to this one?" Mrs. Henderson didn't deserve to have me putting something crappy in her house.

"Depends. How much of a chef are you?" Mel, the repairwoman, asked.

"Well, I set an oven on fire trying to cook a frozen pizza."

Mel burst out laughing as she grabbed her tablet from the counter. "I got you, girl. Solid basics is what you need. None of this starting-your-oven-from-your-phone baloney."

"Dear God, no. I'd blow up the house for sure."

She flipped the tablet around. "Here are the three I'd recommend." She tapped the screen. "But this is the brand I get the fewest callouts about."

"That's the one, then. I feel like I should always buy from appliance repair people. You have the inside scoop."

Mel grinned. "We do see the good, the bad, and the ugly. You want to buy it now?"

I nodded, moving for my bag and pulling out a credit card. This would put a dent in what I'd saved. While my job paid pretty well, New York was an expensive city to live in, and I didn't have buckets of cash squirreled away. My stomach cramped as I thought about how easily I'd let Bradley pay for things. Our condo. Trips. Food. Even my tab at Neiman's.

The cramping sensation turned to nausea, a feeling that came from shame. I'd let it all happen. Allowed myself to become everything I'd promised Linc I wouldn't.

"Ms. Pierce?" Mel asked, concern bleeding into her tone.

"Ellie, please," I croaked. "Sorry. One of those days. Here you go."

She took my card. "I know how that is. Hopefully, it'll get better from here."

"I'm sure it will." Because I was manifesting that shit.

"The install team will call you in the next twenty-four hours to get you on the schedule, but here's my card in case you run into any issues."

"Thanks, Mel. I really appreciate your help."

"Anytime."

I led her toward the door, holding it open as she headed out. With a wave, I shut it behind her and slid to the floor. A headache pulsed through my skull. I knew I should think about making myself something for dinner, something that didn't require an oven or stove, but I couldn't find it in me to push to my feet.

Maybe I should just crawl into bed and start fresh tomorrow.

A knock sounded, sending a startled shriek out of me since it was right above my head. I scrambled to my feet and opened the door, expecting to see Mel saying she'd forgotten something. But what I saw had me wanting to slam it right back in place.

A towering array of white lilies stood opposite me, a delivery guy struggling to keep them upright. "Ellie Pierce?"

I wanted to say no. To lie. But that wasn't fair to the poor driver. "Yes," I croaked.

"These are for you."

"You can keep them." The words were out before I could stop them.

The man frowned. "Keep them?"

"Yes. I don't need them. Maybe you can donate them to a retirement home or hospital."

His frown deepened. "I have to deliver where I'm supposed to, or I'll get in trouble."

"It could be our little secret," I begged.

Panic spread across the driver's face. "I-I'm sorry. I can't."

"It's okay. Sorry I pushed." I took the flowers, even though it was the last thing I wanted to do.

"Have a good day."

I was sure that was the last thing the guy wanted to say to me as I struggled to balance the massive vase. I set it in the open doorway and glared down at the blooms. Bradley's favorites.

A card was tucked into the top of the flowers, taunting me. At least my name was written in an unfamiliar script. I'd memorized Bradley's handwriting over the decades I'd known him, and this wasn't it. Which made me let out a breath. At least he wasn't in Sparrow Falls.

I plucked the card from the arrangement and opened it.

You can't live without me. Come home. – Bradley

Rage washed through me, hot and fierce like some sort of instant inferno engulfing a hillside of dry tinder. I crumpled the card in my fist. What kind of florist delivered that sort of message? They were going on my shit list.

I shoved the crumpled card into the flowers and picked them up with a grunt. Not only was Bradley leveling threats, he was also going to throw out my back. I tried my best to navigate the porch steps with the arrangement and headed toward the side of the house where the trash cans lived, but it was nearly impossible to see around the preposterous bouquet.

I almost tripped when grass turned to the pavement of the driveway but finally caught a flash of blue. The trash can. I flipped up the black lid with a muttered curse, getting a face full of lilies in the process. I instantly started sneezing.

Cursing louder this time, I heaved the vase into the can and grinned when it shattered against the bottom. Justice. But my satisfied smile fell when I heard a deep, familiar voice behind me. One I knew was paired with hypnotic green eyes.

"What'd those flowers ever do to you?"

CHAPTER NINE

Trace

SHE WAS BEAUTIFUL. EVEN SNEEZING AND STRUGGLING WITH a flower arrangement almost as big as her. Nothing could take away from all that Ellie was. And her fierce determination was a big part of that.

She whirled, her hair in two pigtail braids that swung wide as she gaped at me. She'd changed at some point and now wore a neon blue sweatsuit covered in shimmery stars. The sweatshirt's sleeves were pushed up to reveal colorful bracelets in a rainbow array that accented the various rings dotting her fingers.

She opened her mouth to speak, likely to issue some pithy retort, but stilled when she saw my tiny companion. "I'm allergic to lilies."

My eyes narrowed. Something about that wasn't the whole story. "Might want to tell whoever sent those." I gestured toward the trash can.

"Not wasting my breath," Ellie muttered, then turned to my daughter. "Miss Keely, how was your day?"

Keely beamed up at Ellie like she'd hung the moon. "It was the beeeeeest! Everyone wanted to know who did my hair and how."

An authentic smile lifted Ellie's lips, and I nearly stumbled back a step. It was then that I realized I'd never seen one from her before. Not once in the half a dozen or so family gatherings we'd both attended or when I saw her around town. This was the first genuine smile I'd seen Ellie wear. And it was devastating.

"We'll have to see if we can up our game next time."

Keely's mouth dropped open. "There's more?"

Ellie's smile only widened. "Bestie, I got you covered. We'll do Dutch braids next time."

"What are those?" my daughter asked, fascinated.

"Basically, inside-out braids."

"So. Freaking. Cool!" Keely cheered.

Ellie laughed. "What are you two up to tonight?"

Keely jumped as if just remembering what was in her hand. "I made this for you!"

Ellie looked down at the glitter-infested construction paper creation. "You did?"

Keely nodded and handed it to her.

As Ellie read the words I'd helped Keely spell, her eyes got a little misty.

Thanks for making me spunktacular! I love you!

"I love you, too, bestie. And anytime."

"We also wanted you to come to dinner," Keely said. "Dad's making chicken veggie stir-fry, and it's fire!"

Ellie's brows drew together as she turned to me. "Fire?"

"Apparently, it's a compliment," I said, one corner of my mouth kicking up.

"Gotcha." Ellie toed at a pebble with her sneaker. "I, um, I actually don't eat meat."

"You can just have vegestables. Right, Daddy?" Keely offered.

"She's right. I cook them separately anyway." It was the last thing I should've said. I should've told Keely no when she asked if we could invite Ellie for dinner. But Ellie's face from earlier today had flashed in my mind. How she'd seemed somewhat alone in all she was dealing with, even with her brother in town. So, I'd found myself agreeing.

Ellie's gaze lifted to my face. "You don't think that's weird?"

"Why would I? As long as you don't try to steal my cheeseburgers."

Her lips twitched as she lifted a hand into a sort of Boy Scout salute. "I solemnly swear."

"Then come on," I said with a wave.

"Okay, just let me lock up." Ellie jogged for the front door as Keely and I watched.

"Daddy, she is *sooooo* pretty," Keely whispered.

I hadn't missed that fact, but I didn't need my daughter reminding me. "Mm-hmm."

"Even her sweats are pretty."

That had me chuckling because, with their bright and shimmery design, Ellie's sweats could've easily been found in a kids' store. "You should tell her."

Keely's cheeks heated. "She might think I'm silly."

My gut churned. I knew where that doubt came from. Keely's mom didn't have time for the more fanciful stuff Keely was into, and it left my girl uncertain and doubting. It made me want to rage. Instead, I took a deep breath and crouched low.

"Would it make you happy if someone told you they loved your outfit?"

Keely nibbled on her bottom lip but nodded.

"We should always shout out the good in others," I encouraged.

"Okay, I'm ready," Ellie called, jogging over to us.

Keely looked up at her and blurted, "I love your starry sweats and your pigtails and your bracelets. The bracelets are the best because they're like little rainbows. And you're really pretty." Keely snapped her mouth closed, her cheeks turning pink.

Ellie's expression softened, and she crouched to Keely's level, too. "That is the nicest thing anyone's said to me in a long time. And it made my whole day. Thank you."

Keely beamed at her. "Really?"

"Really."

I got stuck on the first thing Ellie had said. *"That is the nicest thing anyone's said to me in a long time."* How the hell was that the case? Ellie was a force to be reckoned with. Funny and fierce. Kind and caring. She should've been getting these kinds of compliments every day of the week.

Keely threw her arms around Ellie in a hug. "I'm so glad."

Ellie chuckled as Keely released her, and her fingers dipped to her wrist. "I think you need one of my bracelets."

"You don't have to," I hurried to say.

"I want to," Ellie argued. "Besties need matching bracelets."

"Duh, Daddy."

Ellie grinned as she slipped the bracelet onto my little girl's wrist. "Yeah, Chief. Duh."

My eyes narrowed on her. "It's Sheriff."

"Whatever you say." And with that, Ellie took Keely's hand, and they skipped off toward our house.

Ellie tugged a leg up onto her chair, hugging it to her chest. "Thanks again. This was amazing."

Keely had abandoned us for her dolls, and I was now in the danger zone. Alone with Ellie. At least there was a table between us.

"Anytime." Apparently, the table didn't keep me from saying stupid, reckless things.

One corner of Ellie's mouth pulled up, and I couldn't help tracing the movement. "Careful. That's a dangerous offer."

She had no idea how much.

Ellie leaned back in her chair, studying me. "Where'd you learn to cook?"

It should've been an easy question. A simple one. Normally, I dodged it, but in this moment, with the soft strains of Keely's voice wafting from the living room as she played, the darkening sky outside, and Ellie's face glowing in the dining room's low light, I found I didn't want to.

"My parents weren't the greatest. Mom would try to cook when she wasn't high. Dad couldn't be bothered. I figured out early that if I wanted to eat consistently, I needed to cook the meals myself."

Ellie stared back at me for a long moment. She didn't look horrified or shocked. She didn't look away like Leah had when I'd tried to share things about my childhood. She just met me where I was. "That had to be scary."

It wasn't what people usually said. They were horrified and offered platitudes. I leaned back in my chair and reached for the one beer I allowed myself. Never more than one. I'd never risk activating the addiction genes running through me. "It made me appreciate the Colsons that much more."

Ellie's thumb stroked her calf in a rhythmic motion. "That's a good way to look at it. Doesn't change the hard, though."

"No. No, it doesn't." And I left it at that. Because giving Ellie these explosions of truth was playing with fire.

"Do you like it? Cooking, I mean."

She was cutting me some slack, and I appreciated it. I took a sip of beer, mulling it over. "I like it. I'd probably like it more if I didn't have to do it every day and account for a tiny human's taste buds half the time."

Ellie grinned. "Linc likes to remind me that I thought dipping grapes in ketchup was the height of cuisine."

I barked out a laugh. "Please, don't give Keely any ideas."

"I promise. What would you cook if it was just for you?"

Interesting question. One I hadn't pondered for a while. Usually, when it was just me, I did the quickest thing possible or grabbed takeout. "Might horrify you, but I'm going brisket, baked mac and cheese with breadcrumbs on top, mashed potatoes, and chocolate cake for dessert."

Ellie stared at me for a long moment, and then those gorgeous lips twitched. "What did vegetables ever do to you?"

"Says the vegetarian. You're probably on the take for Big Kale."

She burst out laughing, and the sound was pure magic—throaty with a little rasp but so damn free. It wrapped around me in smoky tendrils, and I never wanted to lose the feeling of it. How the vibrations clung to my skin.

"Big Kale, huh? I could probably be convinced. Kale is expensive."

I inclined my beer bottle toward her. "See?"

"You can't hate veggies that much. Tonight's dinner was full of them."

"If I don't want my kid or me to get scurvy, sacrifices must be made."

"Especially in the battle of mealtime." Ellie shook her head, dropping her foot to the floor and standing to grab the plates.

"You don't have to do that." The truth was, I didn't want to lose the moment we were having right now. And that made me dumb. And maybe even a little reckless. But there wasn't anything I could do about it.

Ellie smiled, stacking the plates. "You cooked. The least I can do is clean."

I shoved back my chair. "Well, I'll supervise while I get dessert ready."

"Dessert, huh? Chocolate cake?"

"Chocolate cake is a weekend, off-duty festivity. Tonight, you'll have to settle for berry sundaes."

Ellie's pale green eyes sparked. "A berry sundae is not settling. That's just rude to berries."

I chuckled as we made our way into the kitchen. "Apologies to the entire berry family."

"That's a little better." Ellie started scraping plates as I began slicing berries. But when she got to the dishwasher loading, I couldn't help but cringe. Nothing was even. Plates were askew, bowls at odd angles, cups ready to be knocked over by the spray of the machine.

"Chief…"

My gaze flicked to Ellie's face. "Yeah?"

"Why are you staring at me like I'm committing atrocities of war right now?"

I scrubbed a hand over my stubbled cheek. "To be fair, you *are* currently committing atrocities against my dishwasher."

Ellie gaped at me. "I rinsed these thoroughly."

I set down my knife and moved toward the dishwasher and Ellie. "I give you a solid B on the rinsing."

"A *B*?" Ellie asked, offended.

"At least you passed. This Leaning Tower of Pisa in my dishwasher is a D at best."

The shock on Ellie's face morphed into a glare. "All right, Mr. Perfection. Let's see what you've got."

"I thought you'd never ask." My hands flew over the top rack, righting glasses and reassigning bowls to their proper spots. I moved Tupperware from the bottom rack to the top.

"That was perfectly fine there," Ellie groused.

"If you want to melt the plastic, sure. But then again, you did start a fire the last time you utilized kitchen machinery."

Ellie gaped at me for a moment and then moved so fast I didn't have a prayer. She grabbed the spray nozzle connected to the faucet, pointed it straight at me, and turned it on full blast.

The yelp that escaped as the freezing-cold water hit my chest was anything but masculine, but it couldn't be helped. I dove for Ellie, and she shrieked as I wrestled the nozzle from her hands, keeping an arm around her waist so she couldn't escape.

"You deserve worse!" she yelled between fits of laughter.

"I'll show you worse," I said, lifting the nozzle in her direction.

"White flag! White flag! I surrender," Ellie begged.

Those pale green eyes swirled, the color something I'd never seen before—like delicate moss beside a creek or the first shoots of a new plant making its way into the world. Her body pressed against mine, her breasts brushing my chest with each inhale, her heat seeping into me.

"You gonna apologize?" I rasped.

Amusement danced over Ellie's expression. "I'm sorry that I can get the job done way faster than you."

"You mean you're sorry you're about to start a plastic meltdown and ruin my dishwasher."

Her lips twitched, the berry color deepening. "Your top rack looks like a drill sergeant assembled it."

"Is that so, Blaze?"

"Gotta live a little, Chief. You know, mix your bowls and plates, see what happens."

God, she was a little troublemaker. So, I did the only thing I could. I let some of that spray loose over both of us. Ellie shrieked, writhing against me, but I held her tight. "I am going to get you for this!"

"Naw, I got eyes in the back of my head."

"You'd better be using them in your sleep!" she cried, fumbling to turn off the tap.

When she succeeded, she twisted back to face me. It was only then that we realized how close we were. I could smell the hint of bergamot and rose clinging to her, earthy and whimsical all at once. Just like her. I could see those lush lips parting on an intake of breath, the pink color rising to her cheeks.

And all I could think about was what Ellie tasted like. Would the beer she'd had at dinner still cling to her tongue? Or would all that was her overpower it? I wasn't sure, but I wanted to find out.

"Well, well, well," a familiar, older feminine voice cut in. "What do we have here?"

CHAPTER TEN

Ellie

AT THE SOUND OF LOLLI'S VOICE, TRACE DROPPED ME LIKE A
hot potato. I stumbled, nearly crashing into the kitchen counter.
What the hell was I thinking? I'd practically climbed the man like
a tree. I'd given him the *kiss-me* eyes. That was *not* keeping my space
a no-man zone. That was the exact opposite.

Lolli let out a cackling laugh, clapping her hands and making her
copious bracelets jangle. As my head started to clear from whatever
spell Trace had woven around me, I really took in his grandmother.
Always the fashionista with her own unique style, tonight she wore
bell-bottom jeans straight out of the seventies, complete with bedazzled pot leaves at the hem of the flared denim. She'd paired them with
a tie-dyed shirt and rainbow mushroom pins in her hair.

She grinned at me and then her grandson. "I'm here for a kitchen
tango!" She did a little shimmy shake to accentuate her point.

"What's a kitchen tango, Supergran?" Keely asked, poking her
head around Lolli.

I wanted to *die*. I'd practically mounted the man when his *daughter* was in the other room.

"It's, uh, a kind of dancing," Lolli answered.

Keely grinned. "You said Daddy needs to get out and dance."

Lolli gave Trace a mischievous smile. "That he does. You need me to babysit? You two could hit up The Sagebrush. I heard they have a band tonight."

Trace scowled at his grandmother. "No."

It was as easy as that for him. I couldn't deny that it stung a little that the idea of hitting up the local bar with me was so appalling to him. It didn't matter that I was in my single-girl era and needed to stay that way. A woman still wanted to be wanted.

Lolli made a *psh* sound and waved him off, moving toward me. "He's such a stick-in-the-mud. How about you and I hit up the cowboy bar instead? Save a horse, ride a cowboy?"

"Why would you ride a cowboy, Supergran? That seems silly. Or is it like a piggyback ride?" Keely asked innocently.

Trace's scowl morphed into a glare. "Thanks so much, Lolls."

She just laughed. "Just like that, my girl."

Keely looked up at her dad, beaming. "I wanna save a horse and ride a cowboy."

"Dear God, take me now," Trace muttered, pinching the bridge of his nose.

I tried to hold in my laugh but couldn't, not even when I clamped my lips shut.

"I don't know what you're laughing about. You started this," Trace growled.

"Oh, no you don't, Chief. This is on you and your drill-sergeant ways."

"Drill sergeant, huh?" Lolli asked in a stage whisper. "There is something about a man who can order you around."

"Lolli," Trace warned.

"What? It's good to be open and honest about our sexuality. It's healthy."

"I'm going to change my shirt," Trace grumbled, stalking out of the kitchen.

"He's grouchy," Keely muttered. "Is that because he's not dancing enough like you said, Supergran?"

"It's certainly not helping. But what he really needs is some horizontal dancing. Break through that dry patch."

Keely frowned. "I don't know horizontal dancing." She looked at me. "Do you?"

Lolli grinned in my direction. "Yeah, Ellie, you know much about horizontal dancing?"

My face flamed. "I see why your grandkids keep you on a short leash," I mumbled.

"They try, but they fail every time," Lolli said, twirling around the kitchen.

But Keely was still stuck on my dancing abilities—or lack thereof. "Could you take my dad dancing?"

She was the cutest kid and the best daughter, just trying to look out for her dad. "You know what, bestie? I'm taking a dancing break right now."

She frowned. "That doesn't sound like a lot of fun."

"No, it doesn't," Lolli agreed. "Living is for the young. You don't want to miss it."

"I'm not. But my last dance partner wasn't the best, so I'm taking my time with the next one."

Lolli stilled for a moment, and I worried I'd given too much away. But then she moved into my space and wrapped an arm around my waist. "Girls' nights for a while, then. Can't have those boys holding us back."

"Can I come?" Keely begged.

"Of course, you can," I said instantly. "I gotta have my bestie there."

Keely danced all over the kitchen as Lolli turned to me. "You tackle the dishwasher. I'll handle the berries."

My mouth curved as I tugged off my damp sweatshirt. "I'm not sure I can execute it to the sergeant's pleasure, but I'll do my best."

Lolli cackled. "Honey, no one can. He goes to family dinners and rearranges Nora's dishwasher every time."

I sent Lolli a smile that spoke of nothing but trouble. "I'm going to rearrange things in his cabinets."

She let out a hoot. "I gotta get my camera ready for when he sees."

"Ellie," Keely began tentatively as we all sat around the dining room table, empty ice cream bowls in front of us. "Can I ask you something?"

I turned all my attention toward the sweet girl next to me. "Of course, you can."

Her green gaze fell to her lap. "Do you think you could help me with wacky hair day at school?"

A burn lit along my sternum, pure pleasure that she'd asked and utter agony that she was so hesitant to do it.

"Keels, I can help—" Trace started to say, but I cut him off.

"Oh, no you don't, Chief. I was *made* for this mission."

He studied me for a long moment. "You sure?"

"Are you kidding? This is my favorite kind of challenge."

"Really?" Keely asked hopefully.

I turned back to her. "You'd better believe it. How long do we have to plan?"

She grinned. "A couple of weeks."

"Phew." I swiped a hand across my brow. "First thing we need is a theme."

"Unicorns!" Keely cheered. "They're me and my other bestie, Gracie's, *favorite*."

"I'm here for it. I'll start pulling some research images and thinking about what accessories we need."

"You can borrow my magic mushrooms," Lolli offered, pointing to the clips in her hair.

"Lolli, do not get my daughter suspended from school."

She let out a harrumph. "I was just offering to help."

"You were stirring up trouble, like always."

"Someone's gotta make you live a little," Lolli argued.

I pushed back my chair and moved to gather the bowls, but Trace reached out, stilling me. It was the barest of touches, the pads of his fingertips barely grazing my forearm. But the heat of the contact scalded in a way that froze me to the spot.

"You've already helped enough."

I arched a brow at him. "You're just scared I'm going to mix the bowls with the plates, aren't you?"

Trace's lips twitched as he pulled his hand away. "Can't have you messing with a perfectly good system."

"You mean a perfectly good military state," I challenged.

Lolli laughed. "Trace, walk Ellie home. Make sure she gets in safely. Keels and I can handle the dishes. Right, angel pie?"

"I'm a real good helper," Keely agreed.

Trace tipped his head back. "Someone save me."

I grinned at the floor. "I think I can make it next door on my own."

"What if there's a Sasquatch roaming the streets? You could get kidnapped and taken off to a cave in the mountains," Lolli warned.

"Is that a big concern around here?" I asked, amusement lacing my words.

"Well, you never know," Lolli defended.

Trace stood. "Come on, Blaze. Let me walk you home."

Something about the kind offer paired with seeing him at his full height again, his broad shoulders on display, had my mouth going dry. "All right."

I turned and started for the door so I didn't have to be confronted with all that was Trace. "Good night, guys," I called with a wave to Keely and Lolli.

"'Night!" they called back.

I stepped outside, letting the cool night air wrap around me. I tipped my head back, taking in the night sky as I waited for Trace. I felt him before I saw him, his heat bleeding into the air between us. "I don't think I'll ever get used to seeing this many stars."

"Don't get the same view in New York, huh?"

I shook my head. "Too much ambient light. I could see them better at our place in the Hamptons, but it had nothing on this." It was like I could make out the actual shape of each and every star.

"It is quite a show. Good reminder to appreciate it."

I looked over at Trace then. It was a stupid move because Trace bathed in moonlight was even more stunning. I ripped my gaze away and started walking. I needed to get a grip.

Trace caught up to me in two long strides. "Thanks for offering to help Keely with wacky hair day."

"It's just as fun for me as it is for her."

He made a sound in the back of his throat that wasn't agreement or disagreement.

"Can I ask you a question?"

"Just did."

I fought the urge to stick my tongue out at him. "What's the situation with Keely's mom?"

I knew she was in the picture and that Keely spent about half the time with her, but that was it. And I couldn't help but wonder why Keely wasn't asking *her* to help with wacky hair day.

Trace didn't speak right away, and I felt the tension coming off him in waves. But he seemed to read exactly why I was asking. "Wacky hair day isn't really her thing."

That was fair. I loved playing with hair and makeup, but my friend, Sarah, had zero interest. She dyed her hair turquoise and called it a day. We all expressed ourselves differently. But if I had a kid as amazing as Keely, I'd make an effort to be interested in what *she* was interested in. I could tell Trace tried in that arena, at least if Keely's braids the other day were anything to go by.

I wanted to ask a million other questions, but none of them were my business, and Trace's silence was a deafening siren. I realized I'd entered a no-fly zone, so I let the quiet reign and found it wasn't uncomfortable.

When we reached my porch's bottom step, I turned to Trace. "Thanks again for dinner."

"It was no big deal."

"Maybe not to you, but it was to me." I wasn't about to let him erase the kindness he'd shown me.

Trace's throat worked as he swallowed. "You'd better get inside."

"Not good with gratitude or disorganized dishwashers. Noted," I said, a smile tugging at my lips.

Trace shook his head. "Your plastics will thank me."

"I certainly don't need to be replacing another appliance anytime soon."

"No, you don't, Blaze."

I did stick my tongue out at him this time.

Trace grinned. "I can see why you and my six-year-old get along so well."

I flipped him off without looking as I unlocked my door.

"Now, *that* was uncalled for."

"Better than Lolli teaching your daughter about the horizontal tango," I called as I shut the door. I broke into laughter when I heard Trace's grumbling through it.

The Colson crew was chaotic on a good day, but they were *real*. They didn't hide who they were to make each other happy. They lived out loud. And more than that, they lived with love and care for one another.

I flipped the deadbolt and turned off the light in the entryway. As I climbed the stairs to my bedroom, I thought about what it would've been like to grow up in that environment instead of the one Linc and I had been raised in. But then I remembered what Trace had shared. How living the early childhood he had just made him appreciate the Colsons more.

That was the attitude I needed to have. No more what-ifs. I'd let all the weights I'd carried in the past make me value the freedom I had now.

As I stepped into my bedroom, I looked at the white walls. I needed some color in here. Something that reminded me I was no longer in a neutral prison. I glanced at the pile of clothes on the floor and frowned. It should've made me happy, the freedom to have that pile there at all, but something was off about it.

Crouching, I picked up the array of clothing from the past few days and moved to toss them into the dirty clothes basket in the closet. I threw the items in one by one, slowing as I got to the end. I could've sworn those ridiculous rainbow boy shorts I'd worn the other day were in this pile. But I guessed that was what happened when you threw things around your room like confetti. Things got lost.

If Trace had been appalled by my dishwasher organization, he'd have a coronary at the state of my bedroom. I went to sleep with a smile just thinking about it.

CHAPTER ELEVEN

Trace

AS I STEPPED BACK INSIDE, I HEARD LOLLI'S AND KEELY'S VOICES from upstairs. A pang ricocheted through my chest as Lolli voiced a character in one of Keely's books—the same way my mom had when times were good. I battled to carry all the things about my mom. The grief at everything I'd lost. The anger at all she'd thrown away.

Instead, I shoved it all down. If I didn't think about the good, I wouldn't have to think about the bad.

I headed into the living room, picking up behind Tornado Keely. She was pretty good at doing basic tidying after a play session, but there were always things she didn't notice. A forgotten doll behind a chair. Another doll's missing shoe waiting to permanently damage my bare foot in the morning. Crayons shoved between couch cushions. A half-finished drawing she'd dropped beside the television.

By the time I'd picked everything up and took stock of the space, I felt a little more in control. Memories of my mom had been shoved into the box I never opened, and Ellie's scent had begun to dissipate.

Crossing to the kitchen, I opened the dishwasher. Not half bad.

I rearranged a few things, put in a soap packet, and started it up. The image of Ellie shrieking as she tried to escape the water flashed in my mind, as did the feel of her pressed against me.

Hell.

I reached for the cleaning spray under the sink and grabbed a few paper towels.

"I do that bad a job with cleanup?" Lolli asked as she strode into the space.

I sprayed the countertop. "You did fine."

She was quiet for a moment, just watching me. "Even as a kid, you attacked problems this way. If something was bothering you, you'd clean your room, work on tack in the barn, or straighten Nora's pantry."

I tried not to let her assessment get under my skin, but it was damn near impossible. I knew it was me searching for control, a quest to be nothing like my birth parents. But I didn't need the rest of the world to be quite so aware.

"Or maybe I just want to make sure there's no salmonella on the counters," I shot back.

Lolli scoffed. "You could do surgery on those countertops."

She was probably right.

"So," she continued, "how was your evening stroll?"

I sent her a sidelong glance. "You'll be relieved to hear it was Sasquatch-free."

"Can't be too careful," Lolli said with a grin. "You should take that girl to dinner."

My hand stilled on the granite for a moment before I kept cleaning the invisible specks of dirt. "That's the last thing either of us needs."

"Why's that?" Lolli challenged.

"Because Ellie just got out of an engagement, and I need someone more...even-keeled."

I felt Lolli's eyes bore into me and fought the urge to squirm.

"I always thought you were the smart one, but maybe you just hide your stupid with quiet rule-following."

I turned to face my grandma and glared at her. "There's a rule about name-calling in this house."

"If the shoe fits…"

"Lolls," I said with a sigh. "Ellie's great. Keely adores her, and I'm all about them being friends. *I'll* be her friend. But you know what I came from. I need something a little more predictable than what she's offering."

Ellie didn't have the first clue what she wanted, and getting on a train without a known destination wasn't in the cards for me.

Lolli's eyes narrowed. "Because that worked out so well for you last time?"

She didn't mean the words as a slap, but they *were* all the same. A reminder of the failure I already had on my record. "That has nothing to do with why my marriage failed."

Lolli's shoulders slumped. "It's not a failure. How can it be when you two created that beautiful girl upstairs? But you and Leah were never meant to be."

No, we weren't. I'd thought I was making the right decision, the smart play. I'd met Leah in college. She was serious, had a plan for her life, one I'd fit neatly into at first. But after Keely came along, it was like neither of us knew what to do. We'd checked all the items off our list and were simply co-existing.

But I hadn't expected her to cheat on me.

I scrubbed harder at the granite as if I could clear away those memories along with the invisible grime.

"Trace," Lolli said softly. "Love isn't something you can play safe. It doesn't work that way. You want the good stuff, you gotta take risks."

"I've got a daughter to consider."

"Yes, you do. And I like to think you want to teach her to reach for the stars."

I did want that. I just wanted her to do it safely, responsibly, and with as little risk as possible. I tossed the paper towels and washed my hands. "It's not as simple as that."

"It could be," Lolli argued. "You just have to make the leap."

Jumping off cliffs without a parachute was Lolli's thing. Or maybe Cope's before Sutton and Luca came into his life. But I would never take those sorts of risks. I opened a cabinet to get a glass and stilled. Where the glasses should have been, there were bowls on one side and plates on the other, all stacked off-kilter. "What did you do, Lolli?"

She cackled. "Oh, honey. That wasn't me."

An image of Ellie's mischievous smile flashed in my mind. Her threat to get me back. *That little fire starter.*

Lolli knocked her shoulder into my arm. "Tell me again how she isn't exactly what you need."

I leaned back in my chair, the text on the computer screen swirling as a headache pulsed behind my eyes—eyes that burned from a lack of sleep. I reached for the eye drops on my desk and put two in each eye. It took the edge off, but not enough. And it sure as hell didn't erase the images of Ellie swirling in my mind since last night.

My phone dinged, pulling me out of my personal torture. I swiped it off my desk to read the notification.

Kye has changed the group name to Tyrant Trace's Victim Support Group.

I scowled at my device.

> **Me:** *What did I ever do to you?*

> **Kye:** *Narced on me for sneaking out junior year.*

> **Cope:** *I mean, he reported me to Mom for throwing that party while she was gone, but it seems a little long to hold a grudge.*

> **Kye:** *I just thought it was time to bring our wounds out into the open since he's still trying to rule with an iron fist.*

Annoyance and amusement flared as my fingers flew across the screen.

> **Me:** *You're alive thanks to my narcing on you. You could say thank you.*

Kyler had gotten mixed up with some seriously bad people in

his teen years, and it had taken Nora, Lolli, and a family friend who was a sheriff to get him out of it without jail time or worse.

Kye: *I was grounded for six months.*

Rhodes: *For the amount of gray hair you gave Nora, it should've been a year.*

Fallon: *This still isn't funny. Too soon.*

Kye: *Sorry, Fal.*

She'd taken that period of time the hardest, and while Kye could make light of it now, I wasn't sure she ever would.

Fallon: *You're not, but you will be when my next glitter bomb detonates.*

Kye: *Cruel and unusual punishment.*

Fallon: *Mess with the bull and get the horns.*

Shep: *What did Trace do to bring on your wrath, anyway?*

I wanted to know. I hadn't blown his cover for family dinner recently. Hadn't reported any reckless behavior to Nora or Fallon.

Kye: *Nothing. I just heard from a birdie that Ellie rearranged his cabinets and wanted to give him shit.*

"Lolli," I gritted out. Of course, she'd instantly gossiped with Kye. Those two got up to more trouble than the rest of my family combined.

Me: *You know my lockup is looking pretty empty...*

Kye: *You're going to put Ellie in jail for messing with your control-freak organizational system?*

Me: *No, I'm coming for you for starting this.*

Arden: *I knew it would be good to have Ellie next door to you.*

I let out a low growl.

Cope: *Remember how he had to sort all his Halloween candy before eating it?*

Shep: *It's all fun and games until you try to swipe one of his KitKats and ruin his color palette.*

Arden: *Hey, an artist's vision is important.*

Shep: *He replaced my Oreo filling with toothpaste as payback. Now, is that called for?*

Me: *I hate you all, and this chat is going on Do Not Disturb.*

Texts came through in a flurry as I toggled off the alerts.

Arden: *Smart.*

Cope: *You love us.*

Kye: *We keep you from being boring as hell.*

Fallon: *Want me to glitter bomb Kye for you?*

A knock sounded on my open door, and I looked up as I locked my phone. Gabriel didn't wait for a sign to enter—he rarely did. He simply strode in and shut the door. "You look like hell."

"Gee, thanks," I muttered.

Gabriel laughed. "You want me to lie to you?"

I scrubbed a hand over my face. "Might be nice once in a while."

"Gotta get yourself a different bestie, then."

"What are we, five?"

Gabriel just grinned at me. "I could make you a friendship bracelet."

The image of Ellie giving Keely one of her bracelets flashed in my mind. The way she'd so easily slipped it off her wrist to make my daughter feel accepted and appreciated.

"What is it?" Gabriel pushed.

Hell. I needed to watch myself. Around everyone, but with Lolli and Gabriel especially. Lolli because she saw sex everywhere, and Gabriel because he hadn't risen through the ranks of law enforcement for no reason—despite how much of a jokester he was. He had an expert read on people and paid attention to every hint and clue.

I shook my head and leaned back in my chair. "Nothing. You hear any updates on the vehicle that threw the egg at Ellie?"

Gabriel's grin was back, only wider this time. "You're taking a real personal interest in this one, huh?"

I glared at the friend I'd known for half my life. "She's my neighbor, and she's going to be family."

"I don't know, T. I hear she's been wearing too many of your shirts to be considered *family*."

The image of her in my Mercer County Sheriff's Department shirt with her bare legs and wet hair filled my mind. It wouldn't have mattered if the whole house had been burning down around us. All I would've seen was her.

"The woman's a walking disaster," I gritted out.

Gabriel chuckled, a smug smile playing on his lips. "I don't know. I think someone like her could be good for you. Make you live a little. Plus, she's damn nice to look at. Smells good, too."

My teeth ground together, my jaw working back and forth. I knew she smelled good. Like bergamot and rose—scents I shouldn't have been able to peg—but they'd played in my mind until I finally nailed down what they were.

"Okay, okay." Gabriel held up his hands in surrender. "Maybe you're not interested. I might just have to ask her out, then. Take her to The Pop, on a tour of the town. Or maybe a picnic. Really get my swoon on."

My entire body tensed as blood whooshed in my ears. Images of Ellie filling my mind weren't anything new, but this time, she was on a picnic blanket with my best friend, gazing into his eyes, laughing as he told her jokes.

A deeper laugh cut into the nightmare, this one coming from across my desk as Gabriel tipped his head back and roared. "Jesus, Trace. You are so screwed."

My fingers wrapped around the arms of my chair, digging into the padding. "I don't know what you're talking about."

Gabriel wiped tears from under his eyes. "Dude. You looked like you were about to snap me in two."

"Maybe I'm beginning to reconsider my taste in friends," I grumbled.

"Naw, you've got impeccable taste there. And don't worry, I'm not going to make a move on your girl. Even if your ass is too stubborn to."

Your girl.

Why did I like the sound of that so much?

I cleared my throat. "Let's just focus on the case at hand, okay? We don't need to add to the Sparrow Falls gossip mill." One that was apparently working overtime if they were keeping up with how many T-shirts of mine Ellie had in her possession.

Gabriel fought a smile. "Whatever you want, boss."

"Shut up," I muttered.

He just laughed again. "No hits on the APB, but I'm thinking we could hit up a few informants. See if they know of anyone who might drive a vehicle like that. The color makes it unique."

"Good idea. I'm going to make the rounds in town and do the same." I hated the idea of Ellie looking over her shoulder constantly, worried those assholes might show up again. She'd been through enough lately. She deserved to feel safe.

Gabriel pushed to his feet and headed for the door. "You might want to stop by The Mix Up on your rounds."

"Why?" I called.

"Heard your girl got herself a job."

"She's not my girl," I growled.

But I couldn't help but wonder what had prompted that. It wasn't like Ellie could cook. Maybe she simply needed the money. I didn't know what she'd done back in New York. Which just told me how little I knew about her. But I knew Linc well enough to be sure he would've offered to help her out for as long as she wanted or needed.

Shoving my chair back, I stood and slid my phone into my pocket. The din of the bullpen greeted me as I stepped out of my office, officers running down leads or taking calls. The only one not working was Will. I tried not to let that annoy me but failed.

The fact that he'd put his name in the hat against Beth for a promotion just amplified that annoyance. It was as if he thought his presence alone was a gift to the station. The moment he saw me leave my office, he stood. "Need backup, Sheriff?"

"Shouldn't you be working on finding that vehicle like I asked?"

Will's lip began to curl, but he fought it back. "I got some feelers out. Just waiting to hear back."

I'd just bet he was. "Then start your patrol. You're on traffic in thirty anyway."

His blue eyes flashed with an angry heat. "Whatever."

He'd never get the promotion. And unless he had a real wake-up call, he wouldn't last long in this station. You needed to be a team player here. And that was the last thing Will was. He wanted glory and excitement. But law enforcement was a hell of a lot of paperwork and tracking down endless leads until you struck gold.

Beth rolled her eyes as I passed, a phone pressed to her ear as she took notes. Beth had what it took. I knew it wasn't always easy for her, but she handled working in a male-dominated field like a boss. She called assholes on their behavior and never let their BS get her down.

I saluted her as I passed, mouthing, "*Godspeed.*" She struggled not to laugh.

Stepping outside, I took a deep breath and let the mountain air move through me. When I was a kid stuck in that godforsaken cabin miles outside of town that smelled of rotting food and things I hadn't been able to identify at the time, I would sneak out at night just to breathe. The cold mountain air had been my only comfort. The one thing that'd felt like it could wash away everything I was living.

I grabbed hold of that air again and didn't let go. It was the one constant when my world was spinning out of control. And then a single sentence blew it all to hell.

"Well, if it isn't the little traitor."

Hatred and disgust dripped from a voice I hadn't heard in twenty-four years, not since the day they'd locked him up when I was twelve. My birth father was only supposed to be inside for eight years, but that had become twenty-eight when he killed a fellow prisoner two years in and attacked a guard. How he'd managed to get out early was beyond me.

I stared at the man opposite me. He was a stranger and the person I knew best all at the same time. And I knew him best because I'd memorized every mood shift and anger tell. I knew when he would snap even before he did.

But he was smaller than I remembered. When I was a kid, he'd towered over me, this looming evil force. Now, he looked stooped, his skin sallow from all the years he'd spent without a constant source of daylight. It made an angry scar beneath his eye stand out all the more.

"What's the matter, traitor? No hug for your old man?"

Blood roared in my ears as I let his words land. "What do you want?"

One corner of his mouth kicked up, making the scar deepen. "What? I can't stop by for a little family reconciliation? See my son at his fancy new job?"

That was the last thing he wanted. What Jasper wanted was to threaten. Intimidate. But I wasn't twelve anymore, and he didn't have free rein over me.

"Parole offices are a town over. I'm sure you'll be needing to check in." I kept my voice even despite the war of emotions playing out over their battlefield.

Jasper's eyes narrowed on me. "You'd best watch your tone, boy. Looks to me like you've got a lot to lose. Adorable little girl. Hot piece of ass living next door, too. It'd be a shame if anything happened to either of them."

The lunge was instantaneous. Had someone not reached out and grabbed me from behind, I likely would've snapped my father's neck. I had no doubt.

"Shit, T. It's what he wants," Gabriel ground out as he tried to keep me from getting to Jasper.

The man who used to be my father tipped his head back and laughed. "Good to see you, traitor. Can't wait for our next visit."

I lunged again, and Gabriel cursed as Jasper strode down the street. Blood roared in my ears as I fought against my best friend. He got up in my face, giving me a hard shove. "Get it together. You want to give that bastard exactly what he wants? You in a cell or worse?"

My heart hammered against my ribs as I struggled for breath. Gabriel was right. Jasper might be an asshole, but he wasn't as stupid as he looked at first glance. He'd known exactly what he was doing showing up here today.

"I would've killed him," I rasped.

Sympathy washed over Gabriel's expression. "You wouldn't have."

I ran a hand through my hair, tugging on the ends of the strands. "No. I would've." I could see it clear as day. And it was because, as much as I tried to prove we were different, there were ways we would always be far too similar.

"Trace—"

"I need to go check on Keely." Saying the words aloud was like a hot poker to the chest. After everything I'd done to keep my daughter safe, *I* was the one putting her at risk.

"Okay," Gabriel said softly.

"Can—can you check on Ellie?" My throat strangled the words, but Gabriel understood.

He clapped me on the shoulder, not letting go. "I've got your back. Always. No matter what."

I struggled to swallow, and I sure as hell couldn't speak, but I managed a nod before stalking off toward my SUV, trying to ignore the truth of whose blood flowed through my veins.

CHAPTER TWELVE

Ellie

"**O**NE HEIRLOOM TOMATO AND MOZZARELLA PANINI AND A lavender lemonade for you, Deputy Fletcher," I said with a grin as I slid the plate in front of him.

He looked up as he rubbed his hands together like a little kid. "This looks amazing, and I told you, call me Harrison."

"Harrison. Right."

He studied me for a moment, a little of that smile slipping. "You holding up okay after yesterday?"

I tried to fight the sour twist of my lips at the question. It was kind of him to be concerned, but I didn't want to remember the incident at all. Or the fact that my father had put me on a most-hated list. "All good."

"Trace has everyone looking for the car. We'll find them."

I just shrugged. Maybe they would, maybe they wouldn't. It wasn't like I was going to press charges for a drive-by egging. I just wanted to move on. "Flag me down if you need a refill," I said, turning to walk away. I didn't want to give him a chance to talk about it any further.

I was shoving that down with the rest of the shit currently swirling around my life and leaving room for only the good. I rounded the bakery display case to a grinning Thea. "He likes you."

I scowled at her.

"What?" she asked with faux innocence. "I can't point out someone looking at my new waitress with stars in his eyes?"

"And some drool on his chin?" Walter cut in as he stuck his head out from the kitchen.

"Who's eyeing up my girl?" A new voice joined the fray with some grit and a healthy dose of skepticism.

I turned to send Lolli an exasperated smile. "No one. My virtue is safe."

She scoffed. "I'm all for a little virtue defiling, but that pipsqueak over there barely looks old enough to have his driver's license."

Thea choked on a laugh. "I think Harrison's a year older than Ellie."

Lolli glared at her. "Whose side are you on?"

Thea held up both hands in surrender. "I didn't know there was a war happening."

Walter sauntered out of the kitchen, a grin on his face. "Love's the only battle worth fighting. Ain't that right, sweet cheeks?"

Lolli turned her glare to the older cook. "Don't you start."

"A little fiery battle can make things explosive in the sheets," Walter went on.

Thea let out a strangled sound. "I am so giving Shep the play-by-play of this."

"He's not going to thank you," I told her.

She just grinned wider. "That's what makes it so fun."

Lolli's hands went to her hips as she turned to Thea. "I thought you were getting my grandson to live a little."

I leaned against the counter behind the register. "Oh, I heard she's been getting him to live *a lot*. Apparently, the barn at their new place is getting a lot of…*use*."

"Ellie," Thea shrieked, swatting at me with her towel.

Lolli hooted, holding out her hand for a high five, making her bedazzled bracelets jangle. "Now *that's* what I'm talking about."

"Lolli, do you have pot leaves on your bracelets?" I asked, amusement lacing my words.

She held out her arm for me to see. "And my little mushrooms. I'm thinking about opening a shop. Bejeweled Buds. What do you think?"

"That Trace is going to have a coronary," Thea muttered.

I could imagine the shade of red he would turn. A laugh bubbled out of me. "Please, let me help. I am great at designing spaces. We could bedazzle the shop sign."

"Ooooooh, in a psychedelic rainbow," Lolli added.

"Love it. I'm in."

Walter just shook his head. "You two are dangerous."

"That's why I like her so much," Lolli said with a grin.

The bell over the door jingled, making me look up to see Gabriel Rivera striding across the room. He looked a bit more serious than when I'd met him, scanning the space and taking stock of each person inside.

"Gabriel," Lolli called. "Aren't you a sight for sore eyes? Come give me some sugar."

Gabriel shot Lolli a megawatt smile. "I've missed you, Lolli." He moved in and kissed both her cheeks.

"Careful, Casanova," Walter warned.

"You can't pin me down, Walter. I've gotta be free to fly," Lolli shot back.

"Or to get laid," I muttered.

Thea struggled not to laugh. "I wonder if I can get the camera recording from in here and just play it back for Shep. It's not going to be as good secondhand."

"I'd pay good money to see him watch the replay," I said.

She held out a hand, and I smacked it in a high five.

"Gabriel, what can I get you?" Thea asked.

"I actually just need a minute of Ellie's time."

I couldn't help the way I stiffened. If it was something about the egging, why wasn't Trace the one stopping by? Maybe he was putting some distance between us. I should've been grateful but couldn't help the sting I felt. "Sure," I said, moving around the bakery case, trying to fight the blend of annoyance and hurt.

"Are you here to ask my girl out?" Lolli narrowed her eyes at Gabriel.

His lips twitched. "As much as I'd love for that to be the case, I don't think a certain best friend of mine would be all that pleased with that turn of events."

"He's probably got me on the FBI's Most Wanted for rearranging his cabinets. Can't have one of his officers consorting with a criminal."

Gabriel's eyes widened as he turned to me. "You messed with his system?"

I brushed invisible dirt off my shoulder. "Just call me a rebel behind enemy lines."

Gabriel laughed and shook his head. "God, I'm mad I missed that."

"It was glorious," Lolli called as Gabriel led me out of earshot.

"Is everything okay?" I asked, lowering my voice.

Gabriel nodded, but his gaze dropped to the floor before returning to my face. "Anyone give you trouble today?"

I frowned. "No. But I've really only been here."

"No customers gave you a weird feeling? Nobody said anything odd or threatening?" Gabriel pressed.

"No. What's going on?"

"I just wanted to make sure after everything that happened yesterday."

I studied Gabriel for a long moment. Maybe that was the case, but it seemed like overkill. "Did you guys find something?" My stomach twisted at the idea that they might've found something worse than someone playing a prank. Maybe they'd found someone who truly wished me harm. My mind flashed to Bradley for a moment, but an egging wasn't exactly his style.

"No, no. Nothing like that. We're still looking for the vehicle. I just wanted to make sure no one else was giving you a hard time."

My cheeks flamed. If Gabriel was checking up on me, Trace had likely told him what I'd shared: that many people weren't exactly my biggest fans lately. "I'm fine. And I know how to handle myself."

That was a big fat lie on both accounts. Maybe that was the problem. It felt like I'd never truly stood on my own two feet, fought my own battles, or felt strong in doing so. And it was long past time I did.

"All right," Gabriel said. "Give me a call if you run into any trouble."

"Sure." That was a lie, too, but a necessary one. If I was going to start cleaning up my own messes, there was no better time than now.

I hoisted my bag over my shoulder, my muscles already aching from the long day that had started at six and was just finishing at half past four. I slipped out of The Mix Up's back door and locked it behind me, testing the knob to make sure it'd caught. Thea already trusted me to lock up, which seemed like a lot of responsibility. I didn't want to mess it up.

When the lock held, I released the knob and shoved the keys into my bag. My gaze swept the back alley, which was far cheerier than the alleyways in New York. Still, I was on edge, thanks to Gabriel's visit, as if another masked egg bandit might jump out at any moment.

"Stupid," I muttered, squaring my shoulders and starting down the street.

I took three steps before a squeak stopped me in my tracks. I frowned and looked around but didn't see anything. The squeak sounded again. A little closer this time.

I moved in its general direction and the dumpster pressed against The Mix Up's back wall. This time, I heard a whimper. My heart lurched, and I dropped to my knees, peering under the receptacle.

The moment my eyes adjusted to the shadows beneath it, I saw the source of the noise. A tiny dog-like creature trembled there and let out another whine.

"Oh, crap. Crap, crap," I muttered. "It's okay. I'm not gonna hurt you," I cooed as if it could understand me.

The creature let out another whimper. It did look like a dog, but its brown and white fur was really only present on its little head and *massive* ears. The rest of its body was patchy at best.

"You poor thing. I'm so sorry. You must be so scared. But look at how you protected yourself. Found a place to hide where it's safe. But you don't have to hide anymore. I'm going to help you."

The dog belly crawled a little closer and sniffed the air.

"I wish I had some turkey for you, but if you come out a little farther, I can take you to get a snack."

The dog didn't seem so sure about that and stayed exactly where he was.

There had to be a vet around where I could take him to get checked out. But first, I had to get him to trust me. "I know you're scared. There probably haven't been many people you could trust. I know how that is. But I promise I'll never hurt you. And I won't let anyone else either."

The backs of my eyes stung with unshed tears. The only person who had been that for me was Linc. But he was gone faster than I could blink once he graduated high school. Sure, he'd called to check in, but I was basically alone, left to deal with our tyrant of a father on my own.

A little tongue lashed out against my fingers, and I blinked to clear my vision. "That's it, buddy." I forced down the tears and memories. "We're in this together."

The dog came out a little farther, just enough that I could pick him up. He whimpered again, and my heart broke. "It's okay. I've got you," I said, cradling him to my chest as I knelt on the pavement.

The sound of an engine had me looking up, but a window was rolling down before I could place the SUV. "What in the hell are you doing?"

CHAPTER THIRTEEN

Trace

APPARENTLY, MY INNER ASSHOLE CAME OUT WHEN I WAS worried. I'd barked at Ellie as if she'd done something wrong. But why in the hell was she crouched in front of a dumpster? She could've been hit by a car coming through the alley or jumped by someone from behind. But as she straightened, waves of her multicolored hair shifted, revealing the *why*. My jaw went slack as I stared at the…creature in her arms.

I was fairly certain it was a dog, but I wasn't a hundred percent sure. It could've been one of those gremlins after it got wet. What if it bit Ellie?

"El, put the dog down."

Those pale green eyes flashed. "He needs help."

"And I can call in our K9 unit so he gets it, but you could get hurt."

She rolled her eyes, and I had the sudden urge to take her over my knee. "He might not smell the greatest, but he's sweet as can be." The dog licked her chin as if to punctuate the point, and I couldn't help but grimace.

"Ellie."

"Chief."

"Stop calling me that," I growled.

Her lips twitched. "Want to give me a ride home so I can get my car?"

"Are you taking him to the shelter?"

Ellie looked at me as if I'd suggested running the furry little critter over with my SUV. "I would *never* take him there."

"It's a no-kill shelter," I defended. "One of the best in the state." I wasn't a monster.

She rocked the dog against her. "He's been alone for far too long. I'm not about to abandon him all over again."

Ellie's eyes glistened in the late-afternoon light, and I wanted to curse. "Get in."

"Are you taking us to the shelter?" She sniffed.

"No, I'm taking you to the feed store. They've got tubs there where you can wash your dog, and we can get you all the supplies you need."

Ellie stilled for a long moment. "Really?"

"Come on, you and the gremlin get in."

"Gremlin?" she asked as she climbed into my SUV.

"You're telling me you don't see the resemblance? Look at those ears."

Ellie smiled as she ran a finger over the pup's ear. "Gremlin. Kind of fitting. Cute and fierce."

Like someone else I knew. I reached over to give the dog a little scratch, and his head swiveled around as he snapped and snarled. I yanked my hand back. "Jesus."

Ellie sent me an apologetic smile. "Maybe he doesn't like men."

"Whatever," I grumbled, pointing my vehicle in the direction of the feed store on the edge of town. But my head was on a swivel, looking for any signs of Jasper. I'd given the school and Leah a heads-up so they could be vigilant. The school had been concerned, and Leah had been pissed. At least I knew they'd both be careful. But I was on edge, knowing things with him were far from over.

"You okay, Chief?" Ellie asked, breaking into the silence.

"It's Sheriff."

I could feel her smile without looking. That subtle shift in energy warming the space between us. "You're extra growly. Are you all right?"

I was as far from *all right* as you could get, but I wasn't about to tell her that. "Had a long and frustrating day, and now I've got a tiny but vicious mongrel stinking up my SUV and a neighbor whose heart is too big for her own good."

"Gremlin isn't a mongrel."

My gaze flicked over to Ellie. The dog had burrowed into her lap, making himself at home. "No, he's smart. Found the best person possible to take him in."

Ellie beamed at me. "You don't hate me?"

I reared back. "Why would I hate you?"

She shrugged, turning to face the road in front of us. "I don't know. Since I got here, every time I'm around you, you seem…mad."

Hell.

"I'm not mad."

"Okay, supremely grumpy, then."

"I saw your bruise. *That* made me mad." I'd never forget the night she'd shown up at the hospital, worried out of her mind for her brother and Arden and trying desperately to conceal the shiner peeking out from beneath her makeup.

I felt Ellie tense in the same way I'd felt her smile, the energy shifting yet again. But not for the better.

"Oh." That was all she said. One syllable, no explanation.

Ellie had told Linc she'd hit herself in the face with her suitcase in a hurry to get it down, but I couldn't help but wonder if it had happened at the hands of her father. I'd done the math and figured Ellie had lived alone with him for thirteen years while Linc was on the other side of the country. Who knew what Philip Pierce had put her through in that time? And I knew what it was like to live in fear of the people who were supposed to care for you.

But I didn't push. Didn't demand to know Ellie's secrets. I didn't have a right to them.

Instead, we sat in silence until I pulled into the store's parking lot. Sparrow Falls Feed & Friends was a town staple. We loved our animals around here, and they aided the practical and extra pet and livestock owner alike, carrying everything from the staples to dog food that cost more than dinner for Keely and me.

Ellie didn't jump out right away. Instead, she turned to look at me. "Thanks for bringing me, Chief."

Why did that make me feel like I'd won a gold medal, the Nobel Prize, and the presidency all at once? "It's nothing."

"Not to me. To me, it's everything." And with that, she slid out of the SUV.

I hurried to catch up with her, trying not to think about all the ways Ellie slayed me to the bone. I jogged ahead to open the door. One corner of her mouth tugged up. "Such a gentleman."

That was far from the truth, but I'd let her believe the lie. "After you, madam."

Ellie giggled as she passed, and that sound hit me square in the chest. I was so completely screwed.

"Hello, and welcome to Sparrow Falls Feed & Friends. How can I serve you and your pet today?" Curtis, an overly cheery twenty-something, greeted us.

"Hi," Ellie said with a warm smile. "I just found this little guy. We wanted to give him a bath and get some essentials."

Curtis glanced from Ellie and the dog to me, his eyes widening. "Sheriff. You're getting a dog?"

I tried not to let the shock of his words annoy me. Keely had been begging for a pet for as long as she could speak, primarily a dog or a horse. But with how much I worked, it wasn't fair for us to get a dog, and we didn't exactly have space for a horse right now. But she had plenty of access to them at Colson Ranch and Arden's place. Only that didn't stop her from dragging me into the feed store every other week to look at the bunnies and chickens and God knew what else.

"It's hers," I ground out.

Ellie patted me on the shoulder. "Mr. Grumpy Pants isn't the dog dad, fear not."

Curtis chuckled. "Good to know. I'll get you set up. Looks like his fur could use a little help. We've got some naturally soothing oatmeal products I'd recommend."

"That'd be great," Ellie said. "Thank you so much."

"No problem. Here's your stall with some towels, and this is the shampoo and conditioner."

"Since when do dogs need conditioner?" I asked, raising a brow.

"Hey," Ellie clipped. "Gremlin deserves a spa day after all he's been through."

I lifted both hands in surrender. "Okay. Want me to get some cucumbers for his eyes?"

Ellie stuck out her tongue at me before lowering Gremlin into the tub. "Okay, pal. I'm not sure how you feel about water, but I'll try to make this quick."

Gremlin looked up at her with baleful eyes, but Ellie moved swiftly and gently, warming the water before shampooing and conditioning. She had the kind of tenderness you couldn't teach, and it had the contents of my chest cavity shifting uncomfortably.

"Watch him while I grab a towel," Ellie ordered, already shifting to grab one from the stack Curtis had left.

The tub was deep enough that I doubted the tiny dog could escape, but I still stepped forward. And that was a mistake.

Gremlin shook his body like he was trying to get rid of every water droplet that had ever come into contact with him. You wouldn't think so much could cling to his patchy fur, but you'd be wrong. Water flew at me like a fire hose unleashed, soaking my uniform and making it cling to my chest.

Ellie let out a strangled sound of surprise, her hand flying to her mouth.

I slowly turned toward her. "What were you saying about him not being a mongrel?"

She laughed silently and lifted the item in her hands to me. "Towel?"

I took it from her, wiping my face and then my chest. "I don't even want to think about what diseases I could be contracting at this moment."

"Hey, I washed him really well." Ellie grabbed another towel, wrapping the pup in it and lifting him into her arms.

Curtis rushed over, concern written all over his face. "Sorry about that, Sheriff. Those pups can get you. But don't you worry, we've got emergency shirts for just this situation."

"Emergency shirts?" I parroted.

Curtis nodded far too enthusiastically. "Yup. Here you go. I think this is the only one in your size."

In my size, and so bright it hurt my eyeballs. It was a pink Hawaiian print with floofy dog heads where the center of the flower blooms should've been.

"No," I bit out.

Curtis's face fell. "You don't like it?"

I opened my mouth to agree, but Ellie moved right in. "He *loves* it. He's just not sure about how he'll look in pink. But you don't need to worry, Chief. It's going to do amazing things for your eyes."

Ellie pressed her lips together to keep from bursting out laughing, and I glared at her. "Seriously?"

"Buck up, buttercup. We don't want you catching a cold."

I kept right on glaring at her as I unbuttoned my uniform shirt and slid it off. My white tee beneath was completely soaked, too. I grabbed the back of the collar and pulled it off in one swift tug, but it was only to find Ellie staring at me. Not at my face, but at my chest. Her gaze roamed over my pecs and down my abs.

Oh, hell no.

I cleared my throat, and her eyes flew to mine, her face flaming. "Sorry, you put on quite a show, Chief."

Not information I needed.

She shoved the abomination in the form of a T-shirt in my direction. "Here. This'll help."

My mouth twisted in disgust as I pulled the thing on. The second it was over my head, Ellie burst out laughing.

"I'm sorry," she wheezed. "I have to." She lifted her phone and snapped a photo.

My phone buzzed in my pocket as I followed Ellie down yet another aisle at the feed store. Her cart was full, and she was carrying Gremlin in a pink sling she'd found for him. Pulling out my cell, I glanced at the screen.

Arden has changed the group name to Trace's Hula Hounds.

My back teeth ground together as I slid my finger across the screen to open the text chain.

> **Arden:** *Check out Trace's new look.*

The text was followed by the photo I knew Ellie had taken. There I was, in all my scowling, pink-Hawaiian-shirted glory.

> **Fallon:** *I'm asking Lolli to make a diamond painting of this. It needs to be memorialized forever.*

> **Rhodes:** *It's almost as good as Anson's pink kitten shirt. Maybe we can get them in a picture together for the Colson Family Christmas card.*

> **Shep:** *That's a whole new definition of an ugly Christmas sweater.*

> **Me:** *I am putting you all on my deputies' radar. If you speed, jaywalk, or park anywhere you're not supposed to, they're taking you in.*

"My sister, really?" I called to Ellie.

She turned around, grinning widely. Gremlin stuck his head out of the sling. "It was too good not to pass along for sibling torture."

"I'm going to get you back for this," I warned.

"You can try," she singsonged, turning back around.

My phone buzzed with a flurry of new texts.

> **Kye:** *I'm reporting this to the mayor. Abuse of power.*

Cope: *I'm taking out a billboard on the highway and putting this up.*

Me: *You have too much money on your hands, Puck Boy.*

Arden: *I am now engaged to a billionaire. Maybe I should ask Linc to put one up on every road in and out of town.*

Me: *Does anyone know how to get unadopted? *not asking for a friend**

Fallon: *Sorry, pal. You're stuck with us for life.*

Me: *That's what I was afraid of.*

I shoved my phone back into my pocket and moved to catch up with Ellie as she headed for the checkout. "They're never going to let me hear the end of this. You know that, right?"

"That's what siblings are for. Plus, a little shit-talking is good for you."

"The thanks I get for taking you to the pet store." I ticked a point off with each finger I put up. "Soaked by the monster. Have to wear this Pepto Bismol-colored flower atrocity—that smells like a wet dog, by the way. And get mocked for all eternity."

"Oh, come on," Ellie said as she moved up to the register. "It's not that bad."

"Arden and Cope said they're making billboards."

Ellie choked on a laugh. "God, I love them."

"Not helping."

Curtis looked up as he began ringing up Ellie's plethora of items. "I don't know, Sheriff. I feel like you could get a lot of numbers this way. You're styling. And this shirt screams *animal lover*."

"Is that really what it screams?" I asked, dropping my voice so only Ellie could hear.

Her lips twitched as she pulled the price tag off her sling. "Here, don't forget this."

"Little dude looks happy in there," Curtis said with a smile.

"I think he is." Ellie gave Gremlin's head a scratch, and he all but purred.

"All right. That'll be five hundred eighty-six dollars and thirteen cents."

Ellie winced but pulled out her credit card, tapping it on the screen. "Who needs a savings account anyway?"

I hadn't thought about how Ellie was making ends meet with a new rental and moving expenses. I knew The Mix Up paid fair wages, but it wasn't like she'd be rolling in cash from that gig alone. "Why don't I go half with you?" I suggested, pulling out my wallet.

Ellie instantly shook her head, expression hardening slightly. "Gremlin's my dog, my responsibility. I've got this."

I slid my wallet back without another word, sensing that this was a no-go zone for some reason.

"Thanks for all your help, Curtis," Ellie said.

"No problem. When you go into Sparrow Falls Veterinary Clinic, make sure to tell them he was a stray. They'll give you all his shots for free."

Ellie tugged her lip between her teeth but nodded. "Thanks."

What was her deal with help? She'd let me give her a ride easily enough, but any offer of monetary help clearly wasn't welcomed. I mulled that over as I grabbed the bags and started for the door.

Both of us were quiet as we stepped outside, but the moment I took in the parking lot, my steps faltered.

"Trace?" Ellie asked, concern in her voice.

I couldn't take my eyes off the man on the opposite side of the lot. The hunch of his broad shoulders. The silver now threaded through his dark hair. The eyes so similar to mine. And the cigarette dangling from his lips.

Jasper took a long drag of the smoke, exhaling and letting his mouth curve into a cocky grin.

"Who is that?" Ellie's voice dropped low, even though he was too far away to overhear.

"No one," I muttered, guiding her toward my SUV.

I was a goddamn idiot. Spending time with Ellie when Jasper could see us? Stupid. Worse, reckless. It would only put her in his sights more.

I waited as Ellie climbed into my SUV with Gremlin. As soon as the door shut behind her, I shoved the bags into the back seat and got behind the wheel, but I felt Jasper's eyes on me the whole time.

As if it wasn't enough that I'd had to live most of my childhood terrified of what he might do next. What his so-called friends might do. Now, it was like I was back there all over again. I could protect myself, but what about Ellie? My daughter? My stomach roiled, a sick feeling washing through me.

As soon as we were out of sight of the pet store, Ellie spoke. Her voice wasn't angry or harsh, but it had a coldness to it I'd never heard before. "Don't lie to me."

My gaze flicked to her. "What?"

"Tell me it's none of my business. Tell me to take a long walk off a short pier. But *don't* lie to me." Ellie let out a shaky breath, and I could see for the first time that she was far more than angry. "I've been lied to all my life by everyone around me. Don't you lie to me, too."

CHAPTER FOURTEEN

Ellie

MY HANDS TREMBLED AT MY SIDES. I WASN'T SCARED. I WASN'T sad. I was finally feeling what I should've felt all along. Angry. At my mom. My dad. Bradley. Even Linc. They'd all lied. Some because they thought they were protecting me. Some because they wanted to manipulate me. But all thought it would work because I was weak.

And I was done with that.

"Ellie," Trace began.

"Don't," I clipped. I hated the softness in his voice, as if he, too, thought I was some wounded animal.

Trace was quiet for a moment before he spoke, saying words I never could've predicted. "He's my birth father. He's been in jail for twenty-four years, and I'm the one who put him there."

Everything in me stilled and got so quiet I could feel each beat of my heart, the two-part thump at elevated speeds. "Why?"

"He killed my mom." There was no emotion in Trace's voice as he pulled into my driveway, no hint of anything as he stared straight ahead, the engine still running. "He didn't pull a trigger or cut off the air from her lungs, but he killed her just the same."

My heart rate sped up, each beat like butterfly wings against my ribs. "I'm so sorry." I let out a breath and then gave him another piece of my truth. "I know what that's like." I knew it all too well. Just one more lie I'd lived with for most of my life.

Trace turned, the movement slow, his gaze searching. "You do?"

"I do."

He searched my eyes for answers or comfort; I wasn't sure which. But whatever he saw there made him continue to speak. "Jasper was mixed up with drugs. A group of guys that were seriously bad news. He got my mom hooked. I had to watch her fall deeper and deeper into that addiction. One night, he shot her up, cackling as she climbed onto the roof of our cabin, saying she could fly."

A sick feeling swept through me as dread mounted, but I didn't look away. I could be in the awfulness with Trace so he wasn't alone with the truth.

"She jumped," Trace rasped. "She wasn't trying to end her life, just didn't know reality anymore. My dad freaked. Thought he could bury her on our property, and no one would know. Told me if I spoke a word about it, I'd go to jail right along with him."

An image of little-boy Trace filled my mind. Alone and terrified, grief-stricken. I knew how that was. How it felt like everything and everyone in the world was against you.

"You told someone anyway," I surmised. Even if Trace *hadn't* said that he'd sent his father to prison, I would've known. Because that was simply who he was. He didn't stand for things that were wrong, and he'd do whatever he could to make them right.

Trace's jaw worked back and forth. "Went to school the next day and told my principal. Sheriff's department called Child Protective Services. Told them all where he'd buried her and what had been going on at home."

"And he went to prison."

Trace nodded slowly, his fingers following invisible lines on his uniform pants. "Got eight years for manslaughter, concealment of death, and drug possession."

I frowned, doing the math in my head. "Shouldn't he have been out by now?"

"Killed another inmate and attacked a guard his second year in."

My mouth went dry as I thought about my own father currently sitting in a jail cell. I knew now what he was capable of, but it had always been hidden. Carefully constructed lies and facades of pleasantness. Trace's father's violence was in your face, the monster that never hid in the shadows. I wasn't sure which was worse.

"And now he's...what? Threatening you?" Anger surged, boiling over and spreading through each and every vein.

"In not so many words. Made sure I knew that he saw me with you, with Keely. Looking for targets around me."

That boiling turned to pure fire. "I'm not a target. And I hope he comes for me. I'll break his balls and have him singing soprano until the cops get there."

Trace's lips gave the barest twitch. "Break his balls, huh?"

"Damn straight."

Any hint of a smile slid from his face. "If you see Jasper, you get somewhere public and call me. You do *not* engage. Promise me."

It was the panic in Trace's final words that had me agreeing. "Okay. But he's probably just trying to make you worry."

Trace leaned back against the headrest. "I wish I could be sure of that."

Unease slid through me like oil through water. "What about Keely?"

A muscle in Trace's cheek fluttered. "I talked to her mom and the school. We'll all keep a close eye."

God, I wanted to punch Trace's dad. Wanted to do worse. Trace was the last person who deserved this, not when he did so much for others—his family, especially.

He reached out, closing his fingers around the steering wheel until his knuckles bleached white. "I've worked so hard to keep Keely safe. I'd give *anything* to make sure she stays that way. Happy, healthy, secure. But I keep failing."

I whirled in his direction, startling Gremlin in my lap. "The hell, you do."

Trace's eyes widened slightly at the fervor in my words.

I pinned him with a hard stare. "We don't always get to choose our pasts. We definitely don't get to choose what we're born into. But you've created such good out of your heartache. You're an amazing father, brother, and son. An incredible cop."

"Sheriff."

"Whatever. You made good out of the bad, beauty out of the ugliness. I would be proud as hell if I could do that."

Trace stared at me for a long time. "What ugliness are you trying to erase?"

I let out a long breath. Thinking about sharing the truth with Trace was akin to standing naked on the lawn and letting the world see every scar and blemish. But he deserved it.

"My mom died when I was six. Dad said it was a car accident. Later, I found out she'd been drinking."

"I'm sorry, Ellie—"

"That wasn't the whole story. No one told me the truth. Not my dad. Not Linc, not until recently." My fingers dug into the seat cushion. "My dad terrorized her. Belittled her. Stole her life, piece by piece, until she didn't want to live anymore. There were no skid marks at the scene. No signs that she tried to brake at all. She floored it and aimed straight for the bridge railing."

"Ellie…"

My eyes burned as I fought back tears. "I miss her, but I'm so mad at her. And worse…I'm just like her."

Trace reared back. "Excuse me?"

I turned to face him, giving him my greatest shame. "I stayed in situations I shouldn't have. Just for a flicker of affection and acceptance. And I let myself swallow all their lies because it was easier than looking for the truth. Maybe if I hadn't, none of this would've gone as far as it did."

Trace's expression turned as hard as granite. "You wanted your family's love, and that makes you a monster?"

"The day our mom died, Linc and I promised we'd *never* be like them. And that was exactly what I became."

"Bullshit," he spat.

"You cursed, Chief."

"Don't give a damn."

"That's number two."

He pinned me with a hard glare. "You're nothing like them. You may have the good parts of your mom, but your dad? You think he'd be crawling around on dirty pavement trying to save an abandoned dog?"

The image was so opposed to anything my father would deign to do that I almost laughed.

"Didn't think so," Trace said. "You think your dad would give a little girl the bracelet off her wrist just to make her feel accepted, special?"

My dad gave nothing unless it benefitted him in the long run.

"Taking that silence as a no, too," Trace went on. "And I sure as hell don't think he'd jump in to help Thea tackle tables when she was swamped when he didn't even work there." Trace arched a brow. "Yeah, I heard about that."

I pressed my lips into a hard line.

"You're nothing like him. Wouldn't be surprised if you sprang from nothing but magic and fairy dust. Because that's what you leave in your wake."

"Oh." My lips formed the shape right along with the word.

"Yeah, *oh*. And if you keep talking down about yourself, you and I are gonna have problems."

My mouth curved the barest amount. "That so?"

"Yeah, it is."

"I'll keep that in mind, Chief."

"Good."

I couldn't hold back the full grin that formed. "Only you could say *good* like you're still pissed off."

Trace shook his head. "No one can piss me off quicker than you."

"I'm taking that as a compliment."

"You shouldn't."

"I still am," I said, sliding out of the SUV.

"Go inside. You're grounded."

I couldn't help but laugh then. It was the last sound I thought I'd make after sharing what I felt was my shame. But Trace gave it to me anyway.

CHAPTER FIFTEEN

Trace

I STAYED FOR TOO LONG, WATCHING ELLIE GET INSIDE WITH THE dog and her bags. Some people would think I was an asshole for not helping her. Hell, *I* thought I was. But I knew if I let myself get behind a closed door with her after everything we'd just shared, I wouldn't be able to hold myself back from her any longer.

I gripped the wheel, my fingers so tight the material covering it squeaked in protest. I had to walk away. For many reasons.

I threw my SUV in reverse and backed out of the driveway. I scanned the street, looking for any sign of Jasper. There was nothing. No cruel glare or man with a cigarette dangling from his lips. No scar slicing beneath an eye as he scowled.

I hit the phone button on my steering wheel. "Call Gabriel."

He answered on the second ring. "Everything okay?"

"He's following me."

Gabriel cursed. "There anything I need to know about?"

"Are you wondering if you need to help me bury a body?"

"Don't say that shit on a recordable phone line."

My lips twitched. "Love your conspiracy theories."

"They're always listening," Gabriel shot back.

"You realize *we* are the *they* in that statement, right?"

"Just tell me what happened."

I adjusted my grip on the wheel as I made the turn onto Cascade Avenue, my gaze still searching for any sign of the man who'd once been my father. I was attuned now, components of my alert system flooding back, even after twenty-some years of disuse.

"I went to the feed store with Ellie—"

"Wait, you went to the *feed* store with Ellie? The one you hate going to because Keely's always dragging you in there and begging for a bunny or a ferret?"

I shifted in my seat as if that would ease my discomfort. "Ellie found a dog. It wasn't in the best shape, so she decided to take it in."

Gabriel chuckled over the line. "Of course, she did."

I ignored the fact that my best friend was clearly getting to know my neighbor. "Jasper wasn't there when we went in, but he sure as hell was when we got out."

"He approach?"

I shook my head as if Gabriel could see me. "No. Just stared."

"Wants you to know he's watching."

But it wasn't just that. "He wants me to know that he can get to me. Me *and* the people in my life."

"The people *closest* to you."

"Ellie isn't that, Gabriel."

"You sure about that? You two seem thick as thieves lately."

"She's my neighbor, and she's going through some stuff."

Gabriel was quiet for a moment before he spoke. "Maybe you both could use each other. Ever think of that?"

"Could you stop playing matchmaker for five seconds and focus on the issue at hand?"

"Sorry. You want to apply for an order of protection?"

I mulled that over. "Not sure that's the play."

More silence came from Gabriel's end for a beat. "It tells Jasper that what he's doing is working. Might be smarter to ignore him."

"There's always the chance he'll escalate if he doesn't get the reaction he wants."

"He escalates, and he's back inside, finishing out that term," Gabriel reminded me.

That much was true, but it also meant putting Keely and Ellie at risk. That didn't sit well with me. "We put Lavender Lane, The Mix Up, Leah's house, and the school on the regular drive-by list. Forty-five-minute intervals max."

"That's no problem. Especially since you and Miss Ellie are *neighbors*."

"Gabriel," I warned.

"What?" he asked with faux innocence. "Maybe she needs to come over and borrow a cup of sugar. Or her power's out, and she needs someplace to stay."

"Jesus," I muttered. "Pretty sure you should be writing Hallmark movies."

"Maybe I am on the side. It's good to have hobbies."

One corner of my mouth kicked up. "I support your dreams."

Gabriel chuckled. "Such a good friend."

I turned onto a street on the opposite side of town. "I gotta jump. Picking up Keels."

"Tell that girl to give you hell."

"I'd rather not teach my six-year-old a curse word, but thanks."

Gabriel laughed. "I'm pretty sure Lolli has taught her far worse."

"Don't remind me."

"Call if you need anything."

"Thanks, man. Appreciate you," I said.

"Always got your back."

"Same goes." And with that, I hung up.

I was more than lucky to have the people I did in my life. The universe might've put me into a rough situation starting out, but with the family I'd built, one of *choice*, I'd more than made up for it. Gratitude washed through me as I thought about everyone who surrounded me and the support I had.

And then Ellie's face flashed in my mind. I wanted her to have that, too. Because, right now, as bright and cheery as she was, I sensed a loneliness in her. But she'd taken the first step. She was here in Sparrow Falls and building a new life. One I knew I wanted to be a part of even though I should've been keeping my distance.

I made the final turn into Leah's neighborhood. The place she'd chosen to live after the divorce was as different from my house as you could get. The new development was full of modern builds set close together. The yards were minuscule, and the design made me think of a geometry problem. It was just one more piece of evidence that Leah and I had never fit.

Pulling into her driveway, I sat for a minute, tugging my mask back on, making sure every defense was in place. It wasn't even Leah's fault that I needed to do it. It was that she reminded me of all the ways I'd failed.

Taking a deep breath, I slid out of the SUV and headed for her front door. It opened before I reached the front stoop. Leah wasn't glaring exactly, but her mouth *was* pressed into a firm line. It accentuated her blond hair cut in an angled bob just below her chin. She was still in what I thought of as her *work uniform*: tan slacks, a white blouse, and a brown belt. It was some version of this every day unless she had a presentation, then it was a suit.

"You're late," she clipped.

"I'm sorry." It was always best to start there when I'd fucked up. "I told you what was going on."

When I called Leah to tell her about Jasper, I'd asked if she could take Keely for a few hours after school so I could make some inquiries. Since she could work from home, it shouldn't have been a huge deal. Clearly, Leah hadn't been pleased.

Her brows pulled together in confusion. "What are you *wearing*?"

I'd completely forgotten about the atrocious pink Hawaiian shirt. How that was possible when I glowed neon was beyond me. No, I *did* know how it was possible. Ellie.

She'd distracted me in every way imaginable. With her kindness. Her raw honesty. By giving me hell.

"Trace?" Leah's voice cut into my spiraling thoughts.

"Sorry. I, uh, had an incident."

She arched a brow. "And you went to a bad tourist shop in Hawaii to remedy it?"

I shrugged. "Desperate times called for desperate measures."

"Daddy!" Keely yelled, running for me.

There was no greater feeling than when she launched herself at me—complete faith that I would catch her. And I always would.

This time, I caught her with an *oomph* and hauled her into my arms. "Did you grow today?"

She giggled. "No." Then she pulled back slightly. "I looooove your shirt. Pink *and* puppies!"

I chuckled. "I'm glad you approve."

"Keely," Leah said, her voice holding the slightest hint of tightness. "Can you grab your backpack and take it to the SUV? Your dad and I need to talk for a minute."

A wariness settled into Keely's eyes as she looked back and forth between us, and I wanted to scream at Leah. I gave Keely a pat as I set her down. "Everything's fine. We're just talking schedule stuff."

Keely's head dipped as she moved to grab her backpack from just inside the door. "Okay," she said, but the single word was quiet and sounded defeated.

As she headed for the SUV, I pinned Leah with a hard stare. "Don't pull that in front of her. It makes her worry."

Leah bristled. "Because I asked her to give us a moment? That's learning manners. Sometimes, adults need to talk privately."

"Yeah, sometimes they do. But *how* you say it can make a kid who's been through a lot of upheaval worry. So have a mind to that."

Leah's mouth thinned into the hard line I'd memorized over the years. "She doesn't need to be coddled."

"She's *six*."

"Which is why I asked her to wait in the car," Leah snapped.

This was getting us nowhere. "What did you need to talk about?"

Leah clasped her hands in front of her, her knuckles bleaching white. "I know the occasional emergency will pop up, but I need *you* to keep *my* schedule in mind. I've got a lot going on at work right now, and I can't leave at the drop of a hat every other day."

"It was *one* day."

She pinned me with a stare. "What about last week?"

I'd busted a meth-cooking facility, and the arrests and paperwork had been a nightmare. "Fine. I can have my mom fill in when needed."

"Nora shouldn't be your solution," Leah ground out. "Maybe I should have primary custody. If I knew I'd have Keely for the whole school week, I could plan accordingly."

My entire body hardened to granite. "You are not taking more time with my daughter away from me. You try, and you'll have the fight of your life on your hands."

"Trace—"

"I know I'm far from perfect. But I love that girl with everything I have. Not having her with me half the time is like walking around with half my heart missing. I'm not losing any more." I had thought we'd done well with our parenting arrangement. It wasn't typical with Leah taking Keely to all the lessons she was so passionate about our daughter being involved in and me picking her up for horseback riding outings with Arden, despite who had custody that day. But it had seemed to work for us. At least, I'd thought it had.

Leah's hazel eyes widened as I started talking, her complexion paling. "Okay."

"Good." It was all I could say when I wanted to rip into her. But more, I wanted to tear into myself. For messing things up so royally. For not being what Leah needed to stay. For losing my daughter.

I turned and stalked toward the SUV, trying to rein in the ugly stew so Keely wouldn't see it. Swallowing all that ugliness cost me something. But I'd pay it over and over again for my daughter.

CHAPTER SIXTEEN

Ellie

I WOKE TO A PHONE RINGING AND A DOG LICKING MY CHEEK. "Gremlin," I mumbled, trying to grab him and fumble for my phone at the same time. I failed at both. The dog dive-bombed my face, and my phone clattered to the floor.

"Oh, God. Gross, Gremlin. That was my mouth." I tried not to gag as I swung to sitting and swiped my phone off the floor. "Hello?" I greeted without looking.

"Are you okay?" Linc demanded. "You didn't answer, and you're out of breath."

"In overprotective mode much? I was *sleeping*."

"Oh. Sorry for waking you."

"Told you, Cowboy," I heard Arden say from the background. "Not everyone likes to rise at dawn like you."

"And not everyone keeps vampire hours like *you*," he shot back.

I couldn't help but laugh. Gremlin must've liked the sound because he barked and jumped, spinning on the bed.

"What was that?" Linc demanded.

"Breathe, ConCon," I said, swiping up Gremlin and sliding my feet into bright, fuzzy purple slippers covered in hearts. They'd been an impulse purchase in town, and I loved them. "I got a dog."

"A dog?" he parroted.

"I want to meet him or her," Arden called over the line.

"Would you put us on speaker?" I asked with a laugh as I headed downstairs, not bothering to put on anything but the oversized T-shirt I was wearing—a T-shirt that was the perfect amount of worn. One that was just the right level of softness to sleep in. A tee that still smelled like sandalwood and black pepper. Trace's shirt.

"Fine. Putting you on speaker," Linc grumbled.

"I want to see the baby," Arden called.

"One sec. I'm taking him out." I unlocked the back door and stepped out onto the porch, making a beeline for the grass. "There you go, buddy."

"What kind is he? Where'd you get him?" Arden kept going with a rapid-fire list of questions.

I laughed as I watched to make sure Gremlin did his business. "I'm not sure, but he's little. And he found me. He was under the dumpster outside The Mix Up."

"And you just took him home?" Linc barked. "He could have diseases."

"You sound like Trace," I grumbled.

"Then Trace has some sense," Linc shot back.

"Trace has met him?" Arden asked, but I heard a hint of *something* in her tone.

"I ran into him right after I found Gremlin. He took me to the pet supply store," I explained as I snapped a picture of my pup.

"Suddenly, the photo you sent yesterday makes more sense," Arden said, a smile evident in her voice.

"Gremlin?" Linc asked, sounding appalled.

I sent the photo to Linc's phone so they could see.

"Oh my goodness. Those ears," Arden cooed.

"Total little gremlin," I said with a laugh.

"He doesn't even look like a dog," Linc muttered.

"Watch your mouth," I snapped. "You're going to hurt his feelings."

"Brutus will love him," Arden said. "We'll have to have a playdate."

"Yeah, why don't you come over today?" Linc suggested. "I feel like I haven't seen you in ages."

"I'm actually going to the farmer's market with Thea and Fallon this afternoon, but what about tomorrow?" I asked.

"Okay," Linc agreed, but his tone was a little sullen.

"Let her live her life, Cowboy. You're going to smother her."

I couldn't help the laugh that bubbled out of me. "She's good for you, ConCon."

"I don't think I like you two ganging up on me," he muttered.

I headed back inside, Gremlin tucked under my arm. "That's good for you, too."

"Damn straight," Arden agreed.

"I'm ending this call before this gets any worse," Linc said with a groan.

"Love you both," I called.

"Love you, too, El Bell," Linc said as he ended the call.

I set Gremlin down and grinned. My brother was happy. And with a woman who was incredibly good for him. He deserved that more than anyone I knew.

I headed for the kitchen and coffee. I might not be a cook, but I had coffee down—well, as much as you *could* have down putting one of those little pods in the machine and waiting for the caffeinated goodness.

After getting that going, I prepped Gremlin's food. The second I went for the bag, he started dancing around in little twirls across the kitchen. "Good to know you like this ridiculously expensive food."

I put a scoop into one of the bright bowls covered in an adorable pattern of flowers and bones and set it on the floor next to his water. Gremlin dove in like, well, a gremlin. The sounds he made while eating were slightly terrifying but also adorable.

As my coffee started to pour from the machine, I grabbed my cell to check my email and stilled. The little red notification bubbles on my texts read one hundred and thirteen, and the phone app had sixty-seven. My stomach hollowed out as I tapped on the *Messages* icon.

There were only a couple of threads with new stuff: one from Thea, confirming our outing today, one from Linc asking if I was awake yet, and one from Bradley.

I rocked from my heels to my tiptoes as I stared at the thread. I could only read the preview, but that was in all caps. *ANSWER ME! WHERE ARE YOU?!*

I worried the inside of my cheek. I could just delete it and never know what Bradley had to say. But that felt scarier somehow. I held my breath and tapped his name.

> **Bradley:** *I think it's time we talk, don't you?*

> **Bradley:** *We're both adults. And I think we need some closure.*

> **Bradley:** *Stop playing games, Eleanor.*

He always used my formal name when he was pissed. Like he was my parent and not my fiancé.

> **Bradley:** *Where the hell are you? It's after midnight there. Why aren't you answering?*

> **Bradley:** *Are you fucking someone right now?*

> **Bradley:** *Whoring yourself out now that you're penniless*

> **Bradley:** *I'm sorry..youilk just makegjj me so mad89o. Butkl it's cause I lovehui*

The messages went on in an increasingly hard-to-read fashion. Cycling from berating to begging for forgiveness and back again. Something about seeing that cycle in written form had something clicking into place. It made me realize that it had *always* been this way. A pattern of Bradley being an ass and then trying to soothe it away with presents, trips, and flowers.

It had never gotten this bad before. Not until the night I'd ended things. But the pattern was there all the same. Waiting for the right trigger to take it further.

I didn't need to look at my phone app to know the calls and voicemails were from him, too. The majority of them were probably him rambling in a drunken haze. As I stared at the device, it started ringing. It made no sound, still in my sleep setting where only Linc's and Arden's calls went through, but Bradley's call still lit up the screen.

I hit decline. It instantly began ringing again. I rejected that call, too. But it only started the process over again. My heart hammered against my ribs as I once more hit decline. He called *again*.

A sick feeling swept through me as I switched my phone to *Do Not Disturb*, stopping *any* calls from coming through. I quickly maneuvered to my chain with Bradley and hit the *info* button. My finger hovered over the *Block* icon for a second. Something I hadn't managed to do up until this point. As if it were safer to know where his head was at. But I couldn't live like this anymore. Taking a deep breath, I tapped it.

I hoped relief would sweep through me as I turned off *Do Not Disturb,* and no calls started again, but that relief didn't come. Something was seriously wrong, and I didn't have the first clue how to deal with it. I could call his mother to see if she could get him some help. I knew from all the time I'd spent with their family over the years that Helen truly loved and cared about him. But reaching out to her would only entrench me back in that world, and I wasn't sure she would even listen to me.

My doorbell rang, startling a strangled yelp out of me, which only sent Gremlin into a barking fit.

"Ellie? Are you okay?" Trace's voice boomed through the door.

I tried to call back and say that I was fine, but my voice felt rusty, and I couldn't get the words out.

"I'm coming in," he yelled.

A second later, the door flew open, and Trace strode in. Gremlin took it as a call to attack, yapping like crazy and running for Trace's ankles.

"Ow! Jesus, that hurt," Trace clipped as Gremlin nipped at his jeans-clad legs.

"Gremlin, stop," I ordered. "He's a friend." That was the command that always worked with Arden's dog, Brutus. But Gremlin gave no fucks about my command and kept biting away.

"Puppy!" a new voice yelled.

Gremlin's head snapped up at the new intruder. The second he saw Keely, he took off running.

Trace and I yelled, "*No*" at the same time, but it was too late. Gremlin launched himself at her.

CHAPTER SEVENTEEN

Trace

I WATCHED IN SHEER TERROR AS THE TINY, MUTANT DOG launched itself at my daughter. Keely caught him with a giggle, and Gremlin instantly started licking her face.

"That tickles, puppy," Keely shrieked, laughing harder as she cuddled him to her. The dog just burrowed into her like he'd found a long-lost friend.

Ellie caught up to me, stopping just short of Keely, doubling over as she panted. "Oh, thank God." As she straightened, her lips twitched. "Apparently, Gremlin just hates you."

I scowled at her. "Seriously?"

She shrugged, the motion drawing my attention to what she was wearing. A T-shirt she swam in that exposed long, tan legs and ridiculous, fuzzy purple slippers. But my gaze went right back to the tee. *My* shirt. The one I'd given her the night she almost set her house on fire.

The worn cotton skimmed over her form like my hands itched to do. It slid to one side, exposing a smooth shoulder, and the thin cotton hugged her breasts in a way that told me Ellie was definitely *not* wearing a bra. My jeans felt instantly tighter.

Fucking hell.

I squeezed my eyes closed for a second, trying to think of anything but Ellie. My daughter was here, for God's sake.

"You okay, Chief? You kind of look like you're having a stroke."

In for three. Out for three. "I'm fine."

"Then why are your eyes still closed?" Ellie pressed.

I opened them then, trying desperately to hold on to my mask. "You screamed," I accused her. And when I heard that strangled sound, I'd instantly had visions of Jasper breaking in and *hurting* her.

Ellie shifted her weight, rocking on her feet. "I yelped. The doorbell startled me."

"Why?" I pressed. Something was off. Ellie's face was paler than normal, and her hands trembled slightly.

"I don't know. Maybe because I wasn't expecting anyone to be ringing my doorbell first thing in the morning."

"We came to make you breakfast," Keely offered helpfully, now rocking the dog to sleep like one of her dolls. "Breakfasts on Saturdays are the best breakfasts, so you had to get it, too."

Ellie's brows rose, and she beamed at Keely, a smile spreading across her face. "Bestie, that is so nice."

For the first time in my life, I was jealous of my kid. I cleared my throat. "Thought you might like some cooking lessons."

Ellie's pale green gaze, even softer in the morning light, turned to me. "I'd like that. Just give me a second to change."

"Bestie, is that my daddy's shirt?" Keely asked, all innocence and curiosity.

Ellie's cheeks flamed, turning a deep pink. "He, um, let me borrow it. And it's cozy. I'm just going to change."

She bolted for the stairs, but I had the sudden urge to beat my chest like a damn gorilla. I wanted her to stay in the shirt. To wear it all damn day so a piece of me was with her. God, I needed to get a grip.

"Daddy, it's so nice that you shared your shirt with Ellie. Maybe you can be besties, too."

I stared down at my daughter. "Maybe we can, Keels."

The only problem was that I wanted to be way more than *besties*.

"What do you think about learning a scramble? If you're okay eating eggs," I asked, glancing at Ellie. She'd changed into black jeans with tears in them that exposed snatches of skin my fingers ached to trace and boots with laces that had me imagining her keeping those on as I—*nope*. That was a no-go zone.

Keely is sitting at the breakfast table. Keely is sitting at the breakfast table. Keely is sitting at the breakfast table.

"I think that sounds like an ambitious goal, but I'm here for it," Ellie said with a grin.

"Okay, first things first. Since you're a veggie-only fan, we need to make sure you're picking things with enough different flavors." I gestured to the array on the counter.

Ellie saluted me. "Veggie queen, reporting for duty."

"I wanna be a veggie queen," Keely called from where she was coloring with Gremlin on her lap.

"Do you want to give up pepperoni on your pizza?" I asked.

Keely's face scrunched. "A halfsies veggie queen?"

I chuckled. "That sounds like a plan." I turned back to our options. "We'll start with onions and peppers. That gives us a good base. Then, we can add the kale for a little greenery. You're good with dairy, right?"

Ellie pinned me with a hard stare. "Pry cheese out of my cold, dead hands."

I barked out a laugh. "Good to know. Now, here's the secret to cracking eggs. One swift rap on a sharp corner, not too hard, not too soft."

Ellie pulled the corner of her lip into her mouth, and my fingers twitched at my side. "When I crack eggs, I get a million pieces of shell mixed in," she admitted.

"Here." I grabbed an egg, handing it to her.

She took it gingerly as if the egg were a bomb that might explode in her hands.

My lips twitched.

"Don't laugh at me," Ellie grumbled.

I held up both hands. "I'd never." Then I moved in closer, covering her hand with mine. The second my skin touched hers, I realized my mistake. Everything about her was petal soft. But worse, her scent was stronger now. The bergamot and rose wrapped around me like a stranglehold.

"You need to keep a firmer hold." My voice had gotten deeper, a rasp clinging to the words. "Like this."

I gripped Ellie's hand with mine, both of us holding the egg together, then brought it down in one swift rap on the counter's edge. The egg cracked clean in two.

"Sorcery," Ellie muttered.

I chuckled, releasing her to spill the contents of the shell into the bowl. "Now, you try." It took everything in me not to move in again, to cup her hand in mine, to drown in that scent.

Ellie grabbed an egg from the carton, studying it like it held the secrets of the universe. "Firm grip." Her slender fingers tightened around the egg. "One quick rap." She brought the egg down on the counter, and it cracked right in two. Not as cleanly as our attempt together, but close.

She let out a squeal as she poured the egg into my bowl. "I cracked an egg without getting one million shell pieces in the mix."

"You did," I said with a grin.

She let out a soft giggle. "God, I'm such a nerd, getting excited about cracking an egg."

"I don't know. It seems like something to be proud of to me."

Ellie smiled back at me. "Thanks for teaching me."

Her phone dinged on the counter, and Ellie moved to quickly wash her hands. The phone let out another ding. Then another. I frowned as she stiffened and crossed to the device. As she studied the screen, her face paled slightly.

"What's wrong?" I clipped.

Ellie quickly locked the phone, flipping it on silent before shoving it into her pocket. "Nothing."

"Doesn't look like nothing," I pressed. Something had tweaked her. Even now, that slight tremor was back in her hands.

"Just some stuff I still have to sort out in New York. Nothing important."

It was a lie. Maybe not the New York piece, but the rest. You didn't go pale over things that weren't important. Your hands didn't shake. And you sure as hell didn't concoct a lie.

Ellie might've shared pieces of her story with me, but she wasn't sharing everything. And something had terrified her.

CHAPTER EIGHTEEN

Ellie

CANNOT GET OVER HOW CUTE HE IS," FALLON COOED, GIVING
Gremlin's head a little stroke as we explored row after row of the
farmer's market stalls. I'd put Grem in the sling I'd gotten him, and
he was a happy camper.

"And he's so sweet," Thea said.

I rolled my lips over my teeth, trying not to laugh.

"What?" Thea pressed.

"He *hates* Trace. He's tried to bite him twice," I admitted.

Fallon's dark blue eyes went wide. "Seriously?"

I nodded, giving her a sheepish smile.

"Bet Mr. Law and Order looooved that," she said.

"I'm thankful Grem and Keely are besties. I think Trace will just
try to give him a wide berth."

Thea slowed at a display of cut flowers, studying the blooms.
"Moose wasn't all that fond of Shep at first. But they became friends
with time."

Thea's massive Maine coon cat was at least twice the size of

Gremlin and made it very clear when he was cranky about something. I grinned at her. "You mean Shep bought his allegiance with treats."

She laughed and moved us toward a fruit stall. "Whatever works."

My phone buzzed in my back pocket, and I braced. Bradley had obviously realized I'd blocked him because he'd started texting with a new number. I'd blocked that one, too, but I was on edge. Sliding my phone out, I breathed a sigh of relief at the familiar name on the screen.

> **Arden:** *Change of plans for tomorrow. Nora wants everyone at her house for dinner. You in?*

> **Me:** *Sure. Thanks for the invite.*

> **Arden:** *You know you're welcome anytime. And bring your pup. I heard he nearly took off Trace's finger. Smart doggie.*

I scowled at the screen.

> **Me:** *Such a drama king. Grem didn't even make contact. And I think he's only got like two teeth left anyway.*

> **Arden:** *Never letting him live this down.*

"Everything okay?" Fallon asked.

I looked up to find her studying me carefully. In my month or so in Sparrow Falls, I'd realized that Fallon was attuned to everyone's emotions. She read them like others read a book. And she was constantly checking in on the people she cared about.

"Just Arden inviting me to dinner at Nora's," I explained.

Fallon's gaze didn't move right away. "You braced when you pulled out your phone. Were you thinking it was someone else?"

Right to the point. Gentle but not pulling punches either. I tried to choose words that weren't a lie. I felt bad enough for the half truth I'd told Trace earlier, one I *knew* he'd picked up on. "My phone just hasn't been the happiest place lately."

Fallon's expression slid into one of pure empathy. "Is the press still hounding you and Linc?"

"Occasionally. I think I'm still waiting for the other shoe to drop."

That wasn't a lie. It wasn't the whole story either. It had a Bradley-sized hole in it.

Thea moved in, rubbing a hand up and down my back. "It'll pass, trust me. Those buzzards will find something else to circle."

She would know. When her celebrity ex made trouble for her and Shep, the press descended on Sparrow Falls for a few weeks. But after a while of them refusing to comment, the media had gone in search of a juicier story.

"You're right. And I don't want that to cloud our day." I glanced at the next stall and grinned. "I want to see what Duncan has."

Thea looked over and waved at her boss from Bloom & Berry. "I didn't know he was going to be here. Looks like he's got some mums ready for the fall décor hounds."

"Fal, does your mom like mums? Maybe I could bring some as a thank-you tomorrow."

She shook her head but did it with a smile. "You know you don't have to bring anything."

"I *want* to," I argued. "And since my cooking skills aren't exactly up to snuff, flowers are a much safer bet."

Fallon laughed. "How's the new range treating you?"

"I used it safely this morning, I'll have you know. But I did have supervision."

That piqued her interest. Her smile widened. "Sleepover? You dog, you! Who?"

"No, no, no," I said quickly. "Trace and Keely came over this morning." Heat hit the apples of my cheeks. "He, uh, knows that cooking isn't my strong suit, so he offered to teach me how to make a scramble."

Both Fallon and Thea stilled, turning to me.

"Trace Colson?" Thea asked. "The same Trace who follows a schedule by thirty-minute increments and never deviates?"

"I, uh, didn't know about the schedule. But, yes."

Fallon burst out laughing. "You know, he made our chore chart growing up." She turned to me, mischief in her dark eyes. "And I've never known him to deviate from his Saturday pancake routine on the weekends he has Keely."

"Oh." It was all I could manage to say.

"*Very* interesting, him breaking that streak," Fallon said.

"It's not like that," I argued. "We're just…frenemies."

Thea made a choked sound. "Frenemies?"

I shrugged. "I love giving him shit and trying to force him to have a little fun. He loves trying to give me demerits and lecturing me for almost setting my house on fire."

Fallon struggled to keep a straight face. "So, you got revenge by putting him in that truly incredible pink Hawaiian dog shirt."

"Oh, no. I can't take credit for that. That was all Gremlin and Curtis at Feed & Friends."

Thea lost it then. "You are exactly what Trace needs."

"Amen, sister," Fallon said, holding out a hand for a high five.

Thea slapped it. "I feel like they need a reality show."

Fallon nodded. "I could sell that."

But I was still stuck on Thea's words. *"You are exactly what Trace needs."* I held them close for a moment too long because the reckless part of me wanted that to be true.

"Well, well, well, if it isn't the trio of terror," Duncan said with a grin as we walked up.

Fallon moved in to give him a quick hug. "Here to wreak mayhem and destruction."

"Maybe I need to call Kye to keep you in line," Duncan shot back.

Fallon stuck her tongue out at him. "Don't you dare ruin my fun by calling that overprotective oaf."

Thea gave Duncan a hug, too. "Plus, this is a girls' day. No boys allowed."

Duncan chuckled. "Okay, I can take a hint. I'll keep my distance." He turned his smile to me. "You haven't been in to get started on that butterfly garden."

"I know. Things have been a little hectic getting settled in the new house," I admitted.

"Because she almost blew it up," Fallon said on a choked laugh.

Duncan's eyes widened. "Are you okay?"

I sent Fallon a glare. "She lies."

Duncan looked between the two of us. "Somehow, I feel like there's more to this story."

"We'll never tell," Thea singsonged.

"A true friend," I praised.

"Hey!" Fallon protested.

I just grinned at her. "Snitches get stitches."

Duncan scrubbed a hand over his beard. "You three scare me a little."

"Oh, we should," I told him.

He laughed. "Do you guys need anything, or are you just here to give me nightmares?"

"I need two pots of mums. Can I pay for them now but pick them up later?" I asked.

"Sure," Duncan agreed. "What color?"

I scanned the options. "I'm thinking these deep burgundy ones. What do you think, Fal? Will your mom like this color?"

"She'll love them. She's more of a pink than an orange girl."

"Perfect." I peeled off thirty dollars and handed it to Duncan. "I'll be back to grab these."

"Take your time," he called as we headed down the row again.

"Hey," I said, turning toward Fallon as we walked. "Kye's MMA gym…"

She nodded. "Haven?"

"Yeah. Do they do any beginner training for women or self-defense classes?"

Fallon's brows rose. "They do both. And some of the instructors do one-on-one lessons, too."

One-on-one sounded good. Then, I wouldn't have to be as embarrassed with my lack of coordination in front of a big group. "Kye did Arden's training, right?"

She nodded, but an expression I couldn't quite pin down flashed over her face. "He does it for a lot of people."

I glanced at Thea, looking for a clue as to what I wasn't picking up on.

Thea shook her head. "Fal's annoyed that Kye won't train her."

That surprised me. The two of them seemed like peas in a pod. They were always laughing and giving each other a hard time. But Kye was especially protective of her. "He doesn't want you to get into the MMA world?" I asked.

Fallon let out a sound of frustration. "He always makes up some excuse for why he can't teach me. Or tries to pawn me off on one of the other trainers. It's like he thinks I'm too weak or something."

"I know that's not the case," I argued. I hadn't known them all that long, but it was clear that Kye thought Fallon hung the moon.

"I'm not so sure," Fallon mumbled.

I wanted to ask more but sensed it was a sore subject, so I tried to guide us out of it. "I also want to take a yoga class at that studio I saw in town. Want to do that with me?"

Fallon brightened, just like I'd hoped. "I've heard it's really good. It's new. I'm in. As long as we get brunch after."

"I like the way you think."

As we reached the final stalls, I heard a sound. A soft and slightly sad bleat. I turned, trying to find the source. That's when I saw it.

A goat was tied to the very last farmer's stall, looking sad and forlorn as the farmer talked to a customer. As I moved closer, I saw a *For Sale* sign above the goat's little patch of hay. Beneath it read *Final Offer*.

I frowned. Selling a goat at a farmer's market didn't really seem like a great idea. How could you know it would go to a good home?

I found myself making a beeline for the animal. I didn't know the first thing about goats, but I crouched low, holding out a hand for it to sniff as Grem's little head popped out of the sling to investigate. The goat licked me, and I grinned.

"Hi, little one," I cooed, scratching beneath its chin.

"You lookin' for a goat?" the man behind the stall asked, a wad of chewing tobacco in his lip.

"No, not really."

"Shame," he muttered.

I glanced up at the sign again. "What does *final offer* mean?"

"Means she's going to slaughter if she don't get sold today."

My eyes widened as a sick feeling rolled through me. And then I felt my mouth saying the words before I heard them. "I'll take her."

I tugged on the worn lead rope Ethan the farmer had given me alongside enough feed to get me through my first week as a goat owner, but my new goat friend would not be moved.

"Come on, buddy. Please?" I begged.

If any of my neighbors saw me right now, they'd probably think I was completely unhinged. And maybe I was. I'd gotten Gremlin inside and come back out for my new goat. A goat I was appalled to discover didn't have a name. I was going to give her one, but I needed to know what fit her personality first.

I gave the lead rope a little slack. "Come on. There's a whole lot of grass in the backyard. Don't you want to eat some?"

No movement.

Frustration bloomed. She was too heavy for me to carry her. I'd learned that while lifting her out of the back of my SUV. I was pretty sure my back would pay the price for that for the rest of the week.

"How about some of this?" I coaxed, pulling some feed out of my pocket and offering it to her.

She sniffed the air but didn't come any closer.

I straightened and tried tugging again, harder this time. I put all my weight into trying to get the goat to move.

Nothing.

I walked behind her and tried shoving from the rear, attempting to get her to walk through the open gate. The goat kicked back, getting me right in the shin.

I howled in pain, hopping around and spilling some very creative curses like, "Son of a goat nugget," and "Damn it all to hay bales."

A throat cleared from behind me, and I stilled, slowly turning around.

I was greeted by Trace, who seemed to somehow be both pissed off and amused all at once. "What exactly is a son of a goat nugget?"

CHAPTER NINETEEN

Trace

I'D WATCHED ELLIE FROM MY WINDOW FOR A MINUTE AS SHE struggled to get a goddamned *goat* into her backyard. For a second, I worried Lolli had slipped me one of her *special* brownies and I was hallucinating. But after blinking a few times, I knew I wasn't.

What the hell had Ellie been thinking? Trying to wrangle an animal she likely knew nothing about without any help? She could've been seriously hurt. As was evidenced by her hopping, cursing dance.

Ellie froze, her eyes widening at my barked words. I expected her to read me the riot act. To give me absolute hell for being a stick-in-the-mud. What I didn't expect was for those gorgeous pale green eyes to fill with tears.

"Oh, fuck," I muttered, moving into Ellie's space. I pulled her into my arms and held her to me. "Hey, hey. What's going on?"

"Y-you said the F-word," she said between sobs.

I just held her tighter against me, wishing I could take back my words, soften my tone. I was such an asshole. "Yeah, I did."

Ellie kept right on crying as I held her. Each sob was like a knife to the chest, and I would've given anything to fix whatever was wrong. Slowly, her cries lessened, but they didn't cease altogether.

"Can you tell me what's going on?" I did everything I could to keep my voice as gentle as possible.

Ellie pulled back, her eyes bloodshot and still pooling with tears. "I can't even save a goat. How am I supposed to save myself?"

Everything in me tightened, and I battled not to grip Ellie harder. To keep my contact gentle. Instead, I lifted a hand to her face, my thumb tracking under her eye, the same one that had been bruised yet hidden beneath coats of makeup. "Who hurt you?"

My voice was soft, but fury vibrated each word. Because there was more to the story. More to what was going on with her father. Or maybe something else entirely. But I needed to know what it was more than I needed my next breath. Because in that moment, I would've given anything to take away Ellie's pain.

"My ex," she whispered.

My jaw clenched so tightly pain stabbed through the bone.

"Just once," she hurried to add. "When I left."

"He. Hit. You?" The fury vibrated harder this time, my hold on it more tenuous.

Ellie twisted slightly, looking away but not leaving my hold. I wasn't sure I'd have been able to let her go if she tried.

"I don't know what it was about. He never—there was no temper before. It was like this whole other side of him came out," she admitted.

"Tell me you reported it."

Ellie was quiet, which was my answer.

"El."

"It wouldn't have done any good. His family's connected. It never would've made it to court. And even if it had, I couldn't deal with any more attention."

I muttered another curse. Apparently, Ellie made me break all the rules. But I understood her thought process. She already *had* the world's attention, thanks to her father's crimes. Heaping more on would've been more than she could take.

But everything about him walking free made me want to rage. There was no justice in that. And justice was the one thing I needed to count on. That whatever bad in the world happened, the evil would pay for it.

"Did you tell anyone?" I asked, defeat bleeding into my tone.

"No," Ellie whispered. "I just—I was embarrassed." Her gaze lifted to mine. "I made so many mistakes, Trace. Let the wrong people rule my life. My dad. Bradley."

"Don't say his name," I spat.

Ellie's eyes widened a fraction.

"Sorry," I ground out. "I just—I'm too angry right now. I want to hunt him down and—" I cut myself off, not wanting to admit that the same urge toward violence my father had also ran through my veins.

Instead of being appalled, one corner of Ellie's mouth kicked up. "Don't worry, I've thought about a little justice myself. Throwing him into alligator-infested waters. Buying a voodoo doll and giving him a permanent limp dick. Keying his precious Maserati."

My thumb ghosted over the swell of her cheek. "You've got a vengeful streak in you like Fal does."

Ellie gave me a wavering grin. "Watch out, Chief. I'll get you if you cross me."

"Noted, Blaze. Noted." I stared down at her, admiring all her strength but so badly wanting Ellie not to have endured what she had. "I'm so sorry this happened to you."

She didn't look away as she listened to my words. "I *let* it happen, Trace. That's what makes it so awful. What makes me feel so ashamed."

"The hell, you did."

Ellie shook her head. "You don't get it. I might not have let him hit me, but I let him walk all over me from the moment we met. From the moment Bradley and I got together, he treated me like nothing more than window dressing, acceptable arm candy. And I just went along with it."

"You're a hell of a lot more than that," I ground out.

"I like clothes. Makeup."

"Who gives a damn?" I challenged. "There's nothing wrong with liking those things. And that's *one* piece of you."

"Maybe. But I even changed that for him. For my dad. My boss. I was all neutrals and acceptable styles. I never fought to just be…me."

Hearing that killed something in me. Because I could see the sparks of the real Ellie coming through now that she was free. And dimming those would be a loss for the entire world.

"Who do you want to be?"

Ellie's pale green eyes shimmered like dew-covered moss. "I don't know."

"Tell me one thing you want."

"I want a goat."

I barked out a laugh. "Looks like you tackled that one, even though it's illegal to have livestock within city limits."

Ellie winced. "Really?"

"Don't worry. I won't turn you in."

"You breaking the rules for me, Chief?"

"I knew you were going to be a bad influence."

Ellie laughed, the sound easing something in me. "We'll make a rebel out of you yet. I did get you to drop an F-bomb."

I stared at her for a long moment and decided to give her a piece of my own shame. "I don't like to curse because my parents did. All day, every day. It was like every other word in our house. Hearing it reminds me I could be like them."

"Trace," Ellie whispered. Her hands lifted to frame my face. "Dropping an occasional swear word won't *ever* make you like your dad. You didn't let what you came from define you. You let it *teach* you. It showed you the kind of dad you'd never be. The kind of man. And dropping an F-bomb won't change that."

I stared down at her for a long moment. I wanted to kiss her so damn badly. Wanted to taste the words she'd just given me on my tongue. "I've been holding on to these invisible rules like they'll keep me from becoming him."

"You don't need 'em, Chief. You're already a million times the man he could ever hope to be."

Maybe Ellie was right. Maybe it was time to let go just a little. Maybe it was time to take a risk. My head lowered, lips hovering just above hers—

"OH MY GOD!" Keely screeched. "You got a goat! Can we get a goat, Daddy? Pretty please, can we?"

My daughter barreled across the lawn toward us, and I leveled Ellie with a stern glare. "I'm going to make you pay for this."

Ellie just burst out laughing. And it was the best sound I'd ever heard.

CHAPTER TWENTY

Ellie

THE DOORBELL RANG FOR THE THIRD TIME, AND GREMLIN LET out a series of high-pitched barks, running down the stairs. "Just keep your pants on," I grumbled, rubbing sleep out of my eyes. Who rang the doorbell at seven-fifteen in the morning on a *Sunday*?

I picked up Gremlin, tucked him under my arm, and then yanked open the door, wearing my best scowl. "What?" I grumbled.

To add insult to injury, pure hotness greeted me. Trace stood there in worn jeans, and not by a designer's false wear and tear but from everyday use. And given that he'd paired them with honest-to-goodness cowboy boots, I was guessing they were worn from working on his family's ranch. And the soft flannel he wore over a tee had me wishing for one of my own.

Trace's dark green gaze swept over me, lingering on my bare legs for a moment. "What are you wearing?"

It was the first time I'd given any thought to what was on my body that morning. I glanced down at myself, taking in the bright pink shirt with a sparkly rainbow creature emblazoned on it under *I'm fucking magical.* "A T-shirt," I said with a huff.

One corner of Trace's mouth kicked up, pulling it into a slightly off-kilter smile. "I like your unicorn."

I should've been embarrassed that he'd found me in nothing but a ridiculous tee, hair in what I was sure was a ginormous tangle atop my head from going to sleep with it wet, and no pants on. But I found I wasn't. Instead, I lifted my chin. "It's a pegacorn."

Trace stared back at me, unblinking. "A pegacorn…"

"Yes. It's a cross between a unicorn and a Pegasus."

Those beautiful lips twitched. "I didn't know those two cross-pollinated."

"Well, they do, and it's to create the most magical creature in all the land."

Trace laughed then, the sound husky and a little raw. It skated over my skin like what I now knew the pads of Trace's fingertips felt like. "Cute," he muttered.

I pressed my thighs together. This man was going to kill me. "What are you doing here at seven in the morning? On a Sunday."

Gremlin let out a low growl as if to punctuate my point.

Trace wasn't deterred by my menacing dog or my clipped words; he just grinned at me. "Can you keep a secret?"

I wanted to be the keeper of all this man's secrets, and that was a serious problem. Still, I found my mouth pulling into a smile. "I could be convinced. Might take some bribery, though."

Trace chuckled. "I think the bribery will be contained in the secret."

That had my brows pulling together. "Okay…"

"You're going to need pants, though."

I couldn't hold in my laugh. "Now, where's the fun in that?"

Trace raked a hand through his hair, pulling on the strands. But then he stepped into my house, backing me up and closing the door behind him. "You're killing me, Blaze. And there's only so much I can take before I break."

My breaths came quicker, escaping in short pants as Gremlin growled. "And what happens if you break?"

"Neither of us will leave this house for days, and I really want to show you something. So, do me a favor. Turn around and walk that perfect ass upstairs and cover it with some pants, okay?"

I tugged my lip between my teeth, fighting not to laugh. "Okay."

And that's exactly what I did. But it cost me.

Trace was quiet as he drove, his SUV bumping down the gravel road. For a while, I'd thought he was taking me out to Nora's house, but nothing there could've been the secret. Then he'd turned down another road—one called Monarch Way.

Finally, I couldn't take it anymore. "Where are we going?"

My mind had been churning since Trace showed up this morning. And it had taken us a while to get going. I'd had to change, take Gremlin out, feed him and my nameless goat friend—who was already doing a number on my back lawn—and put Grem in the little pen I'd gotten him, complete with chew toys, pee pads, and water. Plus, there'd been the required coffee. Always coffee.

So, over an hour had passed where I was trying to put together the pieces of what Trace could possibly want to show me. I'd tried a handful of questions, but he'd dodged them all.

Trace briefly glanced my way before turning his focus back to the road. "You're not one for patience, are you?"

I did the only mature thing I could and stuck my tongue out at him.

Trace barked out a laugh.

"This is cruel and unusual punishment," I muttered, pulling a leg up onto the seat so I could rest my head on my knee.

"We're almost there. Do I need to promise you candy if you don't ask how long again, just like I do with Keely?"

I pressed my lips together to keep from smiling. "I do have a thing for Twix bars."

"I'll keep that in mind."

We drove for another few minutes, and I let myself really take in our surroundings. To the east, the Monarch Mountains, four craggy peaks that never lost their snow, even in the height of summer. To the west, Castle Rock, golden rock faces looking permanently sun-kissed. And a mixture of fields and forests leading to both.

God, it was beautiful. But more than that, there was power in it. A raw realness that took my breath away every time.

"I love it out here," I whispered.

I could feel Trace's eyes on me. A beat longer this time before he turned back to the road like the responsible driver he was. "Me, too. Can't imagine living anywhere else."

"I can't imagine what it was like growing up here. Having all this wildness around you." Maybe that's what called to me about Sparrow Falls and its surroundings. That it was just a little unkempt, free. Almost dangerous. It tempted me to be all those things, too.

"What was it like in New York?" Trace asked.

I thought about that for a long moment. "There were good things. The Natural History Museum is a dream for a kid. The Central Park Zoo, too. The park itself is beautiful. But how I lived… It was stifling—never experiencing the things that make a city like that so rich. And at some point, it just started to feel like I couldn't breathe."

Trace took all that in, mulling it over before he spoke. "And here?"

"Here, I'm trying to learn to breathe again."

"Seems like a good place to start."

It was. The landscape. The people. The air. It all seemed to help.

Trace flicked on his blinker, even though there wasn't a car in sight, and turned onto a drive. He stopped at a gate and cattle guard, hopping out of his SUV but leaving it running. "One sec."

He unlocked a chain, swung the gate open, and then ran back. Just as he'd promised. I was starting to realize that about Trace. He did everything he said he would. I didn't know anyone else I could say that of.

"I hope you're not breaking and entering," I said, studying him. "I happen to know the sheriff."

Trace's dark green eyes flicked my way. "Pretty sure you only know a chief of police, and we don't have one of those around here."

A soft laugh left my lips. "Touché."

He grinned as he guided the SUV down a gravel road. Trees were scattered on either side of our path, making it difficult to see much beyond what was right in front of us. But after a few minutes, the drive dumped us into a wide-open space.

I couldn't help the audible gasp that left my lips. There were fields and meadows that felt like they went on for miles before morphing into forests and then unobstructed views of the Monarch Mountains and Castle Rock. My fingers were undoing my seat belt before I consciously gave them the command. I opened the door before Trace even shut off the engine, sliding out and into that openness.

A barn stood off to my left, paddocks and pasture beyond it. It looked solid and sturdy but aged—the kind of time-lapse that spoke of weathering storm after storm.

That called to me, and I found myself moving toward it, pressing my hand to the worn wood. Even the feel of it had character. I traced a seam with my fingertips and turned to see something else in the distance. Not a structure but something mapped out on the ground.

Trace sauntered in my direction, not in any hurry. "You want the tour?"

I nodded, heading toward him. His mouth split into a grin like a little kid about to show you his favorite Christmas present. "There will be a walkway here." Trace moved his hands like he was guiding a plane into place.

"Tons of windows so you can see right through the house downstairs. It's shielded from the road, and we'll have a gate with security codes, so no need to worry about people you don't want seeing in."

I grinned at him. "Safety first, Chief?"

Trace shook his head at me. "Always." He turned back to where the house would go, laid out with string and posts. "Walk in here, and you'll see all the way through to a wall of windows at the back."

God, it would be stunning. "Like the mountains are right in your living room."

Trace nodded. "Kitchen and family room there." He pointed to the left. "Living room and office to the right." He gestured again. "Below us will be a basement with a playroom for Keely and a gym for me. Upstairs will be the bedrooms and laundry."

But I was stuck on the view. I could see Trace and Keely here. What an amazing life they would lead. How wild and free Keely could be. My mind painted pictures all around me, Trace cooking in a chef's kitchen, Keely coloring in front of those towering windows. I kept building their beautiful life until pressure built behind my eyes. "It's perfect," I croaked.

Trace moved to stand right next to me. He was so close that his heat bled into me. "I can get water and power in the barn. I thought we could move your goat friend out here as soon as it's running. That way, I don't have to write you a ticket."

He glanced down at me. "But you can't tell anyone. Shep's the only one who knows about it. I wanted to surprise Keely when it was closer to being finished."

Everything hurt in the best way. Trace didn't know what a miracle he was. A *good* man when, except for Linc, my life had been full of so many bad ones. The way he cared for his daughter, making her dreams come true. How thoughtful he was in building their life together. That he would let in someone he barely knew so she could have a place to put the goat she'd rescued on a whim.

I swallowed hard and looked up at Trace. "You're getting Keely a horse, aren't you?"

He grinned down at me. "She's been begging since she could talk."

"You're a good dad."

Something passed over Trace's face. "Best thing you could say to me."

"It's true. And you're a good man."

"Blaze."

"Truth."

"You're killing me."

"Thanks for letting me keep my goat here."

"Stop it."

"And for showing me this beauty."

A muscle fluttered in his cheek. "You can come out here any-time you want."

And I knew that was a gift, too. I turned to the horizon again, letting the unique pine air fill my lungs. "Chief?"

"Yeah?"

"I can breathe."

CHAPTER TWENTY-ONE

Trace

I CAN BREATHE." ELLIE'S VOICE ECHOED IN MY HEAD ALL DAY LONG. When I picked Keely up from riding lessons with Arden. As I watched her play at the park. And it didn't stop as she and I headed to the Colson Ranch for our family dinner.

Something about the admission felt intimate. Like some connection had been forged by me giving Ellie a place that allowed her to breathe. And I'd be a liar if I said it didn't freak me out.

I found myself a little more powerless to resist Ellie with every day that passed and every second I spent in her presence. And worse, I found I didn't want to.

"Daddy?" Keely asked from the back seat.

I jerked myself out of my spiraling thoughts. "Yeah, Keels?"

"Can we teach Ellie blueberry chocolate chip pancakes next?"

My gut twisted. Keely was getting just as attached as I was. "Sure, we can."

"Maybe we can make them into unicorns."

I couldn't help but laugh. "I think you might be overestimating my pancake-art abilities."

Keely beamed at me through the rearview mirror. "You can do *anything*, Daddy."

God, that confidence slayed me. Suddenly, I heard Ellie's voice in my head again. *"You're a good dad."*

I cleared my throat, trying to brush off the emotion. "Just remember you said that when the unicorn looks more like a sad horse."

Keely giggled. "At least it'll still taste good."

I pulled into a spot at the end of a makeshift row next to a bunch of my family's vehicles: Fallon's hatchback that had seen better days. Kye's black truck with its shadow detailing in art that looked like the patterns he inked on people's skin. Anson's equally dark truck with far more dust and dirt on it. Linc's Range Rover. Shep's truck with the *Colson Construction* emblem on the side. And an SUV I'd memorized the sight of by now.

I looked for hints of it all over town. Just like I looked for flashes of the girl with hair that sparkled like a rainbow in the sunlight. My fingers tightened around the wheel.

Everything in me battled, knowing that Ellie was inside. But anticipation won out. Because I was like an addict hunting for his next fix, knowing it was just around the corner.

I switched off the engine, and Keely was already unfastening her booster seat. "Do you think I can go riding after dinner?"

I laughed as I got out of the SUV and moved around to help her down. "You went this morning."

Keely beamed up at me. "Two's better than one."

She jumped, and I caught her easily and set her down. "Let's see how long dinner lasts."

"Daaaaad, it's always forever."

She wasn't wrong there. Colson family dinners always started early because they went long. But I wouldn't have it any other way. It was everything I'd never had as a kid and everything I wanted to give to Keely. I might have failed to give her a two-parent home, but at least she had this.

As if she wanted to remind me of that, Keely took off running for the porch steps of the home I'd lived in from twelve until I left for college. It looked like something out of one of those feel-good movies: a white farmhouse with a wraparound porch, complete with rockers and porch swings. I knew it was worn from years of use, but Nora and Lolli never let so much as a chip show through on the paint or anything else.

Keely hauled open the front door just as I reached the top step. The moment she did, voices and laughter spilled out. Keely didn't wait to be invited in because she knew she always belonged here. And that was a gift, too.

The moment she stepped inside, she yelled, "Bestie!" and charged for Ellie.

I stood frozen, watching it play out. My daughter flew at Ellie, pigtails streaming behind her. Ellie grinned widely, her pale green eyes lighting at the sight of my daughter, her dog dancing at her feet. She'd changed from what she'd worn earlier, and it was so much worse—maybe even more torturous than that damn pegacorn T-shirt with no pants.

She wore a pleated plaid skirt in burnt oranges and browns that hit her at mid-thigh, paired with tights with artful little tears that revealed tan skin. I wanted to slip my hand up that skirt and tear the stockings right off. But I'd want her to keep the heeled boots on. They weren't exactly cowboy boots, but they were close, and with the white turtleneck sweater revealing a sliver of taut skin at her navel, it was like she'd blended New York and Sparrow Falls into something uniquely her.

Someone knocked into me from the side, offering a beer. "You're drooling."

I glared at Kye, taking the bottle and returning my gaze to my girls just as Ellie caught Keely. She spun her around, and Keely giggled as Gremlin barked.

My girls.

It was dangerous to even think the words, but I couldn't stop myself. Because it felt...right.

"Looks like those two have bonded," Kye murmured, amusement in his tone.

"Don't start," I growled.

His lips twitched beneath his dark stubble, and the action made the tattoos on his neck flutter. "What did I say?"

"You know exactly what."

"I can't notice that your neighbor gets along great with your daughter and that you can't take your eyes off her?"

I tore my gaze from Ellie, but it hurt. Like ripping off something that had been superglued.

Kye laughed. "Dude, you are so totally fucked."

"Language, Kyler," Nora clipped as she walked up.

He grimaced. "Sorry."

Nora sent him a quelling look and pulled me into a hug. "Missed you. You've been working too hard."

I hugged her back. "Sorry, Mom. Things should slow down now that we're getting past tourist season."

She pulled back but kept a hold of my biceps, studying me like only a mother could. "You know you don't have to apologize. I just worry about you."

"What he needs is a night out on the town," Lolli called from her spot at the kitchen island, where she drank some sort of colorful cocktail with an umbrella.

"Lolls," I warned.

"What?" she asked, her voice full of innocence. "I can't suggest that my grandson should let loose? You know, I've been working on something that could help with that. It's a special blend—"

"You lost me at *special*," I said.

Rhodes laughed from her spot on the couch, where she sat next to Anson. "Lolli's turning all the ladies into *special* brownie fiends. Two of her girls from yoga came into Bloom yesterday asking if I stocked any of the good stuff."

Fallon struggled to keep her composure. "I can't wait for next week's class. Everyone's really going for that downward dog pose. They'll probably start barking."

Nora pinned Lolli with a hard stare. "See what your influence is causing?"

"I'll try your special blend," Keely piped in helpfully.

I sent Lolli a glare that should've had her cowering. Instead, she just laughed and moved to Keely and Ellie. "How about you help me come up with a concept for Ellie's diamond painting? I need to make her one now that she's in her new house."

"Like that's any less corrupting," Shep muttered, taking a pull from his beer.

Thea smacked his chest from her perch on the arm of his chair. "I love our diamond art."

Shep stared up at her for a long moment. "It's penis pumpkins. We have penis pumpkins in the greenhouse."

"I really prefer the term dick gourds," Kye said, popping a sliced red pepper with some dip into his mouth. "It's more dignified."

Fallon gaped at him. "Seriously?"

"What's wrong with dick gourds?" Kye asked.

"It's better than puck penises," Linc said, handing Arden a plate as he lowered himself to sit next to her on the hearth in front of the fireplace.

"I think you mean your stick dick," Kye corrected.

I lifted a hand to squeeze the bridge of my nose. "Someone save me."

"What's a stick dick?" Keely singsonged.

"I hate all of you," I grumbled.

"Daddy," Keely said very seriously. "We don't use the H-word."

"That's my girl," Lolli praised. "No H-words. But there's nothing wrong with a little phallic expression. It opens up those sexual chakras."

Ellie struggled not to laugh as she set Keely down. "Do I want to know what a sexual chakra is?"

"Oh, darling, we'll work on it. It's your sacral chakra. A little of my psychedelic tea, and we'll get you opened right up. Then we'll hit up the cowboy bar or The Sagebrush."

"Lolli," I gritted out. Though it wasn't only because I didn't want my six-year-old going into school tomorrow talking about stick dicks and sexual chakras. It was also because I was jealous. The idea of Ellie letting loose with someone who wasn't me…had everything in me twisting into knots.

"Just because you're a stick-in-the-mud doesn't mean the rest of us have to be," Lolli shot back.

Ellie just shook her head. "I don't know if I could keep up with you, Lolli."

"Trust me," Fallon called. "You can't."

"But you'll have a hell of a lot of fun trying," Lolli said, shaking her hips in some bizarre dance.

My cell phone rang, and I'd never been so happy for an interruption. Pulling it from my pocket, I saw Gabriel's name on the screen and swiped my finger across the device to accept the call. "Please, save me from the insanity that is my family."

Gabriel was quiet for a moment, and everything in me went on alert. "What's wrong?" I asked, moving out of the open living space and down the hall.

Gabriel cleared his throat. "It's your dad. We've got him in lockup."

CHAPTER TWENTY-TWO

Ellie

I T WAS AS IF MY WHOLE BODY WAS ATTUNED TO TRACE. I COULDN'T help being aware of every move the man made. The second his phone rang. The moment the call turned.

I watched as his shoulders stiffened, the muscles twisting into tense blocks of cement. The way his shields went up as he talked to the person on the other end of the line. And I couldn't stop myself from following him as he walked down the hallway.

It might make me a creepy stalker, but I had a deep urge to help. To ease whatever ate at him the way he'd soothed me more than once.

"I'll be there as soon as I can." Trace faced away from me as he ended the call, but he made no move to turn or leave as he said he would. Instead, he just stood there for a moment, clutching the phone at his side, his breaths coming in ragged inhales and exhales.

I tracked each breath with my gaze, my fingers itching to reach out and grab hold. I wanted to tell him it would be okay, even though I had no idea what was wrong. "Trace?"

Those muscles wound tighter, and he didn't move right away. I felt him putting up layer after layer of walls between us. Each brick he placed to reinforce the barrier was like a carefully placed blow, but I knew there was nothing I could do to stop it.

Finally, he turned, his expression unreadable. "I need to go into the station."

My hands fisted, the nails I'd painted lavender the other day pressing into my palms. "What happened?"

"Case," Trace said flatly.

"What case?" I pressed.

"That's sheriff's department business."

The words were like a slap, but I knew what was beneath them. Over the past few weeks, Trace had given me pieces of himself, tiny slivers I was slowly assembling into an image that revealed more than he might want to show me. But I saw it all the same.

I stared at Trace, not letting my gaze waver for a second. "It's okay if you need help. It's okay if you need someone to lean on. It doesn't make you weak. It makes you human."

A muscle fluttered wildly in his jaw. "Ellie—"

"Let me be there for you. Like you've been there for me."

That jaw worked back and forth, but Trace took a single step toward me. It was all I needed. I closed the distance and slid my fingers through his, squeezing tightly, an invitation for him to lay down his burdens.

"Gabriel arrested Jasper. He's in lockup."

I sucked in a sharp breath. "For what?"

Trace's throat worked as he tried to swallow. "Gabriel busted up a party out at The Meadows. Drugs were present. Jasper was in front of a trailer next door, clearly intoxicated."

"Does that violate his parole?" I asked quietly.

In many ways, that would be a gift. Jasper would have to return to prison, and Trace would be free of him for a few more years at least.

"Gabriel's checking now. Every parolee's terms are different. But they're drug testing him. If he dings positive, he's definitely going back."

Was it wrong that I hoped Jasper tested positive for every controlled substance under the sun? Probably. But I didn't care. I didn't claim to be a noble person, and I would've done just about anything to protect Trace from the world of hurt currently raining down on him.

"Do you want me to go with you?" I asked.

I saw the slightest movement in Trace's lips as if he were trying to smile. "You secretly a law enforcement agent of some sort?"

I huffed out a breath. "I could be a secret agent. I bet they have cool outfits."

Trace chuckled, even if the sound was half-hearted. "Hate to break it to you, but most agents I know wear boxy, oversized, and ugly suits."

"Damn."

"Still bet you'd make it look good."

My cheeks heated, but I didn't take my eyes off Trace. "I could wait in your office or the car, just so you know I'm there."

He stared at me for a long moment. "Means something. You offering that."

I'd have waited twenty hours for Trace if it meant letting him know he wasn't alone.

His gaze flicked down the hall. "Can you stay with Keely? If I'm not back by the time dinner's over?"

I tried to hold back the jerk my body wanted to make. Because I knew that was a whole new level of trust. "I've got her."

Trace lifted his chin in understanding. Agreement. "Nora has an extra set of keys and a spare booster seat if you need it."

"We'll figure it out. Text me if you need anything."

Trace squeezed my fingers and then released them, already moving. He poked his head into the living room. "Got a callout. Be back if I can. Keels, Ellie's gonna stay with you if I'm late."

Keely's green gaze moved to me instantly. "Bestie time?"

"You know it. We can do face masks," I told her.

Keely cheered, spinning in a circle of pure glee.

"Good to know I'll be missed," Trace muttered, amusement lacing his words.

"Be safe," I whispered.

"I'll be fine." And then he was gone.

I wasn't so sure about his words. Didn't quite believe them.

Because Jasper was stirring up memories that I wasn't sure Trace had ever truly dealt with.

When I turned back to the room, it was to find everyone staring at me. I glanced behind me, half-expecting to see a giant green alien or a grizzly, but there was nothing. "What?"

Fallon grinned at me. "Trace doesn't trust people with Keely easily."

Shep lifted his beer to me in a salute. "And by *not trust easily*, she means he runs at least two different background checks, asks for five references, and puts a nanny cam somewhere every time."

My jaw went a little slack at that. "Seriously?"

"Kye still isn't allowed to babysit alone," Fallon said, her delight in the fact clear.

"Hey, Keely loves her uncle Kye. Right, Keels?" Kye defended himself.

Keely plopped down on the couch. "You're my favoritest! Remember when you let me draw tattoos all over my arms?"

Fallon leaned into Kye, looking up at him, her eyes twinkling. "Hence, why Kye is not allowed to babysit alone."

"They were *washable* markers. I don't know why everyone freaked out so much," Kye grumbled. "Plus, my Keels has skills. Could be an epic tattoo artist one day."

Kye would know. His artistry had garnered attention from across the globe, and people came from all over for appointments with him.

Fallon shook her head. "You let her go to sleep with it on. The markers came off on the sheets and seeped into her skin so much Trace couldn't get it off for a week."

Kye just shrugged. "So, she was a little baddie for a week, big deal."

I could only imagine Trace's reaction to that ordeal.

A phone dinged, and Fallon pulled her cell out of her purse, frowning as she read whatever was on the screen.

Kye read her mood instantly. "What's wrong?"

Fallon didn't move her eyes from the screen. "Nothing. Just an update on a case."

While Fallon wasn't law enforcement, she often worked alongside them as a social worker with Child Protective Services. I'd come to realize that while Fal was probably the most sensitive of the Colsons, she was also a badass in her own right. And every kid that crossed her path was better for it.

Kye stiffened. "Tell me you're not going back to The Pines tonight."

The name caught my attention. "What's that? The Pines."

Arden grimaced as she turned to me. "Rougher neighborhood a ways out of town."

"A lot of drug traffic through there," Anson added.

Kye's entire demeanor had changed as he stared at Fallon. His tattooed fingers bleached white as he gripped the bottle in his hand, and a muscle in his jaw pulsed in a staccato beat.

Fallon glanced up at him. "Don't."

"It's not safe," Kye ground out.

"It's my job. And I can't always have a hulking shadow following me around. I know what I'm doing. Trust me," Fallon begged.

"I'd trust you with my life," Kye said without hesitation. "It's everyone else I don't trust."

And there it was. The thing I'd sensed in the time I'd known Fallon. She was the only one Kye *truly* let in.

Something changed in her then. She hooked her pinky through his and squeezed. "I'm not going anywhere tonight. It's just about some follow-up I need to do tomorrow."

Kye's whole form relaxed a fraction. "And you're taking a deputy?"

Fallon sighed. "Yes, I'll take a deputy."

Kye's pinky tightened around hers and then released, sending some silent message only the two of them understood.

"All right," Nora said, clapping her hands together. "Enough bickering for one evening. Dinner is ready."

"It's called shit-stirring," Kye said, pushing to his feet.

"Kyler Blackwood, I will still ground you. Don't think I won't," Nora called.

He just laughed and crossed to the table, but I intercepted him before he made it. "Kye?"

"What's up, buttercup?"

A soft laugh left my lips. "I was wondering if you could help me with something."

"You need ink?"

I shook my head. "I have an aversion to needles."

"You and Fal both."

"I was wondering if you had time for some self-defense training or mixed martial arts instruction?"

Kye's expression morphed again, becoming assessing like an animal gauging my weaknesses. Only I knew it wasn't a lead-up to attack. It was something else entirely. "What are you looking for?"

I swallowed, really thinking about the question. "I want to feel strong."

I wanted that more than anything. To feel like I could stand up for myself and not just with my words. That I could back it up with my body, too.

"That, we can do. Tomorrow, five o'clock?"

"That easy?" I asked, a little shocked.

One corner of Kye's mouth pulled up. "Gonna turn you into an ass-kicking machine."

"Kyler Blackwood," Nora called. "You're in time-out."

"Swear jar, Kye Kye," Keely yelled.

Kye shook his head. "Always the black sheep."

Only I knew he was anything but.

Laughter filled the air as Shep told a story about Lolli getting frisked at an airport thanks to her T-shirt that read *Go Green*, with a pot leaf instead of the recycling symbol.

My phone dinged, and I shifted to pull it out of my skirt pocket. It dinged again before I could even get it out, and then it started ringing.

I quickly silenced it, taking in the unfamiliar number on the screen. Unease slid through me like the oily tentacles of an unknown sea monster. I pushed to my feet, mumbling that I'd be back. As I headed for the back door, the phone started ringing again.

The same unfamiliar number.

My fingers tightened around the device. It could be Trace. Maybe he was calling from a landline at the station.

I hit *Accept*, pressing the cell to my ear as I closed the door behind me and stepped out onto the back deck. "Hello?"

"Eleanor."

Everything in me tightened at the sound of Bradley's voice. "You need to stop calling me."

Maybe he simply needed to hear it. To know that we were truly done.

"You need to stop playing games," he spat.

My fingers gripped the phone harder. "I'm not. I'm saying we're done. I hope you can deal with the things you need to and find someone who makes you happy. But that person isn't me."

I moved the phone away from my ear to end the call but heard him yelling on the other end of the line. "You think you can throw me away, you little cunt—"

I disconnected, but I couldn't stop staring at the screen. I could count the number of times I'd heard Bradley curse on one hand. He'd always thought my letting those spicy words fly was an unattractive habit. Maybe keeping them in my vocabulary was my little rebellion.

A new call flashed on the screen. Same number. I ignored it and moved to block it, too. I'd change my number tomorrow. Cut off access. It would be better for us both.

I heard the door behind me but didn't move. I didn't have the layers of mask I needed for whoever it was. I painted on one after another as the footsteps got closer.

"Everything okay?"

I should've known it would be Linc. He was always checking in. Such a good big brother.

I turned, giving him an easy smile. "Yup. You finish dessert?"

Linc's eyes narrowed on me, clearly not dissuaded from his mission. "Who was on the phone?"

"No one," I said quickly.

"El Bell…"

"ConCon." We could both play the childhood nickname game. I hadn't been able to say Lincoln when I was little, so he'd become *ConCon* to me, much to our father's chagrin. Philip Pierce hated nicknames. *"We gave you a specific name for a reason. Don't sully it, Eleanor."*

Linc didn't smile at my use of his nickname now. "Don't shut me out."

I straightened. "I'm not."

"Ellie, you've barely talked to me since you moved into your new place."

My shoulders slumped slightly, the fight leaving me. "I'm sorry."

"You don't have to be sorry. Just tell me what's going on."

The pleading in Linc's voice nearly broke me. I moved in and wrapped my arms around my brother's waist, giving him the hardest hug I could. "You're too oversized," I grumbled.

Linc laughed as he released me. "Maybe you're just too small."

I shot him a dirty look as I leaned back against the porch railing, letting the night wrap around me like a comforting blanket.

"You ready to talk?" Linc pressed.

I wasn't. Not about everything. Linc was too entwined in it all. Everything felt like a giant knot I was still trying to untangle. But I didn't want to lock him out either.

"I'm trying to figure out how to stand on my own two feet." Truth. It might not give him every detail, but it gave him the core.

Linc's brows pulled together as he studied me. "It looks to me like you're doing that."

"I almost set my house on fire the first night I was in it."

Linc's eyes went wide. "You what?"

I held up both hands, trying to placate him, even while being grateful that I didn't have a soon-to-be sister-in-law who shared all the sibling gossip with her fiancé. "I'm fine. The house is fine. I got a new range, and we're all good."

"Ellie—"

"What?" I asked, cutting him off. "You want me to move out?

Come live with you and Arden at your new place when it's done so you can keep an eye on me? Never learn to cook because I might blow something up? You already moved me in next door to the sheriff without my knowledge."

Linc was quiet for a long moment before he spoke. "You need room to stumble."

The air left my lungs on a giant whoosh because I knew he understood. "Yes."

"And I might've been a little stifling."

My mouth curved as I held up my finger and thumb to show a sliver of space. "Just a tiny bit."

He barked out a laugh. "Arden told me I was being overbearing."

"Have I told you lately that I *love* your fiancée?" I asked.

Linc grinned. "She's pregnant."

I stilled, my hands wrapping around the porch railing and holding on tight. "What?" I whispered.

"Twins. We wanted to tell everyone tonight."

My hands released the beam, and I flew at my brother.

He laughed as he caught me and swung me around. "Happy news?"

"The happiest," I croaked, tears filling my eyes.

"Hey," Linc said as he set me down. "No tears."

"They're happy tears." I sniffed. "I just—you guys deserve this. Every ounce of this happiness."

"They're gonna be so damn lucky to have you as an aunt," Linc whispered.

"Gonna be even luckier to have you as a dad."

Linc gripped my shoulders and held on. "Gonna give them everything we never had. Love they never question. Fun and chaos. Color. The knowledge that they're accepted for whoever they are."

Each statement was a beautiful blow—a knife slicing to the core with joy as its blade. I didn't know how I could hold the two extremes, but somehow, I did. "I know you will."

And I did. I just hoped I could find the same for myself.

CHAPTER TWENTY-THREE

Trace

I STARED UP AT THE STATION FOR A LONG MOMENT. IT WASN'T THE first time I hadn't wanted to go inside. There'd been more than once where I'd faced a case that cut. Important ones, but they hurt like hell to work.

This wasn't that. *This* was me not wanting to face what going inside would bring up. The ugly stew of memories. No, more than memories. Demons.

Ellie's face flashed in my mind. Her voice rang in my ears. Her offer to come with me wrapped around me.

It was such a simple thing—almost *childlike* in its simplicity— extending a hand so I wouldn't be alone.

But I was used to being alone. I was basically alone until I was twelve. When I went to the Colsons', I'd been anything but with all the people filling the space. Yet I'd kept to myself. Dealt with my traumas and fears alone. Even after I married Leah, we hadn't truly let each other in. So, when that ended, it had almost been a relief to be alone again, caring for my daughter on my own.

But there was something about Ellie. She made me wonder what it would feel like to have someone—not someone to complete me, but someone to lean on, someone who would be there when I needed it, not to fix things but to be in them with me.

I switched off the engine and stared at the building for a moment longer. I kept the image of Ellie in my mind and clung to the memory of bergamot and rose as I opened the door and slid out of my SUV. I hadn't bothered with my uniform, badge, or gun. They weren't needed for what lay ahead.

Opening the door, I stepped inside. A deputy who'd only been with us a handful of months greeted me, an uneasy smile on his face. "Sheriff."

He knew. He knew the man in one of those cells was my father. No…my DNA donor.

"Martin," I greeted, not giving any sign that the situation had gotten to me. I was good at that.

Without another word, I headed for the bullpen. It wasn't as full as it usually was on weekdays. Sunday evenings were usually slow all around. Not typically party nights but rather a day for tourist turnover. We got the occasional accident or drunk-driving arrest, but that was about it.

The handful of voices quieted as I entered the room. Damn, that felt like a gut punch. I didn't give any sign of how it affected me. Instead, I moved straight to Gabriel's office. He saw me through the open door and motioned me in, even though he had a phone pressed to his ear.

Stepping inside, I shut the door and lowered myself to one of the chairs opposite his desk. It gave the bullpen my back, and that was a good thing. I wouldn't have to watch every microexpression my face made.

"Thanks, Jim. Yeah, I'll make sure he reports in tomorrow," Gabriel said. "Have a good night."

Gabriel lowered the phone to the receiver and swiped his gaze over me. It was a quick assessment, likely trying to see if I had it together. "That was Jasper's PO. Not sure why, but Jasper's allowed alcohol. An oversight, given his past possession charges."

"What about a public intoxication charge?" I asked. Any charge could potentially send him back to complete his sentence.

Gabriel scrubbed a hand over his tan face. "Technically, he was on his property. He rents a cabin out at The Pines. He was sitting in a lawn chair in front of it."

"Conveniently next to a party you busted."

"That'd be the one. And there's more."

I braced because, with the man who'd once been my father, I could be in for anything.

"The man who rents the trailer next door? The one with the party? That's Rainer Cruz."

I tried to hold back my reaction, but it wasn't easy to do. I knew Rainer—had known him all my life. He was the kind of mean that had to be part of his DNA because I didn't think it could be learned. There was a viciousness to him that always led Jasper to bad places. They'd been a part of the same drug ring back in the day.

"You know him," Gabriel assessed.

"Yeah. One of Jasper's nearest and dearest."

"Looked him up. Looks like he was living over in Roxbury until about a month ago. Arrested a couple of times by their PD, but nothing ever seems to stick to this guy," Gabriel went on.

"What'd you find at the party?" I asked.

"Meth, crack, and a little acid. Conveniently, not *on* Rainer or your dad."

"Jasper," I clipped.

"Sorry. Not on Jasper." Gabriel's face twisted. "But one of the dogs found a stash site in the woods behind the two trailers."

"Tell me you're dusting it for prints," I growled.

"Already sent it to the lab and told the techs I'd treat them to a steak dinner if they can get it on the top of the pile."

I eased back in the chair. "You're a good friend."

Gabriel grinned at me, but it was half-hearted. "You're a lucky fucker to have me in your corner."

"Sometimes," I muttered.

That startled a laugh out of him. "Fair." Gabriel was quiet for a moment. "You want to see him?"

That was the million-dollar question, wasn't it? I couldn't decide what the better move would be. I mulled each over, playing out both sides of the coin in my mind. Finally, I stood. "I want to see him."

Jasper didn't get to think he'd made me cower. The man had lost his power over me a long time ago.

"I'm with you," Gabriel said, pushing his chair back.

There was no room for argument in his statement, and I knew the reasoning behind it was three-fold. He was backup should things go sideways. It meant dotting our i's and crossing our t's for procedure. And he cared about me.

I gave him a chin lift of acceptance, and we moved out into the bullpen—right into Will shooting his mouth off.

"Give me a fucking break. His dad was doing twenty-eight for manslaughter and *murder*, and he somehow got elected sheriff? I think it's time someone ran against his white-trash ass."

It wasn't the first time I'd heard the term tossed my way. Probably wouldn't be the last. But it always landed a little closer to home than I wanted.

The entire room went silent as Will's gaze cut to me. The smart move would've been to cower. He didn't. He stared me down as if challenging me to throw a punch.

"You got a problem with my leadership, talk to the mayor. In the meantime, you will not mess with my station. Clearly, being at a desk is too much temptation for you to run your mouth. So, let's take that desk away from you. Patrol for the rest of the month. I see your ass anywhere close to that chair, you're suspended."

A few officers snickered. Two of them high fived.

Redness crept up Will's neck. "You can't do that."

"Check with the mayor," Gabriel said helpfully. "Because I cosign that assignment."

"I'd like to toss in prisoner trash pickup next weekend," Sergeant Yearwood said as she walked out of the copy room. "My old bones are so over your shit."

Laney Yearwood had been with the department since she was eighteen. Now, at sixty-three, she was ready for retirement, and her tolerance for assholes was practically nil.

I shot her a grin. "Now, that's a mighty fine suggestion, Sergeant Yearwood."

She flipped me off. "You call me Sergeant Yearwood again, we're gonna have problems."

I chuckled. "Noted." All amusement left my expression as I turned to Will. "Why is your ass still in that chair, Deputy? Do I need to relieve you of duty, or can you handle a simple patrol?"

Will's teeth gnashed as he stood and stalked out of the station. Applause erupted as he did. God, I loved my team. At least ninety-five percent of them.

Beth moved into the bullpen from reception. "What'd I miss? Will looks pissed as hell, so I know it was good."

I shook my head and moved toward the back hall and the holding cells we had there. I knew the rest of the crew would fill her in. Gabriel followed behind me, sticking close as we turned into the room that housed the two cells.

They didn't get a whole lot of use. Mostly for drunk and disorderlies, or waiting for suspect pickup on larger cases. We didn't keep people here longer than overnight. They'd get transferred to county.

As I stepped into the room, it felt smaller than normal, the air thick and reeking of sweat and alcohol. A pair of bloodshot eyes lifted to glare at me. "Can't keep me here," Jasper spat.

"I don't have anything to do with this. Conflict of interest and all that."

Jasper stood, wobbling before he struggled toward the bars. "You got your pigs on me," he slurred. "Trumped-up charges."

"Sir," Gabriel began, all false politeness, "you appeared inebriated to multiple officers on the scene. When we ran your ID, we saw you were on parole. It's within our rights to require a drug test because of that. We're just waiting for those results to come back. I'm sure you understand."

Jasper spat through the bars, narrowly missing Gabriel's shoe.

"I understand that my bastard brat put you up to this. Gonna sue all your asses."

"Good luck with that," I muttered.

"You," Jasper sneered. "You think you're so much better than me. But I'm in your blood. Your veins. You'll never get me out."

A coldness swept through me. One so brutal it sliced like a blade. Because despite Jasper's blustering, he spoke the truth.

A twisted smile spread across his face. "You have no idea what's coming for you. But it's gonna be fun as hell watching you lose everything."

CHAPTER TWENTY-FOUR

Ellie

THE SOUND OF A KEY IN THE LOCK HAD ME BOUNDING OFF THE couch and crossing to Trace and Keely's front door. By the time Trace opened it, I was already there. Everything about him looked exhausted, and it had only been a few hours.

"Keely?" he asked, shutting the door and leaning against it.

"Asleep. We took Gremlin for a walk. Did face masks. Read stories. She passed out halfway through *Goodnight Moon*."

Trace let out a breath, leaning harder against the door as if he wanted the wood to swallow him whole.

"That bad?" I asked quietly.

Trace stared straight ahead, but I knew he wasn't seeing me. It was something else entirely. "He's in my head. Worse, he knows it."

I wanted to junkpunch Jasper...whatever the hell his last name was so badly my hands fisted. I pulled in a slow breath, trying to ease my anger because Trace didn't need that right now. Once I was a little steadier, I took a step closer. Then another.

I didn't stop until I stood between Trace's legs—so close I could feel his breath on my face. So close I could smell the sandalwood and black pepper. So close my skin warmed, thanks to the heat wafting off Trace in waves.

I lifted my hands and skimmed them over his face. "Let him go." My fingers ghosted over Trace's forehead, then his cheeks. "He has no place here."

I expected Trace to close his eyes, but he didn't. He kept them locked on my face as I moved. My fingertips skimmed across his face again, trying to clear away the demons that had caught hold.

"Some part of me believes you. Because you're magic," Trace rasped.

"Good," I whispered. "Not afraid to use a little witchcraft to banish evil."

Trace lifted his hand and trailed his thumb across my lower lip as if memorizing the swell. "Maybe I'm the one under your spell."

My heart hammered against my ribs as I leaned into his touch. The rough pad of his thumb sent shivers sparking across my skin. "Somehow, I don't think you can bend to the will of a little ole spell."

Trace tracked his thumb across my lip, first one way and then the other. "Doesn't feel like that. Feels like every ounce of resolve I have is crumbling."

Blood roared in my ears and pounded at my pulse points. "I know the feeling."

He leaned closer—so close our breaths mingled in the space between us. "Ready to tip those scales?"

I opened my mouth to answer, to say "*yes*," to say, "*fuck the man-ban.*" I needed to know what it felt like to have Trace touch me. *Really* touch me.

"Daddy?" a sleepy voice sounded from the top of the stairs.

I jerked away from Trace's sorcery, nearly falling on my ass in the process. Trace caught my elbow and kept me upright, which only made it worse. His fingers scalded, even through the sweater covering my arm.

"I'm home, Keels," he called.

"Can you tuck me in again?" she mumbled.

"On my way." Trace turned pained eyes to me and moved in

again, pressing his lips to my temple and letting them hover there for a beat. "Guess it's the witching hour."

"I guess so." My voice was barely audible as need pulsed through me in angry waves.

"Text me the second you're home. Lock the door behind you."

"Got it, Chief."

"Killing me, Blaze."

I looked up into those beautiful eyes, the green so dark it almost looked black. "Good."

And then, I was gone.

"Maybe I'm the one under your spell."

The words tumbled around and around in my head as I opened the doors to the old shed Mrs. Henderson had left in the backyard, the afternoon sun warming the cool fall air. As a bleating sound came from behind me, I winced. I hoped she wouldn't mind what I was about to do. But I'd replace the shed if I needed to. For now, my goat friend needed somewhere to spend her nights until Trace's place was ready.

Just thinking his name sent the words swirling in my mind again. *"Maybe I'm the one under your spell."*

As if to knock some sense into me, Goaty—as I was calling her until I came up with something better—headbutted my leg. My hand dropped to give her a scratch as Gremlin chased imaginary butterflies. "I know, I know. Focus on the now."

I studied the shed and looked down at the article I'd pulled up on my phone. *So, You Got a Goat: a 10-Step Guide.* "Well, I've got the hay, at least."

I got to work hauling out the few remaining gardening supplies and piling in the hay I'd purchased from Feed & Friends that morning, along with the best goat feed I could find and bright pink pails for Goaty. And I did it all while trying to ignore those words circling.

"Maybe I'm the one under your spell." And the feeling of Trace's thumb on my lower lip.

"We're not being dumb girls, Goaty."

She let out another bleat in answer.

"Yeah, I'm calling bullshit on myself, too," I grumbled as I stared up at the top of the garden shed. The article had said airflow was important. Maybe this next step would help with my sexual frustration. "I'm sorry, Mrs. Henderson," I muttered as I went in search of the handsaw I'd seen in the garage.

After much cursing and effort, Goaty had some vents under the eaves of the shed that should let air get through without allowing too much cold in. "What do you think, baby girl? Fit for the queen you are?"

Goaty hopped up into the shed, sniffed around, circled, and then plopped down. I grinned, a surge of pride filling me. I might not have had the rest of my life together, but at least I was giving Goaty and Gremlin good ones.

"I've got to come up with a better name than Goaty," I mumbled. She just started snoring.

I laughed and then snapped a picture with my phone, sending it to Sarah in New York.

> **Me:** *I have officially entered my country-girl era.*
>
> **Sarah:** *Is that a GOAT?! Should I be calling for an intervention?*
>
> **Me:** *Let me live in my blissed-out state of delusion that I am actually a cowgirl.*
>
> **Sarah:** *Yeehaw?*

Another laugh bubbled out of me when she sent a GIF of a woman on one of those mechanical bulls. Then I cursed as I caught sight of the time on my screen. "We gotta go, Grem." I quickly cleaned up my supplies and got Gremlin settled. Before long, I was in my SUV and on my way to Kye's gym.

The only problem was that the short drive gave those words a chance to swirl in my mind all over again. *"Maybe I'm the one under your spell."* They were the same words that had kept me up for half the night, making my skin too hot and every nerve-ending stand at attention. The fact that I could still feel Trace's lips pressed to my temple didn't help either.

Trace was haunting me. Awake or asleep, it didn't matter. The echoes of him were everywhere.

Turning into the small parking lot outside Haven, I looked for a spot with the most room. Pulling into one at the end of a row, I opened my door to survey my parking job.

Epic fail.

My wheels had overshot the white lines completely. Pressing my lips together, I backed up and tried again. When I opened the door this time, it was a lot better. Not perfect, but good enough.

Turning off the engine, I hopped out and headed for the front door. A genuine smile tugged at my lips when I saw a familiar face. "What are you doing here?"

Arden smiled, and her massive dog, Brutus, thumped his tail. *"Freigeben,"* she told the beast in German. Brutus instantly made a beeline to me for a rubdown. "Kye told me you were coming for your first lesson. I had to be here for moral support and to cheer you on in kicking his ass."

I laughed as I scratched behind Brutus's ears. "A true friend."

"I try," she said with a smile.

"How are you feeling?" I asked, dropping my voice as if someone might overhear. "I'm so happy for you guys."

Arden's smile turned soft as she pressed a hand to her belly. "Mostly tired. A little nauseous. And craving all the french fries and milkshakes."

"I bet Linc is thrilled with that last one."

"He is far too smug that the babies love his favorite combo."

"I bet," I said, giving Brutus one more pat.

"You ready?" Arden asked.

"As I'll ever be."

There was something about her showing up without me asking.

Just because she knew I was trying something out of my wheelhouse. Her silent support meant more than she'd ever know.

Arden pulled open the door. The moment she did, music and foreign sounds filled the air. The music had a distinct rock edge—not the super hard stuff Arden preferred, but the kind meant to prepare you for battle. It was paired with a percussion all its own. And as I stepped inside, I could see what created the beat.

About a dozen or so people were scattered throughout the massive space. A few warmed up on treadmills or jumped rope. Many were at punching bags, their fists making music as they connected with the surfaces. And a couple were in what looked like practice rings. The crowd was primarily male, but I saw one woman sparring and another hitting a bag.

But I was struck by far more than just the patrons. The space itself was stunning. It had an industrial feel that I wouldn't have thought would mesh with the Sparrow Falls vibe, but it somehow did. The majority of the surfaces were black and gray, but the far wall that ran the length of the gym was a riot of color.

No, it was far more than color. It was art that came alive, the sort of mural that could reach out and touch you. It looked like a mesh of graffiti and fine art, the word *Haven* spelled out in massive letters at the center.

"Did you paint that?" I asked, pointing to the mural and then turning to Arden in admiration.

She instantly shook her head. "This is all Kye's magic."

"Seriously?" I asked, my shock evident in the single word. I hadn't seen any of Kye's tattoo work, but the mountain of a man clearly had amazing skills. "Maybe I need to rethink my aversion to needles."

Arden chuckled. "I know, right? He's pretty incredible."

"I am, aren't I?" a deep voice said. Kye moved in with a grin, giving Arden a quick hug. "Miss seeing you around here."

She grinned up at him. "You know I'll be back in action as soon as I can."

Kye turned to me, his gaze assessing. I expected a joke or a tease, but there was none of that. "How are you feeling about being here?"

I glanced at Arden for a moment before turning back to Kye. "Good. Your place is beautiful. You've got a serious eye."

"That's a major compliment coming from a fancy New York interior designer," Arden said.

Kye's lips twitched. "Happy to know I made the grade. Killer, you want to show Ellie the women's locker room? Then we'll get started."

"You got it," Arden said, leading me down a hallway while Brutus hung with Kye. She pointed things out along the way. "Men's locker room. Kye's office. Gear storage room." She opened the door to a smallish room. "Not many women work out here, but we've got these lockers and two showers if you need them."

I nodded, slipping my bag into an empty locker and pulling off my hoodie. I'd thought about going badass black for my outfit, but I couldn't resist the pink workout set with rainbow piping. If I was learning to be strong, I would do it as *me*, not pretending to be someone I wasn't.

Shutting the locker door, I turned around. "Ready."

"Let's do this," Arden said with a grin.

We made our way back into the gym, only to be stopped by a guy wearing low-slung shorts, sneakers, and nothing else. His tanned skin had a slight sheen of sweat, and his blue eyes sparkled as he gave me a head-to-toe scan. "I like the kicks," he greeted.

I peeked down at my white tennis shoes with rainbows on the side. My lips tipped up. "Thank you."

"You must be new around here. I'm—"

"The gym's resident playboy," Arden informed me.

The man turned to her with a look of exaggerated hurt on his face. "Arden, you know it'd only take one crook of your finger to make me a reformed man."

"Mateo, I love you, but I'm not about to expose my soon-to-be sister to your bullshit," Arden shot back.

"Listen to her warning," a younger guy who looked to be in his early twenties called as he pulled on some mitts.

Mateo sent the guy a scowl. "Why you gotta do me dirty like that, Evan?"

A laugh bubbled out of me. "How about I admire the game but politely decline?"

Mateo shook his head. "Sisters. Damn. That's too much hotness for my brain to hold at once."

Kye strode up, his worn Haven tee pulling taut across broad shoulders. "If you spent half as much time working on that slip and duck as you do hitting on my family, you'd have it down by now."

"Brutal, bro. Brutal," Mateo muttered, heading toward Evan.

"I don't hear you saying it's a lie," Kye called back.

"I'm getting the sense this place is like its own sort of family?" I said, but it was more of a question.

"A shit-talking, would-bury-a-dead-body-for-you family," Kye agreed.

I laughed. "I can appreciate that."

"Until they won't stop giving you shit for getting engaged," Arden mumbled.

"Just wait till they find out you're knocked up," Kye said, dropping his voice to a whisper.

"Bite your tongue, Kyler."

"Uh-oh," I muttered. "I don't think I've ever heard one of your siblings call you Kyler."

Something flashed across his expression, but he quickly covered it with a shake of his head. "Only when I'm in trouble. Come on. Let's get you started with a warm-up."

Kye took me through a jump rope warm-up that ignited my lungs and had me questioning my sanity. And then we headed for a practice ring.

"If you get into MMA on the whole, or jujitsu like Arden practices, we'll get you kitted out with sparring gloves, maybe even some boxing gloves for heavy-bag work, a practice gi. But for now, we'll work on self-defense." Kye met my gaze before dropping his voice. "If anything is too much, just say the word, and it stops instantly. There anywhere you don't want to be touched or an approach I shouldn't make?"

A memory flashed in my mind, Bradley's face contorting in rage, his hand rising, the stinging blow that had me staggering back a few steps. I blinked a few times, shoving that down and focusing on Kye.

The way he had asked the question and how he'd empowered me to take control of the lesson told me he'd worked with people with triggers before. He wasn't overly gentle in a way that suggested I was weak, but he *was* thoughtful.

"I'm good with whatever we need to do. I'll let you know if something's too much," I said.

Kye studied me for a minute longer and then nodded. "First thing is something you might expect."

"Okay…" I said, curiosity taking hold.

"Avoidance. Run, scream, do anything to bring attention to yourself and your attacker. Many times, the assailant will be startled and take off. That's the best-case scenario."

It made sense, and I would never be mad that I didn't have to punch someone in the face. "I've got a pretty good screaming voice."

One corner of Kye's mouth pulled up. "That's good. If you can't avoid it, the next step is to guard your face. Someone gets off a bad punch to your head, and it's game over."

I lifted my hand to mirror how Kye had his.

"You want to keep your feet a little wider apart, one in front of the other. That'll give you a strong base and make it harder to knock you to the ground. Do everything you can to keep that from happening."

I swallowed, my mouth suddenly dry, but I copied Kye's stance. "I feel that. It's more stable."

"Exactly. Next thing you need to know is your opponent's weakest spots. It's always eyes, nose, throat, groin, and knees." Kye pointed to each place as he spoke. "I'm going to show you which one to target based on how you're attacked."

I straightened my shoulders and nodded. "Let's do this."

Kye began walking me through different approaches. If I was grabbed from behind or the side. If someone tried to choke me. He showed me how to use my keys as a weapon and told me to always walk to my car with one threaded through my fingers if I was alone at night.

It didn't take long for my heart rate to rise, and a thin sheen of sweat to cover my body. I grabbed a sip from the water bottle Arden had handed me. "I am so out of shape," I wheezed.

Kye chuckled. "It's a different set of muscles. But I can give you a circuit workout to improve muscle strength, too, if you want."

"I do," I said quickly. There was just something about the promise of feeling stronger. I wanted it more than anything else.

"All right. What do you think? Got enough in you for one more?"

I nodded and set the bottle down. "Ready."

"Okay, on this one, I'm going to grab for your wrist." Kye moved to show me how he would approach. "The moment I've got you, I want you to lean back and kick at my knee. It'll make me release you. You might stumble or even fall, but that's okay. Just right yourself as quickly as possible."

I ran through the approach in my mind, what I needed my body to do. I was always clumsy at first, but I was learning. "Got it," I said with a jerk of my head.

Kye moved in, slightly slower than normal speed. He grabbed my wrist tightly, jerking me forward, but I instantly leaned back, not going where he wanted me to. I lifted one leg, kicking in half-force at his knee.

Kye's grip on my wrist loosened, and I stumbled backward. I did my best to stay upright but failed. As I slammed into the ring's floor, the air whooshed from my lungs, and I struggled to catch my breath.

Before I could sit up or say a word, a figure swung into the ring, crossing it in three long strides before giving Kye a hard shove. Rage blazed in dark green eyes. "What the fuck do you think you're doing?"

CHAPTER TWENTY-FIVE

Trace

'D WATCHED ELLIE IN THE RING FOR LONGER THAN I WANTED to admit. I came to Haven to burn through some of the need that had been coursing through me since our almost-moment in my entryway last night. Instead, I'd been met with her explosion of magic yet again.

The way she laughed when she bungled a new move, how determined she was to get it right… I saw her muscles trembling beneath that damn workout outfit, the spandex revealing every dip and curve. My fingers ached to memorize them all.

I couldn't stop my back teeth from grinding as Kye moved her arms into position. I was so goddamned jealous of my brother because *he* was the one touching her. But then the moves had gotten rougher. As Kye jerked Ellie toward him, something in me snapped.

And when she hit the ring's mats with brutal force, anger like I'd never known blazed through me. The fiery beast I always kept firmly in check was thrashing at the walls of its prison.

I was through the ropes in a flash, shoving Kye as I snarled at him. But I could only think about getting him away from Ellie. Keeping her from experiencing any more pain.

She'd been through too much already. Losing her mom. Her dad's cruelty. Her ex laying *hands* on her.

Surprise and a flicker of unease filled Kye's eyes as he lifted both hands, palms toward me, keeping them where I could see them and showing me he had no intention of fighting me. "Breathe. We're just sparring."

"Are you?" I growled.

Ellie struggled to her feet, coughing a little at the loss of air. "Trace, I'm fine."

I turned so I could see them both, suddenly feeling like a cornered wild animal. "He hurt you."

Pink blossomed on Ellie's cheeks. "He was *teaching* me."

I glared in Kye's direction. "She could've been seriously hurt."

Kye's head tipped to one side as if trying to read what was going on with me. "We may have pushed a little hard for day one, but Ellie's just fine. See?"

My gaze skimmed over her again, looking for any signs of injury. But all I could see was her heavy breathing and angry expression. It was then that I realized the entire gym had stopped to watch the show.

"I know what I can handle," she gritted out. "And I don't need you or anyone else telling me what I can or cannot do." With that, she stalked across the ring, ducked under the ropes, and took off toward the locker rooms.

I watched her go, every angry step making me realize just how badly I'd fucked up. A hollow feeling took root inside me, the worst kind of empty pain, at the thought that I'd added to Ellie's feelings of being controlled.

"Dude," Arden said, cutting into my misery spiral. "What is wrong with you?"

When I turned to my sister, I saw her own brand of rage directed at me. But I deserved it. "I freaked," I finally admitted.

Kye moved to my side. "Thought you were gonna deck me for a second."

I sent another glare his way, still not altogether happy with him. "You were pushing too hard."

"I wasn't," he said, straightening his shoulders. "Said that to get whatever demon had a hold of you in check. We were fine until you blew through. You know sparring ends in bumps and bruises sometimes."

"He's right. Think about the black eye Shep was rocking a couple of months ago," Arden cut in, Brutus leaning into her side, not liking the tension in the air.

Kye shook his head. "Not gonna make that mistake again. Thea scares me."

Usually, I would've laughed at the reminder of Thea threatening Kye with garden shears when he gave Shep a black eye while sparring. But I couldn't get my voice to make the sound or my lips to curve into a grin.

Kye didn't miss it. He gripped my shoulder, his hand squeezing hard, bringing me back to the present. His voice dipped low. "I know she's been hurt."

My gaze flicked to him as my face hardened. "She say something to you?"

"Not a word. But you start to get radar for that sort of thing when enough people come through your classes who have been victimized in one way or another. I know how to watch for someone's triggers, and I'm not going to take for granted that someone has given me their trust."

My throat constricted as I struggled to swallow. "I'm sorry. I know you're careful. I just—"

"She means something to you," Kye said.

It wasn't a question, but I found myself answering it anyway. "Yeah. She means something." I dragged a hand through my hair. "I'm sorry. I shouldn't have put hands on you." I shouldn't put hands on anyone in anger, but especially not Kye.

"You're fine. Just breathe." A grin spread across my brother's face. "You were jealous, weren't you?"

"Shut up."

Kye cackle-laughed. "You *really* like her."

"Oh, fuck off," I clipped.

Arden gaped at me. "You *cursed.*"

Hell. I would never hear the end of it now.

Kye's grin only grew wider until he looked like a maniacal evil genius. "You way more than like her, and you are so totally screwed."

Arden winced. "I'm not sure how Linc's gonna feel about that."

I pinned her with my worst big-brother stare. "Do not say a word to him."

Arden worried her bottom lip. "Trace. I don't know exactly what happened, but she's been through it."

"I know," I said, that hollow pain flaring to life again.

"She's been doubting everything about herself. Trying to find her footing again."

"I *know.*" I stressed the second word as I met Arden's gaze.

Something shifted in my sister's expression. "She talked to you."

"We both talked," I admitted.

Arden's eyes misted over. "You talked."

"We did."

Her eyes filled then. "Oh, Jesus, these hormones are killing me. I am not crying," she barked at me and Kye.

Kye held up his hands in surrender. "Of course, you aren't."

"Shut up," she shot back. "I need to go." Arden took off for the front door as Kye and I looked at each other.

"It's gonna be a long nine months," Kye muttered.

He wasn't wrong. But I couldn't worry about that right now. I had to find Ellie and make things right.

CHAPTER TWENTY-SIX

Ellie

SHOVED MY SWEATSHIRT INTO MY GYM BAG AND SLAMMED THE locker door. The force of it echoed around the empty room, even with the strains of rock music still making their way through the wall. I was furious at everyone and everything.

My dad for creating such a toxic and cruel environment that'd started everything. My brother for leaving and breaking free when I needed him. My mom for giving up instead of continuing to fight. Bradley for not giving a damn about who I really was or if I was happy. Trace for doubting what I was capable of.

But most of all, I was angry at myself. The rage I felt pointed inward was so much stronger than anything else. Because I'd stayed. I hadn't fought. I hadn't spoken my needs aloud. I hadn't battled for my own happiness. Anger, guilt, and shame swirled in an ugly stew.

I swiped at the furious tears that spilled over and tracked down my cheeks. I was angry at them, too. Yanking the door open, I stepped into the hall and ran right into a wall of muscle.

I looked up, up, up, and into dark green eyes. The moment Trace registered my tears, his expression turned thunderous. He grabbed my hand and tugged me down the hall.

"What are you—?"

Trace opened the door to what Arden had pointed out as Kye's office and pulled me inside, slamming the door behind us.

I glared up at him—a look dulled by the fact that I could still feel tears in my eyes. "What do you want?"

"You're crying."

"Thanks, Captain Obvious. I know. And you probably think that makes me weak, too—"

"You aren't weak," Trace growled. "That's the last thing in the world you are."

I sucked in a breath, searching for words as I tried to process his statement. "You didn't seem to think so earlier."

Pain streaked across Trace's expression.

But I couldn't let it deter me. I needed him to see. To understand. "What I needed today was to feel strong. To start the process of standing on my own for once. To be in my power. And you came in and tried to take that away."

"I know," Trace whispered. "And I'm so damn sorry. But all I saw was him hurting you. I couldn't take it. It was bad enough seeing that bruise on your face when you got to Sparrow Falls. Trying so desperately to hide that someone had put their hands on you in anger. When you told me what your ex had done, I wanted to hurt him ten times worse because that's the truth of what lives inside me. But seeing it in the present? I couldn't take it. I can't handle you experiencing pain."

My heart hammered against my ribs as I watched each of Trace's ragged inhales and exhales, watched him breathe through the pain all over again. I moved into his space, my hands lifting to his stubbled cheeks. "Life will always have pain. I just want to own mine."

A muscle fluttered wildly in Trace's cheek. "Okay."

"Just that simple?" I pushed.

"I'll always want to keep you safe. That'll never change." He took a step toward me, his hand lifting and ghosting under the eye that had been bruised. "I'd give anything to erase every ounce of pain you've ever felt."

"Trace…"

He leaned in closer, his hand sliding along my jaw. "But I'm not trying to control you the way that douchebag ex of yours did."

My heart hammered against my ribs as his sandalwood and black pepper scent swirled around me. "Good." The single word stuck on my tongue.

"You deserve so much more." Trace's hand dropped to my hip, urging me back slowly until I hit the door. His head bent, his lips skimming my brow. "You deserve to be in your power." His mouth trailed lower, featherlight touches until he reached my lips. And there he stayed, speaking against them. "You deserve someone on their knees for you, not someone forcing you to yours."

I felt the brush of each word, the way they coursed through me, pulling me up and making me brave, and couldn't stop closing the distance. I took Trace's mouth, and he let me, inviting me in. The taste of mint and a hint of coffee played over my tongue, along with something that belonged to Trace alone.

I moaned as his tongue dueled with mine. I let loose everything I'd been holding inside for far too long. Frustration and need warred in equal measure, and the only cure was Trace.

Until he tore his mouth from mine, breathing heavily. I was about to tear into him for some misguided attempt at protecting my virtue, but then Trace dropped to the floor.

"What are you doing?" I rasped.

"Showing you what you deserve." He gazed up at me, his eyes a little wild. "Tell me I can show you."

My heart hammered against my ribs, and my mouth went dry. But there were only two words on my tongue. "Show me."

A fire lit in Trace's dark green depths, making his eyes glow like emeralds. His hands dropped to my foot, pulling the shoe free. "Nothing but rainbows," he rasped. "Magic. Just like you."

My throat worked as I tried to swallow. "Trying to find that magic again."

Trace's expression softened as he removed my other shoe. "Never lost it. It's been there all along. You're just letting the world see it now."

My heart did a ragged stutter-step. Each word he gave me was like a tiny explosion in my chest, pleasure and pain springing to life.

Trace's hands slid up my legs, fingers trailing along the rainbow piping. "Killing me in this fucking outfit. Just like that schoolgirl skirt last night nearly gave me a coronary. Everything about you is meant to bring me to my knees, isn't it?"

My mouth curved. "Good to know my fashion efforts aren't wasted."

Those dark green eyes sparked to life as Trace trailed his thumb over the seam of my leggings at the apex of my thighs. "Blaze, they are very much appreciated."

I sucked in a breath, my head tipping back against the door. As Trace moved his thumb back and forth, teasing me through the spandex, sparks danced across my skin. "The way you move. Back arched. Chest heaving. Want to memorize every line and curve."

"Trace," I breathed.

"Not enough?" he rasped.

"No." It wasn't nearly enough. Because when it came to Trace, I wanted everything. It didn't matter that the timing was all wrong or that there were a million different risks. There was something about him, about this moment. It made me feel like I could find that wildness and freedom again. Like I could find that magic.

"Gonna show you, Blaze. Everything you deserve." Trace's fingers hooked the band of my leggings, and he slowly began pulling them down, his thick knuckles grazing my thighs. A sound that resembled an animalistic growl lit the air. "No goddamned underwear?"

My head pressed harder against the wood of the door as a smile tipped my lips. "Can't really wear 'em with these."

"Fucking hell. You're gonna have to give me your training schedule because I can't be in here when you are. Gonna have a hard-on while trying to spar."

A laugh bubbled out of me and, God, it felt so good. Like a release of everything that had been swirling inside me. But the sound died on my lips as Trace pulled my leggings off one foot and leaned in toward the apex of my thighs.

"Smell like heaven." His lips and tongue trailed across my inner thigh. "Taste like sin."

My lips parted as I struggled for breath. And then Trace was moving again, lifting one leg over his shoulder. The move had me bracing myself against the door, tipping my head down to see him. And something about the sight...the hold Trace had put himself in, made me feel more powerful than I ever had before.

"Trace," I whispered.

"Need better access to worship my girl. Need to see all of her."

My girl. Those two words swirled in my mind like the best compliment and kindest praise. After everything I'd been through, I would've thought the *my* in that statement would've gotten my back up. But it didn't feel like a claim. It felt like...belonging. The best kind.

Trace's tongue darted out, circling my clit. My back arched, head pressing into the door again as my breaths turned to ragged pants. Every swipe set off a series of tiny explosions under my skin—the kind that promised the shattering to come.

I reached out a hand to grab Trace's shoulder, needing to ground myself. He slid two fingers inside me, and my jaw went slack at the delicious glide, the feel of him slowly stretching me, circling wider and wider.

My fingers pressed into Trace's shoulder, my nails digging in. He hummed against that bundle of nerves, driving everything in me higher, winding the invisible cord inside me tighter as the sound vibrations moved through me.

Trace's fingers swirled and twisted, curving as they dragged down my walls. I shuddered against him, against the door. The juxtaposition of Trace's heat and the cool wood was like fire and ice in all the best ways.

He teased that most sensitive part of me, his tongue flicking against my clit. My legs started to tremble, and I knew I was barely holding on. Trace's tongue circled as his fingers parted, stretching me. "Let go," he growled against my sensitive flesh.

Some part of me realized I was scared. To break. To come apart and let loose everything I'd been holding so tightly to. The last slivers that meant some semblance of control.

"Ellie," Trace murmured against me, his hand moving to my hip, fingers digging in. "I've got you. Let go."

His lips closed around my clit, tongue swirling as his fingers pumped in and out of me. Everything in me trembled, a war of control and freedom. My nails dug into Trace's shoulder as his words echoed in my head. *"I've got you. Let go."*

I chose the wild. I let go.

The orgasm hit me like a tsunami, so powerful it hurt to shatter. But the pain was so damn beautiful, and it only pushed the pleasure higher. Everything was more.

I squeezed my eyes closed as Trace rode out every wave with his fingers and tongue. Sparks of rainbow light danced in the darkness, little pieces of freedom.

My whole body shook, and when my leg nearly gave out, Trace simply held me there against the door, never letting me fall. Wave after wave, he didn't let go. Until I finally had no more to give.

Trace leaned back on his heels, slowly pulling his fingers from me, and placed my foot back on the floor. But his other hand didn't leave my hip as he made sure I was okay. Those dark green eyes found mine, and he didn't look away as he licked his fingers clean.

My jaw went slack as I stared down at him. "Trace."

"Heaven," he whispered. And then he moved again, slowly putting my leggings back on, gentle hands moving across oversensitive flesh. But he didn't stop there. He put on one shoe and then the other before gripping me by my hips.

"You deserve the world, Blaze. Don't settle for anything less."

CHAPTER TWENTY-SEVEN

Ellie

I SAT IN MY CAR, STARING AT THE SIDE OF HAVEN, WONDERING what the hell had just happened. I was pretty sure I was having some sort of orgasm-induced break with reality, but as I looked down at my sneaker, seeing the bow that Trace had re-tied, I knew it was all real.

The heat of his lips still hummed on mine—the feel of the words he'd spoken against them. *"Text me when you're home so I know you got there safe."*

Why did something as simple as that feel like such a balm? Because it was so much more.

I stared at the wall in front of me and took in the way *Haven* had been splashed in another beautiful mural. Kye had painted all sorts of flowers and creatures found in the area around the word. Sparrows, hummingbirds, and butterflies floated atop the gym name.

For the first time in forever, I felt lighter. Freer. Like all those creatures there. The corners of my mouth tipped up as I admired Kye's artistry, how he'd created something that fit in with its surroundings but was his style.

Maybe that was it. Maybe it was me finding the wildness with Trace. When I started my SUV, I didn't head for home. I drove toward the hardware store on the outskirts of town as an idea began coming together in my mind. One that might be over-the-top for most, but I didn't care. Because it was me.

Parking in a spot at the end of the row with plenty of space, I headed inside. The shop wasn't crowded since it was the end of the day. A pretty blonde a little older than me waved from where she was restocking a shelf. "Welcome. Just holler if you need help or to check out. I'm just trying to get tomorrow's work done today."

I grinned. "Good luck with that. And thanks."

"Name's Mara if you need me."

"Thanks, Mara. I'll be hitting you up for some paint in a bit."

"I've got you covered," she called as I headed down one of the aisles.

I stopped in front of a display of paint swatches. There were what seemed like endless options. Given how small Sparrow Falls was, the variety had me pleasantly surprised.

Closing my eyes for a moment, I saw the image I wanted to create in my mind. Plucking out specific colors in my head, I opened my eyes again, then grabbed swatches covering just about every color in the rainbow—and a few more for good measure. I compared tones and pigments and finally decided on my choices.

That was when I felt it. The telltale sensation of eyes on me. I couldn't help the stiffening in my muscles as memories of Kye's recent instructions filled my mind. Glancing up, cold hazel eyes met mine—ones narrowed in my direction.

The man was big and broad, wearing jeans that had seen better days and a flannel with a sprinkling of sawdust on it. He had at least fifteen years and a hundred pounds on me and didn't seem especially friendly.

"You're that rich bitch whose daddy killed all those people and stole their money, ain't you?"

My muscles turned to granite. That wasn't exactly what had

happened, but the details didn't matter in a situation like this. Taking a deep breath, I turned to face him.

No more running.

"That's me," I said, not looking away.

The man sneered at me. "And you think you can just live off all his blood money and get off scot-free? You should be hung right along with the bastard. Maybe you need a little local justice."

He took two long steps toward me before someone rounded the corner and moved in front of him. "Now, Jimmy, that sounds a hell of a lot like a threat to me. I might not be on duty, but I still have a responsibility to uphold the law."

I didn't think I'd ever seen Harrison out of uniform. He looked boyishly handsome in jeans, a tee, and a ballcap. Like he was getting ready for a baseball game or, more likely, to do a little yard work.

The man, who was apparently named Jimmy, scowled at Harrison. "None of your business, boy."

"You made it my business. And because our team was part of that case, I can tell you that Ellie had nothing to do with it other than trying to help bring her father to justice. So spread *that* around," Harrison said, his voice hardening.

Jimmy's jaw worked back and forth before he scowled at me and stalked off. "I don't got time for this bullshit."

The air left my lungs in a whoosh, and I realized I'd crumpled the paint swatches in my hand. I tried my best to smooth them out as Harrison turned around.

"I'm so sorry about that."

I shook my head and focused on the paint chips. "Not your fault."

He frowned at me. "That happen a lot?"

I shrugged. "It's not uncommon."

That had a vein straining in Harrison's neck. "You have a run-in, call me. I'll have a word."

I thought about arguing, but it wasn't worth the battle. I didn't want to explain to him that the thing I needed most right now was to stand on my own two feet. "All right."

Harrison sighed. "You're not going to call, are you?"

I grinned, even though it was strained. "What I'm going to do right now is paint a mural."

My early 2000s pop playlist blasted through my portable speaker as I moved my pencil across the massive white wall. I'd moved all the furniture into the center of the room and covered it with plastic drop cloths. I'd even taken time to tape off the molding despite it being the most mind-numbing task. But *NSYNC helped get me through.

Gremlin barked from his bed in the corner, moving toward the door. I frowned. I hadn't heard anything, but I moved in that direction anyway. A pounding let loose on my front door, and Gremlin began barking his head off.

"Blaze, restrain that feral beast because I'm coming in."

"Hold your horses, Chief." Picking up Grem and unlocking the deadbolt, I opened the door to a very grumpy-looking Trace. "Who pissed in your Cheerios?"

His scowl deepened. "You didn't text."

I winced. "Sorry. I got distracted."

"I texted you, and you didn't answer."

I mumbled a curse. "I forgot to tell you. I changed my number to a Sparrow Falls one."

Trace's green eyes darkened, that astute quality taking over. "You changed your number."

"Yeah. I mean, I don't need a New York one anymore, right?" It wasn't a lie, but it wasn't the whole truth either. And given how on edge Trace had been at the gym, I didn't want him worrying any more than he already was.

Trace's gaze roamed over me from head to toe as if looking for answers. Instead, he likely got only paint-splattered coveralls and hair in a rat's nest bun atop my head. "What are you wearing?"

I beamed up at him, relief rushing through me at the change in subject. "My painting outfit."

"Your…painting outfit."

"Yup."

Trace reached out, his fingers moving to a strand of hair that had fallen out of my bun. "You've got pink paint in your hair. And some green." He pulled his hand back to show me, but Gremlin took that opportunity to snap and snarl, nipping at Trace.

He snatched his hand back, glaring at my dog. "Jesus. Are you sure that thing doesn't have rabies?"

"Don't talk about my soulmate like that," I clipped. "And I took Grem to the vet. He's a hundred percent healthy, even though he's a little underweight."

Trace's mouth twisted into a grin. "Soulmate, huh? Fits. You did leave claw marks on my shoulder."

I gaped at him. "I didn't."

He only grinned wider. "You did. Don't worry, I wear your marks with pride."

My cheeks heated, and I couldn't hold his gaze. "Sorry about that. I, um, might've gotten carried away. I haven't—I mean—I'm not used to—"

Trace moved in, ignoring Grem's snarls. His fingers went to my chin to tip it up, so I had nowhere to look but his face. Trace's expression had gone a little stormy, the dark green of his eyes looking almost black now. "You haven't had someone go down on you before?"

I swallowed hard, searching for the right words to explain. "I haven't dated a ton. My dad pushed me in Bradley's direction the second I graduated high school, and he, um, didn't like that."

Trace's eyes turned pure shadow and storm. "Means something, you trusting me with that. And I won't lie; I love knowing I got to give you that for the first time."

"Oh."

"So damn cute," Trace muttered, a little of the storm easing.

The sound of car doors slamming pulled us from the moment, and Trace moved back out to my front porch. "Over here, Keels."

At the sound of his favorite person's name, Gremlin started wiggling and yipping. I followed Trace out and down the steps to see

Keely running across the front yard toward us, backpack smacking against her body as she flew.

Grem's wiggling intensified, and I laughed as I set him down. He went straight for his girl, and Keely squealed as he leapt in the air. She instantly sat, welcoming all the doggy kisses and cuddles.

"I'm pretty sure I've been replaced as bestie," I mumbled.

Trace chuckled and patted me on the back. "I've been there. Brutal."

As I looked up, I saw an unfamiliar woman crossing slowly toward us. She was beautiful, her blond hair cut in a stylish bob that hit just below her chin. Her outfit didn't tell me much, mostly pulled-together business neutrals, but there was a little flare in the form of her belt. The clasp was gold and formed a delicate array of flowers. But when I reached the woman's face, her expression was wary, and there was more than a little uncertainty in her eyes.

This had to be Trace's ex and Keely's mom. And, *of course*, I was meeting her in paint-splattered coveralls and tangled hair. *Awesome.*

"Ellie, what're you doing?" Keely asked, giggling as Grem licked her cheek.

"I'm painting a rainbow on my living room wall," I told her with a smile.

That had Trace's ex pulling up short, genuine confusion spreading across her face. "You're painting a…rainbow…on your living room wall?"

Trace tried to cover a laugh with a cough. "Leah, this is our neighbor, Ellie. Ellie, this is Keely's mom, Leah."

I noticed that he didn't voice what either of us were to *him*. And I wasn't exactly sure how I felt about that. But what did I expect? *"Leah, this is my neighbor, Ellie. I had my fingers buried in her a few hours ago and made her come so hard she thought she was having a stroke."*

I needed to pull it together. "It's nice to meet you, Leah."

"You, uh, too," Leah said.

Keely looked up at me as she cradled Grem in her arms. "Can I help you paint?"

I looked quickly around the group, trying to survey the

temperature and not wanting to step on any toes. "I'm not sure what you've got planned with your parents, but if it's okay with them, it's okay with me."

"One hour," Trace said. "Then we've got our dinner and bed-time routine."

"Yay!" Keely cheered, pushing to her feet and charging toward the house. "Bestie paint party!"

I laughed, ushering her inside, but not before glancing over my shoulder. Trace and Leah looked like they were in some sort of tense standoff. I had to force myself to turn back around and focus on the task at hand. "Not my circus, not my monkeys," I muttered.

"Are you getting a monkey next?" Keely asked, wide-eyed.

I grinned and shook my head at her. "I think I've got my hands full with Grem and our friend Goaty. Who you still have to help me name."

"Oh, oh, oh," Keely cheered as she set Gremlin down. "I thought of the *perfect* one."

"Lay it on me, bestie. I need to know."

"Bumper. Because she's always bumping into things."

A laugh bubbled out of me. "That is perfect. You are a creative genius. What do you say? Want to lend me that genius by helping me with this wall?"

Keely gazed up at my creation. It was mostly a pencil drawing at this stage, with a few paint swatches in places to make sure the tones were right. "Whoa. This is soooooo pretty."

"Thank you. I think it's going to bring a lot of happy."

Kye's murals had given me the idea, but this was my spin on it. A stylized rainbow with all sorts of flying creatures around it. Fireflies to light my way. Sparrows to represent my new home. Dragonflies to bring me luck. Bees to tend the home I was building. Hummingbirds to remind me to be fierce. And butterflies as my symbol of transfor-mation. My favorite of all.

"My mom would never let me do this," Keely mumbled.

Tension wound around me as memories of my father filled my

mind. "This might not be everyone's thing, and that's okay. They might have their own thing."

Keely scowled at the floor. "Her thing is homework and nine million lessons."

I fought the wince that wanted to surface. "Maybe you guys just need to find your thing together."

"Maybe," Keely said, scuffing at the floor with the toe of her shoe.

I hated to see her so dejected. "For now, how about you help me make this wall sing?"

A little of Keely's smile returned. "Let's do it!"

I held out my hand for a high five, and Keely slapped my palm. As we got her covered in one of my old tees, I couldn't help but worry about Keely and her mom—and all the ways *I'd* never felt free to be who I truly was. I didn't want that for Keely. But the only thing I could do was make sure she felt safe to be who she was with me. And I'd let her paint my whole damn house to do that.

CHAPTER TWENTY-EIGHT

Trace

LEAH HELD MY GAZE, A HINT OF HARDNESS SLIPPING INTO HER expression. "You just let our daughter go hang out with a stranger?"

My jaw wound tighter with each word that slipped from my ex's mouth. "I think you know me better than that."

I'd never put Keely at risk. That girl was my life, and Leah knew it.

She shifted uncomfortably as if reading the thoughts swirling in my mind. "Well, she's a stranger to me. Don't you think I should know who Keely's spending time with?"

"I have friends you don't know. Ones that are around Keely plenty. Why is this suddenly an issue?"

Leah's lips pressed into a firm line. "A friend."

"Yes, I do occasionally have one of those." The only problem was that Ellie was so much more than that. I had no idea how to classify her when both of us were running from what I knew it had the potential to be.

I liked things to fit in neatly ordered boxes, and Ellie didn't do that. She scribbled outside every line. She refused to play by any rules.

And slowly, she was making me realize that what I needed wasn't what I'd originally thought.

"Are you sleeping with her?"

The question jerked me from my thoughts and nearly had me rearing back. "You know that's none of your business, Le."

Neither Leah nor I had been in a serious relationship since the divorce. She'd dated here and there but never brought any of the guys around Keely because it hadn't reached that stage. I'd gone on a handful of dates that had gone nowhere because nothing seemed right. But neither of us had *ever* been territorial over the other.

The muscle where Leah's jaw met her cheekbone began to pulse, her tell that her annoyance, anger, or some other emotion was mounting. "We share a daughter."

"We do. And she is one hundred percent your business. Who I have in my bed is not. You'll get a call if I'm moving someone in or getting married. That's it."

Leah let out a frustrated huff, the only expulsion of emotion she seemed to allow. "It's as easy as that for you?"

"Le, talking about who either of us is involved with isn't exactly healthy. Let's stay focused on our daughter, all right?"

"Sure," she muttered and turned, stalking toward her car.

I reached up and pinched the bridge of my nose as hard as I could. Sometimes, the pressure points there could clear the tension headache away. Somehow, I had a feeling this wouldn't be one I could stave off.

Fuck.

None of this was easy. None of it was how I'd wanted it to be when I asked Leah to marry me. But as I watched her walk to her car, get in, and mindfully close the door without even a slam to betray how she felt, I wasn't sorry that we'd ended up here. Because there'd never been the kind of fire between us that there should've been.

And for the first time, I could see why she'd strayed. What she was reaching for when she had. Because I had flickers of that *more*, that fire, with Ellie.

I turned and stared up at the pale purple house, hearing the faintest strains of some god-awful pop music from inside. But it made a smile tug at my lips. I strode toward the front door and opened it, the music intensifying.

Crossing to the living room, I took in total and complete chaos. Furniture was piled in the center of the room in a completely disorganized fashion and covered with a plastic tarp. Trays of paint lay in a haphazard array. But my girls…they were having the time of their lives.

Keely wore what had to be one of Ellie's T-shirts as makeshift coveralls, and they both shimmied and shook as they worked on the lightest part of a rainbow, the yellow. It wasn't your average, in-the-lines rainbow. I could see from a red curve Ellie had been working on earlier that it was imperfect and wild, not playing within expectations. It looked like a watercolor someone had dumped drops of water on.

I could see how it would take shape, and it was perfect in all its imperfections. It was Ellie. It was what Ellie was showing me I could be.

A series of barks tore through the air, and teeth suddenly sank into my jeans-clad ankle. Or should I say *tooth*. Because Gremlin really only had one snaggletooth left, and it was loose on a good day.

I glared down at him as Keely spun around.

"Daddy, look what we're making!" she cheered.

I tipped my head up to take them in again. "Pretty amazing."

Ellie set down her paintbrush and crossed to me, picking up the little beast. "Grem, that's not nice."

"Don't think he gives a damn," I muttered.

Ellie's mouth curved. "You know, Chief, I've heard a few cuss words slipping from your mouth lately."

I shrugged. "Better fine me. We've got a swear jar at my house. It'd be nice to have something other than Kye's money in there."

Ellie laughed, the sound wrapping around me. Even that was a little wild. "Come on, I'll get you something to drink. I already got Keely some strawberry bubble water."

Strawberry bubble water. Jesus, even her water was whimsical. But I followed her into the kitchen.

Ellie set Gremlin on the floor, and he let out a little growl in my direction. "Be nice," she said. Opening the fridge, she gave it a once-over. "I've got strawberry bubble water, beer, Coke, and a half-drunk bottle of rosé."

An image of Ellie dancing around her living room in her under-wear with a glass of wine popped into my head. "I'll take the beer."

She leaned in, those awful coveralls pulling taut across her ass, grabbed a bottle, opened it, and handed it over. "You should really have this in a glass with an orange, but I ate my last one with breakfast."

I took the bottle from her, our fingers brushing, that phantom energy swirling between us. "I think I'll survive." I took a swig of the beer as she leaned back against the counter. "What spurred all this on?" I gestured to her outfit, knowing she'd understand that I meant the mural.

Shadows flickered across Ellie's expression, and I wanted to take the question back, but then they passed, morphing into something I couldn't quite read. "Seeing Kye's murals at Haven reminded me of something I wanted. Reminded me that I could have that now."

I frowned. There was no denying that my brother was talented. His artistry was the kind of thing that held people captive and made them travel from all over the world to have his pieces inked into their skin. But this was more than a search for artistry.

Ellie's fingers curled around the lip of the counter, bleaching white. "My dad hated bright things. Hated anything that didn't fit into his neat and orderly world of what was *acceptable*."

Hell.

"I always wanted a rainbow in my bedroom growing up. Decided it was time I gave it to myself. No rules about rainbows in this house."

I suddenly wanted to pick up a paintbrush and cast her entire house in every color imaginable. But I knew it was more powerful if she gave it to herself. And it said something that she was letting Keely—letting *me*—into it all. "You're finding your magic again."

One corner of Ellie's mouth kicked up, making the specks of yellow paint on her cheek catch the light. "I guess I am."

I moved into her space, unable to resist the pull of everything that was Ellie, dying to catch a little of the sunshine that was her. My lips brushed across hers once, twice, and then I took the kiss deeper. My tongue stroked in, needing more of her taste—a taste I knew would haunt me for the rest of my days.

Ellie moaned into my mouth, and my dick stiffened. I forced myself to pull back, knowing if I didn't, I'd be doing things I definitely shouldn't while my daughter was in the next room. Ellie's eyes were unfocused, and she blinked a few times as if trying to clear her vision. "What was that for?"

"Maybe I needed a little of that magic, too."

Wariness slid into Ellie's expression, instantly setting me on edge, but she didn't look away from me. "What are we doing?"

A fair question, one I'd been wrestling with. "I don't know," I answered honestly. "But for the first time I can remember, I'm okay with that. No plan, no destination."

"Just seeing where it leads and having fun?" she asked, a little of that uncertainty melting away.

I stepped a little closer, into that danger zone. "I know I don't want to hold myself back from you." It was more truth than I normally offered. Because it gave the other person power. And that wasn't something I relinquished easily.

"I don't either. Even though I should."

My gaze roamed over her face, searching those pale green depths. "Why?"

"Trace, I'm a mess. I don't know up from down. What I want to do for a career. What I want my life to look like. Who I want to be. It's not fair to tie you up in that." She took a deep breath. "And I don't want my involvement with you to skew figuring that out."

"Are you listening to some ridiculous pop playlist that makes me want to jab an ice pick into my eardrums?"

Ellie frowned. "Well, that's rude, but yes."

I grinned at her. "Told you I hated that stuff."

"You did…" A glare took root in her expression.

"Baby, you don't give a damn that I hate it. You're still listening. You're being who you want to be. Rescuing a goat and a feral dog and painting a rainbow on your wall. You're you, and you don't care that I wouldn't do any of that."

Ellie stared back at me for a long moment, a million things flitting across her expression.

My grin widened. "Honestly, I think you'd do the opposite of whatever I say because you love pissing me off. You rearranged my cabinets."

A laugh bubbled out of her. "Might do your linen closet next."

I pinned her with a hard stare. "Don't you dare."

Those beautiful lips twitched, and then she sobered, looking into my eyes. "I'm not afraid to go against what you want. Why is that?"

I lifted a hand, my thumb ghosting over the specks of yellow paint on her cheek. "Sometimes, we need a brutal moment to teach us what we won't stand for. You've had a few of those lately. Hate it for you. But it also broke you free."

"Free," Ellie whispered.

I pressed a kiss to her temple. "You stood up to me at Haven. Told me what you wanted and what you didn't. Put me in my place. You're not going to let anyone walk all over you again. Trust yourself. I do."

"Chief," she whispered, emotion clogging her voice.

"Proud of you. You can kick my ass any day."

I felt her laugh more than I heard it as she pulled back. "Thank you."

The genuine emotion in Ellie's voice, in her eyes, nearly brought me to my knees. "Blaze—"

"Daddy!" Keely yelled from the other room.

I wasn't sure what Keely had cut me off from saying, but it was probably a good thing. I grinned down at Ellie. "Always something."

We moved from the kitchen to the living room, Gremlin trailing behind us, grumbling as he went.

"Bestie, you are doing such an amazing job," Ellie praised.

Keely beamed at her and then turned that smile on me. "Daddy, can I do this in my room?"

I sighed, looking at Ellie. "First the goat. Now, a mural. There's going to be payback."

Ellie's eyes twinkled. "Oh, I don't know. I can think of a few ways I could pay up."

She was going to kill me. And I'd gladly let her take me down every time.

CHAPTER TWENTY-NINE

Ellie

I CLIMBED BEHIND THE WHEEL OF MY SUV AND TOSSED MY PURSE onto the passenger seat. My arms were tired, but they'd lost some of the soreness over the past two weeks of working at The Mix Up. And I was learning to balance more than two plates on my tray at once—a true victory.

I'd started to slip into a routine of sorts. Shift at the bakery, working on the house, cooking lessons with Trace and Keely, family dinners with the Colsons, self-defense training with Kye, and time with the girls. It was simple and perfect and *me*.

Now that I'd finished the mural, it was time to put in my butterfly garden. Trace had warned me that it could freeze any day now that we'd dipped deeper into October, but I didn't care. It was the principle of the thing that mattered.

I started the engine in my parking spot behind The Mix Up but paused as my phone rang. Swiping it up, I hesitated at the unfamiliar number. My stomach lurched. I hadn't heard from Bradley since I'd switched my number, but that didn't mean he couldn't have found it somehow.

Staring down at my cell, I flipped through my options. But I didn't want to run. Not anymore. Swiping my finger across the screen, I accepted the call. "Hello?"

"You are receiving a collect call from an inmate at Longfield Correctional Facility. This call is being recorded and may be monitored. To accept this call, press 1."

A vein thrummed in my neck, and a whooshing sound filled my ears. I'd kept as much distance from my father as possible, but I still knew what prison he was at while awaiting trial. I should've hung up. Denied the call. Rejected any contact. But I found myself hitting the 1 on my screen.

"Eleanor." My father's voice sounded older somehow, and the noise in the background—voices and a few shouts—wasn't something I was used to hearing when he called.

"What do you want?" The cold question surprised me, even though it had come from my mouth. Maybe my time in Sparrow Falls had made me bolder, stronger.

"That's no way to greet your father," he clipped.

"You haven't acted like a father once in your life, so I guess that's fitting."

Background noise filled the line for a handful of moments before Philip spoke again. "I can see my sources were correct. You're letting bad influences take control of your life."

Unease slid through me. *Sources.* Ones that could find any phone number or location. The same sort of *sources* Bradley had used to harass me since I'd arrived in Sparrow Falls. But I wouldn't let Philip know that he'd struck a nerve with the information he'd managed to glean while in prison. "That's rich, coming from you. The only bad influences in my life were you and the people you put there."

"Eleanor. That is enough," he barked. "I heard from Henrick that you aren't returning Bradley's calls."

Bradley's father had *tattled* on me? I couldn't help the laugh that bubbled out of me. "Seriously? Bradley told his dad, and his dad called *you*? So you can…what? Tell me to play nice?"

"Eleanor." My name was uttered through gritted teeth, a sign I was getting to him. "The Newbury family is your only hope. Helen already thinks of you as a daughter."

It was a low blow, bringing Bradley's mother into it. She'd always been kind to me, especially after my own mother passed. She'd taken me shopping for new school clothes a handful of times and had been a source of warmth at stodgy society events. Now, I couldn't help but wonder if she was stuck the same way my mother had been. Locked in a castle where someone had thrown away the key. But I saw what Philip was trying for now. He was attempting to play on what I'd always longed for...a family.

"I don't need the *hope* the Newbury family brings me. I wish them the best, and I'll always be fond of Helen." I couldn't say the same for Henrick. He was a pompous ass of epic proportions and a huge reason why Bradley lived with the entitlement he did. "But this is done. Bradley and I are done. That world and I are done."

"Stop throwing a stupid little tantrum," Philip spat. "You need to pull yourself together. Go back to New York. To Bradley. I expect you to live up to the Pierce name." The tone was a jerk of the chain he thought was still around my neck.

How many times had I caved when I heard disapproval in his tone? How many times had I surrendered to his threats? Too many to count.

But I wasn't that scared little girl anymore.

"The only thing I want to do is *hide* from the Pierce name. I'll change it as soon as I can because I don't want any ties to the man who *murdered* innocent human beings for nothing more than a quest for money and power."

Philip scoffed. "They were hardly innocent."

"They didn't deserve what you did. And neither did I. You never cared about me. You taught me to be nothing more than expensive window dressing. And I let myself believe it was true. That I had to be whatever you wanted me to be, so scared I'd lose my last parent if I didn't. But I know the truth now. It would've been the world's greatest gift if I'd lost you."

Blood roared in my ears, and my breaths came in quick pants.

"You're going to regret your insolence, Eleanor. And when you do, you'll remember this moment."

A click sounded, and the line went dead.

I waited for the fear to hit, for a wave of anxiety to come crashing down. But it didn't. As I lowered my phone from my ear, my breaths slowed, and the pounding in my ears lessened. I felt…lighter.

Never—not once—had I told my father how I truly felt. I'd always been too frightened. Of what he would do, of losing him even though he terrified me. But Trace had made me realize something. I wasn't scared anymore. I could be exactly who I wanted to be. Feel the way I needed and share those feelings. And all of that was okay. More than okay. It was good. And it was freeing.

I dropped my phone into the cupholder and plugged Bloom & Berry into my navigation system. Even with how long I'd been here, I still didn't have directions down completely. Thank goodness for navigation. Plus, I'd set the voice to have a British accent, and who could be mad at that?

It took me about twenty minutes to make it to the nursery outside of town. But the second I parked, I knew it was worth the drive. The whole place was like a magical fairy plant land.

Several greenhouses were spread out in the distance, and endless displays of plants and trees lay in front of them. I instantly zeroed in on a section of Cinderella pumpkins in various colors. I'd need several of those. But first, flowers.

I pulled out my phone, bringing up the article I'd found about late-blooming flowers that attracted butterflies. I squinted at the pictures and tried to memorize the way they each looked and their names.

"Everything okay? You're looking pretty angrily at that poor, innocent phone," a deep voice said.

I looked up to find Duncan standing just a few feet away, a flannel shirt open over a Bloom & Berry tee and a ballcap with the same logo pulled low. "I am looking to Google for some plant assistance."

Duncan mimed a knife to the chest. "Brutal. Choosing Google over my offer of help."

I shook my head but did it with a grin. "I wasn't sure if you'd be here, so I wanted to be prepared."

"I'm *always* here. Small business owner perks."

I glanced around the massive spread. "I wouldn't exactly call this small."

He chuckled. "Fair enough. You still looking to plant that butterfly garden?"

"I am."

Duncan scrubbed a hand over his bearded cheek. "It might be getting a little late in the season. We've got some freezes coming that will do many of these plants in."

"Trace warned me, but I want to get at least a few things started. It's kind of the principle of the thing. Even if I have to replant in the spring."

Duncan studied me for a moment. "I've got an idea if you want to hear me out. Also, completely okay if you want to run with your own thing."

I appreciated the options; it didn't make me feel steamrolled while still offering his wisdom. "Tell me what you've got."

"We'll find you some things for pots for now. You can bring them inside on the nights when the temperatures are really dropping. Then, we'll get you bulbs for the garden. They need to be planted in the fall. Come spring, your yard will be full of color."

I mulled that over for a long moment. Something about that idea spoke to me. Laying the seeds now for a bloom to come. "Kind of the perfect metaphor for my life right now," I mumbled.

Curiosity filled Duncan's eyes, but he didn't give it voice. Instead, he said, "Let's get started."

I heaved the bag of soil out of the back of my SUV, grunting at its weight. I might've started Kye's suggested weight training regimen, but apparently, I wasn't in fighting shape quite yet because this bag of soil was doing me in.

"Blaze," a familiar, deep voice warned. "What are you doing?"

"Painting my nails. What does it look like, Chief?"

A second later, the soil was being hoisted from my arms. "You could seriously hurt yourself."

I glared up at the six-foot-something sheriff holding the massive bag with ease. "It's annoying how easy that is for you."

One corner of his mouth quirked up. "I've got some inches and pounds on you."

Did he ever... And that was annoying, too. Or maybe it was the fact that our alone time had been nil since that moment at Haven. A stolen kiss or touch here or there, but that was it. Time with Keely, call-outs and extra shifts, and one emergency trip to the vet after Gremlin ate an unidentified mushroom on a walk had interrupted any attempts at some good old-fashioned one-on-one time. And my sexual frustration was reaching epic proportions.

"Where do you want this?" Trace asked, breaking into my grumpy thoughts.

"By the front porch," I grumbled.

As we walked in that direction, Trace's steps slowed. "Whoa. You know, it's not nice to show up your neighbors with a full fall décor installation."

I took stock of the dozen or so pumpkins currently lining my front porch steps. "You really aren't going to want to look in the back then."

Trace chuckled as he set the bag of soil down. "Go big or go home?"

I rocked from my heels to my tiptoes, taking it all in and wondering if I'd gone too overboard. I hadn't even added the potted flowers yet.

"Hey," Trace said, moving into my space and wrapping an arm around me. "It looks great. I was just giving you a hard time because we haven't even gotten pumpkins yet."

I tugged my lip between my teeth. "I never got to do this growing up. My dad always had a company come in and decorate for fall and Christmas."

Trace muttered a curse and pulled me closer. "Giving yourself the things you never got."

I nodded.

"Well, we're doing your place to the nines, and then you can help me and Keely do ours. Twice the Halloween, twice the fall, twice the cheer."

He sounded so pissed off about it all I couldn't help the laughter that bubbled out.

Trace pulled back, scowling down at me. "What?"

I only laughed harder. "That's maybe the nicest thing anyone's ever done for me, but you sound so angry about it."

Trace brushed the hair from my face. "Blaze, I'm angry at everything that was stolen from you. Rites of passage and experiences that should've been yours. And I'm pissed as hell that you were too scared to ask for what you wanted."

I stretched up on my tiptoes and brushed my lips against his. "Not scared now."

Trace took my mouth, his tongue sliding in, teasing and toying. I pressed myself against him, relishing the feel of his strength. My phone dinged, but I ignored it. Then it let out three more alerts.

I growled against Trace's mouth as I pulled back. "I need a Do Not Disturb setting for life."

Pulling out my phone, I unlocked the screen. I had eight new text messages, each from a different number, and all including a photo.

As I opened them one by one, my heart pounded faster, ice sliding through my veins. Pictures of me. Leaving my house. Walking Grem. Working at The Mix Up. Poking around in shops downtown. At dinner with the girls.

And each image had a message. Cruel and taunting things.

YOUR LIFE IS PATHETIC.

YOU'RE NOTHING.

GO HOME OR ELSE.

And then pure fury sounded from beside me. "What in the actual fuck is that?"

CHAPTER THIRTY

Trace

ANGER BLAZED THROUGH ME, BURNING AWAY EVERY OUNCE OF calm I'd found by having Ellie in my arms. There were pictures on her phone, clearly taken with a long-lens camera, given their slightly grainy quality. A photographer had invaded her life, stalked her. And someone wanted her scared.

Ellie looked up at me, her face pale. "I-I don't know."

I wrapped an arm around her and scanned the street. Nothing popped for me. There were no vehicles that didn't belong or people out of place. And our neighborhood was quiet, where you knew the people who lived around you. If someone saw something out of place, they'd say something. It didn't make sense.

"Keys?" I clipped.

Ellie looked up at me, a hint of confusion in her expression, but she handed over a ring with at least five keys and a charm that looked like the thing on her T-shirt she'd called a pegacorn the other day. I would've found it funny if I wasn't so damn tweaked.

I pressed a button on the fob, and the SUV's back hatch lowered. Beeping the locks, I guided Ellie to her front door.

"What about the flowers?" she asked.

"We'll deal with them in a bit." I did my best to keep my voice even, but I heard the strain in it as the photos swam in my mind. Testing the doorknob, I scowled. "Why is this unlocked?"

Ferocious barking erupted as we stepped inside, and Gremlin dive-bombed my ankles.

Ellie pulled out of my hold. "I was going in and out of the house. There was no reason to lock it."

"You go in the backyard, get distracted, someone could slip through."

Her lips pressed into a hard line before she spoke. "I'm pretty sure Grem here would've alerted me."

The dog tugged at my uniform pants leg as if to punctuate the point. And for the first time, I was glad she had him. He might not be able to do any damage, but he was at least a sort of alarm system.

I pulled my phone from my pocket and hit Gabriel's contact. He answered on the second ring. "What's up?"

"Need you to roll out and check the area around Ellie's house. See if you find anyone or anything that doesn't belong."

An engine started up; Gabriel must've already been in his vehicle. "Gonna give me any more than that so I have a direction to go in?" he asked.

My back molars ground together so hard an ache took root in my jaw. "Someone sent pictures to Ellie's phone. They've been watching her. Could be Jasper, but she's got trouble back home, too." And the long-lens approach didn't read like Jasper. He didn't usually have that sort of patience.

Gabriel let out a stream of curses. "On my way. Try not to break anything in the meantime."

My mouth twisted into a scowl. "Just get here." I hit end on the call, frustration mounting on various levels: having no clue who'd sent those photos, someone being fixated on Ellie, and my wavering control.

Because I cared about Ellie. More than I wanted to admit.

As my gaze found her again, her skin still a little pale and her hands shaking a bit, I *did* want to break something. I wanted to end whoever had put that fear in her.

"Blaze," I whispered. "Come here."

She moved to me as easily as she breathed. I wrapped my arms around her, and Ellie pressed her cheek to my chest. I held on to her, relishing the feel of her breathing, in and out, a rhythm that reminded me she was here in my arms, safe and unharmed. "It's gonna be okay. We'll figure it out."

Ellie didn't say anything, but her hands fisted in my uniform shirt, holding on. And that said it all. Her trust. Her belief. Her leaning.

"Come on. Let's sit down." I guided Ellie into the living room that had come alive under her fingers. I never would've thought a rainbow mural would look anything other than ridiculous, but Ellie made it work.

The room had become a mix of whimsy and art. She'd found a pale blue couch and placed colorful, flowered throw pillows on it. The floor had a color-blocked rug that tied in to the rainbow motif. Across from the couch was a yellow and pink chair with mismatched pillows. But it all worked. Eccentric, over-the-top, and Ellie.

I settled her on the couch and turned to face her. "Can you talk this through with me?"

Ellie bent, picking up Gremlin and settling him next to her. "Sure. I...what do you need to know?"

"Do you think this could be Bradley?" I asked. His name felt like acid in my mouth, and saying it in Ellie's safe space felt like sacrilege.

Ellie rolled her lips over her teeth. "It's possible. Wouldn't be the first time he had someone watch me."

Everything in me stilled as I struggled for composure. "Explain."

She tugged one of the pillows onto her lap, hugging it to her. "He gave me a driver in New York. Said it was so I'd be safe, but the driver kept tabs. Reported on my movements. And then there was the time I found photos of me, long-range ones, kind of like these"— she held up her phone—"in his office."

"You confront him?"

Ellie shook her head. She looked so damn sad. "In hopes of

what? A big, ugly fight? It wouldn't have changed anything." She toyed with a tassel on the pillow. "I had my own little rebellions. Took the subway to work now and then. Left work through the back door and went to dinner with a friend."

"How'd Bradley react to that?" I asked, scared of the answer.

"He was tense, but he never called me on it. The reins would just tighten a little."

The ache in my jaw flared brighter. "Because he couldn't admit what he was doing."

"Not if he wanted to play the doting fiancé card," Ellie muttered.

"Have you heard from him since you've been here?"

Ellie's gaze shifted to the side, a telltale sign.

My gut twisted, but I slid a hand over hers, interlacing our fingers. "You want to talk this out with someone who isn't me? I can have Beth or Laney come take a statement and—"

"No," Ellie said quickly, squeezing my fingers and dropping our hands from the pillow to her lap. "I just want to talk to you."

I would've understood if she didn't. Our relationship had slipped from casual acquaintance to…more. But it meant something that she felt comfortable telling me her story.

"Okay," I said quietly. "You need to stop, just say the word."

She nodded, her grip on my hand tightening. "He texted a lot. After what happened…"

"The breakup?" I knew it was so much more. The time he'd laid hands on Ellie. *Hit* her. *Marked* her. I imagined it in a million different, devastating ways. Each one making the rage I was so at odds with pulse through me.

"After everything that happened," she began, "it was like a roller coaster. Apologies. Explanations. Begging for forgiveness."

"Then it would change," I supplied. I knew the cycle of abuse, had seen it far too many times working the job I did.

"It would change," Ellie echoed. "It became my fault. I'd put us in that position. The stress of what my father had done. Not being what Bradley needed. And then he'd go on the attack. Say awful things…"

Tears began to gather in her eyes, and my rage blazed brighter.

I beat it back. "Hey." I framed her face with my hands. "Nothing he said about you was true. Nothing."

"I know that," Ellie croaked. "I know they were all his projections. But when it happened this time, it was like I could see all the little patterns leading up to it. The ones I couldn't see for so long. The ways he punished me if I didn't do things the way he wanted. All my little rebellions came at a cost. It was never physical, but it hurt all the same."

Ellie leaned into me, her forehead against mine. "Seeing Linc truly happy, coming to Sparrow Falls for those handful of days, it made me realize that I *wasn't* happy. I was living my life for everyone but me. But Arden made me see that maybe—just maybe—I could start over. Topple the damn board."

"I'm so damn glad she did, Blaze." I'd be forever grateful to my sister for that. For helping Ellie find her fight and hook into her bravery.

"When I ended it, and he hit me...it was like it woke me up, clued me in to everything else. Made me realize how I'd been allowing myself to be treated."

My thumbs skimmed the apples of her cheeks, back and forth. "Not anymore. Look how fucking strong you are. You got out. Away. You're starting this beautiful new life for yourself."

I felt Ellie's cheeks move under my hands, her mouth pulling into a smile. "You said the F-word, Chief."

"Someone told me sometimes it's okay."

Ellie pulled back, that smile still on her face, even if it looked a little tired. "Don't tell Nora. I don't want her thinking I'm a bad influence."

I chuckled. "Your secret's safe with me." Any amusement slid from my face because I knew we weren't done. I needed more information. "What about after you got to Sparrow Falls? Can you tell me a little more about how he's contacted you since? What those messages were like?"

Ellie's gaze slid to the side again. "Same cycle. But it was clear he was watching me—or had someone watching me. Said something about me moving into this house. Sent flowers with a note that was more a threat."

My eyes narrowed on her. "The ones you were throwing out the night Keely and I invited you to dinner?"

She nodded. "I changed my phone number, and that seemed to stop it, but…"

"What?" I pressed, trying to shove down the reminder that I'd known something was off about her changing numbers.

"My dad called today."

My muscles wound impossibly tight. "From prison?"

"I don't know why, but I took the call." Ellie's lips twitched, a move that didn't make sense until she continued speaking. "I told him what an awful dad he was. That I didn't want anything to do with him. And it felt so damn good."

My hand found hers again, needing the contact. "Giving yourself that freedom."

Ellie looked up at me. "I guess I am. He wasn't thrilled about it. He wants me back in New York, living up to the Pierce name. What a joke."

I struggled to keep my hand on hers gentle as rage coursed through me like a living, breathing monster. "What'd you say about that?"

"Told him to take a long walk off a short pier. He tried to manipulate and pull strings. But the thing about starting over? Throwing everything away and beginning again? He doesn't have that hold anymore."

"So damn strong, Blaze."

Her mouth curved the barest amount. "I'm trying to be."

She was, but that didn't mean I didn't have one more suspect to add to the list. This felt like more of a Bradley play, but if Philip had her new number, we couldn't know for sure. "Can I get another contact on this?"

Ellie frowned. "Who?"

"Anson has a friend from his days at the bureau. His name is Dex. He was a black hat hacker the FBI…adopted."

"You mean he could either work for the FBI or get charged with something."

My girl was always ten steps ahead.

"Exactly that. But he's helped us with a few different cases now. He might be able to get more information on the numbers and images than I can."

Ellie tapped her feet on the floor but finally nodded. "Okay."

I pressed a kiss to her temple and unlocked my phone, scrolling to Dex's contact information. I tapped the number, and it began ringing. Once. Twice. Three times. Finally, someone answered. "What?" It was more grumble than anything else.

"Afternoon to you, too," I greeted.

"I was sleeping," Dex muttered, an extra rasp to his deep voice. "It's almost six back east."

"I was up all night working on a case."

It was on the tip of my tongue to ask which one, but it was none of my business. Dex's time with the bureau had come to an end, and he was working freelance these days. "Sorry, man. I could use your help."

A rustling sounded in the background, and I pictured a faceless guy surrounded by crushed energy drink cans. "Talk."

"So verbose. No wonder you and Anson are friends."

"You want my help or not?"

I did. More than that, I needed it. So, I laid out the situation to Dex, leaving out as many personal details as possible. I knew from Anson that Dex's justice trigger got flipped when anyone hurt women. I didn't know why; it was just that he wasn't afraid to dip his toe back into those darker waters to help.

"Tell me the numbers the texts came in from," Dex ordered.

I read them off one by one, hearing Dex's keyboard in the background as I did.

"It's software. All these numbers are coming from one software program, so it's likely all the same person. I don't have a lock on the IP address, but let me dig a little more. And get me the photos. I might be able to find something on those."

"You got it." I paused for a moment.

"Something else?" Dex pressed.

"Thank you. I really appreciate your help."

It was Dex's turn for silence. "Who is she?"

That was the million-dollar question. I went with the simple truth. "Someone important."

He chuckled. "Town sheriff bites the dust."

"Are you going to hack some stuff or sit around and gossip?"

"I can do both at the same time. I'm talented that way."

"Goodbye, Dex."

"Buzzkill," he shot back.

I shook my head and ended the call.

"What'd he say?" Ellie asked. "I could only hear a few things."

"The texts came from a software program. Like the kind that sends those political texts or spam bots. It's probably all coming from one computer. Dex is going to try to find out where that computer is."

Ellie nodded slowly. "It could be either of them. Neither are super techie, but they could've paid someone to do it. Philip's assets are frozen, but I'm sure he has bank accounts in places the US government can't touch, and I *know* his lawyer isn't opposed to handling his dirty work."

I didn't miss how Ellie had used her dad's given name, creating more of that distance. I wrapped an arm around her and pulled her into me. "We'll figure it out. I promise. You're already on the drive-by list, but I'll increase the frequency. And I think we need to get an alarm put in here. My brothers have used a great company called Anchor Security in the past. Anson's friend, Holt Hartley, owns it and—"

Ellie pulled back. "Wait, wait, wait. I don't want to feel like I'm living in a prison. I just got out of that."

The tension in my jaw was back. "We need to keep you safe."

"If this person wanted to hurt me, don't you think they would've done it already instead of sending photos? They want to *scare* me."

She had a point. Right now, their game was fear. But when people like that didn't get what they wanted, they did one of two things: They either found a new target, or they escalated.

CHAPTER THIRTY-ONE

Ellie

I F YOU ORDER EVEN ONE MOTION DETECTOR OR LASER BEAM, I will rearrange your entire closet and dresser. I will mismatch your socks and put your boxers in with your T-shirts," I threatened as Trace pointed out to Anson a window he wanted better coverage for.

Arden stifled a laugh with a cough. "You know how to hit him where it hurts."

Trace sent me a quelling look. "Nothing you or the demon dog can accidentally trip."

Gremlin lifted his head from where he'd been snoozing on his dog bed as I narrowed my eyes. "Say no motion detectors or laser beams."

He sighed and held up a hand in a Boy Scout salute. "I solemnly swear, no motion detectors or laser beams."

"You know," Linc began, "this would all be solved if you moved back into Cope's house. Arden and I could stay there with you. It's off the beaten path and has tight security."

Linc and Arden currently lived in a guesthouse on Cope's property while their new house was being built. And the hockey star had been kind enough to let me stay at his place while he and Sutton were up in Seattle as he worked to get back on the ice. But I knew Linc would hover if I went back there.

It was hard enough convincing him that this was likely Philip's play at trying to scare me back to New York while leaving out my painful history with Bradley. After everything he and Arden had been through recently, Linc didn't need that on his shoulders. And given that Arden was newly pregnant, she didn't need the stress of worrying about me or being concerned that her fiancé might lose it.

"I agreed to some over-the-top security system. That's enough. I'm not uprooting anyone," I said.

Trace crossed the room, moving into my space. He slipped his hand under my hair and squeezed my neck. "Just a precaution, but it'll make everyone feel better. This way, we know all our bases are covered."

Gabriel and Dex had found exactly nothing last night. No evidence of a private investigator in the area. No signs of Jasper. No IP address to tell us where the texts had come from. Trace had even made a poor deputy sit in my driveway overnight, just in case.

I felt a little guilty that their presence had eased some of my worry. But I still slept with Mrs. Henderson's trusty bat under my bed.

"Hey," Linc bit out. "What's with all the touching?"

Anson choked on a laugh. "Do we need to have *the talk*?" He gestured to Arden. "Actually, since you knocked her up, maybe we do. When two people—"

"Anson," Arden barked. "I might be pregnant, but I still know twelve different ways to snap your neck, and I have a habit of carrying a switchblade."

He just grinned. The smile was so wide it looked slightly deranged. "Arden in love. Threatening death and dismemberment to anyone who might harm her Lincy-poo."

My brother scowled at the ex-profiler. "Did you just call me Lincy-poo?"

Anson shrugged. "It just felt right."

Linc shook his head and turned back to Trace. "Please explain your hands being on my sister."

Heat flared to life somewhere deep, and not just because Trace was touching me. "Oh no, you don't, buddy. There is no alpha-male, big-brother overprotective nonsense happening. I touch who I touch, and that's that."

Linc blinked a few times. "Okay...I just...you two are..."

"Figuring it out." It was the best answer I had for something I had no idea how to classify. Neighbors with benefits seemed a little ridiculous.

Trace moved, sliding an arm around my shoulders, his silent statement on the matter.

"Oh, come on," Anson said, exasperated. "He called Dex for her. He called *me*. He's bringing in Holt and Anchor Security. He took a day off work to be here, for God's sake. He's a goner."

I stiffened. "Anson...you aren't helping."

He looked back and forth between us and flashed that creepy grin again. "Pleased as punch for you two."

"Who are you, and what did you do with the guy who barely speaks two words most days?" Trace asked. "I think I liked him better."

Anson just shrugged. "Your sister happened. Now, I'm into love and all that shit."

Arden started laughing and leaned into Linc. "He's like a feral matchmaker now or something."

Linc kept looking back and forth between Trace and me as if trying to figure it all out.

"Well, this feral matchmaker has all the measurements he needs," Anson said. "I'll get these to Holt. He's going to send a team down from Seattle and will try to come himself."

"He doesn't have to," I started.

"He wants to." Anson grinned. "He thinks Lolli's a trip. He had her make a donut dick painting for his brother, Nash, for Christmas."

"Jesus," Trace muttered.

I fought a smile. "She's getting a true following."

"Someone save us," Arden said, turning to pat Linc's chest. "Come on, Cowboy. Take me to lunch. I'm hungry."

"But we should stay and—"

"*Cowboy*," Arden warned. "Your sister needs a little time to process. And I need a cheeseburger and to dunk some fries in a milkshake."

Linc's expression changed then, going soft as if a memory were grabbing hold. He ducked his head to brush Arden's lips with his, his hand going to her belly. "Gotta make sure my babies are taken care of."

She smiled up at him and then jumped, wrapping her legs around his waist. "Feed me, Cowboy."

"Vicious to the bone," Linc muttered, not letting her down. He glanced my way. "Call if you need anything."

It was a command, not a question, but I still nodded. "I'm good, ConCon."

"Call anyway," he ordered.

I gave him a salute as he carried Arden out of the house. Anson just stood there, grinning, then gestured to the two of us. "This is good. I like it."

Trace stared at him for a long moment before shaking his head. "I'm telling Rho to put you on a tighter leash."

"Never going to mind that," Anson called as he headed for the front door.

Trace turned, his hands moving to my shoulders. "You okay?"

I wasn't entirely sure how to answer that question. So much was flying around, but I was still standing. "I'm not, but I am. Does that make any sense?"

He brushed a strand of hair back from my face, his fingers lingering. "Completely. Strong as hell."

It meant something that Trace saw me that way. And it meant even more that I could feel that strength building within me.

"You want lunch? Hang with Bumper? Something else? I've got three hours before Keely gets dropped off."

I mulled over the options. Trace had already force-fed me a massive breakfast after dropping Keely at school. And as much as I loved Bumper, there was something else I wanted more. "Can we plant my butterfly pots and bulbs?"

My supposedly happy afternoon had been ripped away yesterday, and I wanted to reclaim some of that.

Trace's expression softened. "Let's plant a garden."

"I think we should map out where the bulbs go," Trace began, studying the front garden beds like he was about to go to war. "We could measure them so they're about eighteen inches apart and—"

Laughter bubbled out of me; I couldn't help it. If I'd thought Trace was orderly in his home, it had nothing on how he attacked my quest for a butterfly garden—the methodical way he'd potted each plant, following the exact instructions Duncan had sent me home with. He'd actually counted the handfuls of gravel he'd put at the bottom of each one.

Trace turned to me, frowning. "What?"

I slowly made my way to him, the sun beating down on my bare shoulders since I'd stripped down to a workout tank. I wrapped my arms around his neck. "Chief. It's a garden, not a military march. It doesn't have to be even or perfectly dispersed or anything else. We can plant them where the spirit moves us."

He stared down at me for a moment. "Are you making fun of me?"

"Maybe a little." But the truth was, he'd helped me find the magic I'd lost yesterday. And the fact that the sun was blazing, giving us what felt like a final dose of warmth before fully submerging us into fall, only made it better.

Trace's lips twitched, making his scruff dance with the movement. "Just wait until you have patchy flower beds."

"The horror," I mocked.

That gorgeous mouth pulled into a grin. "I like you, Ellie Pierce."

For the first time in months, I didn't mind the sound of my last name, because it was coming from his lips. "I like *you*, Trace Colson."

"I think I'll even like your patchy flower beds," he whispered, brushing his lips across mine.

"If they're patchy, I'll just fill them with more flowers come spring."

"I have no doubt you'll make it magic. Chaotic magic."

A laugh bubbled out of me, and I dipped out of his hold, racing for the hose. I flipped on the water and aimed it at Trace without pressing the sprayer handle. "What were you saying about my patchy flower beds?"

He leveled me with a stare that would've had me taking a step back if I didn't know the real Trace. "You wouldn't."

I arched a brow and pressed the trigger. Water flew at Trace, hitting him square in the chest. He let fly a series of curses that would've made a sailor blush, and I couldn't have been prouder.

Trace ducked out of the stream and ran at me like a linebacker. I shrieked as he grabbed me around the waist and pulled the spray nozzle from my hand. A second later, water soaked me from head to toe.

I writhed against Trace, trying to get free. "There will be payback of epic proportions, Chief!"

"It'll be worth it," he yelled, dousing us both.

The water cut off, and Trace grinned at me. "Regretting your life choices?"

I gave him my best scowl, but it died when Trace kissed me. I didn't feel an ounce of the cold as his tongue stroked in, all power and strength. I pressed myself against him, needing more contact, more of everything that was Trace.

A horn honked, and Trace pulled back, instantly on guard. But he eased when he saw it was just one of our neighbors. He ran a hand through his wet hair, his tee sticking to his chest. "I swear the Universe is determined to give me blue balls."

I choked on a laugh but wrapped my arms around his neck. "Thanks for a magical day."

Trace ghosted a thumb over the apple of my cheek. "My favorite kind of day."

And then a new voice broke in. "Daddy, why are you all wet?"

CHAPTER THIRTY-TWO

Trace

I SLOWLY LOWERED THE HOSE AND DROPPED MY GAZE TO MY daughter. Her expression was absolutely gleeful.

"I, uh. We were…" I searched for the words, but nothing came. Ellie and I had been careful not to show any real affection in front of Keely. Which was part of why I was living in blue-balled hell at the moment. But I wasn't about to introduce Keely to someone in that way until I was sure it was serious.

I didn't know *what* Ellie and I were. I only knew I wanted more of the magic that seemed to seep from her pores.

"We're planting a butterfly garden," Ellie chimed in, her hair plastered to her face.

"Where are they?" Keely asked as her gaze tipped up to Ellie.

"Well, they're not here yet. I'm hoping a few stragglers might visit the pots, but I'm putting these in the ground now, and they'll pop up next spring." Ellie bent and picked up one of the bulbs to show Keely.

"Don't you want to get changed?" my ex-wife broke in. It wasn't a mean tone, but it certainly wasn't warm, and the tension radiating through every word had my gaze snapping to Leah.

That muscle right where her jaw met her cheekbone pulsed in a quick-tempoed beat as she locked on Ellie and Keely.

Ellie forced a smile as she stood. "Probably not a bad idea."

"Ellie, can you do the inside-out braids for school tomorrow?" Keely asked, oblivious to the tension swirling around her.

Ellie's smile turned more genuine as she shifted her focus to Keely. "I have to be at the bakery before you get up tomorrow, but I bet I can teach your dad how to do it so he can."

Keely glanced from Ellie to me, skepticism bleeding into her expression.

"Gee. Thanks, kid."

She just giggled. "Your hands are too big. They always get stuck in the parts."

"That's what she said," Ellie mumbled so only I could hear.

My lips pressed into a hard line as I struggled to keep from laughing. "I promise I will do my best."

"That's all we can do," Keely said sagely.

"Just let me go change real quick." Ellie headed for the door. "Good to see you, Leah."

I had to admit, she made the lie sound warm. I forced my gaze to my ex and found her face a blank mask. "Thanks for handling pickup today."

"No problem. You're obviously…busy."

It was meant to be a jab, but I didn't let her pull me into the back-and-forth we often got stuck in. "I was, so I appreciate it. Always happy to return the favor if you've got something going on."

Confusion bled through Leah's mask. "Yeah, sure." She turned to Keely. "See you tomorrow, okay? I'll pick you up and take you to piano."

Keely's face scrunched, making her distaste for her piano lessons clear, but she nodded. "'Kay."

"Love you lots," Leah said.

"Love you, too," Keely echoed.

Leah didn't leave right away, and I got it. When you had a kid, this was the hard stuff that came with divorce. Leaving them to go back to an empty house hurt like hell. It was on the tip of my tongue to invite her in for dinner, but we weren't there. Not yet. But I wanted us to be. Friends.

After everything that had happened, I'd thought it would be impossible. But having Ellie in my life had made me see things in a different light. Realize that things could be messy yet still beautiful and happen in all sorts of unexpected ways.

Leah made herself start walking. "Goodnight, Trace."

"Get home safe," I called.

Something passed over Leah's face. Wistfulness, maybe? But she didn't say anything, simply nodded and moved to her car.

"Hey, Daddy?"

"Yeah, Keels?"

"If you grew your hair out, I could practice braids on you, too."

"Okay, Chief. Do those hand stretches. I know how those big fingers can get in the way," Ellie said with a wink.

I sent her a scathing look as I lowered myself to the couch in my living room. "You sound like Lolli."

"Supergran and Ellie are meant to be besties," Keely chimed in. "She said she's making Ellie a super special diamond painting. She was asking me all about Ellie's favorite things."

"Dear God, help us for whatever is about to be created," I muttered.

"That's not nice, Daddy," Keely said as she crossed her legs to sit in front of Ellie and me. "Supergran's paintings are all sparkly and beeeeautiful."

"And illegal in many states," I whispered under my breath.

Ellie struggled not to laugh, but her cheeks twitched with the effort of holding it back. "What did you tell her my favorite things are?"

"Hmmm." Keely seemed to search her memory as she started brushing out her long, brown hair. "I told her you love goats and dogs and the bakery and rainbows with birdies all around and dance parties. Supergran says she wants to go to the cowboy bar with you so you can save a horse." She looked up at me then. "She's always talkin' about saving those horses. She's real dedicated."

A million different curses circled in my mind. "I'm going to kill my grandmother."

"Daddy!" Keely chastised me. "Do I need to ground you?"

Ellie did laugh at that. "I think that means no dessert for him."

"More for us," Keely cheered.

"But first, braiding lessons," Ellie said. She moved closer to me, her thigh pressing against me. "Pay attention, Chief. You're already on thin ice. I don't think your record can handle one more demerit."

"I'll show you a demerit," I growled.

Ellie's gaze dropped to my mouth. *Hell.* The urge to lean in and kiss her was almost too much to take.

"I'm ready," Keely singsonged, breaking into my lusty thoughts.

Right. My kid was sitting in front of me.

"Okay," Ellie began as she gathered up Keely's hair. "For an inside-out French braid—or a Dutch braid—instead of weaving each piece over the top, we weave the outside pieces *under* the center section."

Watching as Ellie's fingers deftly moved through my daughter's hair, all I could think about was having those fingers on *me*. It was official. I was going to hell.

"Are you paying attention to anything I'm saying?" Ellie asked.

"No, I think you're gonna have to start again," I admitted.

"Daddy," Keely chastised.

"Sorry, Keels."

Ellie shook her head. "Another demerit, Chief. How will you ever pay up?"

My gaze heated as I turned to her. "I'm sure you'll think of something."

"Stop making me want to kiss you," Ellie whisper-hissed, just quietly enough that Keely couldn't hear.

"You started it," I shot back.

"Do I need to separate you two?" Keely asked, like she was our teacher.

"Probably," I admitted.

"Focus," Ellie ordered.

I did my best, but it was a struggle. With an hour or so of tutelage, I was starting to get the hang of it. Keely's braids looked less like lumpy, haphazard rope and more like what they were supposed to.

"I also got something I think will be perfect for her finished look," Ellie said, bending to grab something out of her purse.

Keely whirled around, bouncing up and down on the backs of her heels. "What is it?"

"Keely," I warned.

"I was just asking," she defended.

Ellie laughed as she pulled out a package of something, covering it with both hands. "I like the excitement. I found these on one of my favorite boutique's websites and knew they just had to be yours."

Something happened then. A shifting sensation deep inside my chest. Ellie had been thinking of my girl. She'd gone out of her way to get something for Keely that would make my daughter happy. If I'd wanted to kiss her before, that sensation had nothing on what I was feeling right now.

Ellie uncovered the package. It was a gauzy, somewhat see-through bag, and inside was a set of barrettes with bejeweled butterflies on them. Keely gasped, her hands flying to her face in a move beyond her years. "They're beautiful," she whispered reverently.

"They are." My voice was deeper, carrying a rasp that hadn't been there before.

Ellie's gaze lifted to mine, and I saw something *more* in her eyes. I realized it then. She was giving my girl what she'd never had. There was something so beautiful about that. Something so *Ellie*. She didn't let her lack harden her. It did the opposite. It made her give more freely. To any animal that crossed her path. To friends. To strangers. To my kid. To me.

And we were all better for having her in our lives.

Ellie's pale green eyes glistened. "I was thinking you could put them all up and down your braids. It'll look like butterflies just landed in your hair."

Keely leapt to her feet and hurled herself at Ellie. "This is the best present ever. Thank you sooooo much!"

Ellie laughed as she caught Keely, but I also caught something more in her expression. A joyful pain. "I'm so glad you like them."

"I *love* them."

I couldn't take much more. The two of them like this were going to kill me. Ellie was showing me that my daughter's life could be so damned beautiful, even if I hadn't been able to give her a two-parent home, had callouts that interrupted family time, and whatever else came up that seemed to slip from my control. And it would be beautiful because of the small, unplanned moments we found like these.

Keely released Ellie, taking the butterfly clips. "I wanna see what they look like in my hair." She raced for the stairs.

"Brush your teeth while you're up there. It's time for bath and bed," I called after her.

"Daaaaaadd."

The fact that there wasn't a Y at the end killed me. It was happening now and again, her calling me Dad instead of Daddy. My girl was growing up, and I had no choice but to let her.

My gaze moved to Ellie. She looked so damn pretty. Her hair was in braids, too, still damp from her shower. Her face was bare, revealing a smattering of faint freckles on her nose. And she looked...happy.

"Thank you." I leaned in, my hand sliding along Ellie's jaw so I could take her mouth. I groaned at the taste of her: a hint of after-dinner tea that still clung to her tongue and something that was only Ellie.

She met me stroke for stroke, and my resolve was no match. My hands found her waist, and I lifted Ellie onto my lap so she was straddling me. She rocked against me, the friction making me harden against my zipper. A moan slipped from Ellie's mouth to mine, her nipples pebbling.

"Daaaaaaaddy, where's the toothpaste? Mine's all gone," Keely yelled from upstairs.

Ellie instantly pulled back, her hand going to her swollen lips.

"Hall closet, Keels." My head fell back against the wall. "The Universe is a cockblock."

"Maybe," Ellie said, leaning forward and trailing her lips up my neck. "But there's something about delayed gratification."

My phone dinged, and I cursed.

Ellie laughed against my skin and then leaned back again, shifting to move off me.

My hand tightened around her hips. "Don't. I like you here."

She smiled down at me, a mixture of tenderness and mischief in her eyes I'd never seen before. "Okay."

I shifted so I could pull out my phone but kept Ellie with me. Gabriel's name flashed on the screen. Unlocking my cell, I read the text.

> **Gabriel:** *Heard from Jasper's PO. Negative on the drug screen. No illegal substances at his address.*

My back molars ground together.

> **Me:** *He's keeping it elsewhere. Anything pop on the drugs found in the woods nearby?*

> **Gabriel:** *No prints at all. Sorry, man.*

> **Me:** *Not your fault. We stay on it. He'll fuck up eventually.*

> **Gabriel:** *Did you just say the F-word?*

> **Me:** *I typed it, but regretting it now.*

"What happened?" Ellie asked. She wasn't looking at my phone, even though she could've easily read the texts. She was looking at me. Because what mattered to her was my reaction to whatever it was.

"Gabriel heard back from Jasper's parole officer on the more in-depth drug panel. He's clean."

Her face screwed up. "Is it wrong that I want to plant something so he gets in trouble? Maybe Lolli can loan me some psychedelic mushrooms."

"The two of you are a disaster waiting to happen," I muttered.

"Hey!"

I squeezed her waist as I set down my phone. "I appreciate you wanting to do illegal things for me more than I can say."

"Maybe I just want a pat down from the chief."

My dick twitched. "Sheriff."

"Prove it. Show me your badge."

"You make that sound dirty."

"I meant it to." Ellie leaned forward to kiss me, but just before our lips met, a voice called from upstairs.

"Ready, Daddy!"

I pressed my forehead to Ellie's. "Feeling the urge to kidnap you and take you somewhere there's no cell reception." My fingers tightened on her hips. "Need my hands on you. My mouth. Dying for more of your taste."

Ellie's breaths came faster. "Don't make promises you're not going to keep."

I rolled my hips against her.

"Daaaaaaaad!"

"Fuck my life," I muttered.

CHAPTER THIRTY-THREE

Ellie

T HE MOMENT I STEPPED OFF THE BACK DECK, BUMPER CAME running. She charged right into my legs, which were now littered with bruises, but I couldn't find it in me to care.

I laughed as I bent to scratch her head, Gremlin dancing around us. "Hi, Bumps. How are you feeling?"

Grem let out a low bark, and then he and Bumper were off, racing around the yard. Bumper made a few jumps that looked like she was doing parkour off invisible objects, and Gremlin started to copy her moves. I grinned as I watched their antics. "It's supposed to be bedtime."

They just raced around the yard again in answer. I moved to the little garden shed I'd made into a night shelter for Bumper. Unlatching it, I grabbed the treats I'd set up on the shelf inside.

It only took two shakes of the container, and Bumper came running. She skidded to a halt right in front of me. I laughed and gave her a few scratches. "Don't worry, I'm a ho for treats, too." I gave her one that she gobbled up. "Up you go."

Bumper knew the drill by now. She hopped into the shed and

made her way toward the nest of hay. I knew Trace would have the water and power on at the barn before long, and I'd have to move her out there, but I'd miss having my sweet girl right here. I worried she might get lonely out there. Maybe I needed to get Bumper a friend.

She butted my hand as if to say *yes*. Or maybe she just wanted more treats. I gave her one more and then bent to kiss the top of her head. "Sweet dreams."

I stepped back out of the shed and latched the door. The little slits I'd put at the top of the shed would let plenty of air in, but the solid walls would keep Bumper warm. Gremlin let out a sound of protest, and I bent to pick him up.

"I know. You'd have her cuddling inside if you could." Heading back into the house, I set Grem down, and he went straight for his fluffy bed in the corner. It had been a full day for both of us.

A shift at the bakery, running around town to find all the accessories I needed for Keely's wacky hair day at school, Anson coming by to grab some additional information for the security system parts Anchor Security was ordering, and starting to map out a mural in the kitchen.

I was slowly making this place a home. I was making it *me*. And that felt good.

After quickly washing my hands, I moved to my coffee maker and pressed the button for hot water. I placed a tea bag inside the mug and waited for it to brew. Just as I was reaching for my construction pencil, my phone dinged.

I grabbed it from the counter and smiled when I saw the name on the screen. Trace and I had been ships passing in the night for the past three days. The last image I had of him was his hands struggling to braid and the heated promises he'd left me with—promises neither of us had made good on.

The truth was, I missed him. But it was because of a lot more than a few stolen kisses. I missed time with him and Keely. I missed his scent and his feel. I missed the groundedness he gave me when it felt like my life was spinning out of control.

He checked in every day, usually multiple times, and I hadn't missed the fact a sheriff's department vehicle was still parked outside my house each night. But it wasn't the same as having *him*. In my space. In my life.

Trace: *Miss you.*

Me: *You a mind reader?*

He sent an emoji of a crystal ball, and I chuckled.

Me: *Lolli would argue she has a pot strain that could give you that gift.*

Trace: *Don't give her any ideas.*

Me: *I'll try to refrain.*

Trace: *I'm sorry things have been so crazy lately. Between Keels and work, I'm struggling to keep my head above water.*

I frowned down at my phone, suddenly feeling more than a sense of longing.

Me: *Everything okay?*

Trace: *Mostly. Just some turnover at the station. Don't love that it's keeping me from seeing you.*

That had warmth taking root somewhere deep and blooming through every part of me the way I hoped those bulbs would from the ground come spring.

Trace: *I left you something on your front porch. Open it, then call me.*

My mouth quirked, curiosity spurring me into action. I crossed to the front door and unfastened every lock. Opening the door, I saw a small box on my doormat. It was a sleek, matte black tied with a black ribbon.

I picked it up and shut the door behind me, relocking each latch. I crossed to the stairs and sat, laying my phone next to me as I untied the bow. I paused before I lifted the lid, a buzz of excitement lighting through my veins. The moment I finally opened the box, I stilled. Then my jaw went slack.

A mixture of amusement and heat slid through me as I stared down at what was inside. Not in a million years would I have guessed that *this* was a gift Mr. Law and Order would've left on my doorstep.

"Full of surprises, aren't you, Chief?" I mumbled as I grabbed my phone.

I tapped the call button on our text thread. It only rang once before he answered. "You open it?"

"Did you get me a sex toy?"

A low, husky chuckle sounded across the line, and it felt like echoes of Trace's callused fingertips skating over my skin. "Pretty sure it qualifies," he said.

"Chief…"

"Not going to make promises I can't keep. Might not be able to get my hands on you in real time, but I can control that with an app on my phone."

A grin tugged at my lips. "I admire the ingenuity."

"What do you think, Blaze? You want to play?"

The deep rasp of Trace's voice and the intent behind his words had my skin heating in an instant flush. "Yeah, Chief. I wanna play."

"Where are you?"

His voice was deeper now, the bite of command slipping in. My nipples pebbled in response, pressing against the thin lace of my bralette. "Sitting on the stairs."

"Doors locked?"

"Sir, yes, sir," I mocked.

"Ellie," he growled.

Hell. My nipples tightened again at the tenor of his voice. "They're locked."

"Upstairs to your room," Trace ordered.

Everything in my life lately had been about the quest for freedom, my own choices, my own decisions. But it was exhausting at times. Something about having Trace command me now was like a release. Or maybe it was that it was my choice at every turn, the physical distance between us only giving me more control.

I took the stairs quickly, but each step stirred something. The promise of what was to come paired with the swish of my legs. Thighs brushing against each other. Skin heating like I could feel every nerve ending in my body.

I swore I was out of breath by the time I reached the small bedroom at the end of the hall. It was still chaos inside. Piles of clothes on a chair or peeking out of the dresser. My bed was still unmade from that morning.

"You there?" Trace asked. And I could hear the battle against impatience in his voice. That little tell felt like a surge of power.

"I'm here," I whispered.

"Tell me what you want. Lights on or off?"

My gaze swept around the room. "Off. I want to feel like you could be here. Right next to me."

A rustling sounded from the other end of the line. "My girl misses me."

"I do."

"Lights off. On the bed."

Everything in me wound tighter, but I did as he said. Flicking off the light, I let the moon's glow guide me to my mattress. Each step I took ratcheted my heartbeat faster.

"Phone on speaker, Blaze."

I dropped the box and the phone to the bed and hit the speaker icon. "Done, Chief."

"Need to imagine you. See you in my mind. Imagine what it would be like to peel every piece of clothing off you. Tell me."

I glanced down at what I was currently wearing. "I've got on those starry sweats of mine. The neon blue ones with the embroidered metallic stars." My lips twitched. "Not very sexy."

"Want to know what I think about those sweats?"

I made a humming noise in the back of my throat. "I'm not sure, honestly."

Trace chuckled, the sound skating over the line and across my skin. "All I could think about was pulling those bottoms down, gripping your hips, and sinking so deep inside you that I'd brand myself on your bones."

My lips parted as I sucked in a sharp breath.

"The thing about those sweats is that you can see every curve when you move. How they cup your ass. Curve around your breasts. The only thing that might be better is that kilt-skirt thing you've got."

A laugh spilled from my lips. "I'll keep that in mind."

"You'd better," Trace ground out. "Where are you now?"

"Standing by my bed."

"Take off your sweatshirt and tell me what's beneath."

I lifted the soft cotton over my head and let it drop to the floor, the brush of it against my skin feeling like infinite finger brushes. "My tank top and bralette."

Trace made a sound in the back of his throat. "Lose the tank top, keep the bra. Tell me what color."

"Green."

"Like my girl's eyes. Tell me, are those pretty little nipples poking through the lace?"

The buds pulled up tighter, straining against the fabric as if they had a direct line to Trace. "Yes."

"You like to play," Trace murmured.

I shifted then, my thighs pressing together, my core already aching for relief. "I think I do."

I could hear the smile in Trace's next words. "Kick off your shoes and get out of those sweats. But I want you to take them off slow. Feel your fingers ghosting over your skin. Know they're getting what my fingers are dying for."

My breaths came quicker as I toed off my fluffy boots that wouldn't have stood up to any sort of snow. Then my fingers hooked in the waistband of my sweats and started to tug.

"What do those beautiful thighs feel like? Soft and strong?" Trace rasped over the line.

"Smooth," I whispered. I'd done my shower routine when I got home—shaving, exfoliating. But I often didn't stop to think about how it felt to *me*. I'd so often done it for the benefit of someone else.

"Tease that skin. Glide your fingers over it. Soak in that feel for me."

I did as Trace instructed, sweeping my thumbs over my thighs as I sent my sweatpants sailing to the floor. I kicked them to the side and straightened. "They're, um gone."

"Blaze, what did you have under those?"

I was quiet for a moment, my cheeks heating, even though he couldn't see me.

"Ellie." There was more command in Trace's voice now, more authority.

"Nothing." The word wasn't a whisper, but it certainly wasn't a roar.

"Killing me," Trace said. "Walking around that yard, cooing to a goat, and not wearing any fucking underwear."

"Can I tell you something?" I asked.

"Anything."

"I like when you say *fuck*."

A low chuckle sounded over the speaker. "Fuck, baby."

The best sort of goose bumps skated over my skin.

"Now, climb onto that bed and lie on your back. Knees up. Legs spread."

A shiver racked through me. Anticipation making a home in my body as I climbed onto the mattress. Moving the phone and the box, I felt my pulse thrumming in my neck. "Okay."

"Cup those full tits. Circle your nipples. Tell me if they're hard."

My breaths only came faster as my palms curved around my breasts. They felt heavier in my hands now, and as my fingers teased the peaks, I shuddered, wetness gathering between my thighs. "Like little pebbles."

"Want to taste them. Got my mouth between those gorgeous thighs but haven't tasted your nipples yet. Need to remedy that."

My back arched as if Trace's words were his hands, reaching through the phone.

"Keep one hand on your breast, use the other to get the toy. You press that on switch and hold it to your clit. I'll do the rest."

Blood pulsed in my ears as I fumbled for the gadget. I felt for the button, and a small light came on the moment I pressed it. Positioning what looked like a small cup to that bundle of nerves, I shuddered again. My flesh already felt too sensitive, everything heated to the point of boiling.

"Okay," I breathed.

"How's my girl feeling?"

"Wishing you were here. Wishing I could break." The second thing I said didn't even make logical sense, but Trace managed to understand me.

"You need release. And I'm going to help you find it. Together. You and me. Gotta own your pleasure, every single thing you're feeling."

His words hit like beautiful bombs. Because I'd never owned that piece of myself. Had always been so removed from it. It had been a means to keep someone happy, but that someone was never me.

"I'm with you," I whispered.

"Good," Trace praised. "Take that hand on your breast and slide it between your thighs."

My hand moved instantly because I wanted it there and because Trace had asked.

"Are you wet?"

My fingers teased my slit, and my body trembled. "Yes."

"That's my girl. Getting herself there. Turning herself on. Owning it all. Now, take some of that slickness to your clit."

The words, the feeling, it was almost too much. But I gave myself over to it, relishing it all.

"Gonna turn this on," Trace warned. "Nice and easy, just like my tongue teasing you."

The toy hummed to life, a mixture of vibration and soft suction. A nonsensical noise left my lips as my back arched, feeling it all.

"You like that?"

"Yes." And I wasn't shy about giving him the word. Didn't feel ashamed or worried. I felt free.

"Slide two fingers inside that tight, wet heat, Ellie. Remind me what it feels like."

My hand moved as if it had a mind of its own. Sliding in, feeling that hint of stretch. My body moved as if Trace's hands were guiding it through a symphony, different instruments flaring to life at his command.

"Feel good?" Trace rasped.

"Too good. I—I—"

Trace turned up the intensity on the toy, and I cried out.

"Don't come," he ordered. "Hold it back for me. Hold it back so it's so much better. So we can make it more. So you can break."

My fingers moved in and out as Trace brought the toy back down and then up again. Taking me to the brink and then easing off. "Please," I begged.

"Those moans on your lips. Add a third finger, Ellie. Feel that stretch."

My body obeyed as the toy flared again. I whimpered, my walls clamping around my fingers as the first wave hit. One after another until it took me over the edge. I didn't just break.

I shattered.

More than anything I'd felt before because, even though he wasn't in the room with me, he somehow was. It was Trace who allowed me to fully let go for the first time. My body bent and bowed as he wrung me dry, and I let go. I felt true freedom. Found it with him.

Slowly, the toy eased, and my fingers slid out. My ears rang, and my lungs heaved.

"How do you feel?"

My whole body hummed. "Like a butterfly."

The words were barely audible, but Trace still caught them.

"A butterfly?"

"Light. Flying. Free."

"Love you finding that, Blaze. Love you giving it back to me."

CHAPTER THIRTY-FOUR

Trace

IT WAS OFFICIAL. I WAS ADDICTED TO ELLIE PIERCE. HER LAUGH, her scent, her moans. The way she fit so perfectly into our lives. It wasn't effortless, exactly. It took a hell of a lot of effort to find alone time with her. But the way we came together when we did, or how she folded in with me and Keely when we were all together, something about it felt...right.

More than right, it felt different. But in the best way. As if all three of us were finding parts of ourselves we hadn't before because of each other. For Keely and me, it was all because of Ellie.

I forced my gaze away from the scene taking place at my kitchen island. The breakfast mess had been swept away in favor of hair tools, accessories, and things I didn't even know how to classify. I feared my kitchen would never be the same. Ellie had come over at half past six with a full rolling suitcase. She'd even purchased one of those cape things people wore in salons that was covered in unicorns.

Checking the time on my phone, I grimaced. "Ten minutes."

"I am just putting on the finishing touches," Ellie promised. She reached for a spray bottle. "Every unicorn deserves a little glitter."

I pinned her with a stare. "Is that stuff going to get all over my kitchen?"

Ellie's lips tipped up. "Watch out. Maybe I'll sneak over here and paint your walls with a glitter finish."

"Oooooh," Keely awed. "That would be sooooo pretty."

"Don't you dare, Blaze."

Ellie just laughed and sprayed the glitter in Keely's hair. She'd done pigtails in a style like I'd learned the other day but ended the inside-out braids in ponytails that she'd curled and then added spray color to, promising me it would wash out. She'd placed unicorn and rainbow barrettes throughout the braids and completed the look with a unicorn horn headband that had rainbow ribbons twirling off it.

Ellie pulled the cape off Keely with a flourish. "You are done."

Keely let out a squeal as she hopped off the stool. "I wanna see!" She raced down the hall before I could stop her.

I turned to Ellie. "Thank you. This is going to make her year."

Ellie's expression went soft. "I love doing it. I had way too much fun looking for supplies."

"Thank you," I said again.

"You don't have to thank me."

"I want to."

A mischievous smile played over Ellie's face as she walked toward me. "I'm pretty sure you preemptively thanked me last night."

Memories of her moans and quick intakes of breath played in my mind. "Please, don't make me hard before I have to take my kid to drop-off."

Ellie laughed, the sound wrapping around me in the best way. "Okay, but you do need one thing for drop-off."

I frowned. "What?"

Ellie moved so fast I didn't have a prayer of stopping her. Her arm lashed out, spray bottle in hand, and she let the glitter spray fly. "There. Now you match Keely."

My jaw went slack. "You didn't."

She shrugged. "You needed a little something."

I dove for Ellie, tickling her sides as she shrieked and twisted in my arms. "You look good," she cried.

"I have a meeting with my whole department today."

Ellie only laughed harder. "You'll be a vision."

Pulling into my spot at the station, I switched off my engine and grabbed my cell from the cupholder. A text notification.

Cope has changed the group name to Don't Tell Mom.

> **Cope:** *Gonna bring Sutton and Luca back to Sparrow Falls through the weekend. I have a few days off training. Should be there around noon. Where are you delinquents hiding?*

He was officially back in the throes of hockey since recovering from his incident with Sutton's ex and a teammate, and we'd barely seen him for the past couple of months.

> **Me:** *Come to Keely's Wacky Hair Day parade. It's at 2:30. It'll be the best surprise.*

> **Cope:** *We're there.*

> **Kye:** *You can admit it, Copey pants. You missed us. I get it. We're fucking awesome.*

> **Cope:** *Missing everyone but your annoying ass. And you better not have left anything at my house.*

> **Fallon:** *Why would he leave something at your house?*

Kye sent a series of *shhh* emojis and then a snake, which made no sense.

> **Cope:** *You know I have a thing about snakes. Ever since that scene in Indiana Jones where he falls in a pit of them. This fucker left a dozen fake ones in my bed the last time I came home.*

> **Fallon:** *Kyler Blackwood, you didn't.*

> **Arden:** *Run Kye Kye, she's coming for you.*

Kye: *He bails on us for Seattle, he runs the risk of retribution.*

Shep: *Honestly, with Kye, it could've been a lot worse.*

Arden: *Truth. Do you know that he rigged my showerhead with pink dye when I was in high school?*

Kye: *You kicked my ass in front of my friends.*

Fallon: *You mean your felons?*

Kye hadn't exactly been mixed up with good people when he came to live with us at sixteen. He'd gotten into some seriously dangerous stuff, including an underground fighting ring with ties to organized crime in Portland. It had taken time to pull him out, and it wasn't without more than a few bumps in the road.

Kye: *You know the few of those guys who still live here are terrified of you.*

Rhodes: *As they should be. Fal's vengeful streak should have everyone shaking in their boots.*

Fallon: *I'm not that bad.*

Rhodes: *You wrapped that kid's car in plastic wrap and covered it in Vaseline when he tried to jump Kye senior year.*

Fallon: *Bruce Caruthers is a dick weasel of epic proportions, and he deserved what he got.*

Shep: *Everyone back away slowly and don't make any sudden movements, she's on the warpath again.*

Fallon: *You're a bunch of chickens. Trace, do you have a sneak peek of Keely's hair? I wanna see.*

I knew she was purposefully changing the subject, but I helped her out and sent a selfie I'd snapped of the two of us in the car. Ellie had taken a few of her hair from the back, but I didn't have those.

Rhodes: *Trace, is that glitter in your hair? Did Fal glitter-bomb you?*

> **Kye:** *The sheriff looks like he's about to hit up a rave. Someone text Lolli.*

> **Shep:** *I'm sending her the picture now. I'm sure she'll have some accompanying diamond art for you by the end of the day.*

I groaned. The last thing I needed was one of my grandmother's inappropriate pieces of art. I'd told her the Old-West-themed one she'd done, complete with assless chaps, had been damaged in my move. In reality, I'd hidden it in the back of my garage.

> **Fallon:** *Did you do Keely's hair? It looks amazing!*

> **Me:** *Ellie did. Had a whole plan and a suitcase full of supplies.*

The chat was quiet for a moment, and then it erupted all at once.

> **Rhodes:** *Suitcase, huh? Are there sleepover supplies in that, too?*

> **Cope:** *I want tickets to watch Linc kick Trace's ass. I never got my punch in when he started up with Arden.*

> **Arden:** *I'll show you a punch, Puck Boy.*

> **Kye:** *You paying for that styling in sexual favors, Sheriff?*

> **Fallon:** *I KNEW IT! You two are meant to be.*

> **Kye:** *Your turn to run, Trace. Fal's planning your wedding.*

I pulled a true Arden move and took a picture of myself flipping off the camera.

> **Kye:** *Dude, you've changed.*

> **Shep:** *I heard him curse the other day.*

Shaking my head, I switched the group chat to *Do Not Disturb* and headed into the station.

Fletcher looked up from behind the desk, a confused look on his face. "Morning, Sheriff."

"Morning," I said with a nod.

"Hey," he went on before I could make it to the bullpen, "do you have a minute for me to talk something out with you?"

I turned, curiosity piquing. It wasn't unusual for younger officers to pick my brain on things. Generally, it was something that didn't have legs, like thinking they'd solved a decades-old cold case or something. But that wasn't Fletcher. He was levelheaded, did his job, was thorough, and didn't make trouble.

"Shoot," I offered.

Fletcher rounded the desk and didn't speak until he'd reached me. "I'm worried about Ellie."

Everything in me stiffened, cement pouring into my muscles in an instant. "What do you mean?"

It took everything in me to keep my expression neutral. My fingers itched to reach for my phone and text her to make sure everything was okay. The need for that touchpoint was almost too much for me to take.

"I saw the report about the photos," Fletcher went on.

The cement in my muscles hardened as my back molars pressed together. Deputies had access to our case files, so Fletcher hadn't done anything wrong, but I couldn't help but feel like he was stepping on my toes. *Jealousy*, I realized.

"I was in the hardware store the other day, and Jimmy Banks was giving her a hard time. He doesn't seem like the type who would pick up a long-range camera to shoot photos or use some techy software to send threats, but I thought you should know."

A little of my tension eased. Fletcher was being a good deputy, doing his job.

"I appreciate the heads-up. I'll have Gabriel pay him a visit."

Fletcher's expression shifted slightly. Most people wouldn't have noticed, but I'd had a lifetime of reading the subtlest changes in mood or awareness because it was the best method of protection. I understood the shift. Curiosity about why I wasn't taking the helm on the case and guessing why.

In a community as small as Sparrow Falls, you were bound to know the people whose cases you covered, but my relationship with Ellie was *more*, and I had to let Gabriel take the lead. But that didn't mean I wouldn't be involved.

"Let me know if you need any help," Fletcher said. "I'm happy to take an extra shift at Ellie's."

That had a little of the tension returning to my muscles. "I'll let you know."

Holt Hartley and his team were supposed to be heading down here tomorrow to get the security at Ellie's installed. Then we wouldn't need anyone sitting outside her house.

Fletcher nodded and moved to return to his station. He was a good kid, eager, wanted to help. I needed to stop being such a grumpy bastard just because he'd looked in Ellie's direction.

Crossing the bullpen, I took note of Will's empty desk. Good. I hoped he'd learned his lesson with his temporary demotion.

Beth looked up from her perch, and her mouth quirked. "Morning?"

It sounded like a question, but I couldn't figure out why. "What?"

Frank let out a guffaw. "She's admiring your disco hair."

Gabriel crossed from the break room, coffee in hand. "It's really something. Looks like one of those My Little Ponies my niece loves."

"This could be the new fashion," Laney called from a filing drawer in the corner.

"I hate you all," I muttered.

The parking lot at the elementary school was packed, and I had to find a spot across the street and down a block. But I couldn't be mad about it. The fact that so many people would show up for a Wacky Hair Day parade in the middle of the afternoon on a workday said something about our community, the businesses that served it, and the people who lived here.

I caught sight of Cope's ridiculously over-the-top SUV I used to catch him speeding in every time he was home. Now, it sported a booster seat in the back and a sticker for Luca's youth hockey team. I couldn't help but grin. Sutton and her son had changed him in the best ways. None of us had realized the guilt and demons Cope had been carrying until she came along and helped him heal.

A phantom pressure built in my chest as an image of Ellie at my kitchen counter flashed in my head. I pulled into the last possible spot on the block and hopped out of my SUV, itching to see her, to pull her to my side and feel the heat that was uniquely hers.

Beeping the locks, I jogged across the street and headed toward the school. As I reached the elementary parking lot, my heart lurched. A familiar figure stood on the sidewalk with a cigarette dangling from his lips, making the scar on his face look deeper, more brutal. Jasper's shoulders were stooped, but there was an angry bent to his jaw.

It took everything in me to keep my temper in check—a temper I knew I'd gotten from him. I stalked toward the man. He turned at the sound of my footsteps and pulled the cigarette from his mouth. "There's my boy."

His teeth were yellow with age and lack of care, and everything about him looked hollow. But all I could see were our similarities. The eyes. The jaw. What lay beneath it all.

"I'm not your anything." I said the words, so badly wanting to believe them all. "What are you doing here?"

Jasper's smile stretched wider, making his scar deepen. "Heard there was a kids' thing here today. Never got to meet my granddaughter. I think today's the perfect time, don't you?"

I moved so fast Jasper's eyes widened in shock. My palms hit his chest, shoving him back. "You stay the hell away from my daughter. She will *never* know the kind of monster you are."

A hand gripped me hard by the biceps, tugging me back and creating distance. "Don't," Kye clipped, his voice cold. "I know it's tempting as hell, but he's not worth it."

"Pretty sure that was assault," Jasper yelled, brushing invisible dirt off his flannel.

"Pretty sure you tripped over your own two feet," Kye shot back, turning to face him, the worn and scarred leather jacket pulled taut across his broad shoulders as he glared down at Jasper. "Here's the thing, *Jas*. Can I call you Jas? My brother likes to play by the rules.

It's important to him to color in those law-and-order lines. But me? I don't give one single fuck about that. If you take one step toward my niece? I will end you. And not a single person will miss your sorry ass when you're gone."

There was no denying that Kye and I had a different sort of bond than the rest of our siblings. We'd come from the harshest upbringings. Dealt with the worst sort of demons, thanks to the situations we'd been raised in. But it had been worse for Kye. It also gave him a justice trigger.

If anyone in his orbit picked on, bullied, or tried to harm someone weaker in any way, Kye wouldn't stand for it.

Jasper spat on the sidewalk, barely missing Kye's beloved motorcycle boots. "Brother. You two ain't related in a single way."

"That's where you're wrong, Jas," Kye growled. "I'd do anything for him because what bonds us is far more powerful than anything you'll ever understand. But go ahead. Test me."

Jasper should've been pissing himself. A smart man would've. Kye's six-foot-five, broad form was covered in tattoos from neck to fingertips, and those who didn't know who he really was crossed the street when they saw him coming.

But Jasper wasn't a smart man. His ego and temper always got in the way. He turned to me, eyes narrowing. "Always gettin' others to do your bidding. Cops. Teachers. This goddamned trash. But they won't always be around. Best remember that. You took from me, and you better be damned sure I'm going to return the favor."

Before I could say a word in response, Jasper stalked off down the street. Kye didn't whirl around, his movements were slow, but the tension radiating off him was worse. His amber eyes flashed a brighter gold. "Why the hell didn't you tell me he was out?"

My jaw moved back and forth, the joint popping with each direction switch. "I was dealing with it."

"Yeah, sure as hell looks like it," Kye spat.

I ran a hand through my hair, tugging on the strands. "Gabriel's had eyes on him as much as possible."

"Not good enough."

No, it wasn't. "Gonna have to file a restraining order."

Kye scrubbed a hand over his thickly stubbled cheek. "You know a piece of paper isn't going to do a damn thing for someone like that."

This was where Kye's and my journeys parted ways. I believed in the system. I knew it was far from perfect, but it had helped me when I needed it most, and I needed it to help me here. Kye? He stayed as far away from rules and regs as he could get and didn't trust the system in any way, shape, or form.

"We catch him breaking that restraining order, he goes back inside," I told Kye.

He looked at me for a long moment. "I hope like hell it's not too late."

I did, too.

CHAPTER THIRTY-FIVE

Ellie

I THINK MY HEART IS EXPLODING WITH THE CUTENESS," SUTTON said as she took in all the kids with their adorable and over-the-top hair creations.

"Man, my new school doesn't have wacky hair day," Luca complained, looking up at his mom.

Cope clapped a hand on his shoulder. "Next year, Speedy. We're back here and you can dominate the hair game."

Luca seemed appeased by that, turning a smile to Cope. "I do get to see a lot of hockey games in Seattle, though. That might make it cooler."

Sutton laughed. "Gee, wacky hair or hockey games? I wonder which one wins?"

"Hockey, Mom. Always hockey."

"I keep wondering how they're going to get some of this stuff out of their hair," Shep muttered. "I'm pretty sure that one kid with the purple spikes used glue."

My gaze caught on the older boy Shep indicated, and I winced. "That looks painful."

Fallon leaned in closer so she could see around some kids to get a better look. Then she started laughing. "That is a serious punk phase. And it has nothing on the cuteness you created for Keels."

The first- and second-grade classes were lining up right in front of us, and they looked adorable. But Keely was certainly one of the best with her unicorn 'do. There were some other contenders, though. A quiet little girl with dark hair rocked a Pippi Longstocking replica, her hair sticking straight out in two braids. A boy in their group had sprayed his hair green and had frogs pinned to it. And then there was the brunette whose hair had been made into a legit Eiffel Tower.

Linc moved in on my other side, his hand in Arden's. "How's the new job treating you?"

"Yeah," Sutton called. "I heard the boss is a real piece of work."

I smiled. "Which one, you or Thea?"

Sutton laughed. "Both."

Linc frowned down at me. "You seem...good."

Arden smacked his stomach. "Cowboy."

"What?" he asked, his brows pulling together.

I shook my head. "You say that like it's a bad thing."

"Not bad," Linc said quickly. "Just surprising. I mean, after the photos."

"ConCon, as Lolli would say, stop harshing my buzz."

My brother's mouth quirked in a half smile. "And what buzz is that?"

"The happy buzz. I have a house I'm slowly making my own. A job that's fun. A new dog—"

"And goat," Arden added.

"And goat," I amended. "My brother's making me an auntie. I'm making good friends. I'm happy."

Linc's expression softened. "Trace a part of that happiness?"

I couldn't help the way I braced at the question. Maybe because, as much as I'd been standing on my own lately, there was still a part of me that wanted Linc's approval, and I couldn't decide if that was healthy or not. I'd wasted so much of my life doing what others wanted because I didn't want to lose them.

I rocked from my heels to my tiptoes and let the answer out with my breath. "Yes. He's a part of that."

I felt Linc's gaze on me, but he didn't speak right away. When he finally did, it was a single word. "Okay."

My eyes shot to my brother. "That's it? I was bracing for a lecture or a warning or—or—"

"Some other big-brother overreaction," Arden offered. "I know all about those." She gave Cope a long look as if to make her point.

"Hey, what did I do?" he groused.

"Tried to be all mad that you found Linc shirtless at her house," Sutton reminded him.

Cope shuddered. "Don't remind me."

Linc leaned down and pressed a kiss to the top of my head. "If you're happy, I'm happy. I just want you to have the life *you* want. I don't want you to feel like you have to stay in Sparrow Falls because of me."

"She's staying because of me, obviously," Fallon chimed. "I'm excellent bestie material."

"I heard that," Rhodes called. "I thought I was your bestie."

"I can have more than one," she yelled back.

My mouth kicked up into a smile. "I don't know what forever looks like, but right now, I'm happy. I'm good. And I'm standing on my own two feet. That feels better than good."

The truth was, I couldn't imagine leaving Sparrow Falls. The patchwork family the Colsons had created was the most beautiful piece of art I'd ever seen, and I loved being even a single thread in its fabric. But more, I couldn't imagine walking away from Trace. His quiet strength, the way he kept me rooted in exactly who I was, the care he poured into the world around him...

A woman who had to be the principal began yelling for the teachers to get everyone ready, pulling me out of my thoughts. I glanced around but didn't see Trace anywhere. That wasn't like him. He was always on time—if not early.

"What's wrong?" Fal asked.

"I don't see Trace," I said, still looking around. Nora and Lolli stood with Anson and Rhodes while Cope's crew, Fallon, Shep, and Thea were by me. But there was no sign of Trace anywhere.

Fallon frowned. "Kye isn't here either. He can be notoriously late, but not for something of Keely's."

"There." I caught sight of the two men making their way through the crowd of parents and other onlookers, but neither looked especially happy. The set of Trace's jaw had my anxiety ratcheting up another few degrees.

They stopped to greet Nora and Lolli first, Cope, Sutton, and Luca making their way over to say hello. I didn't take my eyes off Trace. He smiled and chatted, but there was something beneath the surface. A darkness gathering.

Finally, he made his way over to the rest of us. I wasn't sure what I expected, but it wasn't for Trace to pull me to him. He didn't kiss me or make some huge show, but when he tugged me against him, I felt his entire body vibrating.

"What happened?" I whispered.

Trace opened his mouth, and I could see some sort of non-answer forming.

"Chief," I warned.

He knew that tone. I couldn't take lies. There'd been too many in my life. So, instead, he gave me one word.

"Jasper."

I muttered a curse.

"That's gonna get you the swear jar," Trace chastised, his mouth attempting to form a smile but failing.

I looked up into those dark green eyes. "What can I do?"

He stared down at me for a long moment. "Just needed to feel you with me."

Everything in me softened. I slipped my hand under Trace's jacket so I could untuck his uniform shirt and the white tee beneath. Then I moved so my palm was pressed against his back, giving him skin-to-skin contact, telling him without words that I was there and wasn't going anywhere.

Trace let out a shuddering breath and dropped his forehead to mine. "Thank you."

"You don't need to thank me for this."

"You always know what I need. How is that?"

I wasn't sure. But something about Trace encouraged me to follow my instincts. To show up exactly how I was. And somehow, that was just what we both needed.

Music blared—one of the kids' versions of a current pop hit. Trace scowled as he pulled back from me, and I couldn't help but laugh. "Is this worse than my playlist?"

"Definitely."

We watched as the school paraded by, kids dancing to the music as they went. Keely waved like mad when she passed, beaming with pride as she flipped one of her pigtails. Nora took a million photos, and I probably took the second most.

When the parade was finished, the kids had to wind their way through the endless sea of students to find their parents. I could see Keely's unicorn horn bobbing along with frog hair, Eiffel Tower, and Pippi, making their way toward us in the distance. As they did, I felt Trace stiffen.

It wasn't an abrupt movement that made me think danger was near; it was a slow hardening of muscle beneath my hand. I looked up and followed his gaze as Leah approached. "Hey, Le," he greeted.

She nodded, her gaze tracking between us. "Hi. Nice to see you again, Ellie."

There was a pained forcefulness in her words, and I hated it. For her, for me, for Trace. My hand slid out from under his shirt as I smiled at Leah. "It's good to see you, too. Don't the kids look amazing?"

"They do," she agreed and then glanced at Trace. "Did Fallon help you with Keely's hair? It looks great."

"No, Ellie did it," Trace said, keeping his tone light. "She's got a thing for unicorns just like Keels."

The words seemed to hit Leah like a blow, and I felt like the world's biggest jerk. But to her credit, she turned to me, smile still on her face even though it wavered, and said, "You did an amazing job."

"I really like hair stuff," I explained lamely.

"Keely does, too," Leah said quietly.

Shit, shit, shit. I wanted to fix the awkwardness. I didn't want Leah to feel like she was on the outside looking in. Especially not with her own daughter.

I slid my phone out of my pocket and unlocked it. "Here. Give me your number and I'll shoot you my favorite website for hair stuff. They have some really good tutorials on there, too. You and Keely could have a ton of fun with it."

Leah looked from my phone to my face, blinking a few times before accepting the device. "Thanks. That would be, uh, great." She tapped her number into my contacts and handed it back.

"Anytime," I said, my smile coming a little more authentically.

"Mom!" Keely yelled, racing over to her. "Did you see my unicorn hair?"

Leah let a soft laugh free. "I did. You look so incredible."

"Ellie did it! She even made me sparkle," Keely went on.

"I see that. Did you thank her for helping you steal the wacky hair show?"

Keely did a twirl and then ran to me, giving me a huge hug. "Thank you, Ellie!"

"I need to head back to work, baby," Leah said. "Can I get one more hug?"

Keely easily went to her mom, squeezing her hard and leaving some glitter on Leah's business-casual attire. But Leah didn't seem to mind. She kissed the top of Keely's head and then let her go. "Love you."

"Love you, too," Keely called, but she was already running back to Trace and me. "All my friends loved my hair. Benny said I look like a real live unicorn."

Mr. Frog Hair appeared then, blinking up at me. "Maybe next year you can do mine. I bet you can do something epic with frogs."

I chuckled. "I think you're looking pretty great right now."

He shrugged. "My frogs are starting to fall." One plopped onto the ground as if to punctuate his point.

"My main man," Linc greeted, holding out his fist for a bump.

Benny's gaze turned suspicious, but he tapped his knuckles to my brother's. "Are you looking out for my girlfriend?"

Linc chuckled as he wrapped an arm around Arden. "I'm doing my best, but you know she's hard to rein in."

Benny beamed up at Arden as if she'd hung the moon. "You look beautiful, Miss Arden."

"You are just the sweetest, Benny," Arden praised.

"What about my hair?" the Eiffel Tower brunette asked, tugging Pippi Longstocking behind her.

"This is Isabella and Gracie," Keely told me. "They do art with Auntie Arden."

"I do, too," Benny interjected.

Isabella huffed out a breath. "We know. Everyone knows because you never stop talking about how you're Miss Arden's favorite."

Arden straightened at that. "I don't have favorites."

Linc leaned into her, whispering, "That's not what you told me last night."

Lolli let out a hoot as she approached, Nora in tow. "That's my girl. Gettin' herself some of the good stuff."

"What's the good stuff?" Keely asked, all innocence and curiosity.

"Lolli," Trace warned, "we are at an elementary school."

Lolli sent him an exasperated look. "Love, of course, my little pumpkin pie. Love makes the world go round."

"And weed and diamond dicks, apparently," Kye grumbled behind me.

"Kyler," Fallon hissed.

Keely, clearly bored of the adults, joined a huddle with Isabella and Gracie, who hadn't said a word. There was something about the girl's soft quietness that tugged at me. And I didn't miss how her gaze kept flicking to Kye behind me. He probably looked like a towering giant to her.

Benny turned his focus on Linc again, making a two-fingered gesture from Linc's eyes to his. "Don't forget, I'm watching you."

I looked up at Linc, trying not to laugh. "What'd you do?"

"He stole my girlfriend," Benny announced. "Right out from under my nose."

Isabella rolled her eyes. "You said you're in love with Miss Anderson now. Which is it?"

My laughter came harder as Trace pulled me back to his side.

"A real Casanova, huh?" Trace asked.

Benny's face scrunched. "A whatta?"

"He means you're a ladies' man," Lolli said, moving into the group.

Benny puffed up his chest. "I'm a *romantic*." He turned hazy eyes to Arden. "And Miss Arden will *always* be my first love."

"Jesus," Linc muttered. "I don't stand a chance."

Arden patted his chest. "It's good that someone's keeping you on your toes."

Linc dipped his head and brushed his lips across Arden's. "Pretty sure you do that every single day, Vicious."

Keely looked up at the two of them. "Are you two bleep buddies?"

Everyone in the circle froze, slowly turning to the woman with a rainbow extension in her hair and a headband with little mushrooms springing off it...

And almost in unison yelled, "Lolli!"

Keely bounced up and down in her booster seat as we made the drive home from the elementary school. "Can I play with Bumper and Grem when we get home?"

"I think that depends on what plans your dad has," I said, glancing at Trace.

"You might want to take off your horn first," he suggested. "Bumper could think you're a one-horned friend."

Keely giggled. "Bumper doesn't have horns."

"But her cousins do," Trace warned.

Keely began singing some sort of made-up song about goats, and I twisted in my seat to face Trace. "Keely's friends seem sweet."

Trace shook his head. "I have a feeling that Benny is going to be trouble."

A laugh bubbled out of me. "Pretty sure he has Linc running scared."

One corner of Trace's mouth kicked up. "It's good for him."

"What about Gracie? She seems a little quiet."

Something passed over Trace's face. "Not sure about the whole story there, but I get the sense her older sister is the one who mostly takes care of her." His voice lowered so Keely couldn't overhear. "Fallon has been trying to get a better sense of what exactly is going on, but everything has checked out so far."

My stomach twisted at the new information. If Fallon was getting involved as a social worker, Trace was concerned. "Let me know if there's anything I can do."

Trace sent a soft smile my way. "Got the biggest heart."

"Sometimes."

"All the time."

I shook my head. "Sometimes, I'm cranky. And sometimes, I have a you-know-what list."

Trace's lips twitched. "How many times have I made that list?"

I laughed as we pulled into Trace's driveway. "Only a couple. Mostly because it's annoying how gorgeous you are."

That had him grinning. "Good to know, Blaze. Good to know."

I hopped out of the SUV and started toward the street. "I'm going to grab my mail and get Grem. Meet you in the backyard?"

"I'm going for Bumper," Keely yelled, already running in that direction.

Trace let out a long sigh. "When are we moving that goat to her new home?"

"After I find her a friend. She'll be lonely out there all alone," I called as I opened my mailbox.

Trace gaped at me. "Now I'm taking care of *two* goats?"

"Everyone needs a friend, Chief."

I frowned as I pulled out the mail. There was a legal envelope on top with no name and no postmark. I flipped it open and pulled out a stack of what I thought were flyers. Only they weren't.

They were photos.

Of me.

Sleeping.

In my bed upstairs.

Wearing the pajamas I'd worn two nights ago.

And whoever had taken them had been standing right next to my bed.

CHAPTER THIRTY-SIX

Trace

I COULDN'T TAKE MY EYES OFF HER, EVEN WHEN I SHOULD'VE BEEN turning around and clearing out my SUV. Instead, my gaze was locked on Ellie Pierce. The way the late-afternoon sun hit her hair just so, making the red strands hidden beneath the brown flare to life. How the blond wove through it all, creating its own sort of rainbow. And those pale green eyes sparkling with amusement as she gave me hell.

But then it changed. One moment, she was teasing, and the next, her face lost all color. The life and mischief drained from those pale green eyes, and Ellie's whole body started to shake.

I was running before I even knew why; all I knew was that I needed to get to her, had to make sure she was okay. It only took a matter of seconds to reach Ellie, but it felt like a lifetime, an infinity of unknowns and fears swirling in my mind.

By the time I skidded to a halt next to her, my lungs burned, and my heart pounded, making it feel like both could explode from my chest at any moment. But my gaze locked onto the items fanned out in Ellie's hands. Photos. Of her. In her fucking bedroom.

But it got worse. *So* much worse. There were multiple shots, and on the last one, a gloved hand holding a knife reached out in front of the lens. Written on the photo in block letters was: *COULD'VE SLIT YOUR THROAT AS EASY AS 1, 2, 3. GO HOME BITCH.*

Blood roared in my ears as the panic set in. But I did everything I could to keep my voice even. "Ellie, slide the mail back into the mailbox but don't shut it. Try not to touch anything more than you already have."

If there were prints anywhere, we needed to be able to read them. Had to be able to find whoever had done this and nail them to the wall.

"Wh-what?" Ellie asked, her voice trembling as she blinked rapidly.

I placed a hand on her back, needing her to know I was there, that I was with her. That I had her back and always would. "Slide the mail back into the box. Nice and easy."

My gaze swept the street, the houses all around. There wasn't a damn thing out of place. A few families were getting home from school several houses down, but other than that, no movement.

Ellie's hand trembled violently as she shoved the mail back into the metal box that somehow felt like an assault weapon now.

"That's good," I praised as I wrapped an arm around her and guided her toward the backyard. "Keels," I called, still trying to keep my panic under wraps.

"Playing with Bumper, Daddy. It's not time to stop yet, is it?"

My panic eased a fraction, and I breathed a little deeper. "Not yet." Pulling my phone from my pocket, I hit Gabriel's contact.

"I thought you were taking the afternoon to be with your girls. Why are you wasting time calling me?" he greeted.

"Need you to send squad cars and evidence techs to Ellie's. Lights, no sirens. I don't want to scare Keely."

The sound of a chair shoving back came across the line, and I knew Gabriel was already moving. I heard him bark a handful of orders. "On our way. What happened?"

"Photos in her mailbox. Of her sleeping. Someone with a knife." I didn't want to give him any more than that. Didn't want to put the image in Ellie's head again. "I need someone to clear the house, but I don't want to leave Ellie and Keels."

"Be there in less than five. Where are you?"

"Backyard."

"On it." And with that, Gabriel hung up.

I unlatched the gate to the backyard and guided Ellie through it. She didn't speak or make a sound, but I could feel her trembling against me.

"Look, Daddy! Bumper loooooves my horn." Keely ran around the yard pretending to headbutt invisible foes while Bumper danced around her. Barks sounded from inside, and I saw Gremlin pawing at the doors to get out.

"Keys?" I asked Ellie.

She didn't answer right away, and that killed something in me.

"Baby." I crouched, framing her face as I got to eye level. "Can you give me your keys?"

She nodded, but it came in short, jerky movements. It took her a few tries to fish them out of her bag, but she finally handed them to me.

I didn't want to leave her, but I didn't want her or Keely with me in case I saw something inside. I unfastened the gun holster at my hip, happy as hell I hadn't stowed it in the gun locker in the back of my SUV yet. One hand rested there as the other held the keys.

Ignoring Grem's barking, I scanned the living room. Nothing looked out of place; everything was its typical, chaotic rainbow of color. I unlocked the door and sprang Grem from his lockdown. He tore out of the house and headed straight for his pals, Keely and Bumper.

I quickly locked the door again and headed straight back to Ellie. Pulling her into my arms, I held her tightly. It didn't stop the shaking, but at least I could absorb it. I held her as the happy sounds of animals and my daughter swirled around us. I held her as Ellie's world crumbled. I held her, knowing there wasn't a damn thing I could do to erase this nightmare.

But I could protect her now. I could make sure *nothing* like this happened again. And I would. Even if it meant breaking every single law I played by.

Car doors slammed, and I knew the reinforcements had arrived. "Back here," I called.

Keely looked up, a huge smile on her face. "Who's here? Do they want to play with Bumper and Grem, too?"

I kept hold of Ellie. Wasn't sure I could let go if I tried. "Some of my friends from the station are here. They want to see Ellie's house."

Keely's smile widened even further. "Can I tell them I helped paint the rainbow? It's soooooo pretty."

"We can tell them, Keels."

The back gate swung open, and Gabriel and Beth moved inside, shutting it behind them. Gremlin took off running toward them, but instead of attacking Gabriel as I thought he would, he did a little spin and let out happy barks.

Gabriel glanced at me. "This the *attack* dog you keep complaining about?"

I knew he was trying to keep it light for the girls' sake. "He bites me when I come in."

Gabriel grinned and bent to pick up the beast. Gremlin just licked his chin and snuggled in. "Oh yeah," Gabriel said. "Real vicious."

"Is that a goat?" Beth asked, amusement in her voice.

"This is my bestie, Bumper," Keely called.

Beth shook her head. "I'll be damned."

"You got keys?" Gabriel asked, crossing to me.

I nodded, handing them over to Gabriel but still not letting go of Ellie. "Couldn't see anything out of place through the back door. Left the photos in the mailbox with the rest of the mail. Ellie's the only one who's touched them."

Gabriel took the keys. "Beth, you want to get the techs going with the mail?"

She lifted her chin in assent. "On it." But she didn't move right away. She looked at me and Ellie. "We'll get 'em."

My throat worked as I swallowed hard. "Thanks."

"We'll be back. Hold tight," Gabriel said.

I pulled Ellie into my arms, holding on as if that would fix everything.

"Why?" she rasped. "Why would someone do this?"

I didn't have any answers for her now, but I would find out. And whoever was responsible *would* pay.

CHAPTER THIRTY-SEVEN

Ellie

TRACE'S HOUSE WAS TEEMING WITH PEOPLE. MORE THAN HE'D likely ever had in the Craftsman bungalow Shep had modernized. Sheriff's department officials were in and out as Nora energized them with endless coffee, cookies, and other snacks. The entire Colson crew was there, too, apart from Luca, who was at a friend's for a sleepover, and Keely, whom Leah had agreed to take for the night after some initial annoyance at a change in the parenting schedule.

It was all one giant haze. Like an impressionist-style painting I'd see at The Met or MoMA. People were only blurs of shapes and colors as they moved in and out of the space. I was aware of Trace's proximity only by his scent. And my brother's by his occasionally raised voice, which Arden tried to soothe and quiet.

Someone crouched in front of me. I had to blink a few times to register Trace's face. His hands slid from my knees to my thighs, a steady pressure bringing me back. "Do you think you're ready to talk things through with Gabriel?"

My gaze shifted from Trace's face to register just how many people were there. Nora and Sutton hovered in the dining room, looking on nervously and both wearing aprons, caretaking via food as was built into their DNA. Cope moved to Sutton's side, pressing a kiss to her temple and whispering words in her ear.

Shep and Thea were curled up in an overstuffed chair near the doors leading to Trace's backyard. Shep had been sticking close since they'd arrived, and I could see how he watched her now, checking in and making sure she was all right. Guilt pricked at me, knowing she'd been the recipient of her own violating photos and threats. And while different than this, my circumstances had likely brought up memories.

Rhodes busied herself arranging flowers on the dining table as if brightening the space would solve all the problems, while her boyfriend, Anson, spoke with Gabriel in the entryway. They used hushed tones, but their worried expressions gave far too much away.

Kye and Fallon spoke in quiet tones also, tucked away in a far corner of the living room. Kye sporadically tugged a hand through his hair, jerking the dark strands with every movement, until Fallon finally gripped his hand and squeezed tightly. Her dark blue gaze locked with his and held firm, speaking words only he seemed to understand.

But Linc wasn't quiet or calm. He stalked back and forth across the space, his footsteps angry as if taking out all his rage on the floorboards of Trace's house. Arden looked on, worry seeping into her features.

"Ellie, baby. Can you look at me?" Trace's too-gentle voice pulled me back. "Do you want me to clear the room while we talk?"

"No." The word was stronger than I felt. But I knew what I needed to do. I was so damn tired of the lies and half truths, the shame and the guilt. If I was going to talk about everything, it'd be better to do it with the people who were becoming my family around. I didn't want to hide it from them, and I didn't want to lie to my brother anymore.

I cleared my throat, feeling like I was shaking off heavy chains that had been with me for far too long. "I want them to stay."

"Here," a new voice said, crossing into the living room. Lolli offered me a mug that read *World's Best Dad* on the side. "I made you some tea."

Trace's head whipped around. "What kind of tea?"

"Oh, relax." Lolli waved him off. "Sadly, my poppy tea is at home."

"You mean your opium tea?" Kye challenged as though searching for any source of humor at the moment.

Lolli made a *pshh* noise. "Didn't expect you to be a buzzkill. But this is just plain ole chamomile." She leaned into me as she placed the mug on the side table. "With a heavy shot of whiskey to soothe the nerves."

I looked up at her, finding the barest flicker of a smile. "Thank you, Lolli."

She patted my shoulder, then gave it a good squeeze. "I've got your back, honeybunch."

And I could feel that. From every single member of this patchwork family. They all showed up in good times and bad. They each gave in the unique ways that were their strengths. Together, it gave me the strength to dive into the darkness I needed to.

"I'm ready."

Trace waited for a beat as if giving me a moment to reconsider. When I didn't, he stood. "Gabriel. We're ready."

Gabriel looked over, ending his conversation with Anson, and then they both started in our direction. Trace settled in the spot next to me on the couch, weaving his fingers through mine, creating a fabric that was stronger together than anything we could create on our own.

Gabriel moved into the space, but instead of hovering over me, he sat on the floor on the other side of the coffee table. He placed his phone on it and tapped the screen a few times. "Is it okay if I record this so we don't have to go over it again?"

"Yes." My voice sounded rusty, but it was enough.

Anson moved in then, taking a seat in the second overstuffed chair. He was careful not to stare at me, but I felt his gaze finding me in steady intervals as if he were trying to read the meaning behind my every facial expression and movement, his profiler training springing to life.

"Are you okay to begin?" Gabriel asked.

I gripped Trace's hand harder, my fingers tingling from lack of blood flow, but I didn't let go. "We can start."

Gabriel shifted, pulling out a small notepad and pen. "Can you take me through your day? Everything up until you got home."

He'd started me off with a softball question, but I appreciated it. It gave me a chance to steady my voice and my heart rate a minute to slow. I told him about doing Keely's hair for school. My shift at The Mix Up. Thea giving me a ride to the school for the parade, and everything that happened there. My words slowed when we reached the portion of the day where Trace, Keely, and I had arrived home.

Gabriel looked up from his notepad with a gentle smile on his face. "That's great. Very helpful. Tell me, did you notice anyone following you? Have there been any encounters at work that were odd or raised any flags? Nothing is too small."

My mind felt fuzzy, like I was slogging through mud to recall everything.

Trace leaned in, his head dipping so his lips brushed my ear. "Take your time. There's no rush."

With his encouragement, I did, but I still came up empty. "There's nothing. I've had a few unpleasant run-ins with people unhappy about the things my father did—"

"You what?" Linc barked. "Why didn't you tell me?"

Arden took his hand, squeezing. "Easy, Cowboy. She doesn't need your anger, too."

Linc took a steadying breath and seemed to try to rein himself in. But there was a hint of hurt in his eyes now. "Why didn't you say anything, El Bell?"

The use of my nickname nearly did me in. And it was so much worse knowing how much I still had to get through. "I needed to deal with it on my own. You would've had me moving back into Cope's compound and tried to go with me everywhere I went. But that's not a solution. People are mad about what Philip did. They have a right to be. And I'm figuring out a way to deal with it."

A muscle fluttered in his jaw. "If you were living at Cope's, this wouldn't have happened."

I sighed. "Maybe, maybe not. But that was my choice to make."

Gabriel cleared his throat. "Can we talk a little about your father?"

A nauseating sensation swept through me. "Sure."

"Are you two in contact?"

I knew Trace had likely already shared the pieces he knew, but I still went over them. "Not really. He tried right after his arrest, and I never accepted his calls. I changed my number recently, and he tried again. That time, I answered."

My gaze flicked to Linc. His hazel eyes flashed more gold than green as that muscle in his jaw danced. But he held his tongue.

"What did he want?" Gabriel asked, bringing my attention back to him.

My mouth went dry, like all the moisture had evaporated in a single second, leaving me unable to speak. I reached for Lolli's tea, taking a sip and fighting a wince at the bite of whiskey.

"It'll put hair on your chest," Lolli said with a grin, but I saw the uneasiness in her gaze.

"Not sure that's a goal of mine, but thanks."

Shep's lips twitched as he wrapped an arm around Thea, pulling her closer. A few other people chuckled.

I set the cup back on the side table and pulled up my courage. "He wanted me to go back to New York, to Bradley, to that life. I think he still has some unhinged idea that he'll get out of the mess he's in and wants me there when he does."

Images danced in my head, memories of what that life had been like. Michelin-star dinners with Bradley at restaurants I never liked. Charity functions with Helen, where I felt like I was constantly judged and found lacking. Lobster boils at our house in the Hamptons, where my father watched my every move. Wimbledon with Bradley's family and my father, where Henrick would bemoan my lack of tennis knowledge.

I was always dancing on a tightrope, trying to keep them all happy. Everyone but me.

Gabriel focused on the notepad as if to give me privacy for his next question. "And how do you feel about that request?"

"That he can shove it where the sun doesn't shine. And I told him as much. Just like I told him what a crappy father he was. He couldn't hear it, but that wasn't why I told him. I told him for me."

"That's my girl," Lolli cheered. "Stick it to the assholes."

"Lolli," Nora hissed.

"Good luck," Rhodes murmured. "She dipped into the spiked tea."

"Jesus," Trace muttered, pinching the bridge of his nose with his free hand.

Gabriel looked up from his notes as he fought a grin. "Can be freeing, letting loose all those feelings."

"It was."

"And have you heard from him since?"

"No. I haven't heard from him at all."

Gabriel glanced to his right, sharing a silent moment with Anson before returning his focus to me. "And what about your ex-fiancé, Bradley Newbury? Can you walk me through the ending of that relationship and how he took it?"

I stared down at my hands, one still linked with Trace's, the other balled into a fist, the knuckles bleached white on both. As much as I wanted to speak the truth in a room full of people who cared about me, I couldn't take in their faces while I did. But I told myself that was okay. The important thing was that I spoke, even if my voice shook and I couldn't look at anything but how Trace's fingers melded with mine.

"Bradley's and my relationship was never a good one. I can see it more clearly now. It started small. How he would make his displeasure about certain friends or things I wore known. How there would be little punishments if I didn't toe the line."

My tongue stuck to the roof of my mouth as I swallowed. "Nothing huge. But he'd stay out until all hours if I went against his wishes. Or not hold me as we went to sleep. He wouldn't kiss me goodbye. He'd embarrass me in front of his parents or my father, retelling the story."

I forced my free hand to straighten and pressed it flat against my jeans-covered thigh. "It wasn't anything I could've named as more than unkindness. But looking back now…"

"It was manipulation."

The voice that spoke wasn't one I'd expected. I lifted my head to find Anson's dark blue eyes staring back at me. Pissed-off understanding blooming in those dark depths.

"It was a manipulation to get what he wanted. And my guess is that escalated."

I gripped Trace's hand harder but didn't look away from the ex-profiler putting together all the pieces. "Yes."

My brother made a sound low in his throat, but I couldn't look at him. Couldn't look at anyone as I spoke the next words.

"When I told him I couldn't marry him, he hit me. Backhanded me so hard it left me with a black eye."

Movement sounded then. Rustling and then a door slamming. I looked up to see Linc disappearing out onto the back deck and the darkness looming there. My gaze collided with Arden's, and she gave me a sad smile. "I've got him," she said quietly.

I knew she did, but it killed something in me that I'd been the one to cause my brother pain. The one person who'd been there for me growing up. But hiding this from him wasn't a kindness either.

"It's the right thing," Thea said softly. "You have to tell people. Even if it hurts them. Even if it's the most terrifying thing you'll ever do." Her green eyes glittered with unshed tears. "You tell them so they can be there for you. So they can help you untangle all the lies you've been told about yourself."

I battled with my own tears. There was a kindredness between us I didn't want to share with anyone. Because I didn't want another soul to feel the hurt I had. But still, I spoke the words I needed to. "Thank you."

Trace's lips pressed against my temple. "So damn brave."

Gabriel's expression looked a hell of a lot more pissed off now. "I have officers from the NYPD going to interview him, and put a call in to some prison officials at your dad's facility."

"He's also checking into Jasper's whereabouts," Trace added.

There were some sounds of surprise around the room, and I realized that not all the Colsons knew Trace's father was out of prison.

I twisted and turned to look at him. "Do you really think he'd do this just because he's angry with you?"

Trace's jaw worked back and forth a couple of times before he spoke. "He was outside the elementary school today. Made more threats. I honestly don't know. He *hates* me."

I pulled myself into Trace, grasping his hand even harder. Because all of this was weighing on him two-fold. Fear for me and hurt and anger regarding his father. I looked up and brushed my lips across his. "We'll figure it out."

But Trace didn't look like he believed me.

CHAPTER THIRTY-EIGHT

Trace

I STEPPED OUT ONTO THE BACK DECK, SOFTLY CLOSING THE DOOR behind me. Thea was having a quiet word with Ellie, and I wanted to give them that. Because each understood the path they'd walked like no one else could. It didn't matter that the circumstances were different, the digging-out was the same, and I couldn't give Ellie the gift of understanding. I was glad Thea could.

Through the dark, I could just make out Linc and Arden sitting on the deck's steps, leaning into one another. Arden turned at my footsteps. "How is she?"

"Strong as hell. Thea's with her now."

Arden nodded, a sad smile of understanding on her lips.

"Can I have a minute with Linc?" I asked.

Arden stood, but when she did, she stepped in front of her fiancé and bent. She took his face in her hands and kissed him. It wasn't gentle; it was a reminder. "Love you, Cowboy." And then she started for the house.

I took a seat on the steps beside Linc but gave him space. I didn't speak right away. And I was right not to.

"She told you, didn't she? About Bradley."

My throat worked as I swallowed. "She did."

Linc muttered a curse. "I failed her. In so many ways."

"You got her here. Where she needed to be. You gave her the courage to break free. Just because you weren't the first person she opened up to doesn't mean you didn't help her in infinite ways."

Linc slowly lifted his head and turned to me. Even in the dark, I could see the pain in his eyes. It reached out like a living, breathing thing and punched me right in the gut.

"You don't get it. I left. When I graduated high school, I ran. Left for California. I was so desperate to get away I didn't care that I was leaving her with that monster."

I knew he was talking about Philip Pierce. A different sort of monster.

"He manipulated her. Did the same shit Bradley was doing. I know it because I lived it. Cruelty and punishments if you didn't bend to his iron will. He's the one who forced her into that relationship with Bradley. He's the one who took away all his attention and bastardized affection when she tried to leave the first time. And I wasn't there to protect her."

Tears glistened in Linc's eyes, and I reached out, gripping his shoulder hard. "Fuck that noise. Ellie told me how much you were in her life. How often you called and visited. And when she was strong enough to leave, where did she go? Straight to the place she felt safest. You."

His shoulders shook as he let the tears go. "I want to fucking kill him."

"Trust me, I know."

Linc looked up then, the tears fading. "You love her?"

Fuck.

It was a question I purposely hadn't asked myself. Maybe because I was afraid. Maybe because I wasn't quite ready for the truth. But looking at the torture Linc was wading through now, I knew truth was the *least* he deserved.

"She changed what love meant. I don't think I understood until she came into my life. What it could truly be. She's made me a better father. A better brother. A better son. She's made me a better man. And I will do everything in my power to be a good steward of that love. To honor it. To protect it. To protect *her*."

"Fuck," Linc muttered. "Now I know why Cope was so pissed he couldn't punch me."

That startled a laugh out of me—the last sound I'd expected to make. "I can give you a free shot if it'll make you feel better."

"It's no fun if you're letting me have it."

Another chuckle sprang free. "Sorry?"

"You should be."

My phone dinged, and I pulled it out of my pocket.

Gabriel: *Meet me out front? Want to go over a plan of attack.*

I got why he went for the text. He didn't want a bunch of law enforcement personnel pouring into my house while Ellie was so raw. And I appreciated his sensitivity. It was one of the many things that made him such a damn good cop.

"You need to go?" Linc asked.

I pushed to my feet. "Gotta get a planning brief from Gabriel."

Linc stood. "Fill me in after? I'm going to check on Ellie."

"Will do." I headed for the side gate so I wouldn't get waylaid in the house. When I stepped out front, I cringed at all the official vehicles. The lights on at all the houses up and down the street told me the neighbors were all watching the show, and I was sure the rumor mill was running rampant.

Moving toward the street, I found Gabriel, Beth, Laney, and Fletcher all gathered together. I frowned. Fletcher wasn't even on tonight, but I guessed I should appreciate all the extra hands we could get. I scowled when I saw Will headed our way, though. Because even needing extra help, I didn't want his hands anywhere near this.

Fletcher looked up at my approach. "How's Ellie?"

"Hanging in there. Want to bring me up to speed?"

Gabriel nodded, flipping back a page in his notebook. "We've got deputies who will rotate sitting out front overnight."

"That didn't do any good before," I gritted out. Whoever had taken that goddamned photo had snuck in while someone sat in Ellie's driveway.

"Working on that, too," Gabriel said. "Have another batch of deputies rotating one street over. My best guess is whoever took those photos came in through the back. There are pick marks on the lock."

I cursed, and all eyes turned to me.

Will snickered as he walked up. "Guess this prank got the boss spun up if he's cursing."

I slowly turned toward Will. "Did. You. Say. Prank?"

He shrugged carelessly. "If somebody wanted to slice and dice your girlfriend, they would've done it."

I moved so fast Gabriel almost didn't get to me in time. My fist flew, but Gabriel managed to catch my arm at the last moment, just as Beth took my other. Together, they pulled me back, but Laney got right in Will's face. "You're done, pissant," she barked. "Suspended without pay. And I'm filing a complaint with the mayor. I hope like hell Trace fires your ass."

It was more than time. But right now, I was struggling to breathe. Because Will had voiced the deepest, darkest fears that had been stirring inside me since I saw those photos. The knowledge of just how easy it would've been for someone to end Ellie's life. To take her from Linc. From Keely. From me.

"Breathe, Trace," Gabriel ordered.

Will was mouthing off at Laney as she kicked him to the curb. Deputies Allen and Smith gaped at the scene. *Great.* More fodder for the rumor mill.

I shook off Beth and Gabriel. "Her damn dog didn't even wake up. How's that possible?"

Gabriel scrubbed a hand over his stubbled face. "I don't know. I heard that little thing snoring up a storm at your house. It might not have been able to hear the person coming in if they were quiet."

I guessed that was true, but it still bothered me. Someone should've seen *something*.

"I've got more of an update. You want that out here, or do you want me to update you and Ellie together?"

I looked at the friend I'd had for half my life, trying to read into what the update might be. But his poker face was too good. "Together." What Ellie wanted more than anything was to finally be in control of her life, and I wouldn't take that away.

"All right," Gabriel said. "Beth, will you fill everyone else in on the plan?"

She jerked her head in a nod. "On it."

"We've got your back." Gabriel's voice was quiet, but the force behind the words was a vow.

"Thanks." *My* voice was raw, emotion having shredded it to pieces over the course of the night.

As we stepped inside, the various conversations quieted, and all eyes came to us. Linc was seated next to his sister, but he stood at the sight of me, offering me his seat. It was more than just a simple gesture. It was his acceptance of who I was to Ellie, and who she was to me.

She searched my eyes as I sat. "They found something?"

"I don't know. I wanted Gabriel to tell us together."

Surprise lit Ellie's pale green eyes but then she leaned into me. "Thanks, Chief."

"It's Sheriff."

"Whatever you say."

I wrapped an arm around her, pulled her closer, and looked up at Gabriel, waiting.

"Got a few updates for you," he began. "First, Jasper was drinking with a friend after your little run-in at the elementary school. The friend alibied him, but we're looking for corroboration."

My back molars ground together, but I managed a nod.

"Heard back from someone at Philip's correctional facility," Gabriel went on. "The only people he's talked to in the past two weeks are his lawyer and Ellie. Nothing else on the phone or computer logs."

"His lawyer could be a go-between," Linc said, his voice tight. Arden melted against his side and wrapped an arm around his waist.

Gabriel lifted his chin in Linc's direction. "We're looking into that the best we can."

"Bradley?" Anson asked. And the way he did it told me his mind was leaning in that direction on the suspect list.

"That's where things get interesting." Gabriel flipped his notepad page. "The NYPD visited Bradley's apartment. No one home. And the doorman said he hadn't seen Bradley in a few weeks. Doesn't think he's been home because the mail's been piling up."

Ellie stiffened against me, and I pressed a kiss to her hair. "He can't get to you. Not now."

"Police went to his parents' residence," Gabriel continued.

Linc scoffed. "Can't imagine Henrick and Helen were thrilled about that."

Gabriel shook his head. "The detective I spoke to said Henrick Newbury was downright combative. But Helen Newbury was worried. She hadn't spoken to her son in weeks either, and they usually talked every other day or so. We got a photo of Bradley. We'll circulate that around town, but I think you should all take a good look, too."

The Colsons all nodded and offered murmurs of agreement. Gabriel turned to Ellie. "Where do you want to stay tonight? We'll put a detail on you until we find him and know for sure he's the one responsible."

"Holt and his team will be here tomorrow to install the security system," Linc interjected. "But I think you should consider staying at Cope's."

Ellie looked up at me in question.

"I'm where you are," I said. "Wherever you want to be, I'll be with you."

The tension thrumming through her eased a bit. "Here. I feel safe here."

And hell if that didn't make a shot of pride surge through me. I'd built a home that gave Ellie that. *I* gave her that. "Then we stay here."

"It's actually easier to cover this place than Cope's, so that works for us, too," Gabriel said.

"Hey, what's wrong with my place?" Cope pouted.

Sutton patted his chest. "You built that monster mansion in the middle of nowhere, Hotshot. It would take twenty officers to surround it."

"I hope that doesn't mean you're insecure because you're lacking in other departments," Lolli said, arching a brow.

Cope's jaw went slack and then his face screwed up like he was a little sick to his stomach. "Did my grandma just insult my dick size?"

Kye clapped him on the shoulder. "Truth hurts, Puck Boy."

Cope whirled to Sutton. "Tell them that's not true."

She instantly started laughing. "I am not telling your family you have a big dick. Sorry. That's where I draw the line."

"See," Cope demanded. "She said it. Big dick."

"I don't know," Rhodes said, lowering herself to the arm of Anson's chair. "You kind of seem like you're protesting too much."

"If anyone has Big Dick Energy here, it's me," Lolli said with a smirk. "It's rolling off me in waves."

"That's actually the pot smoke," Kye offered.

Lolli winked at him. "Both can be true."

"Dear God," I muttered. "Someone save me from my family."

CHAPTER THIRTY-NINE

Ellie

I PULLED UP THE COVERS ON TRACE'S BED AS GREMLIN SNORED softly on his donut version in the corner. Trace's décor was slightly surprising in its put-togetherness. The blue and gray tones complemented nicely, especially with the stunning black-and-white photo of the Monarch Mountains on the far wall. And the bed itself felt like floating on a cloud.

Lifting the neck of the perfectly worn T-shirt to my nose, I inhaled deeply. Sandalwood. Black pepper. Trace. I wondered if there was a way to put the blend of scents in a candle or room spray. The two T-shirts I'd stolen from him were already losing their scent, and I knew I'd be trying to find a way to bring this one home tomorrow.

Home.

I shuddered at the thought. Because I wasn't sure it felt like that anymore. It didn't matter how many murals I splashed across the walls or how much color I imbued in every room. It would still be the place that someone violated.

Pressure built behind my eyes, dying to break free. I hadn't cried. Not yet. If I broke now, I wasn't sure I'd be able to pick up the pieces this time. There was too much. Finding out my father was more of a monster than I ever could've known. Realizing I'd promised forever to a man who was much the same. Trying to start over. To build a new life. Only to have it broken into.

My breaths started to come faster just as the door to the bathroom opened and Trace stepped out. His hair was still on the cusp of wet from his shower, and he wore blue-and-green flannel pajama bottoms with a Mercer County Sheriff's Department tee that had clearly seen more than a little use. The moment his dark green eyes locked on mine, Trace knew something was wrong.

He was at my side in a second, climbing onto the bed and framing my face with his big, callused hands. "You're okay. You just need to slow those breaths. Focus on me."

I tried to do as he said, to see Trace and nothing else, but the pressure just kept building. In my chest. Behind my eyes. Everywhere. As if with one wrong move, my whole body would explode.

"When is my life my own?" The words tore out of me, garbled by the tears finally breaking free.

Trace's hands dropped from my face but only so he could pull me into his arms. "Ellie."

It was all he said. There was no telling me I was wrong or even trying to soothe my feelings by brushing them away. But my name on his lips was a vow. One that told me he'd be with me through it all.

"W-when do I get ownership of it? Of myself? Even when I start over, my dad's still trying to manipulate me, to move his chess pieces to get what he wants. Bradley won't stop calling, texting, maybe so much worse. When do I get to be free?"

The words tumbled from me like a wave of hot lava, pouring out and burning everything in its path. But Trace wasn't scarred by it at all. He simply pulled back, slid a hand along my jaw and into my hair, and held on. "What do you need?"

I didn't know. Didn't have the first clue.

"Whatever you need, it's yours. Right now. Want to put a pegacorn over my headboard? I'll get the paint. Want to turn my backyard into a goat sanctuary? I'll get the feed. Need to hit something?

I'll take you to Haven and spar with you until you pass out. Whatever it is. I'm here. With you. Always."

Every offer burned into me. And those last words…they were so much more. I could read beneath them to the meaning below. Maybe because I felt it, too. The words neither of us had spoken for so many reasons.

I moved then, straddling Trace's lap, my tee riding up my bare thighs. "I need you. Need this." My mouth met his in a kiss that was more than a little desperate as my fingers threaded through his hair. "I need to feel everything. What it is to come alive and come apart. Because I made the choice."

Trace gazed up at me, searching, checking to make sure this was what I really wanted. What I needed. And then he saw…something. "You need to own this moment. This choice. Because it's your life."

I nodded. "Because *you* are my choice."

Trace's eyes softened then, but heat smoldered in the green depths, turning them to glittering emeralds. "There haven't been many times in my life where that was the case."

His words hit me like painful blows—bombs of realization. Because Trace hadn't been put first much. Not by his mom or dad. Not by Leah. Nora and Lolli had given him that, but Trace hadn't fully let them. I could see how he'd taken it upon himself to caretake all of them. To focus on their safety and well-being and not think about his—or better yet, what would make *him* happy.

"Trace," I rasped, my lips hovering over his, making the barest contact on that single syllable. "I choose you."

His hands moved then, sliding up my thighs and gripping the hem of my tee. He pulled it off in one swift movement, and I watched with pleasure as his pupils dilated, and he let out a sound that resembled a growl. "Ellie…"

My mouth curved the slightest amount. "Yes, Chief?"

"You got into my bed with no panties and no bra?"

"I believe I did."

"Fucking hell," he muttered.

I squirmed on his lap as heat gathered between my thighs.

"Blaze," he warned.

"I told you what your cursing does to me."

Trace didn't wait, he ducked his head, taking my nipple into his mouth and sucking hard. I pushed up on my knees, rising for more contact. My back arched as my lashes fluttered, and Trace hummed around the hard peak.

The sound sent the most delicious vibrations through me, as though that bundle of nerves had a direct line to my core. A rush of heat, wetness, and need pooled between my thighs.

Trace glided a hand up my inner thigh, teasing the sensitive skin until he reached the apex. He grazed his knuckles over my slit, groaning as he did. His fingers delved deeper. Teasing. Toying. Tempting. All as his lips pulled my nipple deeper into his mouth.

My back bowed as every nerve-ending drowned in Trace. His fingers, his lips, his tongue.

Those beautiful, thick fingers slid inside me, stretching as their callused tips teased. I shuddered, and Trace released my nipple, leaning back against the pillows. "Too much?"

I shook my head, my hair moving around my shoulders, the silky feel of it only making my skin pebble more. "Perfect."

A smile tipped Trace's lips as his fingers worked in and out of me. "Love watching you like this. Owning every part of your choices. Taking control of your pleasure."

I shuddered again, his fingers lighting little quakes in me. But my hands reached down and searched for a hold on Trace's shirt. I grabbed at the cotton, pulling it up and over, losing his fingers for a painful moment. But the loss for those handful of seconds only heightened the feeling when they returned.

And wasn't that life? How losing things sometimes made you appreciate their existence all the more.

Trace's fingers swirled inside me, making me whimper. I had to steady myself on his shoulders. My nails dug into taut muscles as those fingertips dragged down my inner walls.

"Don't come," he ordered. "I want to feel every flutter. Every pulse. I need to know what it is to drown in you."

My eyes locked with his. "Please." I needed to feel that. After all the tempting and teasing, the almosts and interruptions, I needed to know what it was to become one with this man. To have *all* of him.

"I've had a checkup, and it's been a long time for me," Trace said, his eyes not straying from mine.

"I have, too, and I'm on the pill. I want to feel all of you. No more half measures."

Trace's hips flexed as he lifted himself and pulled his pajamas down. My hand moved on instinct, wrapping around his thick length and stroking, once, twice, a third time.

"Ellie," Trace growled. "You undo me."

I dropped my mouth to his. "Lose yourself in me instead."

Trace's fingers were gone in a flash. His hands gripped my hips, but there were no forceful movements, not even a guiding sugges-tion. Instead, he let me take the lead as he looked into my eyes. "Your show. Your life. Whatever you need."

Emotion clogged the back of my throat. The way this man saw every last piece of me and let them all shine. Let them all be what-ever they needed to be.

As I sank onto Trace, my eyelids fluttered. I was nearly over-whelmed by the sheer stretch. But I didn't let myself miss a single thing. The scent of Trace all around me. The way his fingers tightened on my hips. How it felt to finally have him filling me.

"Don't steal those eyes from me, Blaze. Need to see you. All of you. Need to see that light green catch fire."

My eyes flew open at his words, connecting with his dark green depths. There was something about us sharing that color. How we were two sides of the same coin. The light and the dark. Balancing each other and coming together to create something neither of us could've done alone.

I rose slightly and then lowered again, this time not losing Trace for a second. He joined me there, hips flexing and helping me find a rhythm that was ours alone. The light and dark swirling together.

Trace's thumb circled my nipple, and then his fingers twisted the hard peak. It was as if someone had lit a sparkler above my head, and all the tiny flickers of light and flame danced across my skin. My body moved quicker now, the stretching glide nearly pulling me under.

But I never lost those dark green eyes. "Please," I begged.

"Need more, Blaze?"

"Yes," I breathed.

Trace gave me what I needed, just like he'd promised. His fingers tightened on my hips as he powered up, muscular thighs driving him into me. My mouth fell open, and my jaw fluttered as I took it all. The power, the emotion, the need.

We met each other in that desperate place, pouring everything we felt into it. The fear at the danger swirling. The anticipation of the unknown at our door. The emotion that we both hadn't yet named out loud.

Trace's finger found my clit and circled. "That's my girl. We find it together."

As the circles drew tighter over that bundle of nerves, the cord inside me wound so tight it was on the brink of fraying.

"Let me see the flames in that pale green. Let me watch you burn." One more flick of my clit, and I burst into flame.

I clamped down on Trace as my orgasm hit, so powerful that tiny flashes of rainbow light erupted in front of my eyes. But I still didn't close them. I didn't lose sight of Trace, not for a single second.

He arched up into me, going impossibly deeper, finding a spot that had another wave of sheer sensation hitting me with enough force that I had to hold on to Trace's shoulders. He thrust again, this time emptying into me but never losing my eyes.

I took it all. Everything Trace had to give. And somehow, through it all, I felt more like the me I was always meant to be because of it.

CHAPTER FORTY

Trace

I HUMMED TO A SONG ON THE OLDIES PLAYLIST ELLIE AND I HAD
settled on as I flipped pancakes on the griddle. We'd found this
was the one genre we could agree on, meeting in the middle of my
classic rock and her 90s pop. And like us, it somehow surprisingly
worked.

Ellie hopped up onto the counter and popped a raspberry into
her mouth. "Those look amazing."

"You look amazing."

Her hair had that tousled look that only came from one thing,
and it just so happened that the disarray made the different colors and
shades spring to life. She wore one of my old Seattle Sparks tees and
a pair of my boxer briefs she'd had to knot with a hair band from her
purse. But she was the most beautiful creature I'd ever seen.

Ellie's mouth quirked in an uneven smile. "You're making me
breakfast. You're already going to get lucky for that. You don't have
to sweet-talk me, too."

I leaned over, pulling her to me for a kiss. "Maybe I want to
sweet-talk you."

"I could get spoiled with this sort of treatment."

"Good," I muttered, just as the doorbell rang, making Gremlin leap from his dog bed and charge to the entryway. "I'll get it." I turned off the heat on the griddle and handed Ellie the spatula. "Put these on the platter, would you?"

"Only bachelor I know who has a platter that actually matches his other dishware," she called as she jumped down from the counter.

I chuckled as I headed for the door. "You admire my design taste, don't lie."

I opened the door to a tense Leah, and a Keely who was already running past me and inside. Gremlin's barks turned happy at his favorite person's return, but Leah seemed less so.

"Le," I greeted, a little surprised.

The tense expression on her face deepened to what could almost be classified as a scowl. "I texted you."

"Shit," I muttered. "I'm sorry. My phone's upstairs."

Leah's brows lifted at that, and I understood why. The curse slipping free, the phone not being on me at all times…neither was exactly characteristic of me.

"Ellie, why are you wearing Daddy's T-shirt?" Keely called from inside.

Ellie's response was muted, but I could still make out her words. "I, uh, got pancake mix on mine, so your dad let me borrow one of his."

"It's way too big on you," Keely said with a giggle.

Storm clouds rolled in on Leah's expression, and the bent of her lips was definitely in scowl territory now. "So, this was just about you getting laid? I turned my schedule upside down to take Keely yesterday when I had a huge presentation to prepare for at work, all because you made up some dramatic excuse to bang your neighbor?"

Anger surged, and I stepped out onto the front porch, forcing Leah to take a few steps back. "Lower your damn voice," I growled. "Ellie isn't just some random woman you can classify as my neighbor and nothing more. She's a woman I care about, and she's been through hell lately. Some creep is stalking her, most likely the ex who gave her a black eye, and he sent her a photo of himself or someone he paid standing over her with a knife while she slept. So, it's not some dramatic excuse."

Leah's face went pale, but it wasn't her voice I heard. It was Ellie's. "You care about me, Chief?"

I froze and then slowly turned around. "Yeah, Blaze. And if you didn't already know that, you haven't been paying attention."

Ellie's pale green eyes glittered like dew-covered moss. "I care about you, too."

"I know."

She let out a huff. "Your ego."

I just grinned at her and opened my arms. She walked right into them, not caring that she was only wearing an oversized tee and my boxers on my front porch in front of my ex-wife. I pressed a kiss to the top of her head.

Ellie looked up at Leah, her cheeks pinking. "I'm sorry. I would've changed if we knew you were coming over."

Leah swallowed, her face still that shade of pale. "It's okay. I'm really sorry for what you've been going through. If I can help in any way, just let me know."

I blinked a few times, trying to read beneath Leah's words to see if there was inauthenticity there. But I couldn't find any.

"Thank you," Ellie said quietly.

Leah's gaze lifted to mine. "We were never right for each other. Too similar and too stubborn."

A surprised chuckle left my lips. "You're right there."

Her expression turned a little wistful. "But we did make one hell of a daughter."

"Never gonna regret that," I told her honestly.

Leah nodded, a hint of sadness creeping into her eyes. "I'm sorry. For what I put you through. It wasn't about you. I had some stuff going on, and I didn't deal with it well. I should've talked to you. Ended things before…"

I knew what she meant. Before she messed around with someone else. But I understood, too. "I wasn't giving you what you needed because I couldn't. Because we weren't…"

I struggled for the right words, but it was Leah who spoke them. "We weren't what we should've been."

"No," I admitted.

"I can take her tonight if you need," Leah offered.

"What about your presentation at work?" I asked.

"I'll deal." Leah sent Ellie a small smile. "Plus, we're working on a fishtail braid from that site you sent. Might not hurt to get a little practice in."

"You two are going to look killer," Ellie said with a grin.

My arm tightened around Ellie. "Might be a good idea until we get this thing sorted out." The last thing I wanted was Bradley or whoever was responsible showing up when Keely was here.

"I've got her. Just text if you need anything else." Leah didn't linger, just gave us both a wave and headed for her car.

"That was...good, right?" Ellie asked, still staring after Leah.

"It was good. I think we're finding our way." My hand slid along Ellie's jaw, bringing her focus back to me. "You make everything better. Make me realize how everything can be more."

"You do, too," she whispered.

My mouth dropped to hers, taking it in a deep kiss that lived out those words.

"Eeeewwwwww," Keely screeched from the doorway.

Ellie and I pulled apart, and I had the urge to let another curse free. This was not how I'd imagined Keely finding out about Ellie and me. I'd wanted to sit her down, explain things. Give her a chance to express anything she was feeling. But, apparently, my kid didn't have any issues doing that here and now.

Keely's hands went to her hips. "I hope you know you both have cooties now. Don't even try to share my drink." And with that, she took off for the kitchen, Grem on her heels.

A laugh bubbled out of Ellie. "Did we just get burned by a six-year-old?"

"She's brutal. Gets it from Auntie Arden," I admitted.

Ellie stretched up on her toes, her lips hovering just over mine. "Worth it."

CHAPTER FORTY-ONE

Ellie

"HERE'S YOUR SECONDARY ALARM PANEL. IT HAS A PANIC BUTTON, in addition to the others strategically placed around the house," Holt Hartley instructed.

"You mean the dozen over-the-top buttons I'll likely hit by mistake and bring every emergency response team in a sixty-mile radius to my door?" I asked.

His lips twitched. "You have to hold it down for five seconds to activate, so don't worry about accidentally bumping anything."

I wasn't sure what I'd expected when the silent partner of Anchor Security showed up at my house yesterday morning along with a team from their Seattle office. Maybe a man in a suit and sunglasses with a gun at his hip? Instead, Holt had arrived in jeans, boots, and a Cedar Ridge Search & Rescue T-shirt, looking like he should be on the cover of some outdoorsy men's magazine.

Trace's arm came around me, pulling me to him and squeezing. "It's not overkill."

I looked up at him and rolled my eyes. "You put a sensor on a window that only Gremlin could fit through."

My dog barked at his name being uttered and danced in a circle. Holt chuckled. "That dog is something."

Grem ran over to the security expert, and Holt picked him up, scratching his belly.

Trace scowled. "Why does that dog like everyone but me?"

"Good taste?" Holt suggested.

I couldn't help but laugh.

The front door to my house opened, and Lolli appeared, carrying what looked like a wrapped piece of art and wearing a tie-dyed workout set covered in countless bedazzled pot leaves. "Oooooh, goody! I didn't miss the hottie brigade."

Holt chuckled. "I'd never miss saying hello to you, Miss Lolli."

I swore Lolli blushed. "You are a sweet-talker, Holt."

"I speak the truth," he said.

"I'm gonna tell Wren you were hitting on my grandma," Trace clipped.

Holt just grinned wider. "She'd understand."

From the little Anson and Trace had shared, Holt and his wife, Wren, had an epic love story. One that spanned decades and had its share of heartache and strife mixed in. But they'd found their way back to each other, and I doubted anything on this Earth could separate them again.

Lolli giggled and offered me the wrapped piece in her hands. "For you. I've been working 'round the clock to get it finished."

A smile spread across my face. "Really?"

"I think it'll go perfect in your living room."

Trace tensed at my side. "If you made it, it probably needs a triple-X warning."

"Chief, be nice," I chastised.

Lolli waved me off. "I'm used to this stick-in-the-mud, but I'm counting on you to loosen him up a little."

"I'm trying, Lolli. Trust me." I ripped into the paper, trying to get to the artwork below.

"I can't wait to see this one," Holt murmured. "But I'm not sure anything can beat diamond donut dicks."

I laughed as the paper fell away, leaving an explosion of color. Across the canvas was a huge rainbow with various flying creatures that mirrored the mural I'd created. But below it was an array of mushrooms in various shapes and sizes, all with a distinctly phallic bent.

"Lolli," I croaked as laughter caught in my throat.

"You have to admit. Their tips just kind of ask for this sort of treatment," Lolli said with a grin.

"Magic mushroom dicks," Holt muttered.

Lolli turned to him. "Have you explored the world of psychedelics much? They can really amp up sexual escapades."

"Lolli," Trace warned.

"You can't haul me away, popo," Lolli shot back. "You might be part of *The Man* but I'm well within my legal rights."

Holt tried to cover his laugh with a cough. "I'm bringing Wren with me next time. I need her to see Lolli in action."

"For the love of God, let that *next time* be because you're on vacation," Trace muttered.

"Deal," Holt said.

I lifted the canvas, making it catch the light. "Thank you for my beeeeautiful diamond painting, Lolli. I'm going to hang it over the mantel."

Trace groaned, but Lolli beamed and leaned in to kiss my cheek. "Have I told you lately that you're my favorite?"

"I'm telling the sibs," Trace said, sounding affronted.

"Buzzkill," she shot back.

I laughed full-out for the first time since I'd found the pictures in my mailbox. And damn, it felt good.

"Marry me." Walter's lips twitched as he flung the towel to rest on his shoulder.

"No." Lolli's face screwed up in annoyance.

"Marry me," he said, not deterred in the slightest.

Chasing SHELTER

303

"I told you, you old coot, *no*. Are you losing your hearing along with your brains?"

Walter shot me a sly smile as I poured a coffee refill into a mug. "I love it when she gets feisty," he murmured.

"I'd be careful," Thea said as she restocked baked goods following the breakfast rush. "Lolli's been taking lessons at Kye's gym."

Lolli took up a fighting stance that looked nothing like the things Kye had taught me. "Damn straight. Cross me, and I'll take you out." Her hand sliced through the air like some bad kung fu movie.

"You know," Walter began, "I could be a hell of a sparring partner."

Lolli straightened, lifting her chin. "You can't keep up with me. I'm training to take down that Mateo fella."

I nearly choked as I set the coffee pot back in place. "Mateo the professional fighter?"

She sent a huff in my direction. "I don't appreciate your skepticism, young lady."

"Watch out," Thea warned. "Her *young lady* is the highest insult."

I couldn't help my laugh. "Sorry, Lolli. I believe in you. But having Walter practice with you might not be a bad idea." I sent him a wink.

Lolli gave him a once-over. "How's your flexibility?"

Walter made a show of lifting his hands in the air and then reaching down to his toes. "Following you to yoga every week has its benefits."

I put a hand over my heart as I turned to Thea. "Swoon."

"I know, right?" she said.

Lolli waved him off. "How about your strength?"

Walter flexed his biceps and held the arm out for her to feel. "What do you think I get from cleaning all the massive pots and pans?"

I tried not to giggle as Lolli felt him up and instead moved to drop the cup of coffee off for Harrison, who'd been seated in a corner for a few hours with what seemed to be casefiles. "Here you go. Is there anything else I can get you?"

Harrison looked up and smiled. "All good. Thanks for keeping me in caffeine."

"Happy to. And the entertainment's free."

He chuckled as he took in Lolli comparing Walter's two biceps. "When is she going to cave and head down the aisle with the poor guy?"

"I don't know, but I can't wait to see her outfit when she does."

"I'm not sure any of us are prepared for that," Harrison muttered.

"You're probably right."

His expression shifted then as if he were trying to study me a bit closer. "Are you holding up okay? Trace said you got the new security system in place at your house."

I shifted as if I could avoid the reminder of what was swirling around me. "I'm good. We're being careful. Maybe not as careful as Linc and Trace would like, but nothing but a twelve-person security team and drone coverage would make them happy."

It had been a battle to get them to settle for the back door being locked and chained and a squad car stationed out front. They'd finally given in.

One corner of Harrison's mouth kicked up, but it quickly dropped again. "You and Trace…"

He let the words hang, and I winced. "It just sort of happened. I wasn't looking for it, but—"

"It found you," Harrison broke in.

"I guess it did. Sometimes, when something's right, it doesn't wait around for you to be ready."

A little hint of sadness filtered into Harrison's gaze. "You might be right about that."

I wanted to tell him that he'd find the right girl. The timing might be inconvenient or the pairing unexpected, but it would knock him sideways in the best possible way. I didn't, though. It felt too much like overstepping or placating. Instead, I just said, "Flag me down if you need another cup."

I headed back to Lolli and Walter's playful bickering and re-stocking with Thea. Soon, the lunch rush hit, and we waded through orders and tables until that eased. As it did, I saw Beth standing by Harrison's table, her iced latte in hand. They traded some words as he packed up, and then Beth took the table next to the one he'd been sitting at, opening her own files.

Realization dawned.

Rounding the bakery case, I headed straight for her table. Beth looked up as I approached, her eyes widening a fraction at what I was sure was the very annoyed expression on my face.

"H-hey, Ellie."

"He's having you guys watch me, isn't he?"

Beth's gaze darted to the side. "I, um. Who?"

My eyes narrowed on her. "Keep with the cop work because you do not have a future in acting."

"Ellie—"

I pulled the apron over my head and tossed it onto the counter. "I'll be back after I get Trace arrested for stalking or false imprisonment or being impossibly overbearing and whatever else I can throw at him."

Thea started to laugh. "I'm surprised it took you this long to realize you had a security detail."

"I hate you all," I called over my shoulder.

CHAPTER FORTY-TWO

Trace

LEANING BACK IN MY CHAIR, I PINCHED THE BRIDGE OF MY NOSE. That convenient pressure point did nothing for me now as I listened to Gabriel walk me through the latest updates.

"How could he have dropped off the face of the Earth?" I ground out. "A camera *somewhere* should've caught him."

"I don't know," Gabriel said. "Bradley's got money and connections."

I sat up at that. "Do you think the parents know more than they're saying?"

Gabriel ran a hand over his stubbled cheek. "Hard to say. The dad, Henrick, told me to call his lawyer, so he's ducking for cover. The mom, Helen, has called me no less than a dozen times to see if I've gotten any leads on her son. She seems genuinely worried."

"So maybe the dad's funding Bradley's getaway," I suggested.

"He wouldn't need to. As far as I can tell, Bradley's got plenty of money socked away. And like many people in that set, a significant amount of it is in Switzerland."

I let out a sound of frustration. Some countries' international banking laws meant tracing money in and out of those accounts was nearly impossible.

"We've got his picture circulating. Hotels, motels, rentals, and every place we can think of," Gabriel assured me. "If he shows in Sparrow Falls or any of the towns in this county, we'll know."

Unless he'd changed his appearance or had a fake ID. But that wasn't something I could control. All I could do now was stay vigilant and trust the people I had looking out for Ellie.

"What about Jasper?" I didn't want to think about my father, let alone speak his name. But I needed to know that, too.

"Restraining order has been served. He has to stay at least one hundred yards away from you, Keely, Ellie, and Leah. It may be enough to send him back inside to finish his term. His parole officer is talking to the board, but if this temporary order becomes permanent, it definitely will."

That was something, at least. Not nearly enough, but something.

"Thank you." That wasn't enough either, but it was all I could give Gabriel at the moment.

"There's one more thing we gotta talk about," my friend went on.

"Not sure I can handle *one more thing*," I admitted.

"Will."

I cursed.

Gabriel tossed a copy of some paperwork onto my desk. "This was emailed to him this morning, notifying him of his termination."

"We get a response to that?" I asked.

"Laney let me know that he replied with a number of expletives and a promise to call his union rep so he could, and I quote, *'fry our asses.'*"

I grunted. "It'll never come back on us."

"Nope. You gave him too many chances, and multiple people witnessed his infractions. We're good there."

"I won't miss having him around here."

"Me either." Gabriel glanced at the door as if he could see through it. "I think we should consider giving Fletcher Will's desk.

He's been showing initiative, has attention to detail, and most of all, he doesn't piss off everyone around him."

I couldn't argue with the points Gabriel made. "Do it."

"All right, then. I'm going to—"

Gabriel's words cut off as my door flew open and Ellie filled the entryway—five foot seven inches of pissed-off glory. "Chief, you are so totally grounded."

Gabriel tried to cover a laugh with a cough. "Told you she'd know before the day was out." He pushed to his feet but stopped to whisper something in Ellie's ear on his way out. I could just make out the words. "Go easy on him. He's worried as hell about you."

A little of the edge to Ellie's anger eased, but she still had plenty of heat behind those pale green eyes as she stepped farther into my office and closed the door behind her.

"Ellie—"

"You said my life was my own."

"It is. Doesn't mean I'm not going to protect it. Keep it safe."

"You need my permission for that."

One corner of my mouth kicked up. "Apparently, I don't."

Those beautiful eyes narrowed on me. "I could make your life very difficult. I could fight you every step of the way. I could turn your organization upside down, undo your linen closet's color-coding system, put the ketchup in the mustard's spot, mess with your medicine cabinet's alphabetized product arrangement. I could make you live in blue-balled hell."

"I'm already in blue-balled hell. So are you."

She let out a huff. "Too attractive and charming for your own good."

"You're so damn beautiful when you're pissed at me."

Ellie softened more. "You don't play fair."

"No, I don't. Now, come here."

"No."

"Ellie."

"No."

"Please?" I prodded.

"Damn you," she muttered but crossed to me.

The moment she was within arm's reach, I pulled her into my lap. She landed with an *oomph,* and I curved my arms around her. "I'm sorry."

"No, you're not."

"I'm sorry I made you feel like I was taking the choice out of your hands. I should've taken the time to make my arguments."

Ellie leaned back in my hold so she could take in my face. "And you think you'd win that argument, don't you?"

"I know I would." I kissed the tip of her nose. "Because it's the smart play. We needed someone inside the bakery in case the unexpected happened. Did Fletcher or Beth interrupt your workday in any way?"

"No," she grumbled.

"Did they make you feel like you were under surveillance or living in a police state?"

This time, Ellie simply clamped her mouth shut, giving me her unspoken answer.

"They were getting paid to sip a latte and have a snack, catch up on some paperwork, and keep you *safe.* Is that really so bad?"

"Why do you have to be so dang reasonable?" she growled.

"It's my superpower." I brushed my lips across hers. "Do you know how hard it was for me to leave you there this morning?" Empathy flooded Ellie's expression. "It was like walking away and leaving my heart right on the counter. It nearly killed me. But I did it because I don't want to steal that sense of normalcy from you."

"Chief," she whispered, nuzzling into me. "I'm sorry."

"You have nothing to be sorry about."

"I'm sorry I didn't think enough about how this might be making *you* feel."

I pulled her tighter against me. "Well, this is why we talk things out."

Ellie smiled against my neck. "That is very adult of us. Pretty sure this is a mature relationship or something."

"Or something," I said with a chuckle.

"I need to go back to The Mix Up. I stormed out and told Thea I was going to perform a citizen's arrest."

That had me laughing harder. "I've got cuffs on my belt. Feel free to use them."

Ellie pulled back and quirked a brow. "I think I could be into that, Chief."

"Good to know." I kissed her, forcing myself not to take it deeper, and then helped her up. "Come on. I'll walk you out."

She started to argue and then stopped herself. "Thank you."

I guided Ellie through the bullpen and out onto the sidewalk. While the temperatures were certainly dropping, the sun shone brighter than ever. "Pick you up in an hour?" I asked as Ellie started down the street.

"I'll be the one with the badass security detail," Ellie called back.

"Tell Beth you called her a badass. It'll make her day."

Ellie laughed. "Will do."

The screech of tires had my head jerking up, trying to find the source of the sound. A sedan with darkened windows but more than a little wear and tear on its body tore away from the curb a block down. I reached for my radio to call it in to patrol when the vehicle veered off course. Not taking off down the road but heading straight for Ellie.

CHAPTER FORTY-THREE

Trace

THE WORLD AROUND ME SLOWED AND SPED UP ALL AT ONCE, everything in supersonic speed until it froze for single snapshots. The sedan jerking to the right. Someone screaming. Ellie's head snapping up. Her eyes going wide with shock.

There was nothing between her and the vehicle other than open road and a curb. Nothing that would slow or stop it. Some part of me was aware of movement. I ran. With everything I had in me.

A burn lit in my thighs, my lungs. I pushed harder as the smell of burning rubber filled the air. I hit Ellie around the middle, sending us both flying. We landed hard, me on my back and Ellie on top of me, but I didn't stop. I rolled us until we reached the cover of a parked vehicle.

I caught the sound of brakes and squealing tires again, then nothing. For the count of one, two, three. Then shouts, a muffled array of voices. But all I could think about was Ellie.

I rolled us one more time until I had her on the sidewalk, being as gentle as possible. Her eyelids fluttered as she looked up at me. "Wha—?"

My hands hovered over her face, where an angry gash sliced her brow. "Tell me where it hurts."

"I-I don't know. Trace, are you—?" She started to sit up, but I held her down.

"Don't move. Not yet."

Her brow furrowed, and then she winced in pain. "You're moving, and you're the one who pulled some Hercules, football-star move."

Relief flooded my system at Ellie's fire returning. "I'm fine," I assured her, but my head thrummed, and my back was on fire.

Footsteps thundered down the sidewalk.

"What the hell happened?" Gabriel barked.

"Tan sedan, darkened windows, some dents and scratches. Didn't get a make, model, or plate, but it wasn't super new." The description poured out of me automatically.

Beth was there, repeating it into the radio at her shoulder.

Gabriel turned to the other deputies and began snapping orders. "Where the hell are the EMTs?"

As if he'd beckoned them by sheer force of will, sirens sounded. An ambulance and a fire truck rounded the corner, blaring onto Cascade Avenue.

"Oh, geez," Ellie muttered, trying to sit up again. This time, she batted at my hands. "I'm fine. I think I got the gash when we rolled. Just let me get up."

I took her hand and gently helped her sit. "How's your vision? Any blurriness or seeing double?"

"No, just an epic headache." Ellie frowned. "But you have some blood on your temple. Did you hit your head?"

"Probably," I muttered.

Two EMTs jumped out of the ambulance, a few firefighters following. The younger woman, Susie, instantly went to Ellie, while the older man, Shawn, made his way to me.

"Trace, I expected better of you than some stunt like this," Shawn muttered as he set down a gear bag.

"You know me, always making trouble."

Susie snorted. "Never broke a rule a day in his life." She turned to Ellie. "I see this nice gash on your brow, but anything else hurt?"

Ellie's lips thinned. "It kind of hurts everywhere, but nothing feels broken."

Both Shawn and Susie began their quick assessments, but it wasn't long before Shawn said, "I think we need to take you both to the ER, just to be safe."

I instantly shook my head. "No. No hospital for me. Let's get Ellie in the rig and—"

"Oh, no you don't, Chief," Ellie argued. "You're not sending me off. Both of us or neither of us."

"Jesus, you two," Gabriel muttered.

"I'll call Dr. Avery. See if he might make a house call. Or maybe we can go to his clinic," I said, trying to placate my friend.

"*I'll* call him," Gabriel shot back. "You call, and you'll classify this as a papercut and a bump on the head."

Ellie snickered. "He knows you so well."

I sent a scowl in her direction, but it died as I took in the gash again. "Are you sure you're okay? I hit you hard, and—"

"Trace," she said, cutting me off. "You saved my life. A few bumps and bruises are a hell of a lot better than getting flattened by a car."

I reached out and cupped her face with my hand. "Don't remind me. Scared the hell out of me, Blaze."

"I'm okay. I promise."

But she wouldn't be if we didn't find whoever the hell was behind the wheel of that car.

"Don't either of you move," Nora instructed in a tone that brooked no argument. She set down a tray stacked high with three different beverages, some soup, fresh biscuits, and pain meds on Ellie's coffee table.

Ellie and I had spent the past couple of hours at Dr. Avery's, where he gave us both very thorough examinations. Ellie's gash had required liquid stitches, and mine the old-fashioned kind since it was on my scalp. We both had our share of scrapes, but overall, we'd been remarkably lucky.

I met Nora's stare. "You know I'm not taking the pills."

She huffed out a breath and pulled two small bottles from her apron pocket. "Fine. Tylenol and ibuprofen for you."

That was all I ever allowed myself to take. Even when I had my appendix removed in my early twenties, I didn't dip into the narcotics my doctor had prescribed. Given my genetic makeup, it wasn't a risk I was willing to take.

Ellie sent me a sidelong look. "Are you sure? Your back looked pretty rough."

That had taken the hit the hardest, and moving quickly anytime soon would be rough, but I'd be okay. I reached over and squeezed her hand. "I'm all right."

A hard knock sounded on the front door.

"I've got it," Nora said, moving quickly in that direction.

A cacophony of voices filled the air, but Linc's rose above it all. "Where is she? Where's my sister?"

"Breathe, Cowboy," Arden ordered. "Having you threatening to burn the world down won't help."

Linc was already moving down the hall toward the living room.

"I'm fine, ConCon. Just a little liquid bandage, and I'm good to go," Ellie assured him before he even reached the room.

Linc stormed over to her, looking back and forth between us. "A car tried to run you over?"

Ellie grimaced. "We don't know—"

"Yes," I said, cutting her off. There was no use in lying to Linc. It would just make things worse in the long run.

"Maybe we need to get you out of here, El—"

"No," Ellie clipped, a finality in her tone. "This asshole doesn't get to make me run."

I reached over and wove my fingers through hers, squeezing as most of my siblings and their partners filed into the room. Shep looked like he'd come straight from a jobsite, while Thea was still in her Mix Up tee. Cope was clad in workout gear, but Sutton and Luca weren't in tow. Given the paint splatters on her clothes and in her hair, Arden had definitely come from her studio. Kye was in sparring attire, and Rhodes had on a Bloom & Berry tee. The only sib missing was Fallon, but she was probably still at work.

I lifted Ellie's hand to my mouth, lips ghosting over her knuckles. "You don't have to go anywhere you don't want to, but we need someone sticking close, given this latest...incident." I glanced at Rhodes. "Where's Anson?"

His take on the situation would be invaluable. This latest stunt was a big step up from terrifying, threatening notes, and I couldn't help but feel it was different somehow. Rasher. Crossing the line to actual harm. Then again, maybe this was the perp escalating.

Rhodes looked from me to Ellie and back again. "He's with Gabriel. He wanted to help."

I knew that help came with a cost. Anson had walked away from the FBI for a reason. There were too many ghosts for him there, demons. But he was putting his profiler hat back on for Ellie. For me.

Before I could say anything else, my phone rang. Releasing Ellie's hand, I grabbed the device from the coffee table and read the name on the screen. *Gabriel.*

I stood, ignoring my back's angry protest, and strode toward the kitchen for a little bit of privacy. "What did you find?"

Gabriel didn't answer right away. That told me whatever it was, it wasn't good. He cleared his throat. "We found the vehicle. Abandoned off County Road 18. Perp wiped it clean but forgot the latch for the trunk. We got a clean print."

"Whose?" It was only one word, but there was so much tension radiating through it that I almost didn't recognize my own voice.

"It belongs to Jasper Killington. I'm sorry, Trace. It was your dad."

CHAPTER FORTY-FOUR

Ellie

THE ENTIRE COLSON CREW THAT WAS PRESENT, WAS TRYING TO keep things light. They talked about my new diamond art proudly displayed on the mantel. The shenanigans Luca and Keely had been up to at Cope's house this afternoon. Anything but accidents and threats and break-ins.

But my gaze was locked on the hallway Trace had disappeared down as if I could see through the wall and into the kitchen. He wasn't gone long; I could tell that by the clock that rested on the far end of the mantel. But it felt like an eternity.

The moment I caught the sound of footsteps through the din of conversation, I braced and sat up straighter. My gaze locked on Trace's face as he came into view. And found nothing there. No lines of tension or ease of relief. The only thing I saw was the absence of... everything. As if Trace had wiped it clean away.

"What is it?" I asked.

Trace shoved his phone into his pocket. "I need to go in. Gabriel thinks he found the vehicle. Wants me to identify it for sure."

"Trace, no," Nora argued. "You need to rest."

"I'm fine, Mom. I've got to go."

I stared hard at him. That all made sense. Finding the vehicle. Needing Trace's confirmation. It was just…something was off.

I stood despite the cries from my abused muscles and bones and moved toward Trace. Most people would've missed it, but I didn't, the slight tensing at my approach. That tiny flicker of movement had my brow furrowing and pain erupting at the reminder of the gash there.

"What's wrong?" I asked, my voice dipping low.

Trace stared down at me but made no move to touch me like he normally would. No caress of my face. No fingers tangling in my hair. No grabbing my hand.

"They need me. I have to get going," he said quietly, still making no move for connection.

"Okay, but—"

Trace leaned in and pressed the gentlest of kisses to the temple farthest from my injury, and then he was gone. My skin tingled at the absence of his mouth, and my eyes stung. Because it felt like a goodbye.

A soft hand landed on my shoulder. "You should sit down. You need to take it easy," Nora said, guiding me back to the couch.

I glanced over my shoulder, hearing an engine start outside and knowing it was Trace.

Nora helped me sit and patted my hand. "I brought my heating pad. It does wonders for sore muscles. Want me to break that out while you eat?"

My eyes stung again, but for a different reason. I'd never had this, not really. The sort of caretaking that was so hands-on. I had a couple of memories of my mom sitting with me and reading me a story when I was under the weather, but she never made me soup or broke out a heating pad. That was something she would've had our housekeeper or cook do.

The simple kindness of Nora's offer had an ache flaring to life in my chest. Missing my mom and longing for the parent she'd never been able to be, even if she'd wanted to.

"Oh, Ellie." Nora moved in instantly, seeing the unshed tears in my eyes. She wrapped a gentle arm around me as the room went quiet. "It's been a day. Just let it out if you need to. We all get it."

"I just—" A hiccupped cry left my lips. "I've never had this." My gaze moved to Linc. "We never had this."

He moved then, coming to sit on my other side and taking my hand. "But we have it now."

I smiled at him through blurry vision. "We do."

The front door opened and closed, footsteps sounding. "What's with the teary eyes?" Lolli demanded, somehow managing to look both worried and affronted. "Are you hurting? Don't worry, I brought my new tea. It's a pot and poppy blend that will knock you out until next week. My taste-tester did tell me she saw pink bunnies for a few days, but you don't mind that, do you?"

Everyone stared at her for a long moment and then burst out laughing. It was exactly what I needed.

Hours had passed with no word from Trace. I'd texted three times and called twice. No response, other than his voicemail message. Every moment that passed had my stomach twisting tighter.

The front door opened, and I instantly leaned forward, praying it was Trace. Instead, Fallon appeared, looking exhausted and more than a little beaten down. I watched as she tried to pull on a happier face as she entered the living room. "Ellie, how are you feeling? I'm so sorry."

"I'm a lot better now." It wasn't a total lie. The pounding in my head had eased, and while I was achy in different parts of my body, it wasn't awful.

"Good. That's good." Fallon let out a breath.

Kye moved into her space, a small scowl on his lips as he took the bag from her shoulder. "Something's wrong."

"Something's always wrong," Fallon muttered. "Nature of the job."

That scowl deepened. "Did anyone give you a hard time? I can—"

"No. Just a hard day," Fallon said, lowering her voice. "It happens."

A muscle in Kye's jaw twitched as his grip on her bag tightened. "Come on. We saved you some dinner."

As he guided her into the kitchen, I leaned back on the couch cushions and grabbed my phone. The screen was still glaringly blank.

"Still nothing?" Arden asked softly.

I shook my head. "I'm starting to get worried."

"When Trace is on a case, he can have blinders on. Nothing but the task in front of him."

I knew Arden was trying to reassure me, but doubt and worry still niggled at me.

The door opened again. I braced, but this time, Anson appeared, with Kye and Fallon—and a plate piled high with food—on his heels.

"Is Trace with you?" I asked instantly.

Anson's jaw flexed before he spoke. "Still at the station. They're trying to find his dad."

"His dad?" I parroted.

"Jasper's prints were in the vehicle. He's the one who tried to hit you."

I pulled the blanket tighter around my shoulders as I sat on the back deck steps, Bumper nosing at my hand. It was past her bedtime, but I couldn't find it in me to put her away in her little shed home quite yet.

"They say animals know when you need comfort," I mumbled. "You're pretty good at that."

Bumper laid her head on my knee and let out a rumbling sigh. I scratched her head as a thank-you.

The door opened and closed behind me, but I didn't look up. Maybe if I didn't, whoever it was would go away. I didn't want words of comfort or platitudes that fell flat. I was too worried about Trace, and too hurt that he'd shut me out.

Heavy footsteps sounded across the deck. Definitely a man. Since that was the case, my best guess was Linc. So, I was surprised when I saw scarred motorcycle boots hit the steps.

"Heard you had a goat back here," Kye said as he sat next to me. He held out a hand for my animal friend to sniff.

"This is Bumper. Keely named her." Even saying that hurt, a reminder of a simpler time.

The goat bumped Kye's hand, and he chuckled. "Appropriate name."

I gripped the blanket and stared out into the dark as Kye stroked Bumper's head. Neither of us said anything for a while, but finally, Kye started to speak.

"He's going to try to push you away. Don't let him."

I glanced over at Kye, but he didn't meet my gaze, just kept petting Bumper.

"Trace and I...we have a different sort of bond than the rest of them."

I frowned. "You all seem pretty close to me." The Colsons shared the kind of bonds that showed what family should be. The kindness and care. The loyalty.

"We are," Kye said. "But that's not what I mean. All of us who came in through foster care have baggage. But mine and Trace's... it's darker."

A hollow feeling took root inside me. "He's told me some." But I didn't know what Kye's story was or what sorts of scars he bore. The way he said *darker* told me it was bad.

"That's good. Good that he's started to share. But I guarantee you it's worse than what he's told you. His old man was a piece of work. Never should've seen the outside of a jail cell or coffin."

That hollow feeling inside me intensified, anguish twisting at everything Trace could've endured at such a young age.

"But it's worse because Jasper got in Trace's head. It's why everything's law and order, playing by the rules, and drill-sergeant tidiness. Everything his childhood wasn't. The opposite of what his dad is."

"He's nothing like his dad," I spat.

Kye turned then, and I saw pain swirling in his amber eyes. "I know that. You know that. But Trace? I don't think he's so sure. And the fact that his father tried to hurt you? It's going to fuck with his head. He'll think he can't have this—the good he has with you. So, he's gonna push you away. Might even try to blow it up so there's no turning back."

Kye let out a shuddered breath. "Don't let him." Those amber eyes glistened. "Trace is the best man I've ever known. He deserves you. Deserves everything good in this world. Don't let him throw it all away because he thinks he doesn't."

My heart broke then. For Trace. For Kye. For all they'd lived through at such young ages. "I won't," I whispered.

"He'll fight you on it."

One corner of my mouth kicked up. "Good thing I've been getting some ass-kicking lessons."

Kye let out a low chuckle. "Good thing."

I laid my hand over his tattooed one, squeezing for a brief second before releasing it. "You know, you deserve that goodness, too."

Kye's gaze shifted, just the barest flick toward the house before returning to the night in front of us. "My head's too fucked up for good."

My lips pursed. "Never heard anything so far from the truth."

Kye grunted and scratched between Bumper's ears. "Go get your man. I'll get Bump in the shed for the night."

I let him have the play for now because Trace needed me. But Kye needed someone, too.

CHAPTER FORTY-FIVE

Trace

I STARED UP AT MY HOUSE, EVERY WINDOW DARK—JUST LIKE IT always was on the nights I didn't have Keely. But the darkness hit harder tonight. It reminded me of how everything had felt before Ellie. How it would feel again now.

But it was worth it. Anything to keep her safe. Because my life wouldn't stop bleeding into hers.

Even if they found Jasper and added a couple of additional years to his sentence, he'd get out again. And if this latest stunt had taught me anything, it was that he would never stop. He was too focused on me.

Now, I couldn't help but wonder again if he'd been the one sending Ellie the threatening photos and notes. If he'd been the one who broke into her house. The tech piece seemed a little above his pay grade, but who knew what he picked up in prison?

My phone dinged, and I plucked it out of the cupholder. There were countless notifications for texts and calls. The number that had come from Ellie had my gut souring, but I zeroed in on the newest message.

Dex: *Still coming up empty on the software. Their servers are in Russia, and it's nearly impossible to get access. But I did find the vehicle you asked about on surveillance footage. Route 66 Gas yesterday at a little after 8 p.m., but the guy paid in cash, so I don't have an ID yet.*

The photo filled the screen, and I fought back a curse.

Me: *No need to get an ID. I know him.*

Dex: *Who is it?*

Me: *My father.*

At least we had a second line of confirmation. Jasper had been in possession of the vehicle yesterday evening. He hadn't reported it stolen today. He'd done this. Because he didn't want me to have even an ounce of happiness and would do anything to take it away.

A numbness settled inside me, and I welcomed it. I'd need it in the days to come. I pulled it over me like a comforting blanket as I'd done countless times as a child when I needed to lock it all out.

Turning off my engine, I slid out of the SUV and headed for my front door. I unlocked it, and my alarm instantly started beeping. I quickly disarmed it and headed toward the kitchen, but before I reached it, a light in the living room flipped on.

My hand went for the holster on my belt—an instinctive reaction—but I cursed when I found it empty. Only, by then, I saw the familiar figure curled up in one of my overstuffed chairs.

I glowered at Ellie. "You know I carry a gun, right? I could've killed you."

"I also know that you stow it in a locker in the back of your SUV because you don't want guns in the house where your daughter sleeps." Ellie slowly unfurled from the chair and stood.

The urge to throw up my hands to ward her off was so damn strong. As if that would somehow stop her. Because if anyone could fight that numbness, it was Ellie. And right now, what I needed was to *not* feel.

She walked toward me, her gaze never straying from my face.

"What are you doing here? You should be resting."

"I should be where you are." Her words weren't angry or loud; they were rooted in a certainty I couldn't share. Not knowing the truth.

"You shouldn't be anywhere near me." It was the only thing I could think to say. The only weapon I had to hold her at bay.

Ellie's steps stilled, and her head tilted to one side as if that change in perspective would give her the clarity she needed. "Is that truly what you think?"

"Yes." The answer came instantly. The total and complete truth.

A sadness swept through Ellie's beautiful eyes. It made the pale green turn almost gray in the low light. "Well, I don't agree."

My back teeth gnashed in a vicious blow. "It's not your choice."

"Isn't it?" she pressed, moving closer—too close.

That bergamot and rose scent swirled around me, nearly strangling me with the promise of her.

She came to a stop right in front of me, her fuzzy boots in some ridiculous color nearly toe-to-toe with my boring-colored ones. "I'm not going anywhere."

"You should. You should fucking run. Because my family is nothing but the worst of the worst, and they ruin everything they touch."

Ellie wasn't cowed; she barely even blinked. "I was with your family tonight. They're everything."

"You know what I mean," I ground out.

"No. I don't. Because family is a hell of a lot more than genes and birth records. It's about the people who show up for you time and time again. The people who make you who you are. And that will always be the Colsons."

My breaths came quicker, ragged grasps at oxygen that never seemed to quite grab hold. "It doesn't matter how much I want them to be mine. Doesn't matter that I made Colson my last name. It's *his* blood running through my veins."

Ellie's eyes flashed a bright green, her temper catching fire. "And you think I don't share that battle? My father *killed* people. He ordered executions for power and sport. *That's* what flows through *my* veins."

I shook my head, stalking around her. "It's not the same."

"Isn't it?" she demanded.

Ellie was nothing but goodness and light. A force so many people had tried to dull over the years. But all had failed. She was so much stronger than all of them, just by her refusal to stop blooming.

"You don't understand." I turned to face her, needing her to see. "He's in me." I slammed a fist against my chest. "That temper. That rage. I fight it back all the time, but I can still feel it. The urge to let it all fly."

Ellie wasn't dissuaded. She only moved in closer, her delicate fingers wrapping around my fist and holding on. "He doesn't get to decide who you are. Only *you* get to do that. You might have anger that lives inside you, but you aim it at injustice. You might have a temper, but you never let it get the best of you. You've taken every bit of pain and turned it into fuel. The best father. The best brother. The best man. I will never run from you because you're everything I ever dreamed of."

CHAPTER FORTY-SIX

Ellie

I COULD FEEL TRACE'S HEART HAMMERING AGAINST MY fingertips. Could feel his breaths coming in ragged inhales and exhales. I could see the anger blazing in those dark green eyes. But I didn't let go. Trace never did, and neither would I. Because he deserved someone who would hold on for him. Someone who would keep him from breaking.

"Not going anywhere." I squeezed my fingers tighter around his fist, pressing both our hands against his chest. Holding him together when he felt like everything was falling apart.

Unshed tears glistened in Trace's eyes. "I can't let him hurt you."

I'd thought my heart had broken when Kye shared those delicate truths on my back deck, but it shattered now. I should've known this was at the core of it all. A need to keep me safe.

My hand gripped Trace's harder. "He's not going to hurt me. Because we're not going to let him."

"No matter what I do, he's always there, haunting me," Trace ground out. "I see him that night. He didn't just make me watch him bury my mother. He made me dig the grave."

Tears pooled, threatening to spill over. "I drove the shovel into hard earth, over and over again, my palms bleeding and begging for mercy. But my father didn't give one damn."

The shards of my heart jerked painfully, a dose of rage rushing through my veins. "Trace."

"When I tried to stop, he hit me so hard my teeth sliced my cheek open. Blood pooled in my mouth, spilling out onto that dirt, mixing with hers."

My tears started to fall, imagining that little boy so scared out of his mind and so traumatized by what he'd seen. There wasn't a damn thing I could say to make it better. All I could do was hold on and let him know that he wasn't in the memories alone. That I'd be with him for whatever he had to face.

Trace's breaths tripped over each other as he struggled to keep his breathing even. "I kept digging, too scared not to, my hands and mouth bloodied. And then he told me to put her in the ground. To erase her as if she'd never lived at all."

His throat worked as he struggled to swallow, his hand spasming in mine. "And I did it. So damn scared of what would happen if I didn't, but so ashamed of not standing up to him."

"Trace," I whispered. "You were twelve. A *child*. He was a monster. And a manipulator. You were doing what you had to do to survive."

Trace's green gaze was nearly black as it locked with mine. "I rolled her into the grave I dug. Covered her with the dirt I'd piled high. And when I started to cry, he hit me again. He hit me until I didn't make any more sounds at all."

Silent tears tracked down my face. I would've given anything to take the pain from Trace. The Trace of all those years ago *and* the Trace now.

"He warned me," Trace rasped. "He said that I was the one who'd buried her. My DNA was all over my mom and the gravesite. If the police came, I was the one who'd go to jail. Not him."

I wasn't sure I'd ever hated anyone the way I hated Trace's father. Not even my own, even after all he'd done to me and others. It took a special kind of evil to put a little boy through that kind of torture. Something I prayed was revisited on him tenfold when he reached the pits of hell.

"But you told the principal anyway," I croaked.

"I thought I deserved what was coming for me. Jail. Death. Whatever it was. But I couldn't leave her there with no headstone, no service. I couldn't do it."

I gripped his hand tighter as if it were the only thing keeping me tethered to this Earth. He was so good. Better than he could possibly know. "A champion for justice, even then."

"I thought they'd take me away. Instead, they brought me to the Colsons. To a place better than I ever could've dreamed."

"And some part of you still doesn't feel like you deserve it."

My words weren't a question, but Trace answered with one devastating word. "No."

I took in a shaking breath. "You don't get it, Trace." I squeezed his fingers as tightly as I could. "You're a miracle for all of us. Every single person you let truly know you. I heard that from Kye tonight. Gabriel countless times. I see it every single day when Keely lights up around you."

"Ellie," he choked out.

"No, you're going to listen. I've been searching for something for as long as I can remember. Looking for belonging, safety. I've been chasing shelter, and you're the one who finally gave it to me."

He let out a shuddered breath and shook his head. "You gave it to yourself."

"Maybe you're right." I lifted my free hand and pressed it to his stubbled cheek. "But I found it in your arms. Because you made me brave enough to finally be who I truly am. Don't take that away from me."

Unshed tears were back in Trace's eyes. "Ellie."

"I love you." I whispered the words into the silence between us, the quiet syllables louder than any scream.

Trace's body jerked as if he'd been struck, but he didn't let go of my hand. "You shouldn't."

"Too bad. I do. And you're just going to have to deal with it."

He stared down at me. "Bossy."

"Damn straight."

"I love you, too."

"I know."

One corner of his mouth pulled up. "Kinda stealing a little of my thunder there."

"You'll deal with that, too." I stretched up on my tiptoes and pressed my mouth to his. "I. Love. You."

Trace pulled back and slid a hand along my jaw. "You showed me what love can be."

Tears pricked my eyes. "Now, who's stealing the thunder?"

"Ellie?"

"Yeah?"

"I need to take you to bed."

"Okay."

"Just like that?"

I shrugged. "Seems I'm agreeable after you tell me you love me."

One corner of Trace's mouth tugged up the barest amount. "That really all it takes to break that stubborn streak?"

"Watch it, Chief. I could turn tonight into blue-balled hell."

He leaned in, his lips hovering over mine. "Naw, you'd never be able to resist me."

"Men," I huffed. But I knew he was right.

CHAPTER FORTY-SEVEN

Trace

I WOKE TO WARMTH AND THE SCENT OF ELLIE. SMOKY HEAT wrapped around me as I held her to me and buried my face in her hair. The scent was stronger there. It must've been something in her shampoo.

Whatever it was, it held me captive as echoes of the night before played in my mind. Finally telling Ellie everything. Having her love me all the same.

It was the sort of gift you could never put a price on, but one I'd always hold sacred. I pulled Ellie closer as if she might disappear if I didn't have that grasp.

A growl sounded from above me, making me realize there was another source of heat and pressure there.

Ellie shifted, rolling as she blinked a few times. Then she blinked again as her gaze lifted. "Why is Grem on your head?"

I reached above me and, sure enough, the damn dog was perched there. The second my hand grazed Gremlin's back, his gummy mouth did its best to bite the crap out of me. "Ow," I clipped, yanking my hand back.

Ellie giggled. "Please, he's got one snaggletooth and it's already loose."

I scowled at her. "Your dog just bit me. Shouldn't you be tending my wounds?"

One corner of Ellie's mouth kicked up as she reached for my hand. "You poor thing. Are you bleeding? Do you think we need to amputate?"

"You're the worst."

"I'm the best." Ellie leaned in, her lips hovering over mine.

But then Grem leapt from my head to right between us, yipping and twirling.

"Seriously?" I groused.

Ellie laughed and snuggled Gremlin to her. "He was feeling left out."

"Now I know why Linc's always complaining about Brutus being a cockblock," I muttered.

"Brutus is the bestest boy in all the land. He would never," Ellie said of my sister's dog. Grem nipped her chin as if to argue the point. "Don't worry, Grem, you're the bestest boy, too."

My phone rang from my nightstand, and I let out a groan. "I hate everyone today."

My plans to keep Ellie in this bed for a few more hours slipped away as I picked up the device and saw Gabriel's name. A weight settled in my gut, spreading into my muscles like molten metal. "Hello?"

"Hey, man. How you holding up?"

I pushed up on the pillows but brought Ellie and Grem with me, even though the dog snarled slightly. There was no more cutting her out. No more holding things in. "I'm better. You find something?"

"I'm glad. Interesting development in one arena."

"Putting you on speaker. Ellie's here." I moved to tap the screen as Ellie looked up at me.

Gabriel didn't speak for a second. "Pretty early for a visitor," he hedged.

Ellie's mouth curved. "Now, Gabriel, are you looking for gossip?"

He chuckled. "Always."

"You two can have teatime later. Tell us what you know," I pressed.

"Got a call from one of Anson's contacts at the federal level. He got some new intel on Bradley."

Ellie tensed next to me, and I wove my fingers through hers, reminding her that I was there and always would be.

"We found out he was arrested for possession in the South of France a few days ago," Gabriel went on. "He's still in lockup, at least according to this guy's source. And what's more interesting is that it turns out he traveled there three weeks ago. It didn't flag right away because he hopped a jet a friend owned."

I frowned. It still should've been in the US Customs system, but who knew what sort of lags happened in the private sector. Or simple errors. Still, something ate at me. Maybe it was this, or maybe it was the fact that we still had no idea where my father was.

Ellie squeezed my hand. "Breathe, Chief. This is good. One threat off the board."

"She's right," Gabriel agreed. "They don't mess around with Americans bringing drugs in. He'll likely do some time."

I took that in. Ellie would get time and distance from Bradley. She'd be safe from him—as long as he wasn't paying someone to do his dirty work. "Do you think we can get a search warrant for his phone records? See if anything pings for someone he could've hired?"

"I can try," Gabriel said. "If we hit a brick wall, there's always Dex."

I grunted at that. The problem was, whatever Dex found wouldn't exactly be admissible in court. "Any leads on Jasper?" I asked.

Gabriel sighed. "Nothing yet. But everyone's looking."

I took everything in. The good. The bad. The hard. The beautiful.

"Come over for brunch. Around ten-thirty," I said.

"Are you having a stroke?" Gabriel asked. "Talk about a one-eighty."

"I'm not having a stroke. Everything's been hard lately. We need to remember the good that's mixed in. So, come over for brunch," I said.

Ellie looked up at me and mouthed, *I love you*. She understood why I needed this. That I wasn't going to let my father or anything else make me lose sight of what was important.

"I'll be there," Gabriel said quietly. "Pleased as hell for you that you've found someone who makes you see the world a little more clearly."

I leaned into Ellie and brushed my lips over her forehead. "Me, too, brother. Me, too."

The sounds of pure chaos reigned in my house. Laughter, oldies music, the din of conversation. The entire Colson crew was here, along with Gabriel, Walter, and even Leah. Ellie had asked if we could invite her, too. And for the first time in a long while, I could see us taking steps toward becoming a truly blended family.

As I moved through the living room, I saw Arden coloring something fantastical with Keely and Luca. Linc hovered close by. Nora and Lolli were in the throes of some card game with Sutton and Thea. I caught sight of more people outside, including Gabriel, who said something to make Leah blush.

That had me shaking my head and moving toward the kitchen, where I found Ellie shaking her hips as she sliced strawberries for our waffle station. "Please note the epic slices. This is chef quality over here."

I chuckled and leaned over to examine her work. "I am *very* impressed."

She beamed up at me. "I think I deserve a reward later, don't you?"

My dick twitched at her sultry tone. "For the love of God, my entire family is here. Please, do not give me a hard-on."

Ellie just laughed, the full-bodied one that said she didn't have a care in the world. And then she leaned in and kissed me. She tasted like strawberries, tea, and *her*. I could've drowned in the combination and been a happy man.

A hoot sounded that had the two of us pulling apart. "There's some nookie happening in the kitchen," Lolli hollered.

"Jesus," I muttered.

Ellie only grinned wider. "I didn't have you pegged as a narc, Lolli."

My grandma straightened her shoulders and let out a huff of air. "I would never."

"I don't know. It sounds like you were throwing them under the bus to me," Kye called as he walked into the kitchen, looking a little worse for wear. Dark circles ringed bloodshot eyes, and I was fairly certain he was wearing clothes from the day before.

That had me frowning. Ellie told me Kye had opened up to her about some of our shared history, and I couldn't help but worry that doing so had reopened a wound for him.

Lolli made a *pshh* noise as she gave him a once-over. "You need a little hair of the dog. You're looking a little rough over there."

Kye moved to the coffee pot and refilled his mug. "I'm not hungover. Got caught up in some sketches and didn't get a lot of sleep. I just need about a dozen cups of the good stuff, and I'll be fine."

The fact that Kye *wasn't* hungover almost made me more worried. It wasn't out of the norm for Kye to disappear for a night or even a couple of days, but the fact that darkness still clung to him set me on edge.

Before I could press him about anything, an excited Keely and Luca raced into the kitchen. "Daddy, can we go to the fall carnival? It starts today, and Luca said there's rides and cotton candy—"

"And corn dogs," Luca said, as if corn dogs were the most important thing on Earth. I didn't blame him.

Ellie rolled onto the balls of her feet like a little kid. "I love carnival rides."

I looked back and forth between the two of them. "I don't know if today is the best day—"

"Pleeeeeease, Daddy," Keely begged. "Benny, Gracie, and Isabella are going, too. Luca said. Please."

I glanced at Ellie, uncertainty digging in. The idea of bringing her somewhere out in the open given everything that had been happening set me on edge. But I also understood that her being cooped up in my house or hers wasn't ideal either.

"I can stay here with Linc and whatever deputy you want. You and Keely can go," Ellie offered instantly.

Of course, she had. Always looking out for my girl.

"No!" Keely protested, instantly running for Ellie and taking her hand. "I need my bestie there."

Luca frowned. "I thought *I* was your bestie."

Keely shrugged, her fishtail braids swinging with the movement. "I can have lots of besties."

Luca's little face pinched at that, and I fought a laugh.

"We can all go," Kye offered. "And we'll stay together."

Before I could answer, my doorbell rang. I frowned. Everyone who might casually stop by my house was already here. I wiped my hands on a kitchen towel and started for the door. "I've got it."

I took a second to look through the peephole, and my frown only deepened at the unfamiliar man on my front porch. Opening the door, I took him in. He looked to be somewhere in his early thirties, and everything about him was a study in opposites.

Tall and broad like he could've been a linebacker in college but wearing wire-framed glasses. Light brown hair in a haphazard disarray, and a few days' worth of stubble on his jaw, not to mention tattoos bleeding out onto his hands. But the messenger bag hanging at his shoulder had more of a business bent to it.

"Can I help you?" I asked.

"Hey, Trace." The man spoke the words like we knew each other. My frown deepened.

"Do I know you?"

"Oh, right. Sorry." He ran a hand through his hair and then extended it to me. "I'm Dex."

My eyes widened a fraction. I wasn't sure what I'd been expecting of the hacker who had the occasional vigilante bent, but this wasn't it. "It's nice to finally meet you. Anson's actually inside."

A grin spread across Dex's face as he glanced over my shoulder. "Shit, I probably should've called. I can get single-minded when I'm on a project. Are you having a party or something?"

"Just an impromptu brunch, and you're welcome anytime. Come on in."

Dex patted his stomach. "I think it's been a while since I consumed anything other than a Redline."

"What the hell is a Redline?" I asked.

He sent me a sheepish smile. "Energy drink. Fuel of computer geeks everywhere."

My steps slowed. "Wait, how did you know where I lived?"

Dex winced. "Hacker, remember?"

"Jesus," I muttered.

"Dex," Anson said with a massive grin as we headed into the living room. "What are you doing here?"

Dex froze. "He's smiling. Why is he smiling? It's freaking me out."

"He smiles now. Don't worry, he's not a pod person or anything," I assured him.

Anson pulled Dex into a back-slapping hug. "It's good to see you."

"You, uh, too," Dex said, clearly still uncertain what to do with this updated version of Anson.

As Anson let him go, Dex's expression shifted, making me realize something I should've noticed earlier. "You have something."

CHAPTER FORTY-EIGHT

Ellie

GONE WERE THE HAPPY VOICES AND LAUGHTER OF A FEW minutes ago. Instead, a nervous energy filled the air as Dex pulled out his laptop and pulled up God knew what. If it was another bombshell of information, I wasn't sure I could take it.

Cope, Sutton, Nora, and Leah had taken Keely and Luca to my house to play with Bumper, making sure the kids didn't overhear anything they shouldn't. But the rest of us stayed put.

Fallon leaned into me. "Not what I was expecting when Anson talked about his hacker friend."

My gaze flicked over to her. "What do you mean?"

She blinked back at me. "Geez, you really are a goner."

"Huh?"

Fallon chuckled. "He's gorgeous. Like some mountain man with a professor-geek-chic edge. There's something about those glasses."

Kye stepped up to our huddle just as Fallon finished speaking, and he frowned down at her. "What's so great about glasses?"

Fallon just sent me a sidelong look. "Men. So oblivious."

That only made Kye's frown deepen. "I wear glasses sometimes when I do the books at the shop and the gym."

I had to fight back my laughter and patted Kye on the shoulder. "Don't worry, you're cool, too."

"Okay," Dex said, his fingers flying across the keyboard as Anson, Trace, and Gabriel looked over his shoulder. "I finally broke into the software company's database."

"I didn't hear that," Gabriel muttered.

I expected Trace to say the same, but he didn't. Instead, he just pressed for more information. "What'd you find?"

"There was a single user in Sparrow Falls," Dex said, his fingers slowing, and his thumb moving over the trackpad on his laptop. "I matched the IP address to a location. This area of The Meadows RV Park & Cabins, in a neighborhood called The Pines."

Trace's form went completely rigid. "That's where Jasper's been living."

"I know," Dex said, clicking on something else. "But his credit card pinged at a bus station two towns over. He bought a ticket to Salt Lake City."

"Getting out of Dodge," Anson muttered.

I couldn't stay where I was any longer. I moved to Trace's spot behind the couch and slid my hand through his. Trace pressed a kiss to my temple. "I'm okay."

I kept a hold of his hand, needing him to know I was there. With him. No matter what came our way.

"The ticket was purchased late yesterday afternoon, and you can see a figure here." Dex pointed to the screen.

In the slightly grainy photo was a man wearing a hat with an unfamiliar sports team logo. But his face was tipped up at an angle just enough to allow a peek at his face, likely looking at one of the departures and arrivals boards. Even with the photo's slight blur, I recognized Jasper Killington instantly. The dead eyes. The scar down the side of his face. The scowl.

"That's him," Trace ground out.

"If he got a ticket to Salt Lake City, he likely got off somewhere before there," Anson said, staring at the screen and trying to put together the pieces. "I'd pick a stop without a station. No cameras. We'd have no clue where. Our only hope is that the bus itself had a camera, but even if it did, it'll take time to comb through the hours of footage."

"Then how the hell are we supposed to find him?" Linc growled, a muscle in his jaw flexing.

"His resources will run out eventually, and someone's going to spot him somewhere. There's only so long someone can run once you have their name and face," Anson assured him.

Linc scrubbed a hand over his face. "And until then, we just wait?"

I sent my brother a soft smile. "Until then, we're grateful he's no longer in Sparrow Falls. And we *live*."

Linc shoved up from his chair. "It's not good enough." He stalked outside and into the backyard.

Arden started to get up, but I held out a hand to stop her. "Let me."

She studied me for a moment and then nodded.

I stood, crossed to the doors, and slipped through them. Even though there was a chill to the air, the sun was blazing, and it was as if the rays cast Linc in the perfect haloed glow as he stood at the edge of the deck, staring out into the yard.

Moving to him, I leaned gently against his arm. "You can't save me from everything, ConCon."

"I haven't saved you from anything."

There was such defeat in his voice that it had my gaze jerking up to his face. "Linc...you saved me from *everything*. You were my respite amid all Philip's manipulations. I *lived* for those Wednesday-night calls."

His hazel gaze swept down to mine. "You shouldn't have had to. I should've done more. Talked to a social worker. Stayed."

I was already shaking my head. "Why? So he could torture us both more? Social workers couldn't have done a damn thing because the pain he inflicted wasn't something you could put down on paper.

And if you *had* stayed…he would've squashed your spirit and killed your soul. He was always worse to you than he was to me."

"You were alone," Linc croaked.

"No. I wasn't." I wrapped my arms around his and held tight. "Because you were always with me. Maybe not in the next room, but I carried you with me. My fearless big brother, fighting for the life he deserved."

Linc's eyes glittered with unshed tears. "I was terrified."

"But you did it anyway. You showed me it was possible." I gripped his arm tighter. "I may not have been ready to fight until recently, but you made me realize I could and gave me the strength to decide it was time."

"El Bell," he rasped.

"Love you."

He pressed a kiss to the top of my head. "Love you more than you'll ever know."

My mouth curved as I looked up at my big brother. "We didn't become like them."

Linc's whole expression softened. "No. We didn't."

"We got free, ConCon."

"We got free," he echoed.

And that was the best gift of all.

Keely and Luca let out shouts of delight as the man walking on stilts bent to give them balloon animals.

Linc let out an exaggerated shiver on my left. "*This* is your idea of living? You know I hate clowns."

I couldn't help the laugh that bubbled out of me as I held tight to Trace's arm with one hand and a massive cone of pink cotton candy with the other. It had a sweet memory of when we were much younger lighting in my mind. Linc, Mom, and me at Coney Island, playing hooky from school and staying out far too late.

I grinned at my brother. "Remember when that one clown startled you at Coney Island? I thought you were going to pee your pants."

Linc glared at me. "He snuck up behind me with that creepy voice and asked if I wanted a balloon. My stranger-danger reflex was instigated."

Arden let out a laugh as she hooked her arm with his. "Don't worry, Cowboy. I'll protect you."

Linc pulled her closer and dropped a kiss to her lips. "I'm counting on it."

A familiar face headed toward us, Bloom & Berry ballcap in place. Duncan shot us all a grin and issued a wave. "Nice to see you guys." His gaze moved to me, lingering on the cut on my head. "You doing okay? I heard about what happened the other day…"

"I'm doing a lot better. And the mums on my front porch are doing amazing," I said, awkwardly trying to steer the conversation away from darker things.

Duncan picked up on my hint and grinned. "Glad to hear it. If you want me to bring anything else by, I'm happy to."

"I can pick more up if Blaze needs them," Trace cut in, none too subtly.

Duncan's lips twitched, clearly having picked up on it, too. "Noted. Enjoy the carnival."

As Duncan headed over to Rhodes to say hello, I sent Trace a death glare. "Seriously?"

"What?" Trace asked with mock innocence.

"You might as well have peed a circle around her," Arden muttered.

Linc sent Trace a commiserating look. "Good luck, buddy. You're on your own."

"Gee, thanks," Trace said.

I pinned him with a hard stare. "He was just being nice."

"Blaze, Dunc's a good guy, but he doesn't offer to make dropoffs for just anyone."

I looked over at the owner of Bloom & Berry. He *had* gone out of his way to help. I nibbled on the corner of my lip.

"I see it's all coming together." Trace gently pulled my lip from between my teeth. "The same way Fletcher's always butting his nose in when it comes to you."

A grimace pulled at my lips. "No, I *know* he was interested."

Trace slowed. "How?"

I shrugged. "He asked me out."

"When?" Trace growled.

"Relax, Chief. It was before we got together. He knows we're a couple now."

"Too fucking cute for her own good," Trace muttered.

Keely ran up to us and tugged at my shirt. "Will you go on the mini coaster with me?"

Trace's expression hardened as he looked at the small roller coaster. "I don't know. That thing looks like it's made of toothpicks."

Cope's hand clapped on his shoulder. "We all know your sensitive stomach doesn't handle coasters well. But don't make excuses."

Kye laughed as he strode forward, carrying some blue cotton candy. "I swear he turned green that one year."

Shep's nose wrinkled. "He barfed on my new boots."

"I tried to warn you not to share one of those cars with him," Fallon said with a grin.

"Way to kick a man when he's down," Trace groused.

Rhodes jumped up and kissed his cheek. "That's siblings, dear brother."

"Don't remind me," he grumbled.

Cope grabbed Luca's hand. "Come on, El Bell, let's do this."

"Hey, that's my nickname," Linc argued.

Cope just laughed.

This was the sort of thing Linc and I never truly had, but standing in the bright fall sun, I knew it only made me appreciate having it now all the more. I handed Trace my cotton candy and kissed him quickly. "Take a video, Chief."

"Ellie…"

But Keely and I were already following behind Cope and Luca as they raced up the marked-off line. They just made the last car of the coaster before us, but that meant we got to watch them race around the smallish track. The whole thing did shake a little as they went.

Keely gripped my hand tighter. "I'm a little nervous."

I crouched so we were eye level. "You want to wait for now? We can try it later."

She shook her head. "No, I want to do it. I just…my tummy's flip-flopping."

"Mine, too," I admitted. "But you know what? That's gonna make it more fun. And your braids are going to fly when you're on this."

That had her grinning again. "Like unicorn hair."

"Just like."

The roller coaster cars came to a stop again, and Cope and Luca hooted and hollered from the other side. We waved to them as we climbed in and buckled up. I gripped Keely's hand as the cars lurched out of the makeshift station.

We climbed higher and higher until we reached the peak. "Here we go!" I yelled to Keely.

She let out an ear-splitting shriek as the coaster dipped down, and I had no choice but to join her. We laughed and screamed the whole way until the cars made it back into the station.

Keely leapt from the car, holding out a hand for me. "That was the bestest ever! Can we go again? Can we?"

I laughed as I climbed out. "I bet we can."

As we started down the winding exit path, something hard jammed into my back as someone grabbed my shirt. "Make a sound, and the little bitch gets it."

CHAPTER FORTY-NINE

Trace

KYE GRABBED MY SHOULDERS AND SHOOK ME FROM BEHIND AS he laughed. "You're looking a little green just watching."

I shrugged off his hold, scowling. "You know they assemble and disassemble these damn things countless times every year, right? Then they cart them around from state to state. The fact that I don't want to ride around in one of those tin cans just shows I have some sense."

Rhodes grinned at me. "Never been a risk-taker, but we love you anyway."

Anson wrapped his arms around my sister and pulled her gently against him. "Not everyone's as much of a daredevil as you are, Reckless."

A familiar figure caught my attention behind them, and the moment his gaze locked on me, an ugly smile twisted the man's lips. Rainer Cruz. Jasper's best friend and the one person who might be darker and more twisted than my father.

"Well, lookie here. We got a real live traitorous pig," Rainer said as he ambled up. He tried to appear as if he didn't have a care in the world, but I could see otherwise. His blond hair had turned a dull gray and was patchy in spots. His teeth had yellowed the way Jasper's had, and he was far too skinny to be healthy.

I knew the look—the impact of drugs over years and years of use. I would've felt bad for the man if I didn't know what evil lived below the surface.

Kye stepped forward, his shoulders straightening. "Keep moving."

Rainer snickered. "Jas told me you had a bodyguard. Still can't fight your own battles, pipsqueak?"

I waited for his barbs to land, but they didn't. Nothing caught hold beneath my skin and ate away at my insides. Because I could see how ridiculous Rainer's statement was now. The same as my father's had always been. I'd been a twelve-year-old kid, scared out of my mind, and had asked for help. I'd reported a wrong I'd seen— one I'd been forced to participate in. It didn't make me weak. It made me a survivor.

So, instead of clapping back or rising to the bait, I simply smiled at the pathetic man opposite me. "It's good to see you, Rainer. Beautiful day, isn't it?"

Rainer's expression turned to confusion as he simply stared at me, clearly unsure how to respond. Anson snickered. *He* understood the game I was playing by throwing Rainer off and confusing the man.

The moment he heard Anson's derisive sound, Rainer's eyes narrowed. "You got somethin' to say?"

Anson sent him an easy grin. "Nope. Just enjoying the show."

Rainer's brow lifted, and he seemed to realize something. "You're that freaky psychic, ain't you?"

Rhodes slipped an arm through Anson's. "Baby, you didn't tell me you could see the future. Why haven't you given me the winning lotto numbers yet?"

"You know what I mean," Rainer ground out. "You see in people's heads."

Anson gave him a long look. "That's one way of putting it. And I'll do you a solid and perform a parlor trick for free."

"Ooooh, goody," Fallon cheered. "I love when he does this."

Rainer bared his teeth at my sister like some sort of animal, but Kye stepped in front of her, blocking Rainer's line of sight. "You don't *look* at her. You don't even breathe her air."

It was Rainer's turn to snicker. "Strike a nerve, delinquent?"

"You were abandoned by your father," Anson cut in. "Likely between the ages of five and seven. Your mother was neglectful at best. My guess is she had a revolving door of men in and out of her life. They didn't treat you well. It's why you have a problem with authority, even now. But what you don't like people to know is that all you yearned for was their approval."

It was as if Rainer had been struck by a bolt of lightning. His body jerked, and then his spine went ramrod straight. "You don't know a damn thing you're talking about."

But the way his face went white told me that Anson had hit the nail on the head.

Rainer spat on the ground the same way my father liked to do. "Keep your freaky family away from me." And with that, he took off.

I turned, following him with my eyes until Rainer was as far from us as he could get while staying on the fairgrounds.

"Did you see how he went all pale?" Fallon all but cheered.

Kye swiveled around to glare at her. "You do not shit-talk a man like that, Fal. He's dangerous and could hurt you just for shits and giggles."

She frowned back at Kye. "We're in public."

"That doesn't mean a damn thing. I need you to be smarter than that." Kye stalked away without another word.

Rhodes reached out for Fallon's arm. "Are you okay?"

Fal shook her off. "I need to go after him."

Hell. A reaction like that meant Kye's demons were working overtime.

Anson wrapped an arm around Rho's shoulders. "She's who he needs right now. They'll work it out."

I knew they would, but I was still worried about my brother, and it was time for us to have one hell of a heart-to-heart.

Luca raced toward our group, Cope following behind at a more sedate pace. "Keels is up there now," Luca yelled. "Get a video!"

I tried to shake off the encounter with Rainer and Kye's reaction and grinned at Luca. "You didn't fall out?"

Luca grinned widely. "Nope. I even put my hands up like this!" He shot his hands into the air.

Cope squeezed his shoulder. "A certified bad—"

"If you finish that statement, I'm grounding you," Sutton cut in.

"Dude," Luca muttered. "Don't get grounded."

We all laughed, and I slid my phone out of my pocket as the roller coaster pulled out of the station and started up the steady incline. *Hell.* Maybe I would upchuck just watching.

"Someone get the barf bag," Rhodes called.

I flipped her off.

"That was uncalled for. And from our sheriff, no less," she said with mock affront.

I recorded every painful dip and roll. The only thing that kept me from tossing my cookies was the fact that I caught Keely's and Ellie's shouts on the air every so often. When the coaster parked back at the station, I breathed a sigh of relief and put my phone back into my pocket.

I tried to see through to the other side of the coaster to track Ellie's and Keely's movements, but I lost them in the throng of people. When they didn't round the roller coaster right away, a hint of unease slid over me.

"Do you see them?" I asked.

Everyone turned in that direction, but I was already walking, then picking up to a jog. That's when I saw her. Keely. She had dirt smeared across her cheek, and her hair was askew. And she was running.

Steps from me, Keely launched herself in my direction. "Daddy!" she wailed. "He took her! The man took her!"

The whole world dropped away. Blood roared in my ears as sheer panic grabbed hold. "Who?" I croaked. "Did you see who?"

Tears rolled down Keely's dirt-streaked face. "He had a scar. Here." She pointed to a spot below my left eye.

The same place Jasper had a scar. My father had Ellie. I'd failed to do the one thing I'd promised.

Keep her safe.

CHAPTER FIFTY

Ellie

AN ACHE THRUMMED IN MY HEAD, AND I COULD FEEL WHERE Jasper had clocked me in the temple with the butt of his gun. I guessed I should've been grateful that he'd hit me on the side that didn't already have a gash. But the steady beat behind my eyes and nausea roiling through me made it hard to feel grateful for anything at the moment.

No. That wasn't true. I was grateful I was breathing. That Keely had gotten away. That Trace was safe. I held on to all three things with everything I had.

Giving the zip ties binding my wrists together a testing tug, I winced. There was barely enough room to move at all, and I couldn't help but wonder what it was doing to the blood supply to my fingers. At least the rope binding my middle to the older wooden chair wasn't tight. Small mercies.

I tried to steal glances around the room as Jasper typed furiously on his cell phone. Making a new getaway plan, perhaps? But it didn't make any sense. Did he truly hate Trace enough to risk prison again?

I did a quick scan to my left. There wasn't a lot to go on. It was clear this was some sort of rustic hunting cabin—one room and a bathroom. The kitchen only had a few cabinet fronts, the ones below simply covered with curtains. But care had been put into the furnishings. What looked like a handmade quilt rested on the bed, and a few paintings hung on the walls. There was even an antique vase and pitcher on a sideboard.

Over the sideboard was a window peering out into a forest, complete with handmade curtains. The only problem was that I had no idea where that forest was. I had no clue how long Jasper had driven because I didn't know how long I'd been unconscious. It could've been mere minutes or hours. But the fact that I hadn't recognized a single thing when I came to wasn't a good sign.

"Don't think about doing anything stupid," Jasper sneered.

I refused to show him any sort of fear. It was exactly what he wanted. Instead, I lifted my gaze and met his stare. "I was actually wondering where they got those antiques. They're charming."

Jasper scoffed. "Charming. Of course, my traitorous son ended up with some rich bitch."

"Don't worry. I'm definitely not rich."

His gaze narrowed on me. He'd lost the fake beard, hat, and sunglasses he'd worn at the carnival, but the angry scar still ran down his cheek. It was something he'd never be able to disguise. I just hoped Keely had told Trace about it so he knew who he was dealing with.

"Don't think you can pull a fast one on me. I'm not a fuckin' idiot. I know aaaaaall about your prick of a father."

I leaned back, feeling the wooden chair press into my spine. I wondered if there was a way to use it as a weapon. As my gaze dipped to the gun clutched firmly in Jasper's hand, I reconsidered the wisdom in that. "You're right. My dad is a huge prick."

My agreement seemed to confuse Jasper at first, but then his face contorted with rage. "No loyalty. Just like my bastard son."

I pulled the zip ties tight, using the flare of pain to keep from saying something stupid. Something that could trip Jasper's hair trigger and have him emptying that gun right into me.

"What?" Jasper sneered. "Nothing to say now, Rich Bitch?"

I inhaled through my nose, the stale air from a cabin that had been locked up for too many days or weeks choking me. "No. I don't."

Jasper smirked then, leaning back in his chair. "Won't lie. I liked messin' with you. Paying those stupid kids to egg you when you came out of the station."

My body jerked slightly in surprise. "*You* egged me?"

The smirk only grew. "Not me. Someone on my behalf. But you'd better believe I took those rainbow panties. Gonna tell that bastard son of mine I know *exactly* how you smell."

My stomach roiled as I fought to keep from throwing up all over my shoes. "What do you want?"

That was the question. The only one I really needed an answer to. And with as egotistical as Jasper was, I thought he just might tell me.

He leaned back, manspreading like he was trying to take up all the space in an airplane seat, and grinned. "I got everything I want. Got the bait to draw out my waste-of-space son. Got the means to serve him up aaaaalll the pain he deserves when I shoot you right in front of his eyes. And I got a cash cow. I'm riding off into the sunset the minute the job's done."

All the calmness I'd managed to hold on to fled in that moment, along with the belief that I'd eventually make it out of this nightmare. Waves of heat replaced it. Burning panic that made my cheeks flame and my lungs constrict.

I'd naively thought that if Jasper wanted me dead, he would've done it already, never once considering that he had some sick, macabre play planned out.

Breathe. I gave myself the one-word order over and over until my heart no longer felt like it might fly right out of my chest.

But Jasper kept right on grinning like a Cheshire cat. He knew the effect his words had, the terror they instilled. And I was right; he got off on it.

That knowledge sparked a renewed fight in me. Kye's warnings about never letting someone get you to a secondary location might be useless now, but the rest of his lessons weren't. I replayed the different strikes and kicks in my head, silently reciting the points to aim for.

Eyes. Nose. Groin. Knees.

Eyes. Nose. Groin. Knees.

"What, are you having a stroke or somethin'?" Jasper barked. "You're no good to me if you keel over before I get to see the pain on my bastard boy's face."

Trace's face filled my mind. The tender way he looked at me that spoke of love, even before he'd given me the words. The gentle encouragement he gave that told me he believed I could do anything. The sense of belonging and acceptance he offered so easily, giving me something I'd never had before.

"He's not your anything," I ground out.

Jasper's brows slammed together. "He came from me. I *own* him."

The rage stewing inside me bubbled over then. Because I knew what it was to have someone think they owned you. But *no one* owned Trace. And no one owned me. It meant the gift was that much greater when they gave themselves to you. Not because of a manipulation or force, but simply because they wanted to. Because you were better together.

I stared back at the man who had tortured Trace, enacting untold pain and torment on him. I wouldn't let Jasper hurt him anymore. "Trace is nothing like you. He's good, kind, giving. He's everything you aren't, and your pathetic life—and his amazing one—shows it."

Jasper leapt to his feet, charging the few steps toward me, just like I'd hoped. "You fucking cunt," he snarled.

It took everything in me to stay seated as his hand rose to strike me. I watched it, waiting until it reached its apex before springing up. The back of the old chair cracked and splintered in half, sending the rope tumbling to the floor. I used the force of the charge to bring my bound fists right into Jasper's nose with a satisfying crunch.

He howled in pain as blood began gushing from his face, but I didn't stop there. I brought my knee up to hit him right between the legs and then gave him a hard shove. Jasper crumpled to the floor, writhing in pain.

But I was already running.

Jasper screamed as I tore at the front door, trying to open it. It took two tries to get a good grip on the knob where I could twist it. But I managed to throw it open. I knew he'd have his gun back in a matter of seconds, and I needed to create all the distance I could between us in these precious moments. I ran awkwardly with my hands still bound but pushed hard for the thickest of the trees.

My head thrummed as I heard cursing behind me. A shot sounded, but it went wide of where I was. I zigged and zagged, trying to make myself a tougher target.

"You little bitch. I'm gonna make it hurt when I kill you," Jasper snarled.

My lungs burned, and my muscles ached, but I pushed harder. I thought about Trace and Keely, Linc, and the entire Colson crew. I fought for all of them, and I fought for me.

My foot caught on a root.

I slammed into the ground so hard light danced in front of my eyes and all the oxygen flew from my lungs. Pain radiated through me, but I struggled to roll over and get to my feet, needed to keep running.

"Don't fucking move."

I squeezed my eyes closed for a moment, not wanting to see.

"Look at me, Rich Bitch. Open your eyes and see me before I end you. It'll be good enough just to have Trace find your mangled body."

Pain rocked through me. Not the physical kind. I was pretty sure I was in shock, and it kept that from setting in. This was the kind of pain that spoke of a shattered heart. Not getting to figure out who I wanted to be. To build a life with Trace and Keely. To see my brother become a father. To *live*.

But I wouldn't hide from my death either. I wouldn't give Jasper the satisfaction.

I opened my eyes.

And the gun went off.

CHAPTER FIFTY-ONE

Trace

THE STATION HAD TURNED INTO A CHAOTIC COMMAND POST, with endless law enforcement personnel moving about the space while even more combed the streets. We'd called in everyone we could think of while my family was split between consoling Keely and peppering the streets with flyers in case someone had seen something.

But it was as if Ellie had disappeared into thin air. The problem with temporary carnivals was that they didn't come with the sort of security and endless cameras a normal amusement park had. Instead, we were left hoping against hope that someone had noticed something.

And all I could do was sit at the damn conference table that'd become the command center and stare at the giant map that had been put up opposite me. Pushpins marked places of interest in different colors. The place Ellie was last seen. Her home. Mine. Linc and Arden's. Colson Ranch.

And then there were the darker ones. The places Jasper haunted. The trailer he rented. The bar he frequented. The residences of all his known connections.

Rainer had been brought in for questioning and held—one less avenue for Jasper to use.

But what was he doing to Ellie in the meantime? What was she enduring because she loved *me*? She'd already paid far too high a price trying to keep the people she loved happy, and now she was paying more. Sure, the circumstances were different, but what did that matter at the end of the day?

Voices swirled around me: the sound of Dex's fingers flying across his keyboard as he stared intently at the screen, the crackle of police radios, and the words hurled across them. Each one built on the other, but I made no move to alleviate the pain. I deserved it all.

So, I just kept staring at the map as if it would somehow miraculously tell me where Ellie was. As if I would feel some flicker of knowing when I looked at a place's name or a landmark. But I felt nothing.

Nothing but the hollowness that was life without Ellie.

"Holding it together?" Anson asked, his voice quiet as he moved behind the chair next to mine.

"Sure." My voice didn't sound like it belonged to me. It sounded numb. The kind of numbing blanket I'd tried to pull on the day my father nearly ran Ellie over. Only I felt everything now. Every ounce of pain and fury. Every flicker of guilt and anguish.

"Might want to work on those acting skills," Anson muttered.

I didn't care. I just kept staring. Waiting for something. Anything.

Anson gripped my shoulder. "You were there for me when I almost lost Rho. You helped me hold it together when I nearly broke. I'm here, Trace. We're going to get through this, and we're going to get Ellie back."

I wasn't sure what finally broke me. The kind touch? The words that felt like a vow? Whatever it was, it was too much.

I jerked back, sending the chair tumbling behind me. "You don't know!" The words tore from my throat like barbed brambles, shredding everything in their path. "You don't fucking know!" I grabbed the chair and hurled it at the wall, making it shatter into pieces.

The room erupted as I reached for another chair. Anson grabbed it from my hands as Dex moved in behind me. I whirled on him, but he was too quick, and I was too out of my mind. He ducked below my swing and moved in to grab my arm and snap it behind me.

The move forced me to bend at the waist, grunting as pain ripped through my shoulder. *Good.* I needed to feel that pain. But I still fought against it, needing to destroy everything around me.

"Breathe," Dex ordered. "Breathe, or I'm gonna use a pressure point and put you down."

That had some semblance of sanity returning to my mind. A little of the fight left me, and Anson stepped in closer, crouching low. "Come on, Trace. Pull it together. She needs you."

His words took the rest of the fight clean out of me. Sobs racked my body, violent and vicious. "I can't lose her."

Dex released me, and Anson grabbed me in a hard hug, holding on and not letting go. "You're not going to lose her," Anson gritted out. "It's not fucking happening."

I struggled to pull it together. To reel it in. Just long enough to find Ellie. To get her back. "She's everything," I whispered. "She made me see what life could be."

"I know," Anson rasped. "I know."

"Trace."

At the sound of Gabriel's voice, I pulled myself from Anson's hug, trying to read my best friend's face. "Tell me you have a lead."

Gabriel looked between Anson and me, uncertainty written all over his face.

"Tell him," Anson said. "You keep something from him now, and your friendship will never recover."

A muscle fluttered in Gabriel's jaw. "I need to know you can keep your head."

I shoved every ugly, roiling thing I was feeling down and locked it away so it couldn't see the light of day. "Under control."

"Ben Vera called dispatch. Someone tripped the camera at his hunting cabin. Feed's black now, but they probably didn't expect it to have a motion-detection trigger."

It was rare for hunters to have any kind of security up there, and if they did, it generally wasn't hooked up to notify at motion because there was too much wildlife that could trigger it. But that cabin was Ben's pride and joy, and he wasn't about to let anyone break into it.

I struggled to swallow, needing to clear the dryness from my throat. "Did he get a visual?"

"It's Jasper. He's got Ellie at gunpoint."

Law enforcement personnel gathered at a tactical point down the gravel road that led up one of the Monarch peaks. It was an area known best for hiking, camping, and fishing. But seeing as the temperatures had dropped lower, and we could be getting snow at any time, those pursuits had waned for the season.

Still, seeing men and women don Kevlar and check a variety of guns felt more than wrong. But I was grateful, nonetheless. Each of these people was putting their life on the line for Ellie. Some knew her. Some didn't. But to them, it didn't matter.

Beth and Gabriel pored over a map, plotting out the different approaches we would make. Laney, Frank, and Allen talked to the deputies who'd volunteered from the next county over. The only person I expected to see but didn't was Fletcher. I started to search him out, but a hand clamped on my shoulder.

I turned to see Gabriel, a worried expression on his face. "Trace, are you sure you can do this?"

I appreciated that he wasn't trying to argue the validity of my being there. It was a conflict of interest, at the very least. But in small communities, emergencies meant all hands on deck.

"I'll keep my head," I promised.

"And we've got his back," Anson said, stepping forward with Dex at his side. Both were kitted out in tactical gear, surprising me again when it came to Dex.

Gabriel's expression hardened. "You swear he knows how to handle himself?"

Anson scoffed. "Hates firearms but knows his way around them better than anyone I know. Best shot I know at the bureau, too."

I couldn't help but wonder how that mix of things came to be, but for now, I was just grateful he was here.

"All right," Gabriel said begrudgingly, then turned to face the crowd. "You all know your groups and your routes. Move quietly and quickly. Only use the radio when absolutely necessary."

Everyone began moving. My group was comprised of Anson, Dex, and Beth. We took a game trail that wove up the eastern side of the mountain, none of us saying a word as we walked. We moved quickly, but at a pace we could all keep. There wasn't time to stop for breaks.

A twig snapped off to the right, and all of us moved into instant formation, guns at the ready. My pulse thrummed as I forced myself to keep breathing. Jasper? Ellie? Both? Three elk appeared through the trees.

Beth muttered a curse, and we all lowered our weapons.

"Come on," Anson said. "We're getting close. Heads on a swivel."

We started up again, the path winding through the thick trees. And then it happened. A flicker of color appeared on the forest floor. My heart hammered in my ears as I picked up my pace.

What had Ellie been wearing this morning? I struggled to remember. A deep orange sweater, maybe? Or was that yesterday?

I pushed into a run when I saw that the form was human. Sprawled across the path, unmoving.

But it was too big to be Ellie. I said the words to myself over and over until we reached the fallen figure. The moment we did, I sucked in a breath. The person's chest had three holes in a tight grouping that spoke of training. And the face was one that had haunted my nightmares.

Jasper lay there, blood seeping into the earth, a cell phone at his side. One Ellie would've grabbed to call for help, even if she was scared out of her mind. *If* she wasn't under duress.

I struggled to keep breathing as my gaze found Anson's. "If Jasper's dead, who the hell has Ellie?"

CHAPTER FIFTY-TWO

Ellie

I STARED AT THE WOMAN FORCIBLY DRAGGING ME UP THE hillside. It was a face I knew, but it looked more like a stranger than anything else now. "You shot him," I rasped.

Helen Newbury whirled on me. Her blond hair was threaded with silver and pulled back in an artful chignon, her attire looking like she was spending a weekend at her country estate, not slaughtering people on a mountainside. She'd holstered one gun like she'd been around them all her life and now had Jasper's in her possession, as well.

She looked down her nose at me in a way I always thought she was above. "He's disposable, Eleanor."

I winced at the sound of my formal name. It felt like it had been years since I'd heard it, even though I knew it hadn't been nearly that long. But that feeling was a mark of the distance I'd gained from my old life.

My brain whirled as I tried to pull together the pieces of the puzzle. Bradley's mother's presence here meant she was involved in some capacity. The question was, what was her role?

"Move," Helen ordered, dragging me up the mountainside with surprising strength.

Every inch of my body cried out in pain. My shock had apparently worn off. I felt like I'd been caught in a riptide and battered against the rocks over and over again. "I can't," I wheezed.

"Weak," Helen spat. "You always have been. I thought you had what it took to be with my Bradley, but you obviously don't."

I bent at the waist, heaving and desperately trying not to throw up. But I managed to steal a look at the woman I'd known for most of my life. "You're here because I broke up with Bradley?"

Helen's hand whipped back so fast I didn't have a prayer of blocking the blow. She struck my cheek with her open palm so hard I tasted blood. "You ungrateful slut. Your father almost *ruined* our reputation by association, and we had the *kindness* not to cast you out. And how do you repay us? By embarrassing our son."

Her knuckles bleached white around the handgun, making the firearm tremble as she towered over me. My mind whirled as I tried in vain to come up with something that would appease her. "It wasn't working," I said desperately. "Bradley and I weren't right—"

"You weren't good enough for him," Helen spat. "I thought you were different from the rest. That you'd be a soft place for him to land. But I should've seen it all along. No drive. No purpose. Just a weakling who always went with what everyone else wanted."

"Then you should be grateful I'm not in his life anymore." I was grasping at straws, and I knew it, desperate for something to bring Helen back from an edge she was clearly already over.

"Grateful?" she snarled. "My son's life fell apart after you left. He started showing up to work drunk. He brought a *stripper* to a charity function."

I struggled to straighten, pain flaring in my ribs. "And that's my fault?"

Helen glared at me. "You broke his heart. He said if you just came back, everything would be fine. That it would go back to normal. And I needed my boy to have everything he wanted. I thought if you just realized how *lucky* you were to be chosen by him, he'd be okay."

My jaw went slack as more pieces came into focus. "You," I whispered. "You're the one who sent the threats. The photos. You were watching me."

"Please," Helen said, sounding disgusted. "I have much more important things to do than watch your pathetic little life. I can pay people to do that."

"Jasper," I muttered.

Helen brushed an invisible speck of dirt from her Barbour jacket. "Eventually. Bradley had some half-priced private investigator on you at first, but it didn't take much of an offer to have the PI send his reports to me, as well. You were spending so much time with that trash of a neighbor that I put the PI on him, as well. That's how I found Jasper."

"The break-in while I was asleep?"

"Jasper," she huffed. "He was already quite transfixed with your downfall to cause that son of his pain."

"The car nearly running me down?"

Helen's lips pursed. "Jasper, too. He got a bit too carried away there. He was just supposed to scare you into going home, back to Bradley, where you belong. Bradley was becoming more and more unglued by the day. I'd hoped sending him off with some friends would help…"

"But it didn't. Because I'm not the problem," I snapped.

This blow was harder, the butt of the gun glancing off my cheekbone. I doubled over as I cried out.

"I should've let Jasper have his way from the beginning and ended your pathetic existence. I should've known he wouldn't be able to do that. But, as they say, if you want something done right, you have to do it yourself," she spat.

Helen's face twisted into a sneer. "Such a tragedy. One of Jasper's *associates* double-crosses him and shoots him in cold blood. Then you try to escape, but you're gunned down, as well. It'll serve as a warning to Bradley. You are the company you keep."

My heart hammered against my ribs as I struggled to breathe.

My face felt as if someone had exploded a tiny bomb just under the surface. But I had to pull it together. I had to fight.

With everything I had, I forced myself to straighten. "You won't get away with this."

"Oh, darling. I already have." Helen's face went completely cold. "Now, start running."

I knew what she wanted now. To paint a scene that fit her narrative. But I wouldn't give it to her. "No."

"Excuse me?" Helen's tone went shrill, full of the entitlement borne of the rich and spoiled.

"I said no. I'm not making this any easier on you." I braced, waiting for her to move just slightly. If I could get the right angle, I could knock her back into the massive boulder to her left.

"Mercer County Sheriff's Department, lower your weapon," Beth called through the trees.

My heart seized, relief and panic warring in equal measure. But Helen moved faster than I'd ever seen her move before. In a split second, she was behind me, and the barrel of her gun was pressed to the underside of my chin.

"Lower your weapon," Beth ordered again, stepping out from between the trees.

Helen started to laugh. "You came alone, little girl? Such a mistake."

"Not alone," Anson said, stepping out of the woods to my left.

Helen cursed and gripped my hair harder, making tears flood my eyes. "You sniveling little bitch. You ruin everything. If you think I'm going down alone, you are sorely mistaken."

"Don't."

The new voice nearly had my knees buckling. *Trace.* If there was one voice I wanted to hear before I left this planet, it was his.

"You," Helen growled. "She would've gone back where she belonged if you hadn't come along."

Trace stepped in from the right, his weapon raised. "There's only one place Ellie belongs."

Helen let out a low scoff. "Let me guess? With you."

"No," Trace said. "Wherever she *chooses* to be."

"Chief," I croaked.

"Love you, Blaze. You showed me what love means," Trace rasped, his dark green irises swimming with unshed tears.

Helen gripped my hair even tighter. "You don't get to love anyone but my Bradley," she cried.

A crack pierced the air. Pain bloomed. And then chaos erupted.

CHAPTER FIFTY-THREE

Trace

REGARDLESS OF HOW MANY HOURS HAD PASSED, IT WAS NEARLY impossible for me to take my eyes off Ellie. It didn't matter that she'd been checked over in the emergency room and miraculously had nothing more than a mild concussion from Jasper's assault, and bruised ribs from her fall. Still, I feared if I took my eyes off her for more than a handful of seconds, she'd disappear in front of my eyes all over again.

But there my girl was. Sitting on my couch piled high with pillows and colorful blankets. Keely was tucked against her on one side, Grem between them. Linc and Arden were curled in a chair on the other side. Rhodes and Fallon sat cross-legged on the floor in front of the coffee table as Sutton and Cope helped Nora in the kitchen. Thea and Shep were doing a puzzle with Luca at the dining room table while Anson took a call out front, and Lolli made a grocery run.

Everyone was sticking close, wanting to make sure Ellie really was okay. Simply needing to be in her presence. The only one missing was Kye. Which wasn't like him. But maybe too many demons had been stirred up for him this time.

And as my gaze moved to the French doors that led to the back deck, I knew he wasn't the only one. Dex stared out into the yard, but I knew he wasn't actually seeing anything.

"He's still out there?" Anson said, moving to my side as he slid his phone into his pocket.

"Yeah. I still can't believe he made that shot."

When Anson had said Dex was a good shot, he hadn't been kidding. He'd managed to take down Helen Newbury with a clean shot through the neck. Anson had tried to keep her alive until the medics arrived, but there was no saving her.

I wanted to feel bad about that because I knew taking a life carried weight—and from what I could see, that weight was somehow more for Dex—but I couldn't.

Anson stared out at his friend as Dex answered a phone call. "He didn't have it easy growing up. This'll stir that up."

Just like it had for Kye. I couldn't help but wonder what demons the two had in common. But before I could ask anything, Dex strode back inside.

All eyes went to him. There'd been a lot of gratitude for what he'd done, thanks that made Dex extremely uncomfortable. But there wasn't a lot I could do to help him there. My family always let people know when they appreciated them.

"Got a call from a friend at the bureau," Dex said, swinging his phone between his fingers. "Turns out Bradley and his friends were part of a little trafficking operation. Serving the wealthy in specific exotic locales. He's going away for a lot longer than a week or two."

"There's Helen Newbury's trigger," Anson muttered.

Ellie's gaze flew to me, but I was already moving. I dodged different family members until I reached the arm of the couch. Lowering myself to it, I bent and brushed my lips across hers.

She stared for a moment, her mouth hovering over mine. "I'm free."

"You're free," I whispered. "To be wherever you want to be."

Ellie pulled back a fraction, her hand lifting to my face. "With you. That's always where I want to be."

Relief flooded me. I hadn't realized until that moment just how worried I'd been that Ellie would want to leave Sparrow Falls when the dust settled, feeling like it held too many painful memories. "Blaze." I took her mouth again, deeper this time.

"Gross," Keely complained, leaping from the couch. "Cooties."

"Watch out," Luca called from the dining room. "They're gonna do it all the time now."

Everyone laughed.

Linc leaned forward so he could see Ellie. "You're really going to stay?"

She smiled at her brother. "My family's here. Plus, I can't miss seeing you covered in spit-up. And I plan to make a serious campaign for favorite aunt."

"Hey!" Rhodes and Thea protested at the same time.

The front door opened, and Lolli swooped in, laden with bags, her whole form jangling with all the jewelry she wore. Dex frowned as he studied her. "Are those…light-up pot leaf earrings?"

Anson clapped him on the back. "Welcome to the Colson family."

Lolli moved to the living room and set down all her bags. "You," she said to Dex as her gaze roamed him. "You know I'm not usually one for the law-and-order types, but I'd climb you like a tree."

Dex's eyes widened, a little fear filling them. "Uhhhhh…"

Lolli pulled out a bedazzled tin decorated with mushrooms and rainbows. "These are a thank-you for saving my Ellie girl. She's the most fun of all this lot, and I'd be lost without her."

Some of my siblings let out sounds and words of protest, but Ellie just pushed in closer to me. "Lolli," she whispered.

"It's true," Lolli said. "And I expect you to recover from those injuries quick so we can hit up the cowboy bar."

Ellie laughed. "As soon as these ribs heal, I'm there."

Lolli turned back to Dex, handing him the tin. "For you. My special brownie blend."

As Dex took it, the entire room shouted, *"NO!"*

Nora handed me one of the pots she'd used to make some veggie chili especially for Ellie, and I systematically started drying it. Everyone else had left as Ellie dozed on the couch. Leah had come to pick up Keely so Ellie could sleep in, knowing she'd need the rest to fully recover. And she'd brought a bouquet of flowers and specialty tea that was supposed to be good for sore muscles.

Our family was becoming even more blended, and something about that had a sense of peace I'd never known settling into my bones. There was gratitude, too. For my siblings stepping up. For Lolli and her mischievous ways, which always brought a smile to Ellie's lips. And for Nora, my mom.

Quiet moments like these had always been our thing. She never pushed or pried; she simply let me know she was there.

As I crouched and put the pot back in its spot, I looked up at her. "Love you, Mom."

Nora looked down at me, her face softening. "Love you, too. Love that you've found the happiness you've always deserved."

I straightened and turned to face her, ready to give her everything. "Ellie made me truly see what has been around me all along. She made me believe I could accept it. That I could really be a Colson. Could be who you taught me to be."

"Baby," Nora said, lifting a hand to pat my cheek. "You've *always* been a Colson. You're the best of what our family is. Loyal and caring. Giving and protective. You make our family better by being a part of it."

Pressure pulsed behind my eyes as I pulled her in for a hug. "Thank you for giving me a place to belong."

"Thanks for letting me." After a long moment, she pulled back, wiping at her eyes. "How dare you make me blubber when I made it all day without losing it."

I chuckled. "I'm sorry."

"You should be. Now, you put these last mugs away and then get in there and get that girl up to bed. She needs to rest on a soft mattress. I'm gonna get on."

I kissed Nora's cheek. "Text me when you make it home, please."

"Always looking out for his people," Nora said with a smile as she headed for the door.

I dried the two mugs we'd used for coffee as we cleaned, but when I opened the cabinet, I stilled. Then I scowled. There were no longer mugs in perfect, precise order in there, but a mix of bowls and plates with a note.

Chief,

Three guesses where I put the mugs. You're welcome for keeping you on your toes.

xx Ellie

I couldn't help it, I laughed. Opting to leave the mugs on the damn counter, I moved toward the living room. Ellie's eyes fluttered as I entered. "Hi…"

She was a little loopy but so damn adorable. I sat on the edge of the couch and gently brushed the hair out of her eyes. "Want to tell me where you put the mugs?"

Ellie's beautiful mouth curved. "Just try to get it out of me."

My lips twitched. "Blaze?"

"Yeah?" she asked sleepily.

"I want you messing with my cabinets every day."

A look of confusion swept over Ellie's face. "Okay?"

"Move in. Move in with me and Keels now and then into the farmhouse when it's done. You can help me finalize the plans with Shep. We can make it something that's truly ours."

Ellie blinked up at me, her eyes turning glassy. "This is a big step. Keely—"

"Loves you," I said, cutting her off. "Nothing would make her happier than having you with us all the time. But if it's too soon—"

It was Ellie's turn to cut me off. She pushed up and kissed me, stealing any additional words from my lips. When she pulled back, mischief danced in her eyes. "Can I have a goat friend for Bumper?"

I laughed. "You can have a whole damn goat sanctuary if you want."

Ellie's mouth hovered over mine. "I'm reminding you of this moment when I bring home a whole herd."

EPILOGUE

Ellie

NINE MONTHS LATER

WITH WINDOWS OPEN WIDE AND MY BELOVED *NSYNC blaring, Keely, Leah, and I danced around Keely's brand-new bedroom in Leah's brand-new house—a house she was sharing with Gabriel. I still couldn't help grinning like a fool when I thought about it. But it shouldn't have been all that surprising.

Gabriel and Leah were the perfect kind of opposites, the way Trace and I were. Gabriel had a mischievous, fun-loving spirit that brought Leah out of her shell and made her embrace the messy, beautiful moments life had to offer. And it didn't hurt that Keely already adored him, and Trace was just happy the two of them had found their perfect matches. Some people might think it odd that Leah ended up with her ex-husband's best friend, but I found it... perfect.

We'd become a truly blended family. One that was all the more beautiful because of its uniqueness and wide array of colors. And the fact that I'd converted both Leah and Keely to 90s pop girlies didn't hurt.

As one song ended and blended into the next, I grinned at the two of them. "Are we ready for phase two?"

Leah pushed her hair back in a glittery hair band Keely had gifted her for Christmas and gave me a salute. "Let's get this pegacorn flying."

Keely grinned at her mom and then at me. "Can I be in charge of the glitter paint?"

"There's no one I'd trust more." I'd found a company that made pure glitter wall paint and sealant for furniture and had gotten the hardware store in town to special order it. Keely's room was a test. If it went well, I'd be using it on other clients' projects.

Word had gotten around Sparrow Falls about my interior wall murals, and I'd slowly found myself back in the interior design business. But this time, I was doing it as me. I got such a charge out of meeting with the clients and finding out who they truly were, then making their homes reflect that.

But I'd never felt more honored than when Leah had asked if we could tackle Keely's room at their new place together. I put everything I had into the design, and there were pieces of all the people important to Keely in the mural. Leah and I had gone to estate sales and pored over design books until we had the perfect vision for our girl. And it only made it more special that we were painting it together.

The music bumped as we got to work, bringing every inch of it to life. It would be a couple of days before we could move the furniture in and make everything complete, but it would be worth it in the end.

And it was all the sweeter that I'd felt free to do it. With Jasper gone and Bradley serving a serious sentence in France, I could breathe. Philip had tried to keep contacting me for a while, but when he was caught with contraband in his detention facility, he'd lost all outside contact privileges. Even Jasper's friend, Rainer Cruz, was doing time after Trace and Gabriel finally located his stash house. And Will the jerk-face had been relegated to the graveyard shift as mall security, where all they'd give the power-hungry fool was a Taser. And Fletcher had gotten his desk just as he should've.

Sparrow Falls was looking brighter, and the Colsons were finally breathing easy. And we all *more* than deserved it.

As the sun sank a little lower in the sky, marking the beautiful deep afternoon of late summer, the music cut off. Gabriel stood in the open door, grinning. "It looks amazing."

"Isn't it the bestest?" Keely called, running for him.

He picked her up without a thought to the fact that she was likely covering his jeans and tee with paint. "You are, without a doubt, going to have the coolest room in the entire second grade."

Her grin only got wider. "I can't wait for all the slumber parties."

I laughed. "You ready for that, Gabriel?"

He grimaced but did it with a hint of a smile. "I've got the snacks covered, but I'm not sure my eardrums are ready."

Leah patted him on the shoulder. "Don't worry. I'll get you earplugs."

Gabriel chuckled, set Keely down, and turned to me. "Trace texted. He's on his way to pick you up."

I frowned, grabbing my phone to check the time. "Already? We've got a few hours left."

Gabriel and Leah shared a look.

"What?" I asked, a hint of suspicion sweeping through me.

One corner of Gabriel's mouth kicked up. "Should've been a cop, El. The crew just got done with the last of the finish work."

"Seriously?" I shrieked.

Shep's crew had been working practically around the clock to finish the last of the new house build. It felt like we'd been close for months, but true to new-build nature, there were endless things that held us up from getting to that completed status. I knew they'd thought they would finish by the weekend, but today was a complete surprise.

"He'll be here any minute," Gabriel said.

"What do you think, Keels? Have the energy for two new rooms in one day?" I asked.

She giggled. "What are we going to put on the wall at your and Daddy's house?"

"We're going to have to brainstorm because I'm not sure we can top this one." I glanced at Leah. "What do you think? Can you help us with round two?"

She cracked her knuckles and did an exaggerated stretch. "I'll be ready."

I laughed and grabbed Keely's hand as I headed for the stairs, my excitement getting the best of me. When I reached the first floor, a horn sounded outside, and I kept us right on going. The passenger window rolled down, and I could just make out Trace's handsome face behind the wheel.

"Ready to see your new digs?" he called.

"We're ready!" Keely cheered.

I opened the back door and helped Keels inside. The minute I was in the front passenger seat, I leaned over and kissed Trace.

"Cooties," Keely said, scrunching her nose.

Trace chuckled. "I hope she always feels that way about kissing."

"Don't hold your breath, Chief."

The drive to the property felt like it took forever, but right as we pulled off to the new gate, one that had *Colson* branded into the rustic wood, Trace glanced back at his daughter. "You're up, Keels."

She let out a squeal of delight and reached for something on the seat next to her. A second later, a pink sleep mask was being placed over my eyes. "Make sure you can't peek," Keely ordered sternly.

"What is going on?" I asked as I reached up, feeling the silk mask.

Trace squeezed my hand before easing off the brake. "Keels and I have been working on a little surprise for you."

My brows pulled together as I tried to puzzle through what it could be. I'd worked hand in hand with Shep and Thea on the design of the house and yard, with Trace chiming in with both practical and the occasional whimsical suggestion. The home was the perfect blend of us, with a healthy dose of our Keely girl, too.

The SUV bounced over the gravel road for what felt like eons until we finally stopped. I heard doors open and close and then Trace was helping me out of the vehicle.

"Careful, Daddy. Don't let her trip," Keely called.

"I won't," Trace said as he took my hand, slowly leading me down what felt like a stone path. I tried to picture where that might be but came up empty.

"Ready?" Trace whispered in my ear as we came to a stop.

"She's ready!" Keely cheered.

Trace laughed and pulled my blindfold free. I blinked at the sudden brightness as the sun painted the land in front of us in rich reds and oranges. And as it did, I couldn't believe what I saw.

An entire herd of goats—including my beloved Bumper—and a few horses for good measure. But taking off from the fence line was a wild garden *full* of color. So many shades and tones I'd never be able to name them all. And butterflies danced from bloom to bloom, happy as could be.

"Trace," I croaked.

"You said you wanted a herd of goats," he murmured.

Keely jumped up and down. "And you love riding with me, so now we have our own horses."

Trace's lips skimmed my temple. "And you needed that butterfly garden."

Tears gathered in my eyes as I took in all the beauty around me. But more, I felt it. Because it came from the two of them. "You thought of everything," I croaked.

"Almost," Trace whispered. "But not quite."

And then he dropped to one knee.

Blood roared in my ears, and my heart thundered as Trace pulled out a ring box. "Ellie, Blaze, marry me, be our family, make this our forever."

My lips were already saying yes before he even opened the

box. Keely squealed in delight as Trace slid the ring onto my finger. That, too, was all color. A ring made up of countless gems in a rainbow of tones that almost looked like it belonged in the butterfly garden.

Tears tracked down my cheeks as Trace stood, and I threw myself at him. He laughed as Keely danced around us. And then he turned me so I could see our beautiful home. The entire Colson crew was there, waving and cheering. Arden and Linc cradled my niece and nephew as Brutus and Gremlin raced around them. All of them raised a glass, and Lolli shook a bottle of champagne, popping the cork and spraying the yard. It was…perfect.

I looked up into Trace's eyes. "I love you."

His lips brushed mine again. "Thank you for showing me what love could be."

For an exclusive bonus scene,
scan the code below and join Catherine's newsletter.
The scene will be delivered to your inbox instantly.
Happy Reading!

https://geni.us/ChsngShltrBnsScene

CAN'T WAIT TO SPEND MORE TIME IN
SPARROW FALLS? READ ON FOR A LOOK AT

Secret HAVEN

PROLOGUE

Fallon
AGE FOURTEEN

I F YOU JUST FINISHED THE LAST OF THE LUCKY CHARMS, I AM going to hack into your Instagram and post that picture of you streaking downtown the night before graduation."

I didn't look up at the sound of my brother Cope's threat. My pencil kept right on scratching across the paper, the sound inaudible above the din in the kitchen. But growing up the way I had, I was used to noise and chaos. The good kind. The kind that came from my mom taking in foster child after foster child—anyone who needed her—even after my dad had passed away. It was just the kind of woman she was.

Sometimes, kids came for only a night or two. Other times, they stayed forever. But there were always a lot of us, which meant noise and chaos.

Shep shot Cope a grin, his amber eyes twinkling with mischief. "Good thing I've got a great ass. Nothing to worry about there."

"Your ass is so pale, it gives *mooning* a whole new meaning," Cope fired back.

"Watch your language. Both of you," Mom warned, eying the newest member of our crew.

Arden was twelve and had only said about two words since coming to live with us a few months ago. But the way she watched everyone with her gray-violet eyes said she picked up on more than someone might expect.

My grandma, Lolli, made a *pssh* noise as she walked into the kitchen wearing a bedazzled workout outfit, tie-dyed in every color of the rainbow. "Foul language is honest."

Mom pinned Lolli with a hard stare. "Foul language is not welcome in this house."

"Just like my naked yoga isn't?" Lolli huffed.

Cope's face scrunched as he shook his head, making his light-brown hair flutter in a way I was sure the high school girls would sigh over. "Please do not remind me. I'm scarred for life."

Lolli stuck out her tongue at him. "It's called a sun salutation, and it's your fault for coming over to my guesthouse unannounced."

Shep chuckled as he lowered himself to the stool next to me. "Bet he won't do that again."

"I'm staying at least two hundred yards away at all times," Cope said with a shiver.

Rhodes ambled into the kitchen, her deep-brown hair a little wild. "Don't let them dull your sparkle, Lolli."

"Never, my babycakes," Lolli called back.

Shep set his bowl of cereal on the island next to me, making his milk slosh over the side. He quickly moved to mop it up as I lifted my journal out of its path. "Sorry, Fal."

"When do you go back to college again?" I asked, my lips twitching.

He made a face. "This morning. And you're gonna miss me like crazy."

"Not when you take the last of the Lucky Charms," Cope called from the opposite side of the kitchen.

"You snooze, you lose," Shep shot back.

Mom looked up from the stove, giving them each a look that said she was exasperated. "You both need protein, not to mainline sugar."

Rhodes sent my mom a smile. "I'll have eggs, Nora."

My mom's expression turned gentle. "Have I told you that you're my favorite today?"

"Kiss-ass," Cope called as he tried to get the last shreds of Lucky Charms into his bowl.

"Copeland," Mom chastised.

"Sorry, Mom." He grinned at Rhodes. "Sorry, Rho Rho."

My best friend was newer to our bunch. She'd come to live with us a year ago after her family was killed in a fire. And even with as much time as she'd spent here growing up, she was still finding her footing in the sibling pack.

"That's pretty good," Shep said, leaning over to look at what I was drawing.

I quickly closed my journal, hiding my sketch of a house. "Not as good as yours, future contractor extraordinaire."

He sent me a lopsided grin. "Let's hope."

"Only if he's not distracted by all the girls chasing after him on campus," a new voice called. Our eldest brother, Trace, ambled into the kitchen, his new deputy uniform looking perfectly ironed.

"I thought you moved out," Shep shot back.

"I'm out of coffee," Trace muttered.

"Move out of his way," Cope ordered. "Trace without coffee is a dangerous beast."

Trace leveled him with a stare. "I don't get my coffee, and I'm much more likely to write you a speeding ticket when you're doing thirty-five in a twenty-five."

Mom straightened, leveling a glare at my biological older brother. "Copeland Colson. I am entrusting you with precious cargo. Tell me you are not speeding."

There was a slight edge to her tone, and I knew why. When I was ten, a car accident left Cope and me in the hospital, and our father and brother, Jacob, dead.

Trace winced and quickly wrapped an arm around Mom. "I'm just giving him a hard time. He's only doing like two miles over the speed limit."

It was a lie. Cope was a speed demon on skates *and* behind the wheel. Always looking for that next thrill. Maybe because we'd come so close to losing it all.

I stood, putting together my things and shoving them into the backpack at my feet. Once that was done, I moved around the kitchen, gathering supplies for lunch. I quickly glanced around to see if anyone was watching before making two turkey sandwiches. But I got caught up making sure they were perfect and didn't notice my mom moving in beside me.

She brushed some hair back from my face in that easy way of hers. "Did you get enough for breakfast? You've been bringing a lot for lunch lately."

My muscles stiffened; I couldn't help it. A mixture of anxiety and guilt washed through me at hiding my mission from her. But if I shared, she'd get involved. I loved her for it, but I also feared it might make things worse.

"Sometimes, I want a snack on my free period," I hedged. It wasn't a lie. I did occasionally want something to eat during my free periods. It just usually came in the form of candy—strawberry Sour Patch Kids, if I had my way.

Cope sent me a look that told me he was about to be a shit-stirrer. "Eating for two, Fal?"

My jaw dropped, and Mom whirled on him. "That is not something to joke about."

"Oh, please," Cope muttered. "Fal's never even kissed a boy. I think you're safe."

My cheeks heated because he was right. Cope's words stung, but he was right. Everyone else in my family seemed to find relationships easily—or at least offers for them. Trace had been dating the same girl since he started college. Shep had endless female interest. Girls waited by Cope's locker every day. Even Rhodes had plenty of boys paying her attention. And I was sure even Arden would have her share of interest if she ever ventured off our property.

But it was never easy for me. I was a little awkward. I didn't care about the same stuff most kids in my class did. It just…didn't seem important. And it didn't help that I was shy around people I didn't know well. More often than not, I faded into the background.

Grabbing the sandwiches, I stuffed them into my backpack and bolted out the front door. My feet hit the boards of the front steps, and I felt the sting of tears in the corners of my eyes. It was so stupid.

"Fal, wait," Cope called from behind me.

I didn't stop—not that I had anywhere to go. Colson Ranch was miles from town, and my only escape would've been into the pastures with the horses or cattle. I slowed at the fence line, staring out at the horizon. The Monarch Mountains were stunning in the morning light, and their staggering beauty and power were reminders of just how big the world was beyond our fences.

Cope moved in next to me, not saying anything for a moment. "I'm a dick."

I didn't respond.

"A dick of epic proportions. And I'll give you my Lucky Charms for the next two weeks as restitution."

My mouth curved slightly at that. "The ultimate penance."

"No kidding," he muttered. He knocked his shoulder into mine. "I'm sorry. Any boy would be lucky to have you at his side. But I'd also kick his ass if he made a move on you."

I made a face at Cope. "And how many girls have you kissed?" I challenged.

"I'm seventeen. It's different."

"Whatever," I muttered.

Cope looped an arm around me. "Forgiven?"

I glanced up at him. "I don't know. You going to get me a milk-shake after school?"

"Lucky Charms *and* a milkshake?"

"You were a dick of *epic* proportions."

Cope burst out laughing but tugged me back toward the line of family vehicles. Trace watched us approach, the edges of his expression hardening. He didn't like anyone around him feeling less than, especially those he loved. It likely came from the events of his life before he came to stay with us. But he'd taken that hardship and turned it into something good.

"Want me to put him on a most-wanted list?" Trace asked, Shep and Rhodes standing next to him.

"I'll settle for Lucky Charms and a milkshake payment," I called back.

Cope pulled me tighter against him and gave me a noogie. "She drives a hard bargain."

"Cope!" I squealed.

"Not the hair," Rhodes yelled. "That's adding insult to injury."

I struggled to get free. "I'm going to put glitter in your hair gel."

Cope laughed. "I don't use hair gel."

"Your body lotion, then."

"Turn him into a fairy nymph," Rho encouraged.

Cope released me. "Brutal."

I tried to right my hair. "And don't you forget it."

The second bell rang, and more students flooded the halls. Kids stopped to offload books in their lockers and grab lunch money or food they'd brought from home. Nearly everyone but me. I kept my backpack on and dodged kids darting this way and that while trying to avoid any teachers who might question why I wasn't headed for the cafeteria.

Who was I kidding? None of them would stop me. They'd assume I was working on a school project or logging some extra hours of homework. They wouldn't be completely wrong. But they wouldn't be totally right either.

"Fal!"

My muscles stiffened at the sound of Rho's voice above the

crowd. I could've pretended I didn't hear her, but Rhodes was determined, and she would've followed me. I slowed in the side hallway, stepping out of the flow of traffic.

"You're fast for how tiny you are," Rhodes said, struggling to catch her breath.

"What's up?" I asked, feigning nonchalance.

Rho's eyes narrowed on me the way only a best friend's could. "Where are you going?"

"I have something to do this lunch period."

"And that is?" she pressed.

I didn't say anything right away.

Rhodes let out a long breath. "You've been MIA at lunch for weeks. What's going on?"

I twisted the strap of my backpack around my fingers and pulled it tight. "I'm tutoring someone."

Rho's brow furrowed. "Why didn't you just say so?"

"He doesn't want people to know he's struggling. That's all."

One corner of her mouth quirked up. "*He*, huh?"

My cheeks heated. "It's not like that." No matter how much I wanted it to be. But even if there were no stolen kisses or anything of the like, we shared something deep—an understanding I'd never had with anyone else. Not even Rhodes.

"I'm just giving you a hard time," Rho said. "I'll cover for you if anyone asks."

I grinned at her and started down the hall. "You're the bestest bestie," I called.

"I know I am!" Rho shouted.

Keeping an eye out for any faculty members, I ducked out the side door and jogged across one of the soccer fields toward the forest. The moment I stepped into the trees, I breathed a little deeper. The clean mountain air, the pine scent clinging to everything, the sound of the creek in the distance...it all put me at ease.

I wound through the trees, following a path I knew by heart. It had been my escape route since high school started a few months ago. I just hadn't realized at the time that it wasn't only mine.

My heart stuttered as I caught sight of him sitting on a log. I recognized him instantly, even from behind, and with the hood of his sweatshirt pulled up. Kyler Blackwood was just that kind of boy. Bigger than most of the guys at Sparrow Falls High, it wasn't only his size that made him so easy to identify.

It was the energy that emanated from him, wafting off him in crackling waves. He seemed to prowl through life in a way that made others keep their distance. But I was never scared of Kyler. He was *real*. He didn't paint on a smile when he didn't feel it. He didn't pretend that everything was okay when it wasn't. He simply was. And I was in awe of it.

Fallen leaves crunched under my feet, and Kyler turned, revealing one side of his shadowed face. Even half-covered, I instantly knew something was wrong.

"Hey, Sparrow."

I didn't say anything right away; I just kept moving, needing to get to him. I lowered myself to the log next to him and let my backpack fall to the ground. "Tell me."

Kyler shrugged off the request, asking a question of his own. "Got any new house drawings?"

He was the only one I'd ever shown my drawings to by choice. Sometimes, living in an imaginary world—one where parents and siblings didn't die, and kids weren't neglected or hurt—was easier. So, I'd repeatedly draw a whimsical house: a place where no bad things happened. It was a cross between a Craftsman and a Victorian, with teal siding and bright blooms covering most of it.

I wasn't especially good at drawing, but I'd gotten good at this one thing. It was my escape. Except that escape had shifted over the past few months. Changed. Because Kyler had become a part of it.

I could feel the anger and pain swirling around Kyler. I took him in. His hand lay on the log, pressing against the rough bark. His knuckles were torn, which wasn't unusual given the number of fights he got into, both inside the ring and out of it. But some of the tears were fresh.

The urge to clean them gnawed at me. I'd taken to carrying a first-aid kit in my backpack for exactly that reason. But it wasn't time. Not yet. Because something was hurting him a hell of a lot more than those knuckles.

I moved, linking my pinky with his and squeezing. It was our sign that we were there for each other. If I needed to rage about how unfair it was that I'd lost Dad and Jacob, or how worried I was about one of my siblings... If Kyler needed to let loose the ugly stew of feelings regarding what he faced at home each and every day: his father's fists, his mother's vitriol. We were always there.

"Tell me." My words had a slight pleading edge.

Something about that made Kyler turn. And that's when I saw it. A sick feeling swirled inside me as I took in the side of Kyler's face. It was bruised and swollen in a way that could only come from someone hitting you over and over again when you were down.

My pinky tightened around Kyler's as if my grip on him was the only thing keeping him with me. "The fights?" I croaked. Kyler was a hell of a mixed martial artist, but he'd started taking some fights for money, and I'd never had a good feeling about them. Looking at his face now, I realized it was more than just the physical toll of those fights.

The light in Kyler's amber eyes swirled, turning darker. "No."

My throat constricted. Worse than fights for money with no protective gear? Worse than getting mixed up with guys who wore motorcycle club vests and Trace said were dangerous?

"Your dad?" I could barely get the words out, my throat weaving into intricate knots I didn't think I'd ever get undone.

Kyler looked at the creek below us. The dogwoods that had been in full bloom months ago when we first met here were now bare, like bony fingers that had been starved of food and affection for far too long. Like Kyler himself.

A muscle along his jaw pulsed in time to a beat only he could hear. "He got the jump on me when I got home. Drunk or high. Maybe both. He got me down, and I couldn't get up. Woke up on the floor this morning."

The pressure of unshed tears was instant, but I shoved them and the rage swirling inside me down as far as they would go. "Your mom?"

The two words were strangled, barely audible, but he heard them. "You know she doesn't give a fuck about me. She's still pissed that I ruined the best years of her life. Sometimes, I think she'd rather he finish me off."

Tears filled my eyes, cresting up and spilling over as I kept hold of Kyler's pinky. But I couldn't speak. Didn't have the words for him living through something so awful.

He turned then, taking in my face. "Fuck, Sparrow. Don't cry."

Kyler tugged his hand from mine. Not holding his pinky made me feel a little sick. Like I could no longer protect him. Kyler covered his thumbs with the sleeves of his hoodie and swept them under my eyes, clearing away the tears. "I'm okay."

"You're not." The words were barely a whisper. "They can't get away with this. We can't let them."

Kyler's hands dropped from my face. "I'm gonna take off. Maybe try to make it to Portland."

Panic flooded my system, fear fast on its heels. Kyler was two years older than me, but sixteen wasn't old enough to make it on your own in a huge city. Anything could happen to him. And the idea of not seeing Kyler every day? Not knowing he was all right?

It made me feel like I couldn't breathe.

"Don't," I croaked. "I can talk to Trace. He's a deputy now. He can help—"

"No." Kyler was on his feet in a flash, pacing. "You can't. I could end up in a group home or, if my dad rats me out for fighting, juvie. I can't risk it, Sparrow. Promise me you won't tell anyone. Promise."

Each word wound the panic tighter. But I knew I couldn't betray the gift Kyler had given me.

Trust.

For the boy who had nothing, he'd given me everything. His trust. His kindness. He'd seen me doing battle with my grief and had come alongside me in the most beautiful way.

"I won't tell," I whispered.

The tension in Kyler eased a fraction, like someone had dialed down an electrical current. "Okay."

I stared at the boy who'd become my haven, taking in his beaten and bloodied face. "I can't stand you hurting," I rasped, pushing to my feet. "I want to fix it. I want to *kill* them. I want to take away all the pain and make it better."

"You do," Kyler said, cutting me off as he moved into my space and linked his pinky with mine again. "You bring me food. You make sure I don't flunk out of my classes." His finger traced the arrow necklace I wore every day. "You make me feel…not alone. And, Sparrow? I've been alone for basically as long as I've been breathing. But you? You make it all better."

My breath hitched as Kyler's hand lifted to cup my cheek, his thumb sweeping away the last of my tears. My pulse thundered in my ears as his head dipped. But he just hovered there, not closing the distance, waiting for me. Like he always did.

And because it was Kyler, I wasn't afraid or even nervous. I just wanted. To know what his lips felt like, what his tongue tasted like, what it would be like to be kissed by this boy.

I closed the distance, my mouth meeting his. The boy everyone thought of as a brute was heartbreakingly gentle as his mouth met mine. Heat hit my lips, spreading out, moving through my whole form, waking me up as if I'd been sleepwalking through life. Kyler tasted like peppermint and a hint of smoke, and his scent was stronger now, too: oakmoss and amber, but with a twist. As though when those scents connected with Kyler's skin, they changed. Just like I did.

His rough palm slid along my jaw as I pressed into him, wanting more of the magic that was only him. His tongue stroked in, just barely. Hesitant, waiting for that permission again. I met his kiss awkwardly at first, but then I found my footing. His long fingers slid into my hair as I opened for him.

"Well, well, well. What do we have here? I knew there was something more goin' on than studying."

At the sound of the voice, Kyler and I jerked apart. He instantly moved me behind him and glared at his friend.

Oren snorted. "Please. Like I'm interested in the little mouse."

Kyler's hands fisted, and the already bruised knuckles cracked.

"It's a good thing you're not. Because if you lay a finger on her, you know I'd snap your neck like a twig."

Oren held up his hands, but I saw a flare of anger in his brown depths. "Touchy, touchy. Save it for your fight this weekend."

That had anger washing through me, hot and fast. "He's not fighting this weekend. Look at his face. He probably has a concussion."

Oren sent a glare in my direction. "You're a real buzzkill, mouse. You know that? He'll be fine by Saturday."

I stepped to Kyler's side, letting my anger burn out any fear. "If I find out you pressured Kyler into fighting, I'll have my brother put you on every sheriff's department watch list imaginable. I'll let the air out of your crotch rocket's tires every day. And I will find a way to sneak pink hair dye into your shampoo."

"She's got a vengeful streak," Jericho said, stepping out of the trees. "I like it."

I wasn't crazy about either of Kyler's so-called friends, but Jericho seemed to have a soul, at least.

Oren's jaw worked back and forth, his gaze flicking to Kyler. "You'd better keep your bitch on a shorter leash and stop telling her our business."

Kyler moved forward lightning-quick. The only thing saving Oren from a knockout punch was Jericho grabbing his jacket and pulling him back.

"All right, all right," Jericho said, getting between them. "Let's just take a breath. Ore, you know Fallon's a no-go zone for you and anyone else. Kye will break you in two. Kye, no hitting the home team, remember?"

"He earned it," Kyler growled.

"Maybe. But Oren's never *not* gonna be an asshole. So, we just gotta deal."

"You're both pricks," Oren muttered.

The school bell rang in the distance, and it felt a lot like a clock striking midnight. I was about to turn into a pumpkin. Kyler turned, his gaze roaming my face like he was trying to memorize it. "You'd better go. You don't want to be late."

I moved in, not caring that his friends were there. I linked my pinky with his. "You gonna be okay?"

One corner of his mouth quirked up. "Always am, aren't I?"

"Be careful," I whispered.

Kyler stared down at me for a long moment. Then he dipped his head and pressed a kiss to my forehead. It was like he was trying to memorize that, too. My insides churned because it felt a hell of a lot like a goodbye.

"Kyler—"

I swung my backpack around and pulled out the extra lunch I'd made, shoving it into his hands.

"Go," he said quietly. "Not letting you be late because of me."

So, I went. But I regretted it for the rest of the day.

A ringing sounded from down the hall and the kitchen below as I stared at the ceiling in the dark like it held all the answers to my problems. Two rings later, it cut off.

My bedroom was two doors down from my mom's, but I could still hear her muffled voice as she answered the phone—not the words but her familiar, sleepy tone. Then I listened to the floorboards creak as she made her way down the hall and the stairs.

It likely meant one thing: a newcomer. And one coming in the middle of the night meant it was bad. An emergency placement.

I tossed off the covers and sat up, sliding my feet into my fluffy unicorn slippers that matched my pj's and padding down the hall. Mom already had the kettle on by the time I made it downstairs.

"Hey, sweetie. Did I wake you?" she asked as she tightened the sash of her flannel robe. It was the one Dad had gotten her a decade ago. She said putting it on felt like getting a hug from him. She'd patched holes and restitched seams, and I had a feeling she'd wear it for the rest of her days.

I shook my head. "Couldn't sleep."

Mom brushed some hair out of my face. "Everything okay?"

No, everything was not okay. But I'd made a promise, and Kyler had given me his trust. I wouldn't ever break that. "Just a lot going on at school."

"I'm making some Sleepytime tea. Drink some of that."

"Okay." I watched as she expertly removed the kettle before it could make a sound and poured hot water into a teapot before pulling out three mugs. "Who's coming?" I asked softly.

Mom's face got that troubled look it often did when we were about to get a bad case. Like when Arden had arrived and couldn't bear to sleep with the lights off. Or when Trace went to the cemetery to visit his mom on her birthday. "A boy's coming to stay with us for a while."

I watched her face for more clues. "What happened?"

She placed a hand-sewn tea cozy over the pot, then rested her hand there. "He was hurt, and he needs a safe place to stay."

My stomach cramped. How were there so many people in the world who wanted to inflict pain? "Did they get who did it?"

Mom nodded. "Trace said the man's in lockup."

"Good." The force behind the word had my mom raising her brows.

She reached out and cupped my face before tapping the arrow necklace Dad had given me. "Always my little warrior for justice." A soft knock sounded on the door before she could continue. "That's probably Trace."

Mom was already on the move, and I followed behind, wanting to see if I could do anything to help. But as the front door opened, my whole world dropped away. It wasn't the weary look on Trace's face that did it, or the sad look on his partner, Gabriel's. It was the boy whose gaze was cast at the ground. The same one who'd given me everything.

I must've made a sound because Kyler's head jerked up. The second it did, pain filled his expression. His dark brown hair looked black under the dim porch light, mirroring the shadowy circles under his amber eyes.

"Careful," Trace said quietly. "The stitches will smart for a while."

Stitches?

My gaze jumped around Kyler's form, taking in new flashes of information: an arm in a sling, taped gauze peeking out from under scrubs, a bandage across his brow, and the side of his face even more swollen.

"Hi, Kye," my mom said gently. "I'm Nora Colson. You're most welcome here. I've got a room ready and some tea brewing in the kitchen. Fallon can show you the way. You might know her from school."

My heart hammered in my ears. A tingling sensation erupted in my fingers, and it felt like the whole world might drop away. Kyler. *My* Kyler was the one who'd been hurt. The one who needed shelter.

"No," Kyler rasped. "I don't think we've met."

It felt like the most brutal blow—worse than waking up in the hospital after the car accident with broken ribs and a concussion.

"Fal?" Mom asked.

"Sorry," I squeaked. "I can show you." I scurried like the little mouse Oren always accused me of being, but Kyler wasn't nearly as quick. Every step he took looked like it cost him, and I couldn't stop the tears that gathered in my eyes.

Mom spoke to Trace and Gabriel in hushed tones as I led Kyler to the kitchen without saying a word. When we finally reached it and had some privacy, I focused on the tea. I couldn't look at him. It hurt too much. In every way.

"Tell me," I croaked.

Kyler didn't say anything for a long moment. "He caught me packing a bag to leave." Kyler's words were rough like sandpaper and full of pain. "Grabbed a knife. Never seen him so mad." His voice caught. "I think he was going to kill me."

I had to look at him then. The shock and fear were too much. "Kyler," I breathed.

His tears came then, running down his face in streaks of agony. "My dad tried to kill me. And my mom didn't do a damn thing to stop him. She just watched like I was nothing to her."

I wanted to touch him, but I didn't know where. Every place I looked seemed like it would cause him pain. Still, like always, I moved for his pinky and hooked it with mine. "You're safe now. We've got you."

A new sort of fear and pain slid into his expression like they were wrapped in panic. He gripped my pinky harder. "You can't tell them we know each other. That I kissed you."

I frowned, trying to understand.

"They'll never let me stay here if they know. Your brother pulled strings to get me in here. They wanted to put me in a group home in Roxbury. If they boot me from here, that's where I'll go."

Pain ripped through me. Kyler didn't deserve that. He deserved to be somewhere he wouldn't have to watch his back. A place he could heal. And he would be. Even if I had to erase the fact that he knew me better than anyone. Even if I had to hide that I'd fallen in love with him the moment he found me screaming in the woods.

Kyler let go of my pinky, and it felt like someone was ripping my still-beating heart from my chest. But he didn't look away when he spoke again, saying the words that broke me. "Sparrow," he croaked, "you were always too good for me anyway. It's better this way."

CHAPTER ONE

Fallon

FOURTEEN YEARS LATER

CUPPING MY HANDS AROUND A MUG THAT READ *WORLD'S BEST Aunt*, I inhaled deeply. The scent of dark roast filled my nose, deep and rich with hints of dark chocolate and almonds. Or maybe I was imagining that. It didn't matter. Only one thing did. "Do your job, sweet, sweet caffeine," I whispered into the cup as if to manifest some sort of wakefulness.

Taking a long pull of coffee, I closed my eyes—eyes that felt like they were full of acid-coated sand. But I felt slightly more human after a few sips.

I opened my eyes and set the mug on the dresser. Countless rings littered the surface from endless mornings just like this one. It drove my mom crazy. She was constantly giving me coasters or offering to refurbish the top. But the coasters got lost in the chaos of my minuscule cottage on the edge of town, and the dresser had character. Or as Lolli said, *"It's seen some things, baby girl."*

Moving around my room, I pulled up the covers on my bed and

winced at the stack of file folders and the laptop on my nightstand. Paperwork. There was never-ending paperwork when you worked for the child welfare arm of the Department of Human Services. And nine times out of ten, it was the reason for my two a.m. bedtimes. I reached for my coffee and took a sip at the reminder of just how little sleep I was going on.

My phone dinged, and I reached over to swipe it from the charging dock, nearly upending the Leaning Tower of Paperwork in the process. I muttered a curse as hot coffee sloshed onto my hand but managed not to do any serious damage. My sibling group chat flashed on the screen.

Shep has changed the name of the group to Cope's Tighty-whities.

I frowned at the screen. My siblings were always trying to one-up each other by changing the chat name, but this was a new one.

Shep: *Look what I spotted at the grocery store this morning. . .*

A photo of a magazine filled the screen. *Sports Today* had one photo on the cover. My brother, the hockey star, shirtless with some sort of oil on his chest and his hair slicked back. He wasn't in his underwear, thank the gods above, but he was in workout shorts that left little to the imagination. My nose scrunched up.

Me: *I really didn't need to see this before breakfast. I feel a little ill.*

Cope: *Rude. Sutton said I look great.*

Rhodes: *Your fiancée can't exactly be trusted to be impartial.*

Kyler: *Did they dip you in a vat of olive oil for this? Give you a rubdown with a tub of Crisco? I need to know the background.*

Everyone in my family called Kyler by his nickname, Kye, but I could never find it in me to switch his name in my phone. Like so many other things, it was a reminder of what could've been. A brand of something I could never let go, even though it would never be mine.

Trace: *That photo is obscene. It's like gray sweatpants but worse.*

Rhodes: *Ah, gray sweatpants. Men's slut clothes. I think it's cold enough for me to leave a few pairs out for Anson to wear.*

That had a smile tugging at my lips.

Me: *Let me know how the hater of sunshine and bright colors responds to having to walk around in lingerie.*

Rho's fiancé was a notorious grump who'd communicated in mostly grunts and scowls until she came into his life. But everything had changed when the ex-profiler found her—when they'd found each other. A pang lit along my sternum. I set my phone on the dresser and rubbed the spot.

Arden: *It's too early for Cope's junk to be in my face. But I'm sure the puck bunnies will be thrilled.*

Cope: *Don't say puck bunnies around Sutton. She gets a little stabby.*

Arden: *I think I'll get her a switchblade for Christmas.*

A soft sound of amusement left my lips as I started on my makeup. In our family, Arden was known for pulling a knife first and asking questions later—which was exactly how she'd met her now-fiancé, Lincoln.

Cope: *Please, don't. I'm not sure I can afford the lawsuits.*

Shep: *You'll all be happy to know that I sent this photo to Lolli, and she said she's going to turn Cope into a fairy prince in her next art piece.*

A grin finally found my lips as I struggled to keep the cover-up where it was supposed to go. Lolli was infamous for her inappropriate diamond art creations. They all had some kind of phallic or sexual bent to them. And no matter how hard a time Mom or my siblings gave her, she never stopped gifting them.

Cope: *There will be payback, hammer boy. She's probably going to have me mounting a poor, defenseless fairy.*

Rhodes: *You could luck out and be part of one of her throuple creations. Remember the elf queen Eiffel Tower piece?*

Trace: *My eyes still haven't recovered.*

I studied my face in the mirror and winced. My dark circles would need two coats of makeup today.

Kyler: *I'm demanding to know her artist's vision at dinner tonight.*

A curse slipped past my lips as I glanced at the stack of work on my nightstand.

Me: *I might have to miss tonight. Sorry, guys. Give me the play-by-play if I do.*

Rhodes: *What's going on? You've been totally MIA lately.*

Guilt pricked at me because she was right. I'd missed more family dinners over the last month than I had in the past five years.

Me: *Sorry. Work's nutty right now. We're down a caseworker, and things have just been...a lot. But I'll try to make it. Promise.*

Kyler: *Let me guess who's picking up the slack.*

I scowled at my phone, both because he was right and because he knew why this was so important to me. Not just because I knew how deep the need for social workers and support systems was for these kids, but because of *him*.

Kye was an invisible brand on my bones. Something I carried with me wherever I went, in whatever I did—even if no one ever knew.

Trace: *You need to take care of yourself, or you won't be able to help anyone.*

That only deepened my scowl. Trace had retained the overprotective-big-brother role for all of us. Now, he was also the sheriff, extending that protectiveness to the entire county.

Me: *I know what I can handle. Love you all.*

Cope: *That's Fal-speak for fuck off.*

Arden: *You'd all better watch your backs, or you're gonna get glitter-bombed.*

I wanted to smile at her reference to my favorite version of retribution but couldn't quite get my mouth to obey. I was too tired. Instead, I locked my phone and finished getting ready. I donned my typical slacks and button-down and wove my blond hair into a braid.

There was only one piece missing. My hands moved to my jewelry tray and the necklace there—the arrow I'd worn every day for as long as I could remember. I fastened it around my neck and stared at the tiny charm. Tracing it with my fingertips, I swore I could still feel the echo of Kye's fingers doing the same thing.

I squeezed my eyes shut and let myself remember those days for a fleeting handful of moments. I called on the ghost of Kyler, letting the memory wrap around me, allowing myself to recall what it had felt like to be his.

When I opened my eyes, he was gone. No more Kyler. Only Kye. The only foster brother I'd never see as what I should: a sibling and nothing more. Because it didn't matter if it had been fourteen seconds or fourteen years, he'd always be the boy who'd given me everything.

ACKNOWLEDGMENTS

This book was one of those that surprised me at more than one turn. The baddie changed when I was about twenty-five percent through my rough draft. Ellie kept challenging me as I wrote. And I had to pivot Trace more than once. But in the end, it feels like I wrote my most relatable heroine to date and a hero who feels more *real* than any of my others. You know, minus stripper firefighting.

All in all, this book stretched me as a writer and helped me to find new colors to paint with, just like Ellie. I hope you loved it too.

Romance books have given me a lot of things, but at the top of that list are incredible friends that I am so lucky to have in my life. Thank you for walking this path with me. A few folks need that extra special shout-out.

My sprinting partners at various portions of this process: Elsie Silver, Laura Pavlov, and Rebecca Jenshak. Thank you for all the support, encouragement, and ass-kicking when needed.

Elsie, thank you for always doling out pep talks and ass slaps. For always having my back. And for being the best friend on this crazy ride. Immunity necklaces forever. Laura, I'm forever grateful for voice memos that make me laugh until I cry and for getting to share this journey with you. You make the highs more fun and the lows easier to bear. LLo Rocky Pavlova, your friendship is the best gift. Rebecca, we're almost done with the year of hard things as I write this, and I know I wouldn't have made it through without you and your encouragement. But let's write less books next year, okay? Love you to the moon and back, my anti-angst bestie.

Samantha Young, who always listens to plot struggles and helps me find my way. I would not have made it through this year without you. The wild ups and downs that had me struggling for equilibrium were more balanced because of you. Thank you for always celebrating my wins and holding my hand during the hard parts. Forever grateful this book world brought me you.

Willow Aster, my most tenderhearted and encouraging of friends, you make this world a better place, and I'm so grateful you're in mine. Thank you for always being there to talk through anything but especially whatever cult podcast we find.

Kandi Steiner, the best cheerleader a girl could ever ask for. Always down for a T-Swift jam sesh or a heart-to-heart, and I'm so grateful for both.

The Lance Bass Fan Club: Ana Huang, Elsie Silver, and Lauren Asher. Thanks for the endless *NSYNC giggles, the advice, and the cheerleading, but most of all, your friendship.

Jess, incredible encourager, brainstormer, hand holder. Thank you for all you do in all the ways. I'm so thankful you're in my life.

Paige B, my warrior, my meme queen, my Swiftie sister. Thanks for cheering me on to the finish line of this book and supporting me in all the ways. I'm so grateful.

To all my incredible friends who have cheered and supported me through all the ups and downs of the past few months, you know who you are.

And to the most amazing hype squad ever, my STS soul sisters: Hollis, Jael, and Paige, thank you for the gift of true friendship and sisterhood. I always feel the most supported and celebrated thanks to you.

My incredible betas: Glav, Jess, Jill, Kelly, Kristie, and Trisha, who helped make these two sing and who always make me excited to dive into that first round of feedback. I'm so grateful for your insights, support, and, of course, the reading reactions!

The crew that helps bring my words to life and gets them out into the world is pretty darn epic. Thank you to Devyn, Jess, Tori, Margo, Chelle, Jaime, Julie, Hang, Stacey, Katie, Jenna, and my team at Lyric, Kimberly, Joy, and my team at Brower Literary. Your hard work is so appreciated! To my team at Sourcebooks: Christa, Gretchen, Katie, and so many others, thank you for helping these words reach a whole new audience and making my bookstore dreams come true. And to my team at Evermore and Century in the UK, especially Claire and Jess, thank you for bringing the stories to stores across the globe.

To all the reviewers and content creators who have taken a chance on my words...THANK YOU! Your championing of my stories means more than I can say. And to my launch and influencer teams, thank you for your kindness, support, and sharing my books with the world.

Ladies of Catherine Cowles Reader Group, you're my favorite place to hang out on the internet! Thank you for your support, encouragement, and willingness to always dish about your latest book boyfriends. You're the freaking best!

Lastly, thank YOU! Yes, YOU. I'm so grateful you're reading this book and making my author dreams come true. I love you for that. A whole lot!

ABOUT THE AUTHOR

CATHERINE COWLES

Writer of words. Drinker of Diet Cokes. Lover of all things cute and furry. USA Today bestselling author Catherine Cowles has had her nose in a book since the time she could read and finally decided to write down some of her own stories. When she's not writing, she can be found exploring her home state of Oregon, listening to true crime podcasts, or searching for her next book boyfriend.

STAY CONNECTED

You can find Catherine in all the usual bookish places…

Website: catherinecowles.com
Facebook: catherinecowlesauthor
Facebook Reader Group: CatherineCowlesReaderGroup
Instagram: catherinecowlesauthor
Goodreads: catherinecowlesauthor
BookBub: catherine-cowles
Pinterest: catherinecowlesauthor
TikTok: catherinecowlesauthor

ALSO AVAILABLE FROM
CATHERINE COWLES

The Tattered & Torn Series

Tattered Stars
Falling Embers
Hidden Waters
Shattered Sea
Fractured Sky

Sparrow Falls

Fragile Sanctuary
Delicate Escape
Broken Harbor
Beautiful Exile
Chasing Shelter
Secret Haven

The Lost & Found Series

Whispers of You
Echoes of You
Glimmers of You
Shadows of You
Ashes of You

The Wrecked Series

Reckless Memories
Perfect Wreckage
Wrecked Palace
Reckless Refuge
Beneath the Wreckage

The Sutter Lake Series

Beautifully Broken Pieces
Beautifully Broken Life
Beautifully Broken Spirit
Beautifully Broken Control
Beautifully Broken Redemption

Standalone Novels

Further to Fall
All the Missing Pieces

For a full list of up-to-date Catherine Cowles titles,
please visit catherinecowles.com.